HONOR
KNOWS NO
BORDERS

John Sharer

iUniverse, Inc.
New York   Bloomington

Honor Knows No Borders

Copyright © 2010 John Sharer

iUniverse books may be ordered through booksellers or by contacting:

iUniverse
1663 Liberty Drive
Bloomington, IN 47403
www.iuniverse.com
1-800-Authors (1-800-288-4677)

ISBN: 978-1-4502-1230-4 (pbk)
ISBN: 978-1-4502-1232-8 (cloth)
ISBN: 978-1-4502-1231-1 (ebk)

Printed in the United States of America

iUniverse rev. date: 6/24/2010

THE NORTH AFRICAN DESERT, 1941
PART ONE

CHAPTER ONE

THE BATTLE HAD RAGED for two days and two nights. When dawn broke on the third day the North African desert was strewn with destroyed German and British tanks, many still burning. Tank crews and supporting infantry lay dead in close proximity to the twisted and broken tanks. Some were killed by gunfire as they tried to escape their mortally wounded tanks. Some were burned to death. The carnage was overwhelming. Hardened veterans on both sides never forgot those terrible days and most could never bear to talk about them.

Early on the third day, the remnants of the German column broke off the encounter and retreated toward their own lines some thirty miles away. The British formed a line facing the retreating Germans, but did not pursue. That decision was necessitated by diminishing fuel supplies and the necessity of reserving adequate quantities to reach their own lines.

Five of the German tanks had been cut off from the rest of their force and had the line of British armor between them and escape. One of the five flew the pennant of the commander of the German column. Despite the dire fuel situation, thirty-five of the British tanks were ordered to pursue the cut-off enemy tanks. It seemed unlikely that the small German force could outrun the larger British contingent when luck intervened. A devastating sandstorm suddenly arose, reducing visibility almost to zero.

The commander of the German column, Colonel Hans Dieter Reichmann, radioed to the other four tanks.

"Continue in your present direction for two thousand meters, then turn right ninety degrees and run laterally for a thousand meters, then another turn of ninety degrees toward our lines. I will run back and forth firing intermittently in the direction of the British. Hopefully they will believe that all five of us have turned and decided to take a stand. With this reduced visibility, you may very well be able to flank the British and get back to our lines without being seen."

"Colonel, we would prefer to stay with you and fight it out. We don't want to leave you here alone," radioed back Captain Kraemer.

"What I just told you was an order—not a suggestion for discussion," barked Reichmann.

His tone was harsh, but inwardly he was proud and grateful for the loyalty of his men.

"Get going. Now!" he shouted. Then in a lower voice, he said, "Good luck."

Reichmann's tank moved back and forth, firing into the wall of sand with no real chance of hitting anything. After twenty minutes his gunner reported that the ammunition was gone.

"What about the machine gun?"

"Half a belt only."

"Short bursts every twenty seconds."

Eight or nine minutes later the belt was gone.

"Run laterally to the British and we'll try to outflank them, but I fear we have less chance than our comrades."

As if on cue, the sandstorm started to lift and visibility improved noticeably. The British tanks were clearly visible as was the lone German tank.

"Turn away and we'll try to outrun them," yelled Reichmann.

It was hopeless. The chase was over in two minutes. One shell tore off the left track, leaving the tank immobile. The second shell scored a direct hit on the turret, setting the tank on fire. It slowly keeled over on its side. Reichmann was stunned and had a deep cut over his left eye. He quickly checked the remainder of his crew. They were all dead. He crawled out of the tank and rolled over on his back. After a minute or two he saw enemy soldiers approaching and he reached for his pistol. A young corporal stuck the muzzle of a rifle in his face.

"Touch that popgun Fritz and I'll blow your bloomin' 'ead off. Your choice, mate."

CHAPTER TWO

───────────────

THE CONSTANT HEAT DURING the day in the North African desert was unbelievably oppressive. It was unrelenting and there was no shelter from it. The sand got into everything—shoes, eyes, ears, armpits, and up a long-suffering soldier's behind. But it was the flies that provided the ultimate torment. An open mouth and one or more flew in. They swarmed around the latrines and there was no way to keep them out of the food. As a result, dysentery was a constant threat. Water was the scarcest commodity. One helmetful was the ration for each soldier per day. With that helmetful, the soldier had to wash, brush his teeth, and save enough for his canteen. It didn't matter if you were a private or a field marshal, all you got was one helmet of water.

Major Bernie Sloan, the commander of a British supply depot, remembered his introduction to the desert when he first arrived. Sergeant Buckley, who was to become his chief clerk and who had been there from the beginning, told him about the way to determine how long a British soldier had been in the desert. It wasn't the depth of his tan or the length of his beard. It was his tea-drinking procedure. With the limited daily ration of water, the soldiers could only spare enough for one cup of tea a day. To any British soldier, that cup of tea was sacred. Buckley said that it was inevitable that a fly would get into the tea before the soldier was finished drinking it. Soldiers who had only been in the desert for a short time would throw the remaining tea away. Those who had been there longer would fish out the fly, throw it away, and drink the tea. "But the real old timers," said Buckley with a straight face, "they would squeeze the fly out before throwing it away and drink the rest of the tea." Sloan had a good laugh at this story and he came to appreciate that Buckley could tell some corkers with his Lancashire accent and always with a straight face.

With sweat pouring down his face and onto the documents he was reading, Sloan was trying to determine whether the supplies the unit had just received were what he had requisitioned.

"Bloody hell!" he exclaimed. "Buckley, get in here."

Buckley came on the run, stopped, stiffened, and threw a perfect salute.

"Sir."

Sloan reluctantly returned the salute less stiffly and definitely less perfectly. "Buckley, you don't have to salute *every* time you come in here. Let's compromise—once a day and that's it."

Buckley was a career man and, while he was not partial to Sloan's disregard for military protocol, he liked and respected him and would do anything for him. Of course he didn't know that Sloan was Jewish. Nobody in the desert did. Sloan had long since convinced himself that he was not hiding the fact, but he certainly didn't go out of his way to reveal it. It probably wouldn't have made any difference to Buckley if he found out now. He had grown to be fiercely loyal to Sloan. He had never known any Jews—at least not to talk to. He had grown up on a farm and had joined the army as a teenager. The pre-war army had few Jews and he hadn't met any.

"Didn't we order a thousand tubes of zinc ointment?"

"Yes sir, we did."

"Well, instead they've sent us a thousand tubes of shaving cream. We've got enough shaving cream lying around here to shave our army, the German Army, and every male over the age of eighteen in Egypt. Are you sure you ordered the right stuff?"

"Yes sir. I have my copy of the 759/3a/498.1 requisition form that I sent in. Do you want to see it?"

"No, that's not necessary. Call around and see if anyone wants to trade any of their zinc ointment for shaving cream. Tell them we'll throw in a few hundred pair of excess socks that we also didn't order. We need that ointment. A lot of the men are coming down with some type of rash on their bottoms and the MO says that ointment is the only thing that will help."

CHAPTER THREE

"MAJOR—MAJOR SLOAN."

Sergeant Buckley was yelling when he was still twenty yards away from Sloan's tent and running as though a raging lion was chasing him. He burst into the tent panting so hard he could barely talk. He hadn't run that hard since basic training and that had been many years ago.

"What in heaven's name is it, Buckley? You look like you've seen a ghost."

Buckley didn't come to attention, didn't salute, and—without being asked—collapsed into the only other chair in the tent. He realized his place and immediately jumped up.

"You've gotta come with me sir—right now," he gasped.

Sloan followed him out of the tent and, at something more than a quick march, followed him past the larger tents that held a variety of supplies. One tent contained soft goods—desert uniforms, knee socks, battle dress, and the like. Another contained non-perishable foodstuffs—powdered milk, powdered eggs, battle rations, etc. There were a number of other tents containing various items. Beyond the tents were rows of tanks and motorcycles. They were replacement vehicles fueled and ready to go when needed.

Beyond the vehicles self-propelled Bofors guns were neatly lined up in rows with the guns perfectly pitched at identical angles. At least that is the way they were supposed to be lined up. But they weren't. The guns were tilted at various angles in a crazy, disorganized pattern. The guns were supposed to be mounted on a platform with four inflated tires at each corner. A small cab with an engine in the back made the guns drivable and maneuverable. At least that was the theory. It was immediately obvious that most of the guns were missing most, if not all, of their tires.

"What do you suppose happened?" asked Buckley.

"I heard about something like this happening a month or so ago at an Aussie supply depot over near Benghazi," replied Sloan. "They never found out what happened, but they suspected it was Arabs. Turns out the tires on the Bofors fit most passenger cars. Rubber is completely unavailable to the civilian population in the Middle East. The Aussies believed Arabs came in the night, removed the tires, and sold them on the black market at exorbitant prices in Cairo."

Sloan stopped and thought for a moment.

"The Aussies got new tires on the self-propelled vehicles and all their guns were due to move up that day and did. Because they had no more Bofors guns, they did nothing about it. Our guns aren't scheduled to move out for some time so we can't just put new tires on and hope that nobody pinches them. Who was in charge of the guard detail last night?" Sloan asked.

"Lieutenant Harris," Buckley replied.

"Tell him to come to my tent immediately."

Harris came on the double. He was a young officer just out of Sandhurst and was the son and grandson of Sandhurst graduates who had gone on to illustrious careers—the grandfather in the Boer War and the father in world War I.

"Have you seen the Bofors guns this morning?" snapped Sloan.

"I have, sir. I was just making out my report," stammered Harris.

"Well, what in blazes happened to the bloody tires?" Sloan said, his voice raising several decibels.

"I don't know, sir. They were there yesterday."

"Really?" Sloan's voice dripped with a mixture of sarcasm and anger. "Didn't your sentries hear or see anything?"

"Sir, we are severely undermanned. I used all the men I can on nighttime guard duty, but that is hardly enough of them to patrol the whole area—and we can't use any lights."

Sloan's voice softened—he knew the debacle was not Harris' fault and he knew that he had used too angry a tone.

"I'll see if I can get you some more men. You can go."

"Buckley," he yelled. "See if you get me Colonel Simpson at the provost's office."

A few minutes later he had Colonel Simpson on the field phone. Sloan explained the situation to Simpson and told him of the similar experience of the Australian outfit. Simpson had heard that story previously. Sloan pleaded with him to send him some additional men to beef up his security perimeter.

"Sorry, old man," said Simpson, "but I've no one to spare."

There was pause and then Simpson said, "Half a mo. I have an idea. A battalion of Gurkhas came in this morning. I think I can spare you ten or twelve. Only for a few nights, mind you. These are combat-tested troops and they are sorely needed at the front. As you know, they are bloody fearless and ruthless. They carry scary looking blades called Kukri knives. If they take those knives from their scabbards they are required to draw blood before returning them to their scabbards – even if means cutting themselves. Maybe they can scare the bastards away."

"Much obliged, Colonel. I owe you one," a relieved Sloan said.

"Well, I'm not taking payment in zinc ointment or old socks, but a bottle of scotch would suffice," joked Simpson.

New tires arrived that afternoon and were installed on the gun carriages. Ten Gurkhas also arrived that afternoon under the command of Sergeant Raviv Singh. Sloan explained to Singh what had happened with the tires the night before. Singh said that he would deploy his men around the entire depot, but would focus specifically on protecting the guns. He assured Sloan that his men were very well trained and would be very diligent. He also asked Sloan to be sure that Sloan's men stayed away from the supply tents and particularly the guns. Singh noted that there was to be little moon that night, that it would be very dark, and that Singh did not want there to be any mistaken identities. After Singh left his tent, Sloan told Buckley to give those instructions to the men.

Sloan inspected the guns in the evening and, with their new tires in place, they were again symmetrically lined up with all their barrels pointed in the exact same direction and at the exact same angle. When Sloan inspected the guns the following morning, they were still symmetrically lined up with all their barrels pointed in the exact same direction and at the exact same angle. There was, however, something completely new and, to Sloan, totally unexpected. Laid out in front of the guns in a perfect row were the bodies of eight Arabs all precisely equidistant from each other and all with their throats neatly cut. While Sergeant Singh and Major Sloan had lunch together that day and dinner that evening, they talked of a number of things, but the killing of the eight Arabs was never discussed. Sergeant Singh and his men left two days later. Sloan never saw them again. The depot was never again bothered by thieves.

CHAPTER FOUR

THE FIELD PHONE RANG in Sloan's tent. Actually, it was more like a loud rattling. No one would confuse the sound of a field phone with one's telephone at home.

"Bernie, that you?" said the cheery voice on the other end. "It's Joe Corcoran."

Sloan had flown into Tobruk from London with a number of officers, including Colonel Joe Corcoran. During the long wait in the holding area at Croydon and the fourteen-hour flight to Tobruk, Sloan and Corcoran had gotten to know each other rather well and had come to be very friendly. They talked incessantly during the flight, interspersed by a couple of short naps by both of them. Their lengthy conversations and their friendliness was all the more surprising in that they appeared to have absolutely nothing in common other than the same uniforms and the same language. Even that latter similarity was questionable. Corcoran was a blue blood, born to wealthy landowners with palatial estates in both London and Cornwall. He had been educated at Harrow and Cambridge—as had his father, grandfather, and several earlier generations of Corcorans. He spoke with what is commonly referred to as an Oxford accent—or more properly, received pronunciation Where Sloan grew up such people were referred to as toffs and the way they spoke was said to be la-di-dah. After leaving Cambridge, where he took firsts in Romance languages and medieval history and got his blue in rugby, his well-placed connections got him a senior position in the city. He had joined the army at the start of the war, had taken officer training, had covered himself in glory (and medals) in the evacuation from Dunkirk, and had been promoted at an amazingly rapid rate. Sloan, on the other hand, had left school at thirteen and worked in his father's tailor shop. Unlike Corcoran who could trace his English ancestors to the crusades, Sloan's parents had emigrated from Poland just before the turn of the century. His accent was unmistakably cockney, although it had become less so over the years. He was ten years older than Corcoran and had got his commission and promotions primarily because of his demonstrated, though unexpected, skill in organization and expediting matters pertaining to the outfitting, arming, and otherwise supplying combat troops.

"Joe, how nice to hear from you." Sloan was genuinely pleased to renew acquaintance with Corcoran. "How is the battle?"

"A bit slow at the moment. I got a bit of shrapnel in the old leg and they've put me behind a desk. I hope it's only for a short time," replied Corcoran. "Bernie, would it be convenient for you to come up and see me at Eighth Army HQ tomorrow afternoon? There is something I would like to chat with you about. I think you'll be confoundedly interested."

Although they were on a first-name basis and the invitation was phrased as a request rather than an order, Sloan knew that it was an order. Senior officers would address other

13

officers who were only slightly below them in grade in such a fashion—particularly those with whom they were friendly and particularly those who were older.

"I'll be there," responded Sloan.

"Smashing!" exclaimed Corcoran. "I'll see you tomorrow around two. Till then, cheerio."

Sloan had never used words like "confoundedly" or "smashing" or "cheerio" before he went into the army, but he was getting used to them and even starting to say them himself. His friends and family would probably think he was putting on airs, acting like a toff and talking la-di-dah.

He told Buckley to organize transportation and a driver for him around noon the next day and he then retired to his tent to write a letter to his wife, Miriam, and his two children, Rebecca and Tom. He wrote them often and they responded immediately. He was desperately concerned about them and continually urged Miriam to get herself and the children out of London. She was adamant or—as he said—obstinate. She did not want to move and she particularly did not want to be too far from her aged parents who could not be convinced to leave the flat where they had lived for decades. Miriam was a fatalist—or at least she tried to convince Bernie that she was. "What'll be will be" she was fond of saying. He was just as fond of saying "that's ridiculous." He sighed and reached for a small glass, which had a quarter inch of water remaining. It also had two dead flies floating in the glass. As he discarded the flies, he smiled, did not squeeze them out, and drank the water with one swallow. *I suppose that means I have not been here long enough,* he thought with a smile. After tossing and turning for the better part of an hour while thinking of his family in London and the blitz, he turned off the bedside light and fell into a fitful sleep

CHAPTER FIVE

CORPORAL EVANS HAD DRIVEN from the supply depot to
Eighth Army HQ a number of times and knew the way.
Nonetheless, covering the thirty miles between the two places
in the half-track took a little over two hours. There were no
roads and, although the Italian and German troops had
fallen back some weeks earlier, there was still the occasional
raid by small parties. There were also some land mines—
both Allied and enemy—that had not been removed. The
Eighth Army HQ was a sprawling compound encircled by
several barbed wire fences some yards apart. The sentry at the
main entry checked their credentials, passed them through,
and directed them to Colonel Corcoran. Evans parked the
half-track beside the large Quonset hut, which had a wooden
marker with Colonel Corcoran's name on it.

"Shall I wait for you're here then?" he asked.

"No sense you sitting out here in the heat," Sloan replied.
"I don't know how long I'll be. Why don't you find the mess
tent and wait there? It probably won't be much cooler, but
you'll at least be out of the sun. Maybe you can scare up a
cup of tea. I understand they have a little more water here
than we do. I'll come and find you when I'm done."

"Thank you, sir," Evan said. The thought of sitting out in the blazing heat for an hour or more was not a pleasant one. "Do you want me to see if I can get you a cuppa too?" Evans asked.

"That's kind of you, Evans, but don't bother. I'm sure Colonel Corcoran will get us some."

Evans liked Sloan, as did most—if not all—of the men under his command. *Most officers in the same situation would have left the poor driver to shrivel up and blow away in the heat,* thought Evans, *but not Major Sloan. He was always looking out for his men. Take the time when Nobby Clark, a mechanic who took care of the engines, came down with a real bad case of dysentery that dehydrates a man and the only real cure is rest and liquids. There never was enough water, but Sergeant Buckley told a lot of the lads that Major Sloan had secretly given Nobby most of his water ration for several days. The major didn't want anyone to know, but not much went on at the supply depot that Buckley didn't find out about and tell everybody. Then there was the time that Sid Shepherd's old lady got badly hurt when her house in Brixton got blitzed. The major worked overtime to get Sid a compassionate leave so that he could see her. He's a good bloke old Sloan even if he is an officer,* thought Evans.

The Eighth Army headquarters was a series of Quonset huts spread over a very large area of desert. They housed the various groups that managed the affairs of the huge operation that was a fully functioning army. There were groups responsible for supplies—a major concern in the desert with troop lines broad and frequently separated from major sources of food, water, arms, and ammunition by many miles. There were groups responsible for battle plans, for engineering, for communications, for intelligence, and for many other necessary elements of a fighting force. Sloan walked into the outer office of Corcoran's building. A bespectacled clerk was busily typing away, presumably on one of the many and seemingly interminable reports that mysteriously seem to be absolutely essential to the war effort. He jumped to his feet.

"Major Sloan?"

"Yes."

"Colonel Corcoran is expecting you. Please go in."

Corcoran's office was quite large and very spartan. There was a metal desk on spindly collapsible legs. There was a series of metal cabinets, which were overflowing with papers, maps, and charts. The desk and the floor on either side had numerous papers untidily sprawled in what looked to be a haphazard fashion. There were three uncomfortable-looking metal folding chairs in front of the desk. On one of the cabinets was an ancient electric fan that made a loud whirring sound as it unsuccessfully tried to cool off the hot interior of the building. It only managed to blow the hot air in different directions. Corcoran was seated behind the desk with his feet rather carelessly plopped on top of some of the papers. He was on a field phone. He smiled broadly at Sloan and motioned him to one of the metal chairs.

"Yes, General," he said into the phone. He then put his hand over the mouthpiece and whispered to Sloan, "General McCaudle."

Corcoran didn't have to tell Sloan who he was talking to. McCaudle was the only person who could be heard all over the room when he was on the other end of the phone. He was a regular little martinet. He was only five foot six, but with his impressive waistline and his even more impressive booming voice, he seemed taller. He was known as "Shorty"

McCaudle in his years at Sandhurst, but nobody would dare call him that now, at least to his face.

"Yes, General. Major Sloan just arrived." Pause. "No, General, I have not yet spoken to him about the assignment."

Sloan could hear McCaudle say, "Took his sweet old time to get there, didn't he?"

"Well, it is long way from his supply depot and the vehicles have to proceed slowly what with there being no road and the threat of left-behind mines."

Sloan could then hear a very audible "harrumph" from the other end of the phone.

"Yes, General, I am going to discuss it with him and I'll ring you immediately after that." Pause. "Very well, General. I'll call you first thing in the morning."

It was a well-known fact that McCaudle liked to have a stiff brandy and soda mid afternoon and a short nap if he could. He was no boozer and certainly no slacker. After his nap he would work into the early hours of the morning.

Corcoran got up and shook Sloan's hand.

"Not too difficult a trip, I hope?"

"Not too bad, thanks."

"I have a possible assignment for you. You know that we have recently taken a large number of German and Italian prisoners. We have been able to transport most of the enlisted prisoners to more or less permanent camps. As you also know, under the terms of the Geneva Convention, officers and enlisted men must be in separate camps. I have never understood the logic of that, but it is what it is. The plans had been to ship the Italian and German officers to Scotland— very far north. A large camp with all necessary huts, baths, kitchens, etc. had been completed several months ago. Oh, by the way, where are my manners? How about a cup of tea?"

"I would love one," said Sloan gratefully. It had been hours since he had left the supply depot and had been a hard, hot ride.

"Corporal Jones, two teas please—and if there are any more of those chocolate biscuits my wife sent, bring some in."

"Righto, sir."

"Now where was I? Oh yes. The camp was completed and then the unexpected happened. The camp was located in a very remote area and enemy bombing was not anticipated. There had been no activity up there since the war started. A German Dornier, part of a raid on the shipbuilding locations in Tyneside near Newcastle, was hit by flak before it had dropped its load. Apparently its rudder was shot away and it drifted north, unable to steer. The crew bailed out somewhere in the Lake Country. The plane continued rudderless and crewless until it crashed, you guessed it, smack on top of the new POW camp. The bomb load exploded and blew the place to smithereens."

Corporal Jones came in with the tea and some of the chocolate biscuits.

"Your wife is lucky to have found chocolate biscuits," said Sloan.

Corcoran laughed. "That's not real chocolate. Stella made them using some mysterious ersatz concoction, some dried eggs, dried milk, and a couple spoonfuls of sugar."

"She's a genius. They taste marvelous."

"Thanks, I'll tell her. She'll be pleased. She was afraid they would taste like cardboard. Anyway, to continue the story— the place was blown to smithereens and it will take several months before we can prepare substitute accommodations. The long and short of it is that the Italian and German officer prisoners are going to have to stay here until the new place is ready. McCaudle was asked to find a senior non-combat officer who has good judgment and who will be able to interact with the enemy officers to command those camps. McCaudle passed the matter to me and I immediately thought of you. What do you think? It will only be for a few months and your second in command, Captain Bosworth, should be able to handle the supply depot until you get back."

Corcoran looked at Sloan quizzically.

"Joe, I have no experience in handling prisoners. Surely there must be someone who knows more about it than I do. Nobody could know less than I."

"That should not be a problem. Captain Lassiter is an old hand MP. He has been taking care of the perimeter security and will continue to do so. He is very experienced and has an elite group of people under his command. He will report to you and you to me. But your task will be to make daily inspections of the camps, discuss any problems or questions with the senior Italian and German officers, attend to the supply needs, and generally command the units guarding the two camps."

"All right, Joe. I'll do my best."

"Good. That's settled then. I'll tell McCaudle in the morning. He will be pleased—although he won't sound pleased. He never does. By the way, Bernie, do you speak Italian?"

"No."

"What about German?"

Sloan hesitated for a moment. His parents spoke perfectly acceptable English, but they preferred to speak to each other in Yiddish. German and Yiddish have some substantial similarities. Yiddish and German speakers can, with some degree of difficulty, make themselves understood to each other. Growing up, Sloan had learned to speak Yiddish with his parents and, while he did not use it frequently after he left home, he could still handle it.

"Oh, I know few words, but not enough to carry on a sensible conversation."

"Not to worry. Lassiter has two non-coms. One speaks fluent Italian. The other speaks serviceable German—not perfect, but good enough for our purposes. Besides, I think the senior Italian and German officers have some English. The camps are only four miles north of here. Can you be in place by the end of the week? Lassiter will show you the ropes. The billets are not the Savoy, but they may be a slight cut above where you are now."

"I'll be here."

"Splendid."

Sloan picked up Evans in the mess tent and they drove slowly back to the supply depot. He felt somewhat uneasy about not having told Joe Corcoran about his ability to speak Yiddish. He had long ago convinced himself that his failure to tell anybody in the military that he was Jewish had nothing to do with being ashamed or guilt ridden about his Jewish background. He did not feel that being Jewish was anything to be ashamed of or to feel guilty about. His rationale was that nobody in the army had asked him if he was Jewish. Nobody just walks up and asks, "Are you Jewish?" Of course, he found it a little more difficult to explain to himself why he had put down on his enlistment papers in the square seeking religious preference "None." He did have a Bar Mitzvah. He didn't want to, but his parents insisted. He didn't go to synagogue often—usually on Yom Kippur, but then most Jews went then. Besides, the nature of his religious beliefs—if any—was nobody's business.

"Almost there, Major," Evans called out over the desert wind.

It was starting to get dark and the desert wasn't the greatest place to be at night, what with their being no lights, no road, and the possibility of mines. Sloan thought of his conversation with Corcoran—what was said and what was not said. Sloan hated all Germans and all things German—and had for as long as he could remember. He had not mentioned this hatred to Corcoran. It wasn't just Germans, it was also the language, the goods they made, and everything else. When Rebecca was five, he had bought her a pink tricycle for her birthday with a wicker basket, a bell, and light blue and yellow ribbons. She was thrilled. It wasn't until the next day when Sloan was adjusting the seat that he noticed for the first time that the tricycle had been made in Germany. He immediately took it back to the shop. It took him a week to find a suitable replacement that was not made in Germany. Rebecca cried the whole week until the replacement came. It was ironic, to say the least, that he was now to be the commandant of the POW camp. He would write his family and tell them the news. They knew how much he hated Germans and they shared his feelings—although perhaps not as intensely. All outgoing mail was opened and censored, but he did not think the censors would object to his news.

"You all right, Major? You haven't said a thing or moved a muscle since we left Eighth Army."

"I'm fine. Just thinking of all the girls I left behind me," he said in a poor effort at humor. Evans gave a little dutiful laugh

CHAPTER SIX

"THIS CHAP SLOAN—IS HE a Jew?" This was the first thing General McCaudle said in his phone call with Colonel Corcoran the next morning.

"I have no idea," said Corcoran, taken aback by the question—although when he had first met Sloan, he had wondered himself. He had quickly dismissed the issue in his own mind as being unimportant and irrelevant. He had always prided himself on his lack of racial or religious bias, although it had not always been easy. His family was a firmly entrenched noble English family who could trace their ancestry to the time of the Romans and they once had firmly entrenched ideas about who was and who wasn't acceptable.

"Why do you ask, General?"

"Oh don't be daft," McCaudle said petulantly. "You're not usually this dense. People say that Jews aren't to be trusted. They're greedy moneygrubbers who are out for themselves and have no loyalty to their country—whatever country they live in. Mind you, I'm not saying that's necessarily my view, but people do talk."

Oh really, thought Corcoran. "The Jews I have known are not like that," replied Corcoran.

He was aware that was not what the old bigot wanted to hear, but he didn't care. When Corcoran started his first year at Cambridge, he was assigned a Jew as a roommate. Corcoran had never met a Jew before and was more than a little wary. His parents were irate when they heard and Corcoran's father—who had more than a little influence at the university—was insistent that he talk to his contacts and get the housing arrangements changed. Corcoran talked him out of it. Not because he wanted to room with Aaron Rosen, but because he didn't want to start his university career with controversy and by being labeled as a bigot. Besides the arrangement would only be for one term. After that, students would be permitted to make whatever change they wanted. In a totally unexpected development, Rosen and Corcoran really hit it off. They found much in common. They loved to hike and they did a lot of it together in their years at Cambridge. They loved the theater and they made many a trip to London to see plays, musicals, and comedies. They both were athletes; Corcoran won his blue as a fullback on the university rugby team and Rosen his blue as a talented half-miler. Most importantly, they loved to talk to each other and they did a lot of that over the years. They talked about their home life, what they hoped to do in the future, the women they had dated, the food they liked and didn't like, their schoolwork, anything and everything. They roomed together for the entire four years and they stayed in close touch with each other after graduation. Indeed, Corcoran was Rosen's best man at his wedding, wore a yarmulke, and even learned a little Yiddish to inject into the mandatory best man speech at the post-wedding banquet.

In an even more unlikely development, Corcoran's parents became extremely fond of Rosen (who was a houseguest at the Corcoran's country estate on a number of occasions). While trite, it was true that Aaron Rosen became like a son to the Corcorans. Aaron was also responsible for teaching old man Corcoran a great lesson.

"You know, Aaron," Joe's father said once, "you are different from other Jews."

"The only difference," Aaron said, "is that you know me and you don't know all the other Jews."

"I looked at his service record," the general said. "He doesn't show any religious affiliation. I thought that was strange—as though he was trying to hide something."

"Lots of people claim no religious affiliation. I don't think it means that they are hiding anything," said Corcoran.

"Well, I don't trust a man who has no religious affiliation—no matter what his reason and that name 'Sloan'—Jews do change their names to hide the fact that they are members of the 'chosen race.' Well, it's your funeral, Corcoran. It's your recommendation and if it doesn't work out well—" his voice trailed off.

They said good-bye and hung up. Conversations with General McCaudle were never pleasant, but this one was one of the worst to that point. There was worse to come.

CHAPTER SEVEN

SLOAN FINISHED PACKING FOR his temporary posting to the POW camps and traveled to Eighth Army HQ by half-track. Cpl. Evans drove and Sergeant Buckley came too. Corcoran had agreed that Buckley and Evans should be assigned with Sloan to the camps until such time as the prisoners were transported to their permanent facilities. At HQ, the three of them were introduced by Corcoran to Captain Lassiter (the MP officer in charge of security), Lance Corporal Anthony Scalosi (the Italian interpreter), and Private Ronald Herman (the German interpreter). Evans then drove them the short distance to the camps.

The Italian camp and the German camp were separated by about two hundred yards. Each camp was in the shape of a square and each took up about four acres. The camps were surrounded by two separate barbed wire fences approximately ten yards apart. There were four towers fifty feet high in the middle of each side of the square. The towers were manned by guards armed with machine guns. In addition, there were four guards on foot, one on each side. There were two gates in each compound, one directly in front of the other, which would permit access by guards into the compounds. Between the two compounds and equidistant from each were five Quonset huts for the British guards; one was the barracks for the enlisted men; one was the quarters for Lassiter and Second Lieutenant Peter Bradshaw; one was the quarters for the commanding officer, Sloan; one was the kitchen and mess hall for the guards, and one was the lavatory facilities.

"Do you want to see the compounds now, sir?" said Lassiter.

"Why not," said Sloan.

"Which one first?"

"You choose."

Lassiter opened both gates to the German compound with keys from a huge chain. As soon as they entered, a young German officer strode up to them, came to attention, clicked his heels, and saluted. Sloan was surprised to see how neat and clean the young officer was. His uniform, though with a couple of tears in one shoulder, was pressed and his boots shiny.

"I want to see the senior German officer," Sloan told him. The German seemed puzzled. Herman translated Sloan's order into German and the officer saluted again and disappeared into the closest hut. Almost immediately, a tall slim officer emerged and approached the English group. He too was as immaculate as one could be under the circumstances. His blond hair tinged with gray, protruding from the back of his cap, was neatly cut. His boots also gleamed and he was clean-shaven. He came to attention in front of Sloan and, without clicking his heels, saluted.

"Tell him that I am Major Sloan, the new camp commandant," Sloan told Herman, returning the German's salute.

"An interpreter is not necessary," said the German officer,

speaking with virtually no accent, "I speak English. I am Colonel Hans Dieter Reichmann."

"Your English is excellent, Colonel. May I ask where you achieved such mastery of the language?"

"Of course, Major. For several years, my father was a consular officer in the German embassy in London. I attended an English grammar school near the embassy."

"I would like to talk to your officers, Colonel, and let them know what I expect."

Reichmann turned to the young officer to whom Sloan had first spoken and who had remained a discreet distance behind Reichmann. Reichmann said something in German to the young man who snapped to attention and immediately ran into all the other buildings shouting instructions in German. At once, German officers came streaming out of five buildings. As Sloan came to know, those five buildings were barracks. In each building, there were sixty bunks—fifteen uppers and fifteen lowers on each side of the center aisle. There was also a building that served as a kitchen and mess hall and a building with a latrine and washbasins. Similar to the Allied troops, the prisoners were allowed one helmet full of water a day. The configuration was the same in the Italian compound.

Reichmann barked out orders to his men and they formed three lines facing Sloan and came to attention.

"I am Major Sloan and I am the new commandant of this prisoner of war camp," Sloan said.

Reichmann started to interpret, but Sloan interrupted him.

"Excuse me, Colonel Reichmann," he said politely, but firmly. "I prefer the interpretation be conducted by Private Herman."

"As you wish, Major," Reichmann said coolly but without any noticeable rancor.

Sloan continued with his presentation, pausing periodically to permit Herman to translate what he had said into German.

"As I said, I am Major Sloan and I am the new commandant of this prisoner of war camp. These are temporary facilities and we are hoping to have a more permanent camp up and running shortly. I can't tell you when that will be, but hopefully not too long in coming. Water is in short supply, but you should know that the amount allocated to each of you is the same as is allocated to each British soldier, officer, or enlisted man. I understand that the Swiss Red Cross will be distributing packages to each of you—perhaps as early as next week. As you can see, there are machine guns in each of the towers and the guards on the ground carry automatic weapons. Our troops are ordered to prevent escape by any means necessary. Are there any questions?"

The German officers remained silent and remained at attention.

"Colonel Reichmann, you may dismiss your men."

Reichmann turned and barked out the command and the Germans all returned to their huts. It was too hot outside to remain longer than necessary.

At Sloan's request, Reichmann conducted a tour of the barracks and the other buildings in the compound. Sloan was impressed. The beds were all made in military fashion, taut enough to flip a coin in the air. The footlockers were neatly arranged and the floors swept clean. The mess hall and the latrine were similarly spotless and in impeccable order.

"I will come back again tomorrow and every day—sometimes more than once," he said to Reichmann.

"Very well, Major," said Reichmann.

When they got outside, Sloan said to Lassiter, "Let's go see the Italians."

"You're in for a shock," said Lassiter.

Even being forewarned, Sloan was not prepared for what he saw. They walked into the Italian compound. Nobody came out to meet them. There was a makeshift clothesline spread between two of the barracks. On the clothesline were two pair of underpants and several pairs of socks. The underpants were covered in polka dots of pink, green, and light blue. The socks had alternating yellow and green bands. Sloan looked inquiringly at Lassiter, who smiled and shook his head.

"You ain't seen nothing yet."

They walked into the closest barracks.

"Cor Blimey! I've not seen anything like this since the brawl after the pillow fight at Aldershot," said Buckley. Six men naked to the waist and wearing garish underpants were playing cards on an upturned footlocker. Other men in a variety of clothing that was never issued to them by anyone's army were sleeping on unmade beds. There were crumpled clothes and bed linens everywhere. Pictures of nude or near-nude women were tacked up on the walls and several other clotheslines were strung across the room with various items of clothing hanging on them.

"Good lord," exclaimed Sloan. "What a bloody mess! Are all the Italian barracks like this?"

"Oh no," said Lassiter.

"Well, that's a relief," sighed Sloan.

"Some of them are worse," replied Lassiter.

"How could they be worse?"

"You'll see," said Lassiter.

"Where did they get the bizarre underwear?" said Sloan.

"I haven't a clue," replied Lassiter.

Nobody got up at attention—or otherwise. None of the Italians even looked at the visitors.

"Corporal Scalosi, tell them I want to see the senior Italian officer right now," Sloan almost shouted.

Scalosi made the announcement. There was general laughter in the room.

"What's so funny?" said Sloan, starting to get angry.

An older man clad only in a towel rose from the top bunk at the end of the room.

"Don't be angry, Major," the man said in very pronounced Italian accent. "We are not laughing at you. You have to understand something. We are not cowards. We fought the good fight as we were ordered to do. We lost a lot of our troops. They were our friends and our comrades, but we are also not heroes and we definitely are not Nazis. Nobody in the Italian compound wanted to be in this war and we are pleased we are now out of it. When you asked for the senior Italian officer, it is probably me—but none of us any longer think of ourselves as military men, only as men. We will not be an escape threat. You really don't need barbed wire or guards. We just want to go home to our wives and families."

There was a long pause, but no further laughter. It seemed to Sloan that several of the Italians were wiping away tears, but maybe it was just the infernal sand that got into everything. Suddenly the escape part of the speech he had given to the Germans seemed unnecessary and he didn't make it.

Chapter Eight

"MAY I SPEAK TO you privately for a few minutes, Major?" asked Reichmann.

"Of course," responded Sloan, momentarily taken aback by the request.

Reichmann's request was made to Sloan during his third visit to the compound. They went into the small hut that was reserved for the senior German officer. It was large enough for a narrow bed and a single chair. Reichmann sat on the bed and Sloan on the chair.

"Well, what is it?" said Sloan.

"I'm not sure where to start," replied Reichmann.

"It's usually a good idea to start at the beginning," said Sloan.

Reichmann gave a little nervous laugh, cleared his throat, and started in. "I'm not a career officer. I am what I think you English call a retread. I was a junior officer in the First World War. In the cavalry and then the infantry. That was when the cavalry was horses—not like now when cavalry means tanks and other armored vehicles, but no horses. Outside of the Hurtgen Forest, we ran into a column of French troops and I got hit in the leg. We had a doctor in our outfit—a Jew named

Meyer Helstein. The bullet broke my femur and nicked the femoral artery. I would have bled to death if it hadn't been for Helstein. Almost everybody with that type of injury died on the battlefield in those days. Helstein stemmed the bleeding and carried me back by himself to the battalion aid station, which was more than a mile away. He was not a large man and, to this day, I don't know how he managed it.

After the war, Meyer and I and our families became very close. A relationship of that sort was very unusual in Germany——even in the twenties. My family is Prussian. They have strict—and you might say very harsh—rules as to acceptable and unacceptable relationships. Meyer had a medical practice in a storefront in Frankfurt. I lived with my wife and children on the other side of the Main River outside of Sachsenhausen. Meyer was an accomplished violinist. I am a less-than-accomplished cellist. We played in a string quartet for many years. We were frequent visitors in each other's houses and our children played together. Things steadily got worse in Germany and Jews began to be taken away to mysterious places. We found out later that they were concentration camps. For a while, the Helsteins were left alone. He was a good doctor and they were in short supply. We knew it was only a matter of time, however. Meyer and I talked a lot about it. One night, a mob attacked his storefront, breaking up his medical office and leaving ugly painted signs on his front door. Meyer was badly beaten and his wife and children terrorized."

Reichmann seemed to have some difficulty and paused. Sloan had no idea where this was going, but he had become deeply interested.

"Please continue, Colonel." Reichmann cleared his throat and went on.

"It was clear that the Helsteins had to get out of Germany immediately or end up in a concentration camp. Meyer told me that he had been told that there was a safe house in a small German village called Leinzen on the Swiss border and that some Jews had successfully been helped across the border into Switzerland by the people who operated the safe house. Meyer no longer had a car. It had long since been confiscated. There was no way he and his wife could get to the village in any event. Even if they had a car, they did not have appropriate papers or travel permits. They would not have gotten twenty miles. By this time, I had been recalled into the army and was stationed temporarily outside Frankfurt. One weekend, and late at night, I took some travel authorizations from the battalion HQ files, filled them out, 'borrowed' an army lorry, hid Meyer, his wife, and children under some packaging in the back of the lorry, drove them to the safe house in the border village, and then drove back to Frankfurt. Somehow I was not discovered and shortly thereafter I was posted elsewhere. To this day, I have no idea what happened to the Helsteins and I have been terribly concerned about them. I wonder if there is any way you could find out for me. They are my friends. They are wonderful people. I would not be alive today if it wasn't for Meyer."

"Very interesting story, Colonel," said Sloan. "Of course, I can't promise anything and I don't even know where to start, but I will see what I can find out."

"Thank you. I can't ask for more than that," said Reichmann.

Very interesting, thought Lieutenant Heinrich Von Steuffel who had been listening to the conversation with his ear pressed against the thin hut wall. *Our esteemed colonel is a Jew-lover and a traitor."*

CHAPTER NINE

"A REMARKABLE STORY," SAID Corcoran. "Maybe even true, but I doubt it."

It was several days after Sloan's conversation with Reichmann about the Helsteins and Sloan was having dinner with Corcoran and other officers at Eighth Army HQ. Sloan had recounted the story at length to a very interested group.

"Why do you doubt its truthfulness?" said Sloan. "Although, I must say I had some misgivings about it myself."

"We have heard similar stories from other captured German officers before," cut in Major Nigel St. John who had listened with a somewhat cynical expression on his face. "They want to ingratiate themselves with their captors."

"To what end?" said Sloan. "There is not much we can do for them. Do they think we'll give them more rations or let them take showers more frequently? What's the point of manufacturing such fantastic stories?"

"Good question," said St. John. "We don't know. Maybe they think we'll let our guard down. Maybe that would help them with escape plans. Who knows?"

"I'll tell you what," said Corcoran. "Let's check his story."

"How can that be done?" asked Sloan.

"My father is on the board of directors of several international charities," said Corcoran. "I think, with his contacts, he could have the Swiss Red Cross try to run down Reichmann's story. With so much going on these days, it may be very difficult to come up with anything, but it's worth a try."

"I'll wager a fiver that, if they can find out anything, it will be that the story is a phony. Any takers?" said St. John.

There were no takers.

CHAPTER TEN

THE GENEVA HEADQUARTERS OF the Swiss Red Cross had always been a busy place. Since the late thirties it had become a virtual beehive of activity. It was swamped by inquiries from people desperate for any information about their relatives who they believed had sought to escape from Germany. After the war started and Western European countries fell to the Nazi invasion, the inquiries increased from people seeking information about Jewish relatives seeking to flee—not only from Germany, but also from occupied countries. Crossings into Switzerland were attempted from many locations, but principally in the area of Basel and from Ferney Voltaire into Geneva. There were several other places, including the small German village of Leinzen, which bordered Switzerland in a mountainous area sparsely populated and physically difficult to traverse.

Frederic LaVienne, the *chef de bureau* for alien registration, had taken a call from a consular official at the British embassy seeking information about a family named Helstein. He walked down the hall into a large room full of numerous small desks loaded down with papers, files, and boxes. A large number of people moved around the room from metal filing cabinets to desks and back to the filing cabinets. They pulled out documents, briefly read them, and then added them to the piles on the various desks. The scene was one of semi-organized chaos. The only relief from the drabness of the room was the view from the windows of Lake LeMan and the mountains. Nobody in the room seemed to have much time for the view.

LaVienne looked around the room and spotted a young man poring over some documents at a desk close to one of the windows.

"Etienne," LaVienne called out above the din of chatter and the incessant rattle of paper. "I have an inquiry that needs immediate attention."

Etienne groaned, "They all need immediate attention. There's a lot of inquiries ahead of that one."

"We had better give this one priority. It was forwarded to us by the British Embassy. It comes from an Englishman named Rupert Corcoran—Sir Rupert Corcoran to be precise. He is somebody of importance apparently. These people he is inquiring about—name of Helstein—were supposedly taken to Leinzen by a senior German officer who was apparently helping them escape," said LaVienne.

Etienne looked considerably more interested. "A senior German officer!" He looked around the crowded room with the myriad of paperwork. "Well, that is one for the books. I've never heard of anything like that before. Even with priority, it's going to take a while."

The records were understandably incomplete and somewhat haphazard. Efforts had been made to systematize the information, but it was difficult. There were misspellings, holes in the data and many of the names had slipped through cavernous cracks.

"When did these people try to cross?" asked Etienne.

"I don't know," replied LaVienne.

"I'll get started. Leinzen you say. I just remembered. My cousin works in our embassy in Berlin. He was on holiday here in Geneva some time ago. He stayed at my house. He told me he was at a reception at the embassy for something, I don't remember what. One of the German attaches was there and had too many schnapps before he arrived. He was bragging about a raid the Gestapo made on a safe house in Leinzen. He said that that house never had a chance. Only one person had ever been transported there and he was a man. No women and no families. He said there were guides there also, I forgot how many. The Gestapo shot the lot of them right then and there."

"Is your cousin still in Berlin?" asked LaVienne.

"Yes, he is still at the embassy."

"Call him. See if you can get any more information and ask him, if he knows, when the German says the raid took place."

Later that day, Etienne came into LaVienne's office. "I spoke to my cousin. He said that he didn't get much more information. The German ambassador heard the attaché talking about the raid and yelled at him to shut up, then took him out of the room and he was not seen again. Before he was silenced, the attaché told him the raid took place on March 4, 1940. My cousin clearly remembers that date because it is his birthday. Doesn't sound like that German officer was telling the truth about saving the lives of those Jews. By the way, the only name I came across that's anything like Helstein is a family named Hernsen or something like that. Obviously, if our information is correct, they didn't cross at

Leinzen. They were sent to England. I have an address. That's the best I can do."

All of the information gathered by the Swiss Red Cross was forwarded to Sir Rupert Corcoran who immediately went to the address of the Hernsen family. It was in a rundown block of flats in a seedy area of Stepney. Sir Rupert's rap on the door was answered by a tall, middle-aged, dark-haired man who looked at the caller with marked suspicion.

"What do you want?" he said with a thick accent.

"Are you Mr. Hernsen?" Sir Rupert asked.

"What business is that of yours?" The man said belligerently.

"I'm looking for a family who escaped from Germany into Switzerland and was helped by a German officer named Reichmann."

The man whose prior expression was dour and inhospitable broke into peals of laughter. "Ingrid, come here," he yelled. A short gray-haired woman came running to the door. "This man asked whether some German officer helped us to escape. Mister, you are either joking or you're mad. No German officer would ever help a Jew and, believe me, no German—officer or otherwise—lifted a finger to help us. I'm sure they would help us to the closest concentration camp. Now go away and play your silly jokes on someone else." And with that, he slammed the door in Sir Rupert's face.

CHAPTER ELEVEN

"Bernie, it's Joe," said Corcoran. "I got a letter from my father. He has been in touch with the Swiss Red Cross. I have good news and bad news for you. The good news is that you were smart not to take St. John's bet. The bad news is that St. John was right. Your Colonel Reichmann is a liar. He didn't help any Jews to escape. While the information is a little questionable, it seems likely that only one potential escapee was ever taken to Leinzen and he almost certainly wasn't a Helstein. No one got over the border from Leinzen. Everybody at that safe house was shot on the spot by the Gestapo. My father also went to see a family named Hernsen in London who had apparently escaped to Switzerland from Germany, but not from Leinzen. The man laughed at my father and said he must be mad if he thought that any German officer would ever help a Jew escape."

Sloan could not contain his anger. "I knew it. The filthy murderous German bastards. They're scum," Sloan exploded.

Corcoran was not surprised that Sloan was angry, but he was taken aback by the ferocity of his reaction.

"Calm down, Bernie," he said soothingly. "It's not like

a long-lost friend has just been shown to have feet of clay. It's just some German prisoner trying to get something. Besides, we are not 100 percent certain that our information is correct."

"Oh, it's correct all right. I suspected this. I'll call you later, Joe," Sloan said and hung up.

Sloan jumped up—knocking his chair over—and strode out of the office.

"Anything wrong, Major?" Buckley called after him.

"Nothing. I'm going to the German compound," said Sloan.

"You want me to come with you?"

"No."

"You forgot your sidearm."

Sloan just kept walking. Buckley scratched his head. *I wonder what made him so upset,* he thought.

Sloan stormed into the German compound and caught up with Reichmann who was walking in the yard. "Reichmann, I want to talk with you in your hut right now."

"Certainly, Major."

After they got in the hut, Reichmann said, "Won't you sit down?"

Sloan ignored him. "You made the whole damn thing up," he shouted.

"What are you talking about?" Reichmann said, looking puzzled.

"Don't play the innocent with me, Reichmann. There are no Helsteins, no friendship with Jews, and no trying to help them escape. You made it all up. Every last thing. What I don't understand is why. What did you hope to gain? You are just another murderous Nazi. You bastards are all the damn same." Sloan's voice started out loud and got louder.

Reichmann sat down, his face a bright scarlet. "You're wrong, Major. You couldn't be more wrong. I don't know where you got your information, but it is wrong, wrong, wrong."

"Shut up," yelled Sloan, "I don't want to hear any more about this—not now and not ever."

He stormed out back to his office past a startled Buckley who only stood there with his mouth open.

That night, Sloan wrote a longer letter to his family than usual, detailing the events of the day and closing with, "I hate every one of them. There is not a good one anywhere. Love to all." After he had taken the letter to the post, he regretted the degree of vituperation. Not that it didn't clearly express his thoughts—but it was not right to say such angry things in a letter to his wife and children and phrased in what he now thought was a childish manner.

CHAPTER TWELVE

As TIME PASSED, SLOAN's volatile anger subsided somewhat—but by no means completely. His hatred for Germany and all things German persisted, but it was controlled and did not influence his ability to perform his job. Corcoran, who continued to be puzzled by the extraordinary explosiveness of Sloan's reaction to Reichmann's deception, helped calm Sloan.

"Yes he's a deceptive bastard. Yes, he's despicable and yes, he tried to pull the wool over your eyes. I still don't know why or what he hoped to gain. Maybe he thought you and your men would relax their guard and they could escape. Where they would go if they got out of the compound I have no idea. It's a hundred or more miles across desert to their lines and they could never make it. But, let's face it, he's a Nazi officer and he'll play all the cards he has—or thinks he has. He wasn't just picking on you. Relax. Let it go. I'm sure it was nothing personal so don't take it as such. If the positions were reversed, we would do whatever we could to gain an advantage."

Sloan continued his daily inspections of the two camps. His relationship with Reichmann was icily formal. Neither

44

one of them mentioned the aid that Reichmann had claimed he had provided to the Jewish doctor and his family. The one adjustment that Sloan made was that he was no longer willing to discuss any camp matters with Reichmann in English. Despite Reichmann's known fluency in English, Sloan insisted that all conversations be conducted through Sloan's interpreter.

Running the camps settled into an almost boring routine. No escapes were attempted. No disturbances occurred. While water remained in short supply, the amount available remained the same and food was relatively plentiful. Even the Italian camp became slightly more presentable. The colorful underwear remained and the lack of organization still existed. However, the beds were made daily and formations were slightly more military than they had been.

Even General McCaudle offered some grudging, backhanded praise during his weekly staff meeting. "Corcoran, your selection of Sloan to run the POW camps may not be the worst thing you've done. At least they haven't fallen completely to pieces and nobody has escaped or killed anyone."

For McCaudle, that was the equivalent of awarding Sloan the Victoria Cross.

Chapter Thirteen

The intercom buzzed.

"Mrs. Chapman, I told you I didn't want to be disturbed," Sir Rupert Corcoran said irritably. He was meeting with a delegation of the School Emergency Preparedness Committee concerning funding for more onsite air-raid shelter protection. It was one of the many civic functions that Sir Rupert immersed himself in.

"It's Mr. LaVienne from the Swiss Red Cross calling from Geneva. You talked to him some time ago about the Helstein matter. He says he has some further information for you," she said. "I thought you would want to take it," she said gently. She had worked for Sir Rupert for many years and she knew the many projects in which he was involved and the great pressure he was under.

"Thank you, Mrs. Chapman. I apologize. I'll take it in the reception area. Ladies and gentlemen, please forgive me. This is a call I must take. I will be with you in a moment," Sir Rupert said.

"Sir Rupert, I am sorry to bother you, but I have some additional information for you," a heavily accented French voice said. "It is probably of no help in your inquiries about the Helsteins, but I thought I would pass it on for whatever it is worth."

"It's very kind of you to call and I'm most appreciative of your interest in this matter," Corcoran said.

"My colleague, Etienne Bernois, was troubled by the source of the information that his cousin passed on about the safe house at Leinzen and so he expanded his search to include all refugees who came into Switzerland regardless of their point of entry. You remember he came up with the name Hernsen, but that was almost by accident. He has since delved much deeper, examining hundreds of documents. It was an arduous task and I'm not sure it bore any worthwhile results. The closest we have is to a family by the name of Holstern who crossed into Switzerland from Germany— although we are not exactly sure when that happened. The spelling is different from the information we got from you and they are probably not the people you are seeking. However, spelling of names of refugees sometimes is in error. I fear that, despite Etienne's efforts, this new information about the Holsterns, if that is their names, will be of no more help than the information about the Hernsens."

"Do you have any information about their whereabouts?" asked Sir Rupert.

"Mr. Holstern and members of his family were sent to England some time ago. We do not have a telephone number, but we have an address. It is 147 Carron Gardens in Poplar."

"Thank you so much. This is extremely helpful. Please express my gratitude to Monsieur Bernois. He has made a truly yeoman effort," said Sir Rupert.

"I hope these are the persons you are looking for."

The meeting seemed to go on interminably, but finally concluded. He rushed out and jumped in a taxi.

"147 Carron Gardens, Poplar. Do you know where that is?" Corcoran asked the cab driver.

"Do I know where it is?" the cabbie responded with mock incredulity. "I took 'the Knowledge' thirty-five years ago, guv. There is no place in this bloody town I can't find. Of course, the German bastards have rearranged a few things. You sure you want to go to Poplar. There was a lot of bombing there last night. It'll take a while. There's a lot of detours."

The trip from Holborn to Poplar should ordinarily take twenty minutes. It took an hour and fifteen minutes. There was a lot of bomb damage, particularly close to the river. Much of it had not been cleared from the roadways. Finally, after some skillful maneuvering, the cab arrived at 147 Carron Gardens. This was a low-income area of row houses all inseparable one from the other. Despite the recent bombing and a light drizzle, groups of children were playing in the street and small groups of women in aprons were chatting with each other. They looked up mildly interested. It was rare for a cab to stop in Carron Gardens and even rarer for a well-dressed toff to get out and go to one of the houses.

A painfully thin woman in her fifties answered his knock. She was wearing an apron and her graying hair was pulled back severely into a bun. Corcoran thought she would be quite attractive if she wore makeup and had her hair done.

"Yes?" she said inquiringly.

"Are you Mrs. Helstein?" he asked.

"Why do you want to know?" she asked suspiciously and in an understandable, but strong German accent.

"My name is Rupert Corcoran. Please don't be afraid. I

mean you no harm. I am really here on a mission of mercy," he said reassuringly. "Do you spell your name H-E-L-S-T-E-I-N?"

"Yes, that is my name and that is the correct spelling," she said.

"Eureka!" he exclaimed excitedly.

"Pardon?" she said.

"Oh, I am sorry. Do you know a German officer named Hans Dieter Reichmann?"

Her eyes widened and, for a moment, he thought she was going to faint. "You know Hansi?" she said excitedly. "Where is he? Is he all right? Oh, please tell me he is alive and well."

"Yes, he is alive and well," said Corcoran with a smile. "You call him Hansi, do you?"

"Oh, thank God. Thank God. Yes. We always called him Hansi. The children called him Uncle Hansi. Please come in. Do come in. My husband will be home any minute."

Sir Rupert was just finishing a cup of tea that Mrs. Helstein insisted he have when Meyer Helstein arrived.

"Meyer, this is Mr. Corcoran." Sir Rupert did not correct her misuse of the title. "He has wonderful news. Hansi is alive and well."

Corcoran thought that Helstein was going to cry. His eyes welled up and his voice quavered.

"Oh my! That is wonderful news. I am so happy. Where is he?"

"He is in a prisoner-of-war camp in the North African desert. He has told the commandant of the camp that your family and his family are close friends."

"The closest," said Helstein.

49

"And that you saved his life during the First World War."

"Oh, I don't know about that," Helstein said modestly, "but maybe I helped a little."

"I'm sure it was more than that. Colonel Reichmann said he helped you and your family escape from Germany."

"If it wasn't for Hansi, we would all be in a concentration camp and probably dead by now," exclaimed Mrs. Helstein. "He took an enormous risk. If what he did was discovered, he might have been executed. We owe everything to him. I wish the children were here, but they have been evacuated to Devon. They will be so excited when we tell them."

Meyer Helstein told Sir Rupert how he and his family knew Reichmann and related the full story of the trip to Leinzen, which was precisely as Reichmann had told Sloan. He also told Sir Rupert how the Helsteins made it across the border into Switzerland and how it came about that they ended up in London. Dr. Helstein was practicing medicine in the East End under a special license from the British Medical Association. Over a second cup of tea, which Mrs. Helstein again insisted he have, Sir Rupert asked the Helsteins if they could remember the date that they crossed into Switzerland. Mrs. Helstein thought for a moment.

"I am sure it was March 2, 1940. Remember, Meyer, Hansi told us not to take the children out of school in the middle of the week for fear that the authorities would be suspicious. March 1 was a school holiday, I don't remember why, and that was the day we left our house. We crossed the border the next day. We were lucky," she said.

You don't know how lucky, Sir Rupert thought. March 4 was the day the Gestapo raided the safe house and killed everybody. He decided not to tell them that.

He had to walk a long way in the rain before he could find a cab rank. He was kept dry by use of an umbrella that Mrs. Helstein insisted he borrow, laughingly saying that the loan would ensure that he would come back in order to return it. His step was light and his mood buoyant. Not all the moisture on his face was the result of the rain.

Chapter Fourteen

"It's Colonel Corcoran on the field phone," called Sergeant Buckley from the outer office.

"Bernie, are you sitting down?" said Corcoran.

"No. Why?" queried Sloan.

"Well, maybe you should. My father has found the Helsteins. They are living in London. They are close friends of Reichmann. They were saved by Reichmann. He did take them to the safe house in Leinzen and they did cross the border from there into Switzerland. Everything Reichmann said is true."

Sloan was silent for what seemed to be five minutes, but was only a few seconds. "What have I done?" he said softly.

"What do you mean?" said Corcoran.

Sloan related his angry attack on Reichmann.

"Don't beat yourself up, Bernie. We got the wrong information. It's as simple as that. It's nobody's fault. The Swiss records are not the clearest and that's not their fault either. Look, we all know that the Germans have committed the most widespread, the most cruel, the most bestial acts in the history of the world. It's understandable that we would not accept and would reject the idea that an isolated German would perform an incredible act of kindness, of humanity," consoled Corcoran.

"We—I shouldn't have accepted the word of some drunken German attaché. I should have taken that with a grain of salt. But we were told that the one escapee who was killed there was the only one who ever came to that house."

"The Helsteins left the safe house on March 2. The Gestapo raided it two days later. The drunk was wrong. We were all wrong—not just you, Bernie. Tell Reichmann we were wrong and let it go. No harm done."

Let it go? No harm done! Sloan thought later. *How can I? I have let my hatred for Germans and all things German control me. I should have waited. I should have let Reichmann explain. For anyone other than a German, I would have done that.* Sloan paced up and down his small hut for an hour or more. *What am I going to tell him? How can I face him?* He rehearsed a number of different explanations and apologies. None of them seemed adequate or sounded sincere enough. There are a lot of unexpected twists and turns in life. Some more unexpected than others. *No one could have told me that I would be desperately trying to develop a satisfactory apology to a German officer,* he thought.

After he hung up, Corcoran pushed his chair back, put his feet on the desk, and lit a cigar. He took a big puff, let it out, and stared at the ceiling. Life does create some strange and unfathomable connections. Here he was, a British colonel, the scion of a landed family whose conservative-minded family was as far removed from the Jewish community as was possible and yet his college roommate and his best friend was a Jew. Four miles away was a German colonel, the scion of a conservative Prussian family whose conservative-minded

53

family was as far removed from the Jewish community as was possible—and yet his best friend and closest confidant was a Jew. Maybe there was still hope for the world. One nagging thought troubled him. Why had he not told Sloan of this incredible irony?

CHAPTER FIFTEEN

"COLONEL REICHMANN, I HAVE done you a grave injustice and I have come here to apologize to you. I really don't know what to say. I never thought I would be apologizing to a German officer for anything. The Helsteins are in London. They are fit and well and the doctor is practicing medicine at a clinic in the East End. Colonel Corcoran's father met with them and they were ecstatic to find that you too are fit and well."

Sloan stood awkwardly, not knowing what else to say, but feeling that the incredibly heroic act of Reichmann and the angry tirade that he had launched at Reichmann was worthy of more than the halting apology he had just given.

Reichmann, who had been standing in his hut, stood silently for several seconds, sat down on his bed, and covered his eyes. Finally he spoke, "Thank you, Major" he said. "There is no need to apologize. Given what has happened in Europe, it is perfectly understandable that you and your colleagues would doubt what any German would say to you. It was extremely kind of you and your comrades to go through all this trouble. I cannot begin to tell you how much this means to me."

"I must tell you something, Colonel. What you did for the Helsteins probably affects me more than most people."

"Why is that, Major?" asked Reichmann.

"Because I am a Jew."

"I thought perhaps you were, but your name confused me."

"I feel that you are different from other Germans. You have a sensitivity and a compassion that other Germans don't have."

Reichmann smiled and said, "The difference between me and other Germans is that you know me, but you don't know all the other Germans. We are not all cruel, rampaging inhuman beasts—although I don't need to tell you that many of us are."

On the short walk back to his office, Sloan reflected on the amazing events of the day. He had found out that a Prussian-German colonel had saved his best friend, a Jew, and his friend's family from certain death at substantial risk to his own life; that while a large number of Germans were cruel inhuman monsters, his hatred of *all* Germans was itself a kind of bigotry; and, perhaps most remarkable, he had told a German officer something he had not told anyone in a British uniform; that he himself was Jewish.

The additional irony, which he did not know and which he probably would never know, was that Joe Corcoran's closest friend, Aaron Rosen, had told Joe's father virtually the same thing that Colonel Reichmann had just told him. When Sir Rupert told Rosen that he was different to all other Jews, Rosen's response was that the difference was that Sir Rupert knew him, but didn't know all the other Jews.

That night Sloan wrote a letter to his family that surprised them greatly. While he continued to denounce the Germans and the monstrous atrocities that were being conducted by them, he told them the story of Colonel Reichmann and advised that it was not right, as he had done, to automatically condemn all Germans since there were some—or as he said, a few—who we might not know, who were "different."

LONDON—1941
PART ONE

CHAPTER SIXTEEN

"RIGHT ON TIME," HAUPTMAN Heinrich Leuzinger exclaimed.

"What's that?" asked his copilot.

"Rain—it's almost inevitable. You get close to England, it starts raining. It's always raining here. It's what I like best about England. What's that poem about a green and pleasant land? No wonder it's so green."

Large drops had started to splatter on the Heinkel's cockpit glass. Leuzinger turned on the wipers. His feeble joke brought a few dutiful, but nervous laughs. This was a veteran crew. They had been together for eighteen bombing missions—fourteen over London and four earlier ones over industrial areas and shipbuilding yards in the north. It had become routine. The crew performed their assigned tasks professionally in what was a highly tense, but outwardly calm, atmosphere. They had seen many other bombers get hit and go down frequently with men—who were their friends—dying. They knew that their turn could come at any time, but somehow they had convinced themselves that it wouldn't.

"There's the coast and there's the river," called out the navigator.

They had taken off from Schoningen in the late evening and, although it had become quite dark, they could still make out the estuary of the Thames. The fifty Heinkels making up the squadron would follow the river into London and drop their bombs indiscriminately over built-up areas frequently, but not always, close to the river. Several squadrons had preceded them and several more would follow—all with the same non-specific targets.

Fingers of bright lights probed the sky, constantly moving and searching. Puffs of smoke appeared around the planes, sparse at first, but denser as the planes continued toward London and as anti-aircraft batteries increased in number. Two nights earlier, the plane directly to Leuzinger's right took two hits in rapid succession, burst into flames, spun out, and exploded. Nobody got out. Leuzinger had eaten dinner earlier that evening with the young copilot of that plane. He was a replacement who had just graduated flight school and this had been his first mission. During dinner he had not stopped talking while bubbling over with enthusiasm. He couldn't wait to get into action. Leuzinger remembered thinking that he would grow out of it after a few missions. He never had the chance to. Now Leuzinger could not even recall his name—Johann or Juergen or something like that. Leuzinger shifted uncomfortably in his chair, stretched, and yawned. Two more missions and he and his crew would have a three-week leave. There was even talk of his being reassigned as a senior flight instructor. He smiled wearily. He could turn out more Johanns or Juergens.

In all his missions, Leuzinger had never seen as much ack-ack fire. *They must have been moving some batteries into the area from the north,* he thought. The Heinkel immediately ahead of him got caught in the crossbeams of several searchlights and, almost immediately, fire erupted from the right engine. It banked sharply and went down rapidly. Leuzinger saw men getting out of the doomed ship and parachutes opening. He counted them. There were not enough. Half the crew did not get out. Fighters could evade the enemy by diving, climbing, and making a variety of different turns. Skill had much to do with their survival. Bombers were different. Evasive tactics were far more limited and luck was of much greater importance than skill.

London sprawled out beneath the bombers. Earlier squadrons had left their mark. There were fires all over, but more prevalent closer to the river. He maneuvered the plane slightly to the north. While he was given no specific target, he did not want his bombs to end up harmlessly in the water.

"You've got it, Ernst," he called to his bombardier.

Ernst Raeder hunched over and peered through his bombsite. He was very experienced and skillful, but dropping bombs with no particular target in mind required no experience and little skill. He pressed the button and watched a large stream of incendiary bombs leave the belly of the plane. They were like a multitude of thin sticks tumbling around with no apparent precision. He watched as scores of small fires erupted, some separated by large distances, some not.

"All gone," Raeder yelled.

"Let's get out of here," Leuzinger yelled back.

Simultaneously, he put the Heinkel into a wide banking turn. Almost immediately, he felt a violent tremor and the controls froze in his hands. He pulled hard, but they would not move. He looked over his shoulder and saw a gaping, jagged hole in the fuselage at the precise spot where a few seconds earlier one of the two waist gunners had been. His radio operator was lying at an unnatural angle, his eyes wide and staring with his right arm and most of his right side gone. Flames were licking up through the floor and coursing along the right wing. The plane started to keel over and then dropped abruptly.

"Out! Out! Out!" he shouted. "Everyone out. Go! Go! Go!"

Leuzinger was the last to leave as the plane's angle of descent and speed increased. His chute opened and he looked around for his crew. He saw no one. He looked down, but he could see nothing. He crashed into something that gave way under him. He landed hard and at an angle. He heard something snap. Intense pain coursed through his body and he passed out.

CHAPTER SEVENTEEN

THE ROADWAY WAS COMPLETELY quiet. Rationing of petrol in 1941 England was very tight and few non-essential uses merited any ration at all. At this late hour, no vehicles of any kind were seen. Although not recommended, one could lie down at night in the middle of the road for a two-hour nap and have a very good chance of not being run over.

The pavement was deserted. A quarter of an hour ago, it had been teeming with shoppers searching through the meager contents of the various shops. In 1941 England, everything was in short supply or, more frequently, completely nonexistent. The shoppers, deliverymen, and clerks had left on trains, buses, trams, and trolleys for their homes in Hackney, Bethnal Green, Stepney, Clapton, and other areas in the East End of London. They lived mostly in small flats or row houses. As night approached, bombing attacks by German planes were almost inevitable. Most frequently the bombers followed the Thames from its estuary into London airspace, resulting in many of the bombs falling in the dock area and the East End.

When the East End residents reached their homes, they ate hurriedly and many of them set off for the protection of deep underground train stations. Some with back gardens had built bomb shelters buried in the ground and spent the nights in them. Some brave, or foolish, people stayed in their homes— in the mistaken belief that their hallways were fairly safe or because they didn't have a shelter or because they couldn't tolerate the discomfort and claustrophobic atmosphere in the deep underground stations. In the mornings, after the bombers had departed, the people exited their shelters or the underground stations and returned to their homes, washed, ate, and went about their normal daily routines of working, going to school, searching the shops for whatever foods were available, and, in many instances, clearing away the debris at their homes caused by the previous night's bombing— assuming their homes were still inhabitable. It was a routine that seemed impossible to get used to, but they did.

The street was dark. There were streetlights, but they had not been turned on in more than a year. In 1941 England, a strict blackout was enforced nationwide. The object was to hinder German bombers in finding and hitting their targets. Since the German target at that time was London in general with no specific areas designated and since the German navigators did not require London to be lit up in order to find it, the blackout was of limited assistance as a deterrent.

The young boy moved quickly, sticking close to the darkened buildings, which made him less visible. Being alone at nightfall in a more or less deserted area of the East End of London in the early 1940s was an invitation to danger— particularly if the lone individual was Jewish. Anti-Semitism was rampant. Some if it was merely verbal insults, but much of it was physical. Isolated bashings of defenseless old men and young boys was frequent—as was more systematized attacks by groups such as groups of black-shirted fascist thugs. Their targets were open-air markets with stalls operated by Jewish tradesmen, old orthodox Jewish worshippers returning from synagogue with characteristic beards, black hats, and dark suits, and anyone or anything that appeared Jewish and appeared defenseless.

Tom Sloan had been playing football with a group of friends and classmates at London Fields. All of them were Jewish and all lived close to each other. There was very little grass and no goalposts and the players used their jackets to signify the outer limits of the goals. That led to interminable arguments as to whether shots were actually inside the ersatz posts or not. There was no time limit on the games. The boys quit when it got dark or when it was time for dinner and sometimes when the arguments became too intense. Ordinarily, they would walk home together after the game— both for companionship and for protection—even though a large number of fourteen-year-old boys would be no match for a group of twenty- to thirty-year-old bullies armed with clubs and sometimes knives. They were halfway home when Tom realized that he had left his jacket at the field. He halfheartedly thought of leaving it, but it was relatively new and his mother would be furious if he didn't go back and get it. He ran back and got it and then quickly walked toward his house alone sometimes looking over his shoulder and always trying to be as inconspicuous as possible.

The gathering darkness and the shadows from the storefronts were not his only defenses from marauding savages. They were not even his best protection. That protection was his looks. He had none of the claimed stereotypical Jewish traits. His hair was not dark or curly. His lips were not thick and fleshy and his nose was not long or hooked. While he could not be mistaken for the classic blue-eyed, blond

Aryan, he also could not be mistaken for what was widely, and mistakenly, believed to be the typical Jew. He had a fair complexion. His hair was light brown and straight; his lips were thin and pink and his nose was patrician. His father, Bernard, whose hair was dark and curly, although graying at the temples, and whose features were somewhat more characteristic of what were claimed to be Semitic, frequently said in jest that his son must be the illegitimate son of the milkman. His mother was not amused by her husband's joking reference to her son's allegedly suspicious ancestry. She was proud of the fact that her grandparents had immigrated to England from Lithuania in the last decade of the nineteenth century to avoid pogrom-like attacks on Jewish people in that country; that they were tall, fair-skinned, handsome people; and that her son took after them both in physical appearance and in brains.

Her son got very high marks and the masters at his school rated him as one of the top students. Despite her annoyance at her husband's "milkman" gibes, she was proud of the fact that he was a major in the British army serving with the Eighth Army in the North African Desert. This was a singular accomplishment for a Jew whose parents had arrived from Poland shortly before he was born and who had left school at thirteen to work in his father's tailoring business. It was also a singular accomplishment for her to resist responding to the frequent and prideful statements of Mrs. Goldstein next door about "my son, the doctor" with "my husband, the major" or even "my husband, the war hero." While the "major" part would have been accurate, the "hero" part would have been a bit of a stretch since he was in the Royal Army Ordnance Corps and responsible for ensuring that the troops got enough supplies, including such things as blankets and clean socks. The postman, who was not partial to Mrs. Goldstein's bragging, would loudly announce, "Mrs. Sloan, you have another letter from *Major* Sloan."

When the major's parents arrived from Poland, their family name was Slonenstein. Bernie Sloan's father changed the name because, as he claimed, when he bought the small store on Commercial Road, the title "Slonenstein's Suit's & Alterations" was too large to fit above the window. Secretly he told friends, family, and Jewish clients that it was better for business. He did quite well, mostly with alterations, but also with the occasional made-to order-suits, trousers, and sports jackets. That success was probably unrelated to the name change. The yarmulke that he always wore in the shop was a dead giveaway anyway.

Tom climbed the stairs in the flats two at a time, thankful to be home and, as usual, hungry. The Sloan flat was on the tenth floor of the twelve-story building. There was no lift and, most frequently, there was limited lighting. There was one bulb on each landing and—even when they were all working—the floors were not well lit. Most of the time, a number of the bulbs had burned out and they were replaced very slowly. A lot of the steps were cracked and had pieces missing. Even during daylight and even during the summer, there was a cold, dank feel to the building, which had been constructed in 1912. It was not a showplace when new— and it had certainly not improved with age. A sour smell reminiscent of old cabbage and rotten eggs was a constant. Of course, everyone knew it could not have emanated from rotten eggs. Nobody in the flats had seen a real egg since the war started. Whenever complaints were made to the landlord about the smells, the state of the stairs, the peeling paint, the lights, and a myriad of other problems, Mr. Cohen on his rare visits to the flats from his palatial home in Golders Green would place the blame repeatedly on "the war." While Hitler was blamed for most things, it did not appear to be his fault that nobody cleaned the rubbish dump behind the flats frequently enough, which might have eliminated—or at least minimized—the smells.

"Where have you been, Tom? It's almost six o'clock. I told you not to stay out after dark."

Her tone was sharp, but it was born of worry rather than anger. The thugs searching for unprotected Jews were only one concern. Every night, the bombers came and every night, buildings were destroyed and people killed. She and her children had once tried the underground station at Bethnal Green, but she couldn't stand it. She couldn't sleep on the cold, hard platform even though she had brought thick blankets and pillows. She was agitated by the mass of people packed closely together. The toilet facilities were inadequate and the smells and noise were more than she could bear. Thereafter, they stayed in the flat and when the air-raid warning went off, they would go into the small hallway next to the kitchen, try to sleep on makeshift beds, and wait for the all clear. Being in the hall with two sets of walls between them and the outside and having the supposed protection of two floors above them gave Mrs. Sloan an uneasy sense of security. In truth, they would have been safer if they had slept in the open air on the pavement outside the flats.

Chapter Eighteen

Miriam Sloan had been born in Stepney in East London in a small flat above the kosher butcher shop owned and run by her parents Jacob and Leah Lichtenberger. Miriam was tall, very slim with a light complexion. At forty three she was still strikingly handsome and turned heads on her shopping outings. The Lichtenbergers were still alive and relatively healthy. Although they continued to live above the shop, they had long since retired and the shop was under different ownership and had been converted into a combination newsagent and sweetshop.

It had been a long and tiring day. She had left the house at half past seven in order to get to the grocers at the time it opened at quarter to eight. She had Tom's, Rebecca's and her ration books in her purse and two string carrier bags. Although she got to Samuel's five minutes before it opened there were already eight or nine people in line ahead of her. There were no supermarkets; no ability for customers to tool up and down long aisles pulling items off shelves, putting them in carts and paying at check out stands. They went to small neighborhood grocers, butchers, bakers, fishmongers and greengrocers. They ordered items from clerks, usually the owner and his wife, gave those people their ration books and the money; had the owner take the appropriate ration card vouchers; put their pitifully small amounts of groceries, bread, fish, meat and vegetables in their own carrier bags and left.

Leah Samuel was a nervous little woman made more so by the long lines in the store and the repeated necessity of having to tell long time customers that much of what they wanted she didn't have and, to the extent that she did have it, they couldn't have nearly as much as they wanted. By contrast her husband Joe was a big man with a huge waist line and a booming voice.

"What can I do for you Miriam?" he bellowed.

She looked at her list knowing it mostly comprised wishful thinking and that if she could get a small percentage of what she needed she would have to be satisfied.

"Two pound bag of sugar please Mr. Samuel."

She was uncomfortable using first names with the Samuels although Joe had no such compunction.

"Sorry everybody is limited to one pound."

"All right," she said resignedly. "I'll take the one pound bag and a pound of butter."

"Half a pound only," he answered taking a large spatula and slopping a small amount on a piece of grease proof paper and then onto the scales.

"How's the major?"

It was unusual for a Jew, particularly from the East End, to be a fairly high ranking officer in the British Army. There was a grudging respect for Miriam among her friends and acquaintances because of her husband's exalted status. Nobody, other than her family, would say "have you heard from Bernie?" or "How is Bernie." It was always, "Have heard from the major?" or "How is the major?"

She left Samuel's with the sugar, butter, two tins of condensed milk, a package of ersatz cheese, two tins of beans and a tin of peas. She hadn't bothered to ask for eggs or tinned fruit because she knew there would be none. She next went to Rubens's the fishmonger whose stock was worse than usual. Essentially all Ruben had was fish heads which he said would make a good soup. She declined. Three blocks away was Herman Marks Kosher Butcher Store. All he had was beef fat. She bought a couple of pounds. She would cut it up into small pieces and fry it. The unhealthy nature of such a meal was not well known and, besides, that was all there was. Despite the unpleasant sounding concept of eating fried fat it really didn't taste that bad. She next went Weinstein's Bakery.

"Two loaves of brown bread please."

"Sorry Only white bread today and one loaf per customer."

The white bread tasted as though it's major ingredient was cardboard but she took it.

"You want it sliced?" Weinstein asked with an expectant look on his face.

He had just got a electric slicer and he proudly proclaimed his was the only bakery in the entire East End that had an electric slicer.

"Too bad you don't have something worth slicing," an elderly tired looking customer said.

Miriam ended her dismal and very marginally successful shopping venture at Ted's the greengrocer. In the 40s in London shopping for food was pretty much a day long occupation. There was no possibility of buying everything in one place. One had to go to the grocer, the greengrocer, the baker, the butcher and the fishmonger. Because most East Enders did not have refrigerators including Miriam, shopping for perishables, to the extent any were available, had to be done virtually every day.

Ted was more or less unique in Miriam's neighborhood. He was a gentile shop owner. He had a bustling business although almost all his customers were Jewish. He had a friendly reassuring manner about him and treated everybody with courtesy and respect. The community had long forgiven him for not being Jewish although some of the more orthodox residents still regarded him with cool suspicion. He greeted Miriam warmly, asked about the major and told her he had just got a rare shipment of apples and could let her have four. She also bought a cabbage which looked a little worse for wear and four medium size potatoes.

She walked home carrying the foodstuffs she had bought at the various shops. She had covered quite a distance. The bags were heavy and had cut welts in her hands. She wearily climbed the stairs, resting periodically on several of the landings. She unloaded the bags, plopped down in a chair, had a cup of tea and afforded herself the luxury of a little milk and a spoonful of sugar.

CHAPTER NINETEEN

"SO WHERE WERE YOU? It's almost six."

"I was----"

"You don't care about your mother. You want to put her in an early grave."

"I was----"

"I told you to be home by half past five. The dinner will be ruined."

This conversation, with some slight variations happened most nights and this night was no exception. The boys played too long. They dawdled coming home. Sometimes, if they had a few pennies, they stopped in the arcade on the way home and played the machines. The saving grace this night was that there was no way to ruin fried fat. It came ruined. Miriam fried the small cubes of fat until they were crispy. She baked two potatoes and split them into three. She boiled one half of a tin of peas and that was dinner. Rebecca came in just before dinner was put on the table. She had been studying with her best friend Sarah Goldberg who lived with her parents on the eighth floor of the same building. They were classmates at Brookhurst School for Girls which was within walking distance of the flats. Tom was a student at

Brookhurst School for Boys which was a few hundred yards from the girls school. Rebecca was almost exactly one year older than Tom; an inch or two shorter than Miriam and pretty; not as striking as Miriam but pretty nonetheless. Like Tom she was very bright but unlike Tom she applied herself diligently to her studies. She was number one in her class and was almost certain to go onto university even if it meant that the Sloans would have to borrow money from their parents. Tom's grades were also very good but with greater application could have been better. He was more interested in sports. He was on the second eleven football team at school and was the goal keeper. He would have been on the first team but George Robinson played that position and was generally believed to be the best player Brookhurst had ever had in it's seventy year history.

As they finished their dinner and as if on cue the air raid warning sounded. It was always frightening. It increased and decreased in decibels almost rhythmically and lasted for three or four minutes. Almost immediately the bursts of anti aircraft fire could be heard. Gun batteries stretched from the Channel coast up to and encircling London and the south east counties.

"Get in the hall," Miriam shouted, her voice high pitched with tension.

The three of them went into the hall which was narrow and short with barely enough room for them. The flat was tiny. There were two bedrooms. Miriam and Rebecca slept in the double bed in the front room and Tom in a room adjoining. There was a bathroom and a kitchen. That was it. The kitchen which also doubled as the sitting room had a coal burning fireplace which was the only source of heat in the flat. Once a month the coal man with a horse drawn cart would deliver a 100 pound sack of coal to the flat. There was no proper storage place for the coal and the man would empty the sack into the hall closet. The supply of gas and electricity to the flat was controlled by meters. In order to maintain the supply a shilling had to be placed periodically in the slots in the meter. If shillings were not available in a timely fashion the supply of gas and/or electricity would stop until the meters were again fed. The flat had no refrigerator; no radiators or electric fires and no garbage disposal. Food scraps and other rubbish was placed in a chute which unfortunately was directly outside the Sloan's front door. Miriam could tolerate the rubbish chute, the foul smells that emanated from it, the lack of heat, no refrigerator, coal in the closet, the need for shillings to keep the house lit and the stove burning, the burned out lights on the landings, the unsafe stairs, the peeling paint, the interminable shopping nightmare and even Mrs. Goldstein's "my son the doctor." What tormented her was the lack of a telephone. She worried for her parents and Bernie's parents. She wanted to call them after every raid but there was no possibility of any phones being installed in the flat. Both sets of parents had phones but nobody in Miriam's building had one. The closest pay phone was at Poplar Street where it intersected with Reese Avenue. It was three quarters of a mile away and there was always a line waiting to use it.

CHAPTER TWENTY

MIRIAM LOOKED LOVINGLY AT her children sleeping as though there was not a thing to concern them. As usual, the three of them were crammed in the small, narrow hall lying on makeshift beds of blankets and pillows piled on a clean, but threadbare, carpet. The bombing this night seemed further away than usual and the sounds of bombs and ack-ack fire was barely discernible. Also, as usual, Miriam could not sleep. She had dozed off around eleven, but Arnold Lucas who lived in the next building had awoken her. The local council had made the mistake of making Lucas an air-raid warden for the flats and the area immediately surrounding them. His primary job was to walk the area after dark and ensure that no lights were showing from any of the residences. Black curtains were available at any council office at no cost and cardboard cut to fit windows that had been blown out by the force of nearby explosions was also available. Like everything else, glass was in short supply and it took months to replace the many broken windows in the East End. All able-bodied males between the age of eighteen and into mid forties were in the military. Men in their late forties, fifties and even into their sixties were performing all manner of war work and most often living away from their families in temporary housing. The only males around were young boys, babies, and old men. That is how Lucas became air-raid warden.

He was in his mid sixties, short, bald, fat, and arrogant. He had achieved nothing of the slightest importance in his entire miserable little life. His wife, Henrietta, was a scrawny, nervous woman with the unpleasant habit of constantly picking at her face. They lived in the next block of flats from the Sloans. They were childless. His appointment as air-raid warden was to him the greatest event of his life—and indeed it was. It had nothing at all to compete with. He made the absolute most out of his self-perceived importance and let no one forget it. He enjoyed nothing more than to see a slight sliver of light peeking from the window of one of his neighbors. He would bang on the door repeatedly until someone answered and—in his loud, squeaky voice— would require, no order, the poor victim to correct the matter immediately on pain of his pulling out his citation pad and writing up the infraction. Air-raid wardens were required to give one warning before citing the perpetrator. Most of the wardens would be most reluctant to give a citation even after several warnings. The fine was ten shillings for the first citation and an additional ten shillings for further violations. Lucas had no such compunction. He could hardly wait until he could detect, or thought he could detect, the very slightest tinge of light from someone he had already warned so that he could slap them with a fine that most people in the flats could not afford. Lucas was far from the most loved person in the neighborhood before he became warden. Thereafter, he was hated. To make matters worse, he was sweet on Miriam. He would invent excuses to visit her and would hang around outside her block of flats in an effort to see her. She tried everything to get rid of him—including outright rudeness—but he remained a repulsive pest.

"Miriam," he yelled, even before she had opened the door, "you've got light showing. Cover it up right now."

"All right, Arnold, all right. You don't have to shout," she said angrily.

"Don't let me have to tell you again," he yelled even louder, even though the door was now open.

"Go away, Arnold. You will wake the children."

Arnold magnanimously declined to issue citations to Miriam—even though he claimed that she had shown light on several occasions. She denied that she had ever violated the blackout regulations, but Arnold could see light when no one else could.

One of the reasons that she had taken the children to the Bethnal Green underground station was to avoid Arnold. Her claustrophobia however made Arnold slightly more bearable. Arnold's repeated nighttime official and officious visits were rubbing her nerves even more raw. She was thinking of trying to overcome her fear of being in close proximity to a host of strangers and trying the station again when an event at the Bethnal Green underground station eliminated that possibility from her mind. That underground station was particularly deep and had very long, straight escalators. Early one morning, the people who had sheltered there all night were leaving to return to their homes. The up escalator was packed from top to bottom with people. Suddenly, a woman at the top of the escalator heard a plane and screamed, "They're coming back." People who heard her turned and tried to push their way back down. A woman at the base of the escalator was carrying a baby and fell. People, in a panic, were being pushed back and fell on her. More and more people fell and, when the carnage was over, many were dead and even more were injured—a large number critically. Thereafter, that tragedy was known as "The Bethnal Green Tube Disaster." Ironically, the plane that had started the panic was an Australian aircraft on a training flight. The woman who fell at the base of the escalator died in the crush of bodies. Her baby survived. Of the two unappetizing alternatives, suffering the insufferable Arnold Lucas was marginally preferable.

CHAPTER TWENTY-ONE

TOM AND REBECCA WALKED to school together wearing Buckhurst blue blazers with the school emblem on the pockets. Boys and girls wore the school tie—the girls with gray skirts and the boys with gray trousers. Since Tom was now in the fourth form, this was his first year wearing the school regulation long trousers. All boys in the first, second, and third forms had to wear short trousers. The graduation into long trousers was a treasured moment and an important rite of passage.

Tom's first class was geography. The master was Nigel Winters. He was a big, burly, barrel-chested man in his late forties. His weathered face was a testament to hard living and his early career as a big game hunter and safari guide in Kenya. He regaled the class with stories about tracking tigers, rhinos, and other fierce beasts. He showed them photos of himself and his clients with some of the trophy animals he and they had killed. Once he brought in the thirty-caliber rifle that he had used in the African wilds. It created quite a stir and drew a reprimand from the headmaster who told Winters that he should not bring such things into school again. Winters' right ear was missing. He told the boys, more than once, that he had lost it wrestling a lion that had charged him from cover and had knocked his rifle away before he could use it. He killed the lion with his bare hands, but not before he had been badly mauled and his right ear had been torn off. He called the boys by their first names, which no other master did. They loved him and hung on his every word.

Tom's second class was history and it could not have been more anticlimactic. The history master was Lionel Riggins. He was bald with long wisps of unsightly hair peeking over his collar. His clothes looked as if he had been dragged through a hedge backward and his shoulders were always flecked with dandruff. He spoke in a high-pitched, whiny tone and lisped. However, his most noticeable attribute was his extraordinary thinness. He was not just thin—he was emaciated. His clothes hung loosely on him. His sunken eyes peered out through thick and always smudged glasses that were perched on the end of a long beaklike nose. He had continuing difficulty controlling his class. The boys made no pretense about talking to each other and laughing while Riggins would plead with them.

"Boys, boys, you must pay attention. I will not tolerate any more of your misbehaving."

But tolerate it, he did. Other masters faced with misconduct would take a ruler and rap the knuckles of the miscreants several times—and very hard. That was ordinarily enough to stop any cutting up—at least for the rest of that class. Riggins couldn't bear to inflict such punishment on his class and discipline suffered as a result.

Although the war was still in its fairly early stages, the horrors of the German concentration camps had become known in England. Stories about the widespread extermination in such places were a subject of newspaper reports and radio broadcasts. The names of Dachau, Auschwitz, Bergen-Belsen, and others were mentioned. With the Germans only a few miles away across the Channel and invasion a serious possibility, the reports of the death camps had struck fear into the large Jewish population in England. Riggins was not only a figure of fun in the boys' eyes; he was also a source of ridicule because of his physical appearance, particularly his emaciated look. One of the boys had created the nickname "Belsen" and all of the boys took to calling him that. It was cruel, mean-spirited, and particularly unthinking on the part of the Jewish students, including Tom, who joined in the name-calling. In years to come, when he had matured, Tom developed a deep sense of shame for his participation. That sense of shame would be with him for the rest of his life.

Chapter Twenty-Two

Spending nights in the hall was taking its toll. Rebecca could sleep anywhere—even on the hard floor. Miriam and Tom were not so fortunate. Miriam was lucky if she slept fitfully on and off for a few hours. Tom seemed to have the same pattern. For once, Miriam decided to let everybody sleep in their own beds that night.

Two hours after the air-raid warning sounded, a bomb struck two streets away. The explosion was deafening. The windows in the bedroom shared by Miriam and Rebecca burst inward, covering the bed with shards of glass and pieces of wood. Plaster rained down from the ceiling in both bedrooms, baring wood supports. Inexplicably, the toilet flushed. Flames were clearly visible through the shattered windows and the immediate sounds of emergency vehicles could be heard. Tom came running into Miriam's bedroom. Miriam was on her feet, but Rebecca had not moved.

"Oh my god! Oh my god!" screamed Miriam. "Rebecca, are you all right. Please say something." She was bordering on hysteria. Tom shook Rebecca hard. She was covered from head to toe with pieces of glass, wood, and fine powdered plaster. Rebecca stirred, sat up, and sleepily asked, "What's the matter?" Miriam burst into tears. "That's it. Tomorrow night we'll go down the underground." But they never did. There was noise all night long. Bombs fell in the distance, but none was as close as the one that blew out the windows. Ambulances came and went with sirens blaring. People ran up and down the stairs of the flats anxious to know about the damage. Nobody got any sleep the rest of the night

The three Sloans listened to the BBC News on the radio the following morning. They always did before the children went to school. Almost every London household did likewise. In part, they did so to find out what had happened the previous day and to find out about the bombing and what was happening with the war. The newscasters always stated their names. "This is the BBC and here is the news and this is Stuart Hibbert, (or Alvar Lidell, or one of the others). They all had Oxford accents and calm, reassuring, almost soothing voices. That calm reassurance was another prime reason why people listened. Hibbert told the listeners that six German bombers had been destroyed the previous night—five by ack-ack fire and one had flown too low and had its wing ripped off by the cable attaching a barrage balloon to the ground. Barrage balloons were large, inflated oblong-shaped devices that were spotted at various locations all over London. They were sent aloft at different heights and attached to the ground by cables. The object was to confuse the enemy planes and make them fly higher on their bombing runs than they might otherwise have done. This was hoped to make their aims less accurate. Since Hitler's objective at that time was to strike terror in the hearts of the English citizens and cause panic, it was of no concern to the German bombardiers exactly where they dropped their loads. They had no specific military targets in mind and they counted success if they hit schools, housing, churches, hospitals, roads, etc. For that reason, the barrage balloons had little success. By the same token, Hitler's random bombing concept was also unsuccessful because the Londoners, though understandably apprehensive, never succumbed to terror and never panicked.

Rebecca left early for school; she had a class on Wednesdays that started at eight. Tom left a little later and ran into his friend and classmate, Josh Rosenblatt.

"That bomb hit a house on Fleming Street. Let's go have a look," said Josh. "We're early and Fleming is only two streets over."

When they got to Fleming Street, there were police barriers at each end of the block. The scene was chaotic. Josh and Tom tried to slip under the barrier to get a better look. A stern-faced police officer grabbed them both by the scruffs of their necks.

"Just where do you boys think you're going? Nobody is allowed down there. You could get hurt. Get on to school," he said firmly.

They could see halfway down the street that the bomb had obviously landed on top of one of the houses and reduced it to rubble. The houses on either side were practically destroyed—although several of the walls and part of the roofs were still intact, less extensive damage was done to other buildings on either side of the street. There were emergency vehicles up and down the street and helmeted police and firemen were clearing debris and searching for bodies. Arnold Lucas was striding imperiously up and down, his ARP armband in place and helmet on his head with no visible function and making a bloody old nuisance of himself, as usual.

When they got to school, the rumor was that a third former, Archie Sanders, had been killed in the bombing on

Fleming Street. Tom knew Archie vaguely, but he was in a lower form and upperclassmen did not ordinarily associate with their juniors. Although their part of London had not had the same extent of damage as others, their damage was by no means inconsequential and they had a number of fatalities. The children and their parents had become used to hearing of people they knew having been killed or wounded by the bombing. They never got accustomed to the horror of it, although they did become somewhat hardened. Despite sad news, men, women, and children went about their daily activities; worked, shopped studied, played and, once in a while, sometimes secretly and sometimes not, they cried. The children were told not to listen to rumors and they tried not to. But the rumor about Archie Sanders turned out to be true.

CHAPTER TWENTY-THREE

"DO YOU WANT TO go look at the bomb damage on Fleming?" asked Tom as he and Josh walked back from school several days after that bomb fell.

"I can't today," said Josh. "I've got to go to the dentist and get my braces adjusted. I hate it. Every time I go, he tightens them so much it hurts to eat—not that there is much worth eating."

"There's got to be some good shrapnel in there," said Tom.

"It's probably pretty well picked over by now. I know there were a lot of boys going through the houses a couple of days after the raid," Josh said.

Collection of pieces of bombs was a prime pursuit of boys in London, particularly in the East End. It had surpassed stamp collecting and was fast catching up on cigarette cards. Cigarette manufacturers put cards with pictures mostly of football and cricket players in packs of cigarettes. Complete sets were quite valuable if in good condition and trading of duplicates in order to get full sets was rampant. Conker fights were also a significant pastime. Boys would bore holes in horse chestnuts (conkers), hang them on individual strings, and challenge other owners of conkers to battles. The first boy would allow the second boy to swipe at his hanging conker once with his own conker and then the favor was returned. Alternate bashing of the two conkers went on until one or the other was knocked off the string. When one conker was destroyed, the other conker was the winner. After its first victory, a conker became a 'oner.' If that same conker vanquished a second victim, it became a 'twoer' and so on. A 'niner' or a 'tenner' was an object of awe. There were also attempts to strengthen conkers by heating them, covering them in ointment, or—the most favored—soaking them overnight in vinegar. Old, damaged conkers—particularly those with a significant number of victories—were often retired to a place of honor on the mantelpiece.

Collecting shrapnel was fast becoming the activity of choice. However, unlike stamp collecting, cigarette cards, and conkers, shrapnel collecting was dangerous and occasionally even fatal. The "best" places to find shrapnel was in bomb-damaged buildings. Those places were frequently unstable and the smallest vibration could bring down tons of debris. To get to the most likely areas, one had to climb over rickety, heavily damaged walls and beams. Sometimes, unexploded bombs and shells were know to be triggered and explode at unfortunate times. The pieces of bombs were dangerous to handle. They had sharp, jagged edges that readily cut into flesh and, depending on size, were hard to pick up and carry. Despite all that and parents scolding, threatening, and pleading, boys—and sometimes girls—frequently placed themselves in harm's way to pick up essentially useless pieces of twisted metal. Tom was an occasional collector and not as avid as many others. He was more interested in football and conkers, but was not reluctant to explore through the damaged rooms of partially destroyed buildings.

Tom and Josh parted company at Raleigh Avenue as Josh reluctantly headed to the dentist and Tom continued on his way home. For some reason, he decided to detour down Fleming Street. The barriers had come down and the debris had been piled up against the damaged houses. The street was again open for vehicles, although with petrol being unavailable except for public transportation, some limited taxi services, and private cars with special documented needs, there were very few vehicles around. There were signs outside the destroyed house and the two adjoining ones, which were severely damaged, prohibiting entrance and warning of extreme danger.

Tom looked around. There was no one on the street and no vehicles approaching in either direction. He quickly went into the severely damaged house, which was to the right of the one that had been totally destroyed. There were fallen beams everywhere. This had been a house primarily constructed of bricks and wooden beams. The interior walls were, for the most part, still standing although they were cracked and parts had fallen. The roof was gone and the exterior wall closest to the destroyed house was only partially standing. Even though the bomb had fallen several days earlier, there was still dust floating around everywhere that made it a little difficult to see.

Tom carefully picked his way toward the back of the house. There was no shrapnel to be seen. Suddenly his leg slipped between two large broken beams and got stuck. He pulled and pulled, but he was firmly stuck. It was getting dark and he started to panic. He could envision himself stuck there overnight—maybe longer. The house had long since been picked clean of shrapnel and anything else of worth and it was unlikely that anyone would be coming through in the near future—or ever. Maybe after a month or so, some workmen would come through to finish demolishing what was left of the house and would find his skeleton. Just then, one of the beams let out a groan and shifted enough to permit him to free his leg. But the groan didn't come from the beam. It came from further back in the house toward where the small garden used to be. He heard someone in a weak voice—but with a strong accent—call out something that sounded like help. He picked his way, agonizingly slowly, toward the sound of the voice. He did not want to get stuck again. Finally, he got to what had been a small room in the back of the house. The door was wedged shut.

He called out, "Is anyone in there?"

The answer came back, "Yes. Please help me."

He pushed and pushed on the door with no result. He shoved it with his shoulder until it hurt. He kicked it several times, but only succeeded in scratching his shoes. Finally, he took a broken piece of beam, ran toward the door, and rammed the beam into the door as hard as he could. The door cracked, but did not open. He repeated the ramming three more times and suddenly the door swung open.

He went in. The room was even dustier than the areas he had just left and visibility was even poorer. There was a large piece of white material now partially buried under the open door. It had strings or cords attached to it. He thought that it looked like part of a parachute. In the far corner of the room closest to the garden, a man was lying on a pile of debris. When he was within a few feet, he could see that the man was wearing a uniform and had boots with some kind of fur at the tops. His right leg was twisted at an awkward angle. The man's hair was so blond that it was almost white. He looked up at Tom with light blue eyes and smiled.

He said one word, "*Danke.*"

Tom's mouth dropped. He stared at the man, not knowing whether to say something or turn and run.

"You're a German," he finally blurted out.

The man smiled again and said, "And you're not."

"No, I'm not," said Tom, feeling very stupid for saying something so obvious. "I've never seen a German before except on the newsreel at the cinema."

"Well, that makes us even," said the German. "I've never seen an English boy before." His English was excellent, although it was spoken with a pronounced accent.

"Who are you? Where did you come from? What are you doing here?" The questions just streamed off Tom's tongue.

"Whoa! Not so fast. I'll answer all your questions one at a time," said the German. "I'm Hauptman Heinrich Leuzinger—same as a captain in England. I am a pilot in the Luftwaffe. I was shot down. I bailed out and landed in this bombed-out house. I think I broke my leg when I hit this pile of rubble and I've been here ever since. I don't know where the rest of my men are. I know two of them died in the plane, but the others bailed out before me."

"I'll go and get somebody," said Tom, not knowing what else to say.

He started to turn to go when Leuzinger raised himself up, pushing down with his hands on the rubble. He tried to stand, but could not and fell back with a loud groan, his faced contorted with pain.

"Wait, please," he gasped through his pain. "Let me tell you something. I have a wife and children in Germany. I would show you their pictures, but my wallet must have fallen out of my pocket when I jumped out of my plane last night. My boy is three and my girl is almost two. We live on a farm out in the country. That's what I am—a farmer" His words were coming fast and tumbling over each other.

"My wife—she's so ill and she can't take care of the children." He stopped. His eyes filled with tears. "Look, promise me you won't do anything tonight. Don't tell anybody I'm here. I'll explain it all to you tomorrow."

"I don't know," Tom said, looking at Leuzinger curiously. "I should tell my mother. She will know what to do."

"Please don't," said Leuzinger. "I promise you I will tell you the full story tomorrow and I know you will help me. I'm not a Nazi—I'm a farmer. I hate this war. I am so unhappy with what the Nazis are doing. I'm so ashamed. Just come back tomorrow and you'll know what I mean. Can you get me a blanket? I am very cold and I haven't eaten or drunk anything for a long time. Can you? Please I beg of you."

"I don't know. All right, I'll try to get you something. What about your leg?"

"It will be all right for a while. Tomorrow, if you bring me a straight piece of wood and some string, we can probably fashion a splint of some sort."

As he turned to leave, the German called out, "What's your name?"

"Tom. Tom Sloan," Tom replied.

By the time Tom got home it was dark. All the way home he was thinking that he was probably doing the wrong thing. He remembered his father's recent letter about the German colonel who had saved the lives of a Jewish family at the risk of his own. He remembered his father saying that not all Germans were bad people and that there were others that he did not know who were as brave and good as the German colonel was.

Tom thought to himself. *Well, one day can't hurt. I'll hear what he says tomorrow and then decide what to do.*

"Tom, where have you been? School has been over for two hours. You're getting home later and later. I won't stand for it. It's dangerous to be out by yourself after dark. I've told you that a dozen times." Miriam was clearly furious and was very worried.

"I'm sorry, Mum," he said. "I was with Josh. We were just talking and I was looking at his cigarette cards." He could see by the look on his mother's face that he had made a mistake.

"Don't lie to me, Tom. I saw Mrs. Rosenblatt an hour ago and she told me Josh had gone to the dentist straight from school."

"Well, I didn't want to tell you, but I went to the park just to kick the ball around with some of the lads for a little while."

That really made Miriam even angrier.

"I have told you and told you not to go to the park after school. There are some bad people that hang around there and it's not safe for Jewish boys."

He couldn't remember lying to his mother before. It was one of the things that he was proud of. He hadn't told her the truth. He hadn't told her about going in the bomb-damaged house. He hadn't told her about the German. He hadn't told her that he was going back to see him again the next day—and he hadn't told her he was going to steal food, drink, and a blanket from the flat to give to him.

CHAPTER TWENTY-FOUR

THE SCHOOL DAY AFTER his meeting the German pilot seemed interminable. He could not concentrate and his mind kept wandering back to the events of the previous evening. He even got his knuckles rapped in Mr. Winters' geography class. Geography was his favorite subject and Mr. Winters was his favorite schoolmaster. He got his best marks in that class. They had been studying world mountain ranges and Mr. Winters had asked him a question about the Atlas Mountains—their height and location. Tom hadn't even heard the question—even though Mr. Winters repeated it twice. The teacher walked over to him, took a ruler, and rapped him sharply twice on the back of his hand. It woke him from his reverie, but not from his great concern about what he had done.

At recess, a group of Tom's classmates were talking about the bomb-damaged houses on Fleming Street.

"I went through all three houses with some friends and couldn't find anything," said one boy.

"I was there the day before. There were a whole lot of boys rummaging around. I found a couple of very small pieces, but nothing worth keeping. There was a room at the back of one of the houses and the door was stuck. We didn't try real hard to get it open. Maybe I'll go back with a hammer or something and try to break it down."

Tom said loudly so all could hear, "I knocked that door down last night with a broken beam. There wasn't anything in that room except a lot of bricks and wood. I looked very hard."

Tom's heart beat faster. He knew that what he had just said was intended to deter anyone else from going back in that house and probably finding the German flier. He was, in fact, protecting an enemy pilot who only days before had dropped bombs on London. It unnerved him. He decided right then that he would go back that evening and tell Leuzinger that he was going to report the matter to the police. He thought for a moment that he would go straight to the police without first telling Leuzinger, but he dismissed that thought. It wouldn't be fair, he concluded.

That night, his mother and Rebecca were going to the cinema. The Empress was on the corner of Ryder Street and Leicester Road. It was double feature that started at half past five and, with the newsreel, would be over by nine o'clock.

The three of them had an early dinner of scrambled powdered eggs and cabbage. Miriam had made a small treacle tart with the rest of the flour. It was fairly sparse, but it was enough. Nine was later than Miriam ordinarily would want to get home. She never wanted the children to be out after dark, but she liked to go to the cinema once a week. The cheapest seats were one shilling. They were the closest to the screen. The one shilling and nine pence seats were further toward the back. The expensive seats (two shillings and thruppence and three shillings and sixpence) were in the balcony. Miriam always wanted to sit in the shilling seats—both because they were cheaper and because she saw better close up. She wanted to get there early because the shilling seats filled up quickly.

"You sure you don't want to go, Tom?" Miriam said. "It's a good picture. The main feature is a mystery. You like those."

"No thanks. I want to arrange my stamp album," Tom said not telling her that Mr. Winters had given him extra homework for his inattentiveness and definitely not telling her about his plan to go to see the German pilot.

"Well, don't you dare go out tonight. We will be back at nine." With that, Miriam and Rebecca put on their coats and left.

Tom looked in the larder, took two slices of bread, a small lump of cheese, and a tin of beans. He wrapped the items in a part of the *Daily Express*. He poured water into an empty glass jar and tightened the lid. He took a tin opener out of the same drawer. He then went into his bedroom and looked in the old armoire. It contained clothes, extra blankets, shoes, and, on the top shelf, three gas masks. He took one of the blankets and put it, the food, the jar of water, and the tin opener in a carrier bag his mother used to bring groceries from the various stores.

He would return the tin opener and the carrier bag before his mother got home. She probably wouldn't miss two slices of bread, the glass jar, or the small piece of cheese. Nor would she miss the blanket, at least not for a while, and maybe he could get it back surreptitiously in the next few days. He was more worried about the tin of beans. That would be more immediately obvious. He breathed a deep sigh. He would figure out some explanation, but he didn't know what. For a moment, he wondered why he was collecting all this stuff if he was going to tell the police about the German. He wasn't sure in his own mind. Maybe he was wavering on telling the police. Maybe it was because the German must be ravenously hungry and thirsty by now. After all, he hadn't eaten or drunk anything in a couple of days. But why the blanket? Well, he is cold and it might take some time to report to the police and have him picked up.

He peeked outside the front door. No one was around. He went to the window on the landing and looked out. There was no one on the street. It wouldn't do to be seen by the nosy neighbors leaving the flats and walking down the street with a full carrier bag. They were bound to tell his mother. After one last look, he quickly headed down the stairs, out the front, down the street— and headed for Fleming Street and the German pilot.

CHAPTER TWENTY-FIVE

THERE WERE NO STREETLIGHTS on anywhere in London. The blackout extended to the all houses and any other buildings which had to have curtains preventing light from being seen from outside. It extended to all forms of illumination, including streetlights, theater signs, and all forms of displays and other lighting from stores. Traffic signals were reduced to slits that could be seen from the ground, although barely, but not from above.

Tom had brought a flashlight, which also should not be used where it could be seen outside. He didn't turn it on until he got inside the house and screened it with his hand as much as possible in an effort to make in indiscernible from the sky. Picking his way through the house was much more difficult at night. The flashlight offered only minimal help. He tripped several times over breaks in the concrete floor and pieces of beams. Once he fell flat, breaking his fall with his hand and incurring a rather deep cut in the process. He wrapped his handkerchief around it to stanch the flow of blood. He would now have to explain to his mother the cut on his hand, which was not there when she left for the cinema, and the blood-soaked handkerchief as well as the mysterious absence of some of their food.

As he cautiously poked his way toward the back room, he bumped into a couch. He turned his light on it. It was a bit dusty and had a few pieces of shattered wood on it. Otherwise it was in pretty good condition. It was long and large enough for four people to sit comfortably. He tried to see if he could move it, but it was too heavy for one person—particularly a thin fourteen-year-old boy.

He found Captain Leuzinger in the same place and in the same position that he had left him the previous evening.

"Tom," he exclaimed. "I have been wondering all day whether you would ever come back and that if you did whether you would have the police with you."

"I told you I would come back and I told you I wouldn't tell anybody about you—at least until we talked some more," Tom said. "I have been thinking about it and I must tell the police. You're the enemy and I'm hiding you. Maybe they would shoot me for that. Maybe they would say I was a traitor. Besides, you can't just sit there with a broken leg for very long. They would give you medical care and treat your leg. You would be in a POW camp with other Germans and get food and a bed. You just can't stay here."

"Tom, let me tell you some things which I think will change your mind. Things you don't know and things you should know. But before I tell you everything, did you bring me anything to eat and drink? I don't think I can go much longer without at least something to drink," the German said.

"I did," replied Tom. "It's not much. We don't have much. Everything is rationed."

He handed the carrier bag to Leuzinger who reached for

it and groaned with pain as he did. Tom sat quietly while the German hastily wolfed down both pieces of bread and the small lump of cheese. He washed it down with half of the water in the glass jar and then carefully tightened the lid back on.

"I think I'll save the beans and the rest of the water for later," he said. "That blanket will come in useful. It was bitter cold last night. Did you happen to bring any wood we could use for a splint and something to tie it on with?"

"Oh, I didn't. I was in a hurry to get out of the house and I forgot all about it. I also forgot a spoon so you could eat the beans."

"Don't worry about it. I'll eat the beans with the top of the tin as a spoon. We need to splint my leg. There's probably a decent piece of wood and some sort of fabric lying around. Would you mind taking a look around and seeing what you can find."

"I'll look," said Tom.

He went back to where he bumped into the couch, remembering that there were some straight pieces of wood on it that might be the right size. There were also some torn curtains still attached to a rod where one of the windows used to be. He took several pieces of wood and a piece of the curtain, which he ripped off the rod, back to the German.

"That looks excellent, Tom. Can you tear some strips off that piece of cloth? You could use the sharp end of the tin opener to start the cut." Tom did as Leuzinger suggested. The curtain material tore easily.

"You're going to have to come up on my right side and straighten my leg. The break is between my knee and my ankle. Then you will have to place the wood alongside the leg, again between the knee and the ankle, and tie the wood at several places with the curtain material to keep the leg immobile. Tie the material securely, but not too tight or you'll cut off the circulation. When you straighten my leg, it will hurt a lot and I might even yell out. Don't let that stop you. I hate to ask you to do this. It's a tough thing for a young boy. but you've got courage. I knew that the first moment I saw you. Do you think you can handle it, Tom?"

"I don't know," Tom said with considerable doubt in his voice. "I'll try."

"Good lad," said Leuzinger. "I'm ready when you are."

It took longer than Tom anticipated. Leuzinger had been in one place for a long time without much movement. He was lying on rubble comprised of pieces of wood, concrete, and brick. Tom tried to move some of them to make Leuzinger more comfortable, but there wasn't much he could do. Apart from the broken leg, his body was stiff and sore. Any movement was excruciatingly painful.

"You'll have to take my boot off on that side," said Leuzinger.

Tom had seen the type of boot on the newsreels at the cinema. It seems that German and Allied airmen wore the same type of flying boots. It was a difficult, lengthy, and painful process to ease the boot off Leuzinger's leg.

Finally, Tom got the broken leg straightened and, after several muffed attempts, got the makeshift splint properly positioned and securely fastened to the broken leg. Throughout the entire time that Tom was going through the efforts to straighten the leg and apply the splint, Leuzinger had not cried out or made any sound at all. His pale face had turned bright red and he was sweating profusely.

"Thank you, Tom." His voice was weak and shaky. "You did a wonderful job. Now I must tell you all about me, my family, the reason that I must get out of here as soon as possible, and why I cannot go to a POW camp. I told you a little last night. I am a farmer," Leuzinger started. "My wife, Frieda, and I have lived there for ten years. My son is three and my daughter is going to be two. I was drafted in the Luftwaffe at the start of the war and was compelled to go to flight training. I didn't want to. I was—and am—opposed to the war. I detest what Germany is doing in Europe. I know of the atrocities that are being committed there and I detest them. If I didn't have a wife and children, I would have deserted long ago and tried to leave the country. But I can't do that. My family would be made to suffer, perhaps even killed."

Leuzinger's eyes filled with tears and there was a catch in his voice. "My wife, my dear Frieda, has been diagnosed with a fatal illness. I can't even pronounce it. The doctor says she has only six months to live. That was two months ago. We've taken her to specialists all over Germany. They all say the same thing. If they send me to a POW camp, I'll never see her again. I love her so. I must see her again—just one more time. That's why you must help me."

"If I agreed to help you, what could I do? You can't walk. You can't hire a taxi and tell him to drive you to Germany."

Leuzinger smiled. "You have a good sense of humor, Tom. I like that. No, a taxi wouldn't work. I lost my wallet when I jumped out of the plane. I believe it fell out of my pocket shortly before I landed here. In it is the name and address of a friend who would help me."

"I'm not promising to help you escape, but I'll look for the wallet."

CHAPTER TWENTY-SIX

THE SCHOOL PROVIDED LUNCHES at both the boys' school and the girls' school. The cost was sixpence a day if parents had only one child in school and five pence each for two or more. For parents who could demonstrate a certain low level of income the meals were paid for by a fund established by the London County Council. Since Tom and Miriam both went to Buckhurst, it was a total of ten pence. Tom usually had lunch with Josh and three or four others at a corner table. The day after he had placed the splint on Leuzinger's leg he deliberately delayed going to lunch for fifteen minutes.

"Where have you been?" said Josh who had already eaten his lunch and was finishing the small piece of pie that was part of the meal.

"Oh, Belsen wanted to see me," he lied. He had lied more in the last couple of days than he had in a year.

"What did the old geezer want?" asked Paul Roth, his friend who lived in the same flats.

"Something about a paper he said I hadn't turned in. But I had."

The four friends sat and talked for a few minutes while Tom, who was usually a fast eater, uncharacteristically toyed with his food. The others got impatient. They only had three quarters of an hour between classes and they wanted to kick a ball around on the playground as they always did.

"Are you ever going to finish?" said Ronnie Feldman, another friend who was fairly new to the school. He, his mother, and two sisters had been living in Portsmouth to be close to their father who had been called into the Royal Navy. He had been assigned to a cruiser which had been sent to the Middle East. Their family then moved to London to be close to their grandparents.

"You go ahead. I'll be out in a few minutes," said Tom.

After they left, Tom looked around the cafeteria. There were only three boys left in the room and they were at a table at the far end of the room. The lunch consisted of a small stringy piece of meat of uncertain ancestry and age, a small dollop of mashed potatoes, and a tablespoonful of tinned peas. Tom quickly slipped the rest of the meat and the peas into a paper bag lined with greaseproof paper that he had brought from home. He then pushed the bag into his pocket, hoping that the greaseproof paper would keep the grease off his trousers. Then he joined his friends for a kick around.

He went straight from school to the house on Fleming Street. As he stood outside and looked around, a female voice shouted, "Boy, you stay away from that house. Do you hear me?"

He looked toward the sound of the voice. It came from a fat grey-haired woman in a flowered apron with pins in her hair.

"One of you boys is going to get killed in those houses. Don't you know that whole thing could come down on you any minute?" she barked.

"I wasn't going in. I was just looking."

"Well, get on your way or I'll call the police. You don't belong around here." Then she turned around and walked into the flats opposite the damaged houses.

"Nosy old twit," Tom muttered under his breath, but he walked away and around the corner. Ten minutes later he came back. There was no one on the street. He quickly went in the house, made his way to the back, and found Leuzinger exactly where he had left him.

"Tom, I was getting worried about you," said Leuzinger.

Tom took the bag out of his pocket and handed it to Leuzinger. "It's not much, but it's all I could get."

"It will taste like a fine feast," said Leuzinger, reaching for the jar of water and taking a sip.

"While you're eating, I'll look for your wallet."

Tom spent about twenty minutes looking through the rubble, both in the remains of the room where Leuzinger was and in other parts of the house. It wasn't easy. It was hard to move around over all the debris and even harder to locate anything as small as a wallet. After the lapse of twenty minutes, Tom told Leuzinger that he had no luck. Leuzinger looked desperately disappointed, but smiled, thanked Tom, and asked him to sit down.

Leuzinger then said, "I have a friend, an Irishman. He lives in the North of England or the Midlands somewhere. I met him years ago when I was on holiday in England. We have stayed in touch and our families have visited each other several times. His name is Eamon Shaughnessy. He could get me to Ireland if I could get in touch with him. It would be difficult—and perhaps dangerous—but I know he could do it. Mind you, he is not a Nazi sympathizer. Like me, he hates what's going on over there. He'd do it for me as a friend. If he got me to Ireland, I would perhaps be interned and spend the rest of the war in Ireland. We had a lecture in flight training about some convention or other and how it related to the treatment of escaped prisoners in neutral countries. I don't remember much about it. Maybe they would let me go. I just forget."

"What does 'interned' mean? I never heard that word," asked Tom.

"You see the Republic of Ireland, unlike Northern Island, is not part of Great Britain. It's a separate country."

"I knew that, but what has that got to do with being interned?"

"I'm getting to that. The Republic of Ireland is a neutral country. That means it is not in the war on either side. If I get there, the authorities either would put me in a camp for the duration of the war or maybe even let me go back to Germany. I'm just not sure."

"If they put you in a camp, isn't that just the same as if you were in a POW camp in England?"

"In some ways, yes. I would, in effect, be in prison. But in the most important way—no. My wife couldn't come to England, but she could go to Ireland. I could see her and the children and the Irish government might even let them stay with me in the camp, at least for a while. None of that would be possible if I were in a POW camp in England."

"The trouble is I don't have Eamon's address. It is in my wallet and I know that his address and telephone number are not listed in any telephone book. Maybe if you look some more you will be able to find it. I know I had it on the plane before it crashed because I looked at it there. It was in a front pocket of my flight jacket and it ripped when I brushed against something sharp as I fell through what was left of the roof. It's getting too dark now, but would you look for it again tomorrow or the next day?" asked Leuzinger.

"I will," said Tom.

"And will you help me get to Ireland?" pleaded Leuzinger.

"I think so, but let me think some more about it."

CHAPTER TWENTY-SEVEN

"TOM, REBECCA, HAVE YOU seen a tin of beans? It was in the larder and I can't find it. We were going to have baked beans on toast for dinner," said Miriam.

"We had it the other night," said Tom, suddenly angry with himself for not being able to think of a better excuse.

"I don't think so," said Rebecca. "We haven't had baked beans on toast for ages."

"Maybe you just thought you had bought a can of beans. Maybe you accidentally threw it out," said Tom, now totally out of ideas.

"I know you bought a tin of beans. I saw it and I know you wouldn't have thrown it out. Don't be silly, Tom," said Rebecca.

Tom thought angrily, *I wish she would shut up.*

"It must be here somewhere," said Miriam, standing on a chair and poking around in the back of the top shelf. "No, it's not there. Tom, take a shilling out of my purse, run down to Samuel's, and see if he'll let you have another tin."

Tom ran all the way to the grocer's and got there a few minutes before it closed.

"Mr. Samuel, my mum would like a tin of baked beans, please," said Tom.

"You're lucky. I have one left. Here, ninepence," he said. "Want a bag?"

"No, thanks."

He ran as fast as could because he wanted to stop at Fleming Street. He didn't know how long this could go on. If he could only find the wallet, maybe he could contact Mr. Shaughnessy and he could get Leuzinger out of Fleming Street and off to Ireland. He had an idea that might help out on the food situation and the search for the wallet.

"Captain Leuzinger, it's Tom," he shouted.

"Hello, Tom. I didn't think I would see you today."

"I have an idea, actually three ideas," Tom said. "I would like to tell my friend Josh about you because—"

"Do you really think that's wise?" said Leuzinger with a very worried look on his face.

"Josh—that's my friend's name—wouldn't tell anyone. He's my best friend. It's not easy for me to get enough food for you without making my mum and people at school suspicious. My mum already doesn't understand what happened to a tin of beans she was going to cook for us tonight. I don't know how much longer you'll be here. I hope not long. Josh could help with the food. He could also help find your wallet—if it is in this house somewhere. The other thing is there's a sofa toward the front of the house. I can't lift it by myself. Josh could help me bring it back here. You would be much more comfortable on it than on the floor," Tom blurted out breathlessly. He was in good physical condition, but he had run hard to and from Samuel's.

"If you think it's a good idea and you are certain you can trust Josh, I suppose it's all right."

111

"I'll try to bring him by tomorrow. I have to go now. I'm already late for dinner."

Tom ran the rest of the way home.

"That took you a long time," said Miriam. "What kept you?"

"Mr. Samuel had already closed up and he had to reopen for me. That took him a while," Tom said.

This was now the third or fourth lie he had told his mother in the last twenty-four hours. He couldn't keep it up for much longer. Apart from his deep sense of guilt, he knew that sooner or later he was going to be caught out—probably sooner rather than later. Josh was his big hope. In addition to the help he could be, as he had told Leuzinger, it would be a relief to be able to tell someone.

CHAPTER TWENTY-EIGHT

TOM COULD HARDLY WAIT for chemistry class to finish. He wanted to talk to Josh Rosenblatt. It was difficult for him to contain himself or concentrate on what he was doing. Chemistry class was not the best place to woolgather. There were flames, acids, and a variety of items that could burn, scar, and otherwise give anyone a very unpleasant afternoon. The class sat on high stools with an assortment of beakers, Bunsen burners, glass tubes, chemicals, and probes on the desks in front of them. The desks were pockmarked and stained with chemicals spilled by generations of students. Mr. Turner, the chemistry master, walked among the students as they performed elementary experiments with a wide variety of skills.

"Sloan, pay attention to that beaker. I don't want to have to mop you up and send you home in a paper bag. I don't think your mother would like it and, besides, I'm a little short of paper bags," Mr. Turner shouted at Sloan.

Tom had been heating a mixture of chemicals over a Bunsen burner and had let the beaker get too hot—even though the class had been warned not to do so. Ordinarily, Tom liked chemistry—particularly the experiments that Mr.

Turner let the class perform. It was a welcome respite from lectures, many of which he found profoundly boring. This afternoon was different. He was anticipating letting Josh Rosenblatt in on his unbelievable secret.

Before the war, Tom and Josh's parents had been good friends. Leonard Rosenblatt was unusual for this part of London. He had a college degree and was a chartered accountant. He and his partner had a small office in Whitechapel High Street under the name of Rosenblatt & Cohen Ltd, Chartered Accountants. They specialized in handling tax filings and business planning for small companies. Mr. Rosenblatt was called up into the army and was a sergeant in the Finance Corps stationed in Aldershot. He was able to come home on weekends to the Rosenblatt's semi-detached house on Slaven Gardens, which was about a half mile from the Sloans' flat. Slaven Gardens was what passed for an upscale area in the East End. To people in Belgravia, Kensington, and Hampstead, Slaven Gardens looked like something only slightly better than the slums. To the people who lived in the austere flats of the East End, Slaven Gardens was the type of place that they aspired to— and they harbored fervent hopes that their children would someday grow up and live on such a street.

Josh's and Tom's fathers were big football fans and, whenever they could, they would take the bus to White Hart Lane and buy tickets to stand on the terraces to watch their idols—the mighty Tottenham Hotspurs—play against the hated opponents. Often they would take Josh and Tom. If they didn't get to the ground early, they would have to stand behind men (and there never were women at professional football games) and have absolutely no ability to see the game. Sometimes their fathers would lift them on their shoulders for short periods of time so they could see five or ten minutes of the game. Sometimes kindly men standing in front of them would let them through to stand against the rail in the front. Most of the time they were walled in behind a sea of people and could only see the trousers of the men immediately in front of them.

Tom and Josh had been friends since they were eight years old. Josh had a fabulous collection of miniature tanks, planes, and ships that he had put together from kits that could be bought at specialty shops. The ships were aircraft carriers, destroyers, and battleships. He had all kinds of planes—Spitfires, Hurricanes, and Lancaster bombers. They were all to scale. They would play for hours in the small garden behind the semi-detached house on Slaven Gardens launching attacks on the Germans and always prevailing.

While Tom was tall, fair, slim, and athletic, Josh was short, dark, slightly pudgy, and definitely non-athletic. He wore thick horn-rimmed glasses, which caused him to frequently be referred to as "four eyes" or sometimes, depending on the religion and meanness of the speaker, "four-eyed Jew boy." Despite his size and lack of athleticism, Josh was not easily intimidated. That type of bravery endeared him to Tom, but it also resulted in a number of fights, none of which Josh ever won. Josh probably held the record for number of times returning home with a bloody nose, a black eye, and torn clothes.

As soon as they got out of chemistry class, Tom pulled Josh aside.

"I've got to talk to you about something real important. But it's got to be real private," said Tom.

Josh was suitably intrigued. "Nobody's going to be at my

house until six o'clock. My mum and the others have gone to my grandma's house."

When they got to Josh's house, Tom said, "You have to promise me you won't ever say a word of what I am going to tell you to anyone."

"I won't tell. Trust me," Josh said, barely containing his curious excitement.

"Swear on your mother's life that you won't tell a soul no matter what," Tom insisted. Why poor mother's lives had to be security or collateral for the promise has always been a puzzle. Never the father's life, much less the life of the promisor.

"I swear," said Josh.

Although nobody was anywhere near them and the doors and windows were closed, Tom recited the whole Hauptman Heinrich Leuzinger saga in a voice barely above a whisper. Josh just sat there with his eyes wide and his mouth agape.

"Are you sure you didn't make all this up?" Josh said at the end of the story.

"Of course not. It's too late now, but I'm going to take you over there tomorrow," Tom said.

"But he's a Nazi and you're helping him escape," said Josh.

"I told you—he's not a Nazi. He hates them. It's not his fault he's a German. He just wants to see his wife before she dies of this terrible disease."

"But Germans are killing all the Jews. They're all a bunch of murdering swine," cried Josh.

"Most of them—yes, but not all of them. Let me tell you about Colonel Reichmann," Tom said and then told him the story that his father had told.

"How do you know that Reichmann is telling the truth?" said Josh.

Tom was exasperated. "I told you Colonel Corcoran's father found the Jewish doctor and his family. He went to see them. They're living in London now. They confirmed that Colonel Reichmann saved their lives and risked his own in doing that. We're not just taking Reichmann's word for it. We have the Swiss Red Cross and an important English bloke vouching for the accuracy of his story."

"Well, all right. Colonel Reichmann is what you say he is. But I didn't hear you say that Captain Leuzinger saved any Jews or that there is anyone like Colonel Corcoran's dad to back up his story. How do you know he's telling the truth?"

"I didn't say he saved any Jews. He never said he did. I think he would if he had the chance. I know there isn't anybody to back up his story. I just believe him. Sometimes that's all there is. What more do you want?"

"Let me think about it for a minute. Don't rush me. This is important."

"I've told you everything there is to tell. Do you think I would be doing what I'm doing if I didn't believe him?"

"All right. I'm in."

CHAPTER TWENTY-NINE

As THEY GOT CLOSE to the Fleming Street house, Tom said to Josh, "We've got to be awful careful that nobody sees us going in. There's an old lady that lives across the street who saw me and said she'd call the police if I went in."

When they were about to turn into Fleming Street, they saw a man with a horse and cart delivering coal to the flats across from the bomb damage. The man would pull a sack off the cart, sling it over his shoulder, and take it into the flats.

"Don't turn," hissed Tom. "Keep walking straight. We'll wait 'til he's gone."

They walked to the corner and looked at the pictures of coming attractions at the cinema. They then walked slowly around the corner and stopped to look at the cobbler in the window of his shop repairing a pair of boots. The cobbler looked up from his last, rather surprised at the boys' apparent show of interest in his craft. Finally they circled back to Fleming Street just in time to see the horse and cart turning the corner and disappearing. No one else was on the street and Tom and Josh quickly stepped into the house and made their way to the back.

Leuzinger had shifted his position slightly and was

leaning more on his right side. His blond hair was covered in dust. There had been some gusty wind the night before and apparently some of the debris in the ruins had blown around.

"Captain Leuzinger, this is my friend I was telling you about, Josh Rosenblatt," Tom said. "I've told him all about you and your wife's illness and he has agreed to help."

The name "Rosenblatt" seemed to momentarily startle the German, but he smiled and said in a friendly voice, "It's very nice to meet you Josh. I deeply appreciate your coming. I know the situation is difficult."

For a few moments, Josh just stared at the German airman, his gaze principally focused on the Luftwaffe uniform. He had seen such uniforms on the newsreels at the cinema, but he had never expected to see one so close with a live German airman inside it.

"Yes, I—yes—um, Tom told me—said he had found you," Josh stammered, upset that he was so unnerved by this encounter and by his inability to say anything intelligent.

"Tom, you didn't tell me that your friend was Jewish. I think it's wonderful that you have Jewish friends. It's very important that people of all religions get along with each other. That's what the world needs. I compliment both of you," Leuzinger said, smiling even more broadly.

"You're right," said Tom. "It would be good if people of different religions got along and didn't hate each other. But I am Jewish—same as Josh."

The smile didn't leave Leuzinger's face. "I didn't know that. I just assumed with the name 'Sloan' that you weren't," he said. "Not that it makes a bit of difference to me. I deplore religious bigotry of any kind as I told you," he added hurriedly.

Josh had recovered his composure and pulled a brown paper bag out of his pocket. "I brought some crackers and cheese," he said. "It's not much, but it was all I could get today. I think I can get some more tomorrow."

"Well, thank you, Josh. This is most kind of you," said Leuzinger.

"How is your leg feeling?" Tom asked.

"It feels much better today. Thank you for asking. I think in a day or two, I might try to stand up. I'll probably need something to prop me up."

"Josh and I will go and try to bring that couch in here. I think the two of us can handle it. We'll also rummage around and see if we can find your wallet," said Tom.

The two boys struggled with the couch after first removing the debris off it. It was quite heavy and the rubble all over the floor made the trip to the back room long and difficult. The two of them cleared out an area of the back room so that the couch could rest on a flat surface. They placed it as close to Leuzinger as they could. They then helped him onto the couch. They placed his arms over their shoulders, lifted him from the ground, and, with some considerable effort, laid him down on the couch. The effort exhausted all three of them. The boys sat down on the ground—out of breath and sweating profusely—and for a few minutes nobody said anything.

"This is so much better and a whole lot more comfortable," said Leuzinger. "Now, if only we could find my wallet, I could probably quickly arrange to have my Irish friend pick me up and relieve the two of you of any more responsibility for me. I wish there was some other way to get in contact with Eamon, but I know of none other than my wallet. I still think it is somewhere in this house. I can almost feel it falling out of my flying jacket as I came through the roof."

"Josh and I will look today, but I can't stay long. My mother wants me to go with her and my sister to see my grandparents," said Tom. "If we don't find it today I'll come back tomorrow. I can spend more time here then. My mother and sister are going to see an old friend of hers in Stoke Newington. I don't think they will be back until quite late. What will you do if we can't find it?"

"I've given that a lot of thought, but I have not come up with any good ideas. Even with crutches, I won't be very maneuverable. I have no papers that would get me past any suspicious policemen or military people. I can't stay here indefinitely. I suppose I will just try to get to the coast and try to get on some boat bound for Ireland. I understand there is still transportation between England and Ireland."

"I don't see how that will work," said Tom, "and you can't even try it in your uniform. We could probably get you some civvies, but you would almost certainly get caught and shot. I saw in a film that if an enemy soldier is caught in civvies, he is shot as a spy."

"Well, as I said, I can't stay here much longer—and I if I have to die trying to see my wife, I will. I don't know how I can live without her anyway."

CHAPTER THIRTY

"YOU BOYS COME OUT of there right now," yelled Air-Raid Warden Arnold Lucas.

"Blimey, it's the warden," gasped Tom.

Several days later, Josh and Tom were in the back room with Leuzinger. They had been very careful every time they came to the house. They always looked down the street before they turned into it. They always stopped outside the house and looked around again before they went in. If they saw anyone on the street, they kept walking. Their success at having gone undetected had made them careless this time. They did not notice the nosy old lady from across the street who sometime earlier had shouted at Tom to stay out of the building. When she saw Josh and Tom go into the house, she ran around the corner and found Lucas in his flat having his tea. Although, unnecessary to his mission, Lucas put on his ARP helmet and his ARP arm band and hurried with the old lady to the house.

It had been a couple of weeks since Tom had found Leuzinger and the German's living quarters had improved. In addition to the couch, they discovered a pillow under one of the fallen beams. They had rigged up a canopy out of an old piece of canvas from the shed in the small back garden. Fortuitously, the canopy was in place just hours before a fairly heavy rainfall. For a long time they had ignored a door leading from the back room because it was stuck tight. Finally, they forced it open and found a small bathroom, which was virtually undamaged. To their surprise, water was still available in the washbasin and in the lavatory. Electricity and gas had long since been turned off, but not the water. There was soap, towels, and paper. They had put together a crude crutch that enabled Leuzinger to ambulate from his couch to the bathroom. With Josh's help, food had not been as much of a problem as it had been earlier. Tom had stopped taking any food from his flat and, instead, both he and Josh would furtively put portions of their school lunch in bags when they were sure that no one was watching.

Lucas continued to yell, "I know you're back there. Don't make me have to come back and get you."

"Quick," Tom said to Josh. "Let's go. We can't let him come back here."

They threaded their way toward the front where Lucas was standing with his arms folded across his chest looking very stern.

"I'm surprised at you, Tom. You should know better. You could get killed. This place is not safe. Your mother is going to be very unhappy with you when I tell her. And what's your name?" he said to Josh.

"Josh Rosenblatt," Josh replied.

Lucas whipped out his little notebook, which he carried with him everywhere. "What's your address? I'm going to tell your mother too. And don't lie to me. You give me the wrong address and I'll easily find the right one and it will go harder on you," said Lucas in his most officious voice.

Josh gave him his correct address. "Mr. Lucas, I wish you wouldn't tell our mothers," said Tom. "We won't come back here again."

Tom knew there was no chance that Lucas would honor that request. One of his pet activities was telling tales on people.

"I wish I could, Tom. But it's my duty under these circumstances and I have a very important obligation to this community to protect it," Lucas said pompously, monstrously overstating his insignificant responsibilities.

Just then, there was a noise coming from the back of the house.

"What's that?" said Lucas, taking two steps toward the rear. "Is there someone else back there?"

"There's no one else here," said Tom, trying not to sound too anxious. "There's a beam across the middle of the house that sounds like it might fall. It's been creaking like that and looks a bit wonky."

That was the exact right thing to say. There was no way that Lucas' concept of his "important obligations" included putting himself at any risk.

"All right," said Lucas. "I'll take your word for it this time. But now you see what I mean. This is a dangerous place and nobody should be in here."

They went outside. The old lady from across the street was waiting. "See, I told you," she said. "They're a couple of rascals and that tall one was here before and I told him not to go in the house. They deserve a good caning—both of them."

Lucas walked them to the top of the street, shook his finger at them, and left.

"That was a close one," said Josh. "My mother is going to be furious."

"So is mine," replied Tom. "We are going to have to be even more careful from now on."

"The 'now on' bothers me," said Josh. "There doesn't seem to be any end to this. How is he ever going to get out of there? This can't go on 'til the end of the war. What are we going to do?"

"I wish I knew," said Tom and went home knowing that Mr. Lucas had wasted no time in telling his mother and had undoubtedly embellished what had happened and probably had claimed that he had saved both boys' lives. *If only there was some way that Captain Leuzinger could get out of there soon, but I just don't see how it's going to happen,* he thought.

The truth was that Captain Leuzinger would be leaving Fleming Street a lot earlier than either he or the boys had any reason to expect.

CHAPTER THIRTY-ONE

"MY MOTHER IS FURIOUS with me," Josh told Tom as they were walking home from the school the day after Lucas found them at the house. "Mr. Lucas told my mother that the house is very dangerous; that we have no business being there; that we are violating the law and that only terrible things can happen if she doesn't stop me from going there again."

"What terrible things?"

"He said either the house would fall down on me and kill me if I went back or if it didn't and he found me there again he would report me to the police and they would do something—I don't know what," Josh replied.

"Well, he told my mum, too," said Tom. "She told me not to go near the house again or she would tell the school that I am not to be allowed to play football again for the rest of the year."

"What are you going to do?" asked Josh.

"I don't know," said Tom. "I can't just leave him in that house."

"Why not?" said Josh. "He'd probably be better off if he was in a prisoner-of-war camp. He would be with his own people and he would have regular food rather than the scraps we get him and a real bed to sleep in with real blankets and sheets rather than that old dirty couch. He could have a hot shower rather than washing in cold water. I know you and I would be better off if we didn't have to worry about him anymore."

"What about his wife? She's gonna die and he'll never see her again if he goes to a POW camp."

"But he's a German, an enemy. He bombed London. He's killed people over here. Jews are being killed over there by Germans. I don't know why we're helping him anyway."

"We've been all over that. I thought you understood when you agreed to help. He's different," said Tom. "He doesn't believe in what his country is doing. He hates it. He's told us he wouldn't have anything to do with it and he'd leave of it wasn't for his wife and children. If he had left, the Nazis would have harmed his family. He said if he gets to Ireland, he'll be interned and his wife and children can visit him there. They can't here. He won't be dropping any more bombs and he'll be in a camp just like he would be here—only in a country that is not at war with Germany or England or anyone else and that's the reason his wife and children can visit him. Maybe they can even live with him in the camp in Ireland."

Josh looked down at his shoes. "I'm sorry, Tom. I can't go back there again. I promised my mum. She made me swear on her life."

"Mums always do that," said Tom "It doesn't mean anything. I know boys who always swear on their mother's lives and always break their promises. Nothing ever happens to their mums."

"I know, but I just can't go back there," Josh said forlornly. "Are you angry with me? Are we still friends?"

"Of course we are," Tom reassured him. "You have to do what you think is best."

"What are you going to do?" said Josh.

"I'm just going to be more careful. I'm going to see if I can get into the house a different way so that I don't have to go down Fleming Street. It backs onto an alley. I haven't been there in a long time, but I remember that the backs of the houses are separated from the alley by high walls. I'll see if there is some way I can get over the wall and whether I can get into the house from the rear. No harm in taking a look."

"I'll still sneak some food from school lunch for you if you'd like," said Josh.

"Thanks. That'll help."

Chapter Thirty-Two

"I HEARD THAT MAN yell at you," said Leuzinger the next day. "Who was he and what happened?"

"It was the air-raid warden. Some old lady saw Josh and me come in here and she told the warden. He wanted to come back here, but we told him there was a beam across the back of the house that was making noises and sounded like it was going to fall and he backed off," said Tom.

"Good thinking, Tom," said Leuzinger smiling. "Where's Josh?"

Tom explained how the warden had reported the incident to both his and Josh's mother and that Josh couldn't come any more.

"I'm really sorry. I don't want to get you boys into any trouble. What about you, Tom? You came back. What are you going to do?"

Tom had come down the alley behind Fleming Street. The houses on Fleming and Ramsey both backed onto the alley. Before the war, people who lived in those houses and who had cars would park in the alley. There were no garages. Even before the war only a few people who lived on those streets could afford cars. Now, with gas rationing being so tight, nobody on those streets had cars. The alley was deserted almost all the time. Rubbish had built up and was not collected and there was little point for anyone to walk down there. Tom had come up to the back of the Fleming house and had found that the six-foot-high brick wall went the width of the house where Leuzinger was. The wall next door had been partially demolished. Bricks from that part of the wall were strewn all over and no one had cleared them up. In one part, the remainder of the wall was only three feet high. Tom found he could shimmy up that height and, when he did, he discovered that the two houses were separated by a wire fence that had partially collapsed. Tom was able to cross into the backyard of what had become known to Tom and Josh as "The German's House."

"I don't know, Captain. This won't work forever. If we can't get you out of here, it's worse than you being in a POW camp. You won't see your wife and you'll be here in this bombed-out place, sleeping on a dirty old couch, eating scraps of food, and washing in cold water. Sooner or later, they are going to find you anyway. Maybe sooner would be better than later."

"Tom, let me think about it for a few days. Maybe I can come up with a solution. Right now, I don't know what it will be, but I'll try. If only we could find my wallet—that would solve everything.

Chapter Thirty-Three

Every Monday at nine o'clock, all students gathered in the main hall for what was termed assembly. The headmaster, Mr. Slocum, would make announcements. Mostly they concerned new masters, substitute teachers, planned field trips, changes in class schedules, and things like that. With many of the younger masters away in the armed forces, it was always difficult for the school administration to have adequate staffing. There were also announcements about those masters and former students who were in the military. Sometimes it was about medals that had been won. More often it was about casualties, deaths, injuries, and missing in action. Sometimes it was about civilians—present and former staff and students who had been killed or injured in the bombing. There were also presentations by civil defense people about always carrying your gas masks, what to do if caught in the open during an air attack, and stuff like that. Sometimes Tom had heard of certain of the dead and injured, but had no close contact with any of them. Today was different.

After some dull announcements about air raid practice

drills and when to get under the desk Slocum cleared his throat.

"I am sorry to have to announce an unfortunate event that happened yesterday evening. One of our students, Joshua Rosenblatt, was attacked by some thugs on his way home and was severely beaten. He is in Hodgson Hospital. I received a report from the hospital a little while ago. He has suffered a concussion and a broken arm. He also has numerous cuts and bruises; the doctors say he will recover, but will be in the hospital for several days. The attack was seen by a lady who was watering plants in her front garden. She has given a description of the thugs to the police and they are investigating. Mrs. Browning in our nurse's office is putting together a get-well letter. Any of you who wish to sign it may do so at recess or during lunch period."

Tom fought back tears. Poor Josh. He never did any harm to anybody. It was probably a group of anti-Semitic fascist bastards. They look for defenseless Jewish boys who are by themselves. The irony was not lost on Tom. Josh was trying to help a German pilot and was beaten by a bunch of ruffians who never helped anybody but themselves in their whole miserable lives. He could not wait for school to be over for the day so that he could go to see Josh. After his last class, he ran home as fast as he could. His mother was waiting on the street outside the flat wearing her hat and coat.

"Mum, Josh has—" he started to blurt out.

"I know, Tom, I know. I've been waiting for you so that we can go to the hospital to see Josh," his mother said quietly.

For the second time that day, his eyes filled with tears. She always knew the right thing to say and the right thing to do. Hodgson Hospital was several miles away and they had to change buses to get there. Tom knew that Josh had taken a fearful beating, but he was not prepared for what he saw. Josh was lying on his back with his right arm in plaster and in some sort of swing contraption. His right eye was puffed up, completely closed, and surrounded by a huge, deep purple bruise. His left eye was open, but blackened and there was a large bandage around his head about two inches above his eyebrows. Both lips were swollen and, when he opened his mouth, there was a gap where a front tooth used to be. Josh's mother was sitting next to him, holding his hand.

"Tom," Josh said in a muffled voice through swollen lips. "They called me a dirty Jew and said I ought to be in the gas chamber."

Tom, who had been on the verge of tears all day and had been able to control himself with great difficulty, could no longer do so. He sobbed uncontrollably and the tears flowed down his cheeks unashamedly. His mum pulled out her handkerchief and gave it to him while trying desperately to control her own emotions.

CHAPTER THIRTY-FOUR

Tom had gotten to the German's house later than usual. His mother and Rebecca were going to a friend's house to listen to some of their favorite radio programs. They wouldn't be back until after dark. The alley, as usual, was empty. He climbed over the damaged brick wall next door, slipped through the hole in the wire fence, and came into the room the back way.

"What's the matter, Tom? Are you all right?" asked Leuzinger. Tom was pale and his eyes were puffy from crying. He told Leuzinger what had happened to Josh and how the assailants had called him a dirty Jew and that he ought to be in the gas chamber. Leuzinger listened without a word, his gaze focused unblinkingly on Tom and his face taut with concern.

"That is truly awful," he said when Tom was finished. "How can a bunch of moronic ruffians gang up on a young boy and do such horrible things to him. Have they caught them yet?"

"Not yet," said Tom. "A lady saw them attack Josh and gave a description to the police. They're looking for them now. She said there were four and they were big and maybe in their twenties."

"When they find them, they should be put in prison for a very, very long time," Leuzinger said. "But there is a lesson there."

"What lesson? I don't understand what you mean."

"Remember when we were talking a while back—you, Josh, and me—about how you must judge people on their individual merits and you can't condemn a whole country by what some of the people in that country do. You remember that, don't you?" asked Leuzinger.

Tom nodded, not sure where all of this was leading.

"I told you boys that not all Germans condone the terrible atrocities that are being carried out by Hitler's thugs—that not all Germans can be labeled as inhuman beasts because of the acts of many of their countrymen. Well, it wasn't Germans that attacked Josh. It wasn't Germans who ganged up on him and beat him to a pulp. It wasn't Germans that put him in hospital and told him he was a dirty Jew who belonged in the gas chamber. It was a group of Englishmen. Do you think those Englishmen are better than the German fiends who are massacring innocent people in Europe? Do you think because those English thugs are vicious, anti-Semitic animals, that all Englishmen are vicious, anti-Semitic animals?"

Tom thought about his father's letter and his 180-degree change in attitude from hating all Germans after he found out what Colonel Reichmann had done.

"I suppose what you say is right," said Tom.

"Of course, it's right," said Leuzinger. "I think it was some philosopher or statesman who said, 'You can't visit the sins of the fathers on their sons and you can't visit the sins of your countrymen on you. You are only responsible for the sins you commit—not the sins others commit just because, by accident of birth, you share the same nationality."

Tom gave Leuzinger the scraps of food he had brought and said good night. It was getting dark and he was not anxious to go out the back way into the deserted, unlit alley. He thought about Josh and, at that point, decided he would chance detection by going out the front way onto Fleming Street.

It was difficult to pick his way through the rubble, broken bricks, and pieces of lumber. His foot caught a large piece of wood and it flipped over. He looked down to see what he had struck and, in the twilight, thought he saw a small, black object that had been hidden by the piece of wood he had knocked over. He leaned over and groped around. His hand touched a soft piece of material. At first, he thought it was part of a pillow or a piece of curtain.

He picked it up. In the gathering darkness, it felt like a small, thin wallet.

Chapter Thirty-Five

Tom felt inside the wallet. There was nothing in at all. It couldn't be the captain's wallet. He remembered Leuzinger saying that he had pictures of his wife and children in it. It must belong to the people who lived in the house. Tom decided that he would not go back and show it to Leuzinger that night since it clearly was not his.

Right after dinner he went to his room and looked at the wallet more carefully. It was just two pieces of black material, perhaps leather or probably some cheap imitation. It was sewn together on three sides. It had some numbers and letters printed on the outside in three rows. Tom had no idea what they represented, but he guessed that it was some means of identifying the manufacturer of the wallet.

Disappointed that his discovery was of no use and could not help get the captain any nearer to reuniting with his wife and children, Tom went to bed and promptly fell asleep. There was no bombing that night. There had been thick fog over London and the Southern Counties and the German planes had been silent for several days. He woke up with a start. It was two o'clock in the morning. *How silly I am,* he thought. There must have been something in it, whether it belonged to Captain Leuzinger or the owners of the house or anyone else. Nobody goes around with an empty wallet. The boys who first searched the house must have found the wallet and taken its contents. But if it was Leuzinger's, why would they take the family pictures. They would be of no value. If it contained German money, they may not have told the police for fear that they would have to surrender it. His mind went over and over the possibilities without settling on a logical solution. He needed to talk to someone, but he couldn't do so without running the risk of giving away the captain. He would go to the hospital tomorrow and talk to Josh. He was much better and was going to be released in a day or two. Maybe Josh would have some ideas.

Josh was looking much better. He was sitting up in bed, sipping some kind of drink in a glass through a straw. His right eye was no longer swollen shut, although it was still discolored. The bandage around his head had been removed and the cuts and bruises were starting to fade.

"Hello, Josh. You all right, mate?" Tom asked in a concerned tone.

"I'll tell you what," replied Josh in a hushed, conspiratorial voice, "the food here is bit of all right. A lot better than I get at home. I had a nice piece of beef last night and they even gave me seconds on pudding. I might stay a week or so—." He paused, "just joking. I'm going home tomorrow."

Tom looked around to make sure that no one was in the room or close by. He fished the wallet out of his pocket and handed it to Josh.

"I found this in the German's house last night. I haven't shown it to the captain. What do you make of it? There wasn't anything in it."

Josh looked carefully at it. He turned it over, ran his hands through the inside and outside, looked hard at the letters and numbers printed of one side, and said, "It's German."

"How do you know that?" said Tom.

"Look at the number 7. It's got some kind of line through it. You never see that in English writing. At least I never have. Germans write like that."

"I never knew that. How do you know it?"

"I saw a motion picture a while ago. It was about this German bloke who was in love with some English lady. My mother took me to see it. I was never so bored in my life. I don't remember what it was about."

"What has that got to do with whether this wallet is German?" Tom said impatiently.

"Half a mo! Half a mo! Don't rush me. I'm getting to that."

"Don't take all day. I've got to go to the house before I go home."

"Well, this German bloke wrote this English lady a letter. I don't remember why or what it was about, but it was real important to the story. He put the date he was writing the letter at the top of the letter and it was on the screen so the audience could read it. I remember the date had a 7 in it and it had this funny little line through it just like on this wallet."

"All right, young man. It's time for you to leave." The stout, motherly looking nurse with the starched uniform and white cap called out from the doorway.

"Just few minutes," pleaded Tom.

"Not even one," she said in her best authoritarian voice. "Out now."

Chapter Thirty-Six

"Captain," Tom said, "I've found what I think is your wallet, but somebody got to it before me and has stolen everything out of it."

"Let me see," Leuzinger said excitedly. He almost grabbed the wallet out of Tom's hands. He read the letters and numbers on the outside then looked up at Tom. "It's mine. You've done it. You've found my salvation."

Tom looked confused. "But what good is it? There's nothing in it."

"The pictures were important. There was also some English money to help me in any escape. But the most important thing is still here," he said exultingly. "If you promise not to tell anyone, I'll let you know what it is. Do you promise?"

"I've not told anybody anything about you—except Josh."

"I know. I'm grateful and I'm sorry I asked you for another promise. I know you won't tell anyone. Now, Tom, look at these numbers and letters on the outside of the wallet. They are a code for the address of my friend Eamon. I devised it when I was in Germany." He took his right boot off, lifted the support layer inside, and took out a small piece of paper that had two columns with numbers and letters on one side and numbers and letters on the other.

"This is the key to the code. I can now use it to get Eamon's address. Remember I told you that Eamon is a friend of mine and will help me to get to Ireland. He's not a Nazi and has no sympathy for what's going on over there. The only reason he would help is because he is a friend who knows my wife and knows how sick she is. I don't want to be caught with his address on me. He might get into trouble with the British authorities and that's the last thing I would want. Just the same as my not wanting to get you or Josh in trouble. That's why I want you to help me get in touch with Eamon and he will come down and get me out of here."

"How can I do that?"

"Get me some paper and an envelope and I'll write two letters. One letter will tell Eamon where I am in hopes that he can come and fetch me. I'll also enclose a letter for my wife. She'll have been told I was shot down and she'll be very worried. Eamon will send it to his family in Ireland and they'll send it on to my wife in Germany."

"I'll bring paper and envelopes tomorrow when I come."

"The only thing I'll miss is you and Josh. I've grown very fond of the two of you. After the war, I'll invite you and Josh to come spend your holidays on my farm in Germany. We have animals—horses to ride, cows to milk, and goats and pigs. We also have a pond full of fish. My wife is a wonderful cook. She makes the best strudel." He stopped and looked down for a moment. "Hopefully she'll get better. The doctors say no, but you have to have hope."

Tom was both happy and sad about Captain Leuzinger's

now seemingly imminent departure. He was glad that the captain had a realistic chance of seeing his wife and family, but was sorry that he would be going out of Tom's life. Though he was scared much of the time that he would be found out and punished, maybe even put in prison for helping an enemy pilot, there was a strange exhilaration, a sort of excitement that he had not previously experienced. Although everything militated against it—he was a young English Jew and Leuzinger was an Aryan—a German pilot and someone who, by all accounts, Tom should hate. But he didn't. The only adults he had ever associated with were uncles, aunts, friends of his parents, teachers, and rabbis. Some of them were nice and some weren't, but none of them related to a fourteen-year-old boy like Captain Leuzinger. He now had another reason to want to see the war over. He would look forward to spending at least one of his holidays on the captain's farm.

He ran home to get the paper and envelopes. He would take them to the captain the next day and either wait for him to write the letter or come back later for it. Either way, he would make sure the letter was on its way to the captain's friend as soon as he could.

Chapter Thirty-Seven

His mother had long since stopped puzzling over where the tin of beans had gone. The weather had been unseasonably warm in England and no one had wanted an extra blanket. Although Josh had stopped coming to the German's house, he continued to save part of his school lunch for Tom to combine with the part he had saved to give to the captain. Tom was sure that his mother would not miss a few sheets of writing paper and an envelope. The only person to whom his mother wrote was his father and she wrote to him every day. However there were special letterforms that were sold for posting to members of the armed forces overseas. He decided that six sheets of paper would be enough. He also took two envelopes in case the captain made a mistake writing the name and address. He didn't know whether the captain had a pen or a pencil so he took his fountain pen out of the drawer, made sure it had enough ink, and put it in his pocket. It was a Bar Mitzvah present from his grandfather. He would have to be sure to tell the captain that he would have to have it back after he had written his letter. Finally, he took an old magazine so that the captain would have something firm to place the paper on while he was writing. He didn't want to leave anything to chance. The letter would be on its way to the captain's friend tomorrow and he would be on his way to Ireland and a meeting with his wife and children.

"Thanks for bringing all the supplies. I am glad you brought a pen. I forgot to tell you I didn't have anything to write with. I had a pen, paper, stamps, some English money, and Eamon's coded phone number in a small satchel in the plane, but that satchel was still in the plane when it crashed. Now you don't have to sit around here waiting for me to finish writing the letters. It will take me some time to write both. I have so much to tell my wife. She will be so relieved to hear I am alive and that we will soon be back together. I also have to tell Eamon exactly where I am so that he can come and get me. If you could arrange to be back here about this same time tomorrow, I can give you the envelope and you could post it. I'm afraid I'm going to have to ask you to put the stamp on. It'll be another in a long list of things I owe you. All of which I fully intend to repay some day with interest."

Tom went out the back way, through the wire fence, over the bomb-shattered wall, and down the dark rubbish strewn alley toward home. That night, the fog had lifted and the German bombers were back in force. The sky was lit up with searchlights probing the night and sometimes finding the profile of a Heinkel or a Dornier. Bursts of anti-aircraft fire were interspersed with the sound of exploding bombs. Young boys in the heavily bombed cities could identify the type of German or English aircraft solely from the sound without even seeing anything. Each make of aircraft had a distinctive sound, which, over the course of time, could be distinguished. Identifying the different planes, bombers, fighters—theirs or ours—became a kind of macabre game. During the day, there were frequent dogfights between British Spitfires and Hurricanes and German Messerschmidts, Focke-Wulfs, and the occasional Stuka. Identifying planes one could actually see was too easy and the older boys scornfully allowed the younger boys to master the art of plane identification by practicing on the visual before they graduated to the non-visual.

It's funny in a way, thought Tom. *In a few days, the captain will be in Ireland with his family where there is no war and no bombing and I will still be here with my family and without my father where there is bombing and where there is war.*

Actually a lot of the children from the cities had gone to Canada to avoid the bombing. They had gone on hastily requisitioned troop ships and old liners. Tom's mother had been torn as to whether to let Tom and Rebecca go to Canada. Neither of the children had wanted to go. While Miriam was still agonizing about what to do, one of the outbound liners loaded with children had been torpedoed with enormous loss of life. That convinced Miriam.

They had briefly gone to stay in a coastal village where they were uncomfortably crowded into a small cottage with another family. Tom, Rebecca, and their mother had to sleep in one small bedroom and share a tiny kitchen with the other family, which comprised of a mother, four badly behaved children, and a scruffy looking dog whose favorite habit was yipping several times during the night. When Messerschmidts started using the small coastal towns as target practice for their machine guns and cannons, Miriam had had enough. The village experiment was over and they returned to the flat in the East End.

CHAPTER THIRTY-EIGHT

"HERE IT IS, TOM," said Leuzinger, handing Tom a sealed envelope. "Do you think you can get it in the post tonight?"

"I looked at the post box on the corner," said Tom. "The postman doesn't pick up tomorrow, but he does the next day at half past two in the afternoon. My mum says the post is so slow and the pickups every other day because so many postmen are in the armed forces and because of the bombing."

"Well, that will have to do," said Leuzinger. "I've told Eamon to come for me in some type of workman's lorry with markings that would be consistent with his need to be in a bombed-out building, like the gas company or something to do with water mains or electricity. I know in Germany those types of things are always a problem after buildings are bombed. Gas leaks or water mains break or something happens. A lorry identified with that type of work won't cause any curiosity."

"Is your friend in such a business?" asked Tom.

"No. He runs an Irish pub up there in the Midlands, but I'm sure he could borrow a lorry from a friend in one of those businesses. He's lived up there for years and publicans know lots of people."

"How's he going to get you out with you in a German uniform?"

"He'll bring me some overalls or some kind of work clothes so I won't be conspicuous. He'll probably bring a mate with him to help me with my game leg."

"What if they catch you in civilian clothes—won't they shoot you? I saw a picture show once about the First World War. I think it was an American picture show where they shot an escaped prisoner as a spy because he wasn't wearing his uniform."

Leuzinger laughed. "I think that is only at the picture show. It makes the film more exciting. I'm not a spy. I'm a German pilot trying to escape. You know it is the duty of all prisoners—whether they are English or German—to try and escape. Anyway, if they capture me and execute me, I'll just have to chance it. I have to get to Ireland and see my wife and children. That's all I live for anyway. Now off you go. Will you come back tomorrow and tell me you posted the letter and bring me a little food? I ate that piece of chicken and the slice of bread you brought me yesterday. It was good."

"I'm not sure I can be here tomorrow. After school, I promised Josh I would go and see him. He went home from the hospital, but he has to rest for a couple of days. Do you have enough to eat if I don't come tomorrow?"

"I'll be fine. I still have some of that cheese you brought and a piece of bread. That will be enough. It's more important that you go and see Josh. I hope he is feeling better and I hope they soon find the swine that did that to him."

Tom looked down at the envelope. It had Eamon's name and a P.O. box number in Burton-on-Trent.

"What's a P.O. box?" asked Tom.

"Oh. That's where they deliver letters to the local post office rather than the person's home. I don't know why Eamon prefers to have his letters delivered like that. I know a lot of people do though."

It had started to rain by the time Tom had climbed the wall and had started down the alley. By the time he reached the flats, the rain had started to come down quite hard. He went into his bedroom and took out the envelope to put a postage stamp on it. He had "borrowed" it from his mother's drawer. "Bloody hell!" he exclaimed.

"What did you say, Tom?" his mother called out from the kitchen.

"I tripped on the rug," he said, coming up with the first thing he could think of.

"Well, you know I don't like that kind of language."

"Sorry, Mum."

He had let out the expletive because some raindrops had landed on the envelope and smeared the writing. He could still read it with some difficulty, but to be safe he would have to make out another envelope and put the captain's letters in the fresh envelope. He carefully tore open the envelope and took out the sheets of papers and put them on the bed. Fortunately, Captain Leuzinger had only had to use the one envelope and had given him back the unused one. Tom would copy the address from the smeared envelope onto the blank one. He took a quick glance at the letters on the bed. His mother had told him it was very bad to look at letters that were not sent to him. However, when he put the letters on the bed, the first folded page opened.

He couldn't help but look at the writing, at least that's what he told himself. It started "Dear Sir." That's a funny thing to call a friend, thought Tom. It would be like writing a letter to Josh while away on holiday and saying "Dear Mr. Rosenblatt."

Tom read on. "My name is Heinrich Leuzinger; I am a Hauptman (Captain) in the Luftwaffe." Tom's curiosity was now getting the better of him. He's known Eamon Shaughnessy for years. The captain and his family are great friends with the Shaughnessys. They went on holidays with each other before the war. Why would he think it was necessary to explain who he was to a chap who is an old friend? Tom sat down on the bed. He had decided to read both letters in their entirety. For some reason, he no longer felt guilty about it. If he thought he was surprised by the beginning of the letter, the rest of it would be a total shock.

CHAPTER THIRTY-NINE

THE ROOM WAS SPINNING and Tom thought he was going to faint. He made a dash for the bathroom. Thank goodness nobody was in it. He barely made it to the toilet bowl before he started to vomit. His mother heard him and came running.

"What is the matter? What happened?" she said with concern etched on her face.

"It's all right, Mum," he said between violent heaves. "It must be something I ate."

"I'm going to the phone down the street to call Dr. Schwartz."

"Don't do that, Mother," he urged as the heaving started to subside. "I'll be all right in a minute. Really, I will."

"Well, if you are not better in a few minutes, I will call Dr. Schwartz. I'll pull down the covers on your bed and bring you a nice cup of tea. You go in and rest."

While chicken soup was the Jewish mother's traditional panacea for all types of ailments, the war had made chickens and even tins of chicken soup very scarce. A "nice cup of tea" had become a worthy substitute. Miriam made a move to the door. Tom panicked. He had left the letter on his bed. If she saw it, she would not be able to resist reading it despite her pronouncements about the impropriety of reading other people's letters.

"I'll pull down the covers. I'm feeling much better. You make the tea," he almost pleaded.

"All right, but you get into bed right away."

He hastily got into bed and put the letters under the blanket. Although he hadn't wanted it, the tea tasted good. He would have preferred it with another lump of sugar, but it was rationed and more than one lump would indeed be an unaffordable luxury. After he finished the tea, his mother removed the cup. She admonished him to rest and to try to get a little sleep before leaving and closing his door. The nausea had passed, but the rancid taste remained. He pulled out the letters to re-read them. In truth, there was only one letter and not one to his supposed wife. The letter read, in its entirety:

"Dear sir,

My name is Heinrich Leuzinger. I am a Hauptman (captain) in the Luftwaffe. My serial number is 184396. I was shot down over London. Your contact information has been provided to me, as it is to all German aircrews, by Luftwaffe bomber command. The code number is 6gh598ld103. I understand that your organization has the ability to get me back to Germany. I am in the back of an abandoned, bombed-out building on Fleming Street, six houses south of Hadley Street in Hackney, East London. I have a broken leg and will need help to walk. Please come and get me as soon as possible.

I have been assisted by a Jew boy, which is intensely distasteful to me, but has kept me from capture. He found me by accident and, in order to enlist his help, I have been compelled to make up a story. Since he may by chance be present when you arrive to get me, I must tell you what I have told him. I have told him I am married, that my wife is ill, and that I have two children. In fact, I am not married and have no children. I have told him that I sympathize with the plight of the Jews, that I am opposed to what is happening to them in Germany and in occupied Europe, and that I am anti-Nazi. I am, in fact, a loyal member of the Nazi party and have been since before the war. I wholeheartedly support the fuehrer's policy with respect to the Jews. I have told him that this letter is written to an Irish friend of mine, Eamon Shaughnessy, who lives in England and who can get me to Ireland where I will be interned and my wife and children can come to me. I have no Irish friends—in England or elsewhere—and expect to rejoin my unit in Germany.

I tell you all this so that if the boy happens to be with me when you arrive, you won't inadvertently reveal the truth about me. If he were to become suspicious, he would have to be killed. While I have no compunction about killing the Jew, it would be ill advised. There would be a fairly immediate search made for him if he did not return home and it might impact my escape and your security. You are at liberty of course to verify the accuracy of what I have told you about myself through the contacts in the German high command, which I know you have.

I don't mean to tell you your business, but it would be advisable if you use a lorry with signs indicating involvement in the type of business frequently found working on bomb-damaged buildings. I would also recommend that you and your assistant wear work clothes and bring some for me to wear.

The boy tells me there is an alley behind the house and he has come in that way by climbing over a wall. With my broken leg, it would be difficult for you to get me out that way.

Heinrich Leuzinger

Chapter Forty

He felt another wave of nausea come over him. He fought it off. He didn't want his mother calling Dr. Schwartz. Another trip to the bathroom and he wouldn't be able to dissuade her from making the call. Finally the nausea subsided, the room stopped going round, and he was able to think more clearly.

What was he to do? There were a number of alternatives. He could tell the authorities. If he did that, there would be all kinds of questions about his conduct. He may be labeled as a traitor. Maybe put in prison—maybe even hanged. Did they hang fourteen-year-old boys? He could go on as before. Bring Leuzinger food. Post the letter. Let him be picked up and spirited off to Germany. Nobody would ever know that he and Josh even knew the German had been in the bombed-out house. Maybe he should not even go back to the house at all. Maybe not go back to the house *and* not send the letter. Let him starve to death there. Or maybe someone else would find him or he would hobble away and get caught. Leuzinger might then tell his captors that Tom—and perhaps Josh— had helped him. There was no easy answer.

He ate very little for dinner, went to bed early, and

tossed and turned all night. In the morning he thought of something his father had once told him. When he was nine, he had found a purse in the gutter on his way home from elementary school. It had nothing inside to identify its owner. However, it did contain a lot of money—at least to Tom it was a lot of money. There were three crisp one-pound notes and several coins totaling five shillings and eight pence. He asked his father what he should do with it. His father, who Tom thought was the wisest man on the planet, told him there were two things he could do. He could keep it or he could turn it in at the police station. He told Tom that he should consider that you never go wrong by doing the right thing. The adage was trite, but it had stayed with Tom ever since. He had turned the purse into the police station and had left his name and address. The sergeant on duty had told him that if no one claimed it within two weeks, it was his. Two days later, there was a knock on the door and a very old lady asked to see Tom. She wanted to thank him for his kindness and honesty. She told Tom and his mother that she lived alone on a small government pension and the money was all she had to buy food for herself for the rest of the month. She wanted to give him a shilling as a reward, but Tom and his mother gently refused. His mother gave Tom a big hug and kiss and he floated on air the rest of the day.

I've made up my mind, he decided. *I'm going to tell the authorities. They can hang me if they want.* But who should he tell? The local police station was staffed by a couple of old part-timers. They wouldn't be the best people to talk to. He had listened to a radio serial that had something to do with the war. He thought it was "Dick Barton, Special Agent." It came on the BBC at half past six every night. He remembered that there was talk of a branch of Scotland Yard that dealt

155

with espionage. He learned that that was a fancy word for spying. That's what he would do. He would go to Scotland Yard, show them the letter, and tell them everything. He wouldn't tell his mother. No sense in worrying her until he had to. He wouldn't tell them about Josh. There was no need to involve him.

It was all my fault that Josh got involved in the first place. It won't help Scotland Yard to know that Josh had been to the house and knew what was going on. That's it. I'll skip school and go to Scotland Yard first thing in the morning.

THE NORTH AFRICAN DESERT, 1941
PART TWO

CHAPTER FORTY-ONE

THE FIVE BARRACKS IN the German compound were identified as A through E. The day after Lieutenant Von Steuffel overheard the conversation between Reichmann and Sloan, there was a hurried and secretive meeting called in Barracks B. All of the men assigned to Barracks B were present—as well as a large number of the men from the other barracks. Noticeably absent was Colonel Reichmann; he had not been told of the meeting and was not invited. Great care had been taken to ensure that Reichmann did not know the meeting was taking place. Two junior officers had been assigned to watch Reichmann's movements and when they were satisfied that he had returned to his hut, the officers gathered in Barracks B.

"Okay, Steuffel. You called this meeting. What's it all about? I can tell all of you I am very unhappy about us sneaking around behind the colonel's back. This better be good," Major Gruber said angrily.

Karl Gruber was the second-ranking German officer and, like Reichmann, was a retread, having served in the First World War and having been in civilian life between the two wars.

"The colonel's a Jew-lover and a traitor," shouted Von Steuffel.

"What are you talking about?" shouted back Gruber over the sudden rising murmurings among those present.

Von Steuffel then related the conversation he had overheard between Reichmann and Sloan about the escape of the Helstein family. Significantly absent from Von Steuffel's recitation was the fact that Meyer Helstein—who was a medical officer during the First World War—had saved Reichmann's life.

At the conclusion of Von Steuffel's description of the conversation, there were a lot of surprised conversations between groups of the listeners.

"Quiet, all of you. Quiet down," said Gruber. "Are you sure you have told us everything you heard during your eavesdropping?"

"Yes, that was all of it," said Von Steuffel.

"Well, I know a little more than you do about the relationship between Colonel Reichmann and Doctor Helstein," said Gruber. "I was not only the colonel's adjutant here in the desert, but I was in his unit in France during World War I. Doctor Helstein was the medical officer and saved Reichmann's life—and a lot of others including me."

Gruber angrily ripped off his shirt and showed an ugly scar just below his right shoulder.

"I took a bullet in the Ardennes campaign. Helstein was bleeding from grenade fragments in both of his arms, but he took care of my wounds while running back and forth treating other injured soldiers. It was a month later that he saved Reichmann and carried him back to the aid station. The doctor was awarded the Iron Cross."

"Yes, but he's a damn Jew," said one of the officers. "It's treasonous to help Jews. We all know that."

"Are you listening to me, you idiot," yelled Gruber. "Helstein is a war hero. He saved our lives. You can't forget that. If anything takes priority, that does." He turned to Von Steuffel. "Are you asking us to believe that Reichmann didn't tell the English officer anything at all about what Helstein had done for him?"

"He might have said something about that. I can't remember," Von Steuffel sounded a little less aggressive, but very defensive. "What difference does that matter anyway? Reichmann is a liar and a coward."

The veins in Gruber's neck were standing out and his face was bright red.

"First of all, it's *Colonel* Reichmann to you, Lieutenant. Have you got that? *Colonel*. Second, he never denied helping the man who saved his life and I don't know of anyone who asked him—did you?" Without waiting for an answer, Gruber went on. "Third, you say he is a coward. Do you know that the Fuehrer personally invited Colonel Reichmann to Berchtesgarden to decorate him with the Iron Cross First Class for repeated bravery above and beyond the call of duty in various campaigns in Europe? I don't see any Iron Cross around your scrawny neck, Steuffel," Gruber said with scorn oozing out of every pore.

Von Steuffel's face turned even redder than Gruber's. "Well none of that detracts from—" he started, but Gruber interrupted him.

"I've heard enough from you and I don't want to hear any more. If you want to question Colonel Reichmann's conduct, you take it up with him face to face—not behind his back."

Captain Gerhard Steinhalter, sitting on a bed close to the two disputants, rose and said in a level, moderated voice.

"If he had been caught aiding the Jew doctor and his family, he would have been shot as a traitor. You know the law is clear that helping Jews to escape is a capital crime. Major, are you condoning Colonel Reichmann's conduct. If you are, you're condoning the commission of a crime."

"I am neither condoning it nor am I condemning it. I am not a judge. Would I have aided Jews to violate German law? No, I would not. Would I have done so even in the case of Doctor Helstein? That's a much harder question—probably not, but I wasn't a close personal friend of the doctor when it was legal for a gentile and a Jew to be close personal friends. Meyer Helstein probably saved my life too and I am grateful to him for that. People could say that saving people's lives is what a doctor is supposed to do. Nonetheless, when it is your life that is being saved, it takes on a greater and more personal significance. Faced with the same circumstances as the colonel, I don't know what I would have done. I like to think I would have obeyed the law and done my duty, but I don't know," said Gruber. "I believe that no man can say for certain what he would do if was in the shoes of another man with the same history and feelings of the other man. All I am saying is that the matter is now closed. Have I made myself clear?"

Without another word, Gruber turned around and strode out of the hut. There were a few murmurings, but by and large the discussion was over. While the discussion was over, Von Steuffel's anger and resentment was not nearly over.

CHAPTER FORTY-TWO

LIEUTENANT VON STEUFFEL HAD again been eavesdropping and heard Major Sloan tell Colonel Reichmann that he, like Dr Helstein, was a Jew. Several days after the Barracks B meeting, Von Steuffel again confronted Gruber. This time, both of them were outside and the other prisoners were scattered all over the area—some just walking around, some sitting on the ground reading or talking to each other, and some kicking a soccer ball to each other. There were, however, a number of prisoners in the close vicinity to Von Steuffel and Gruber who could easily hear the ensuing conversation.

"Major Gruber, you are apparently willing to tolerate the fact that the senior German officer here is a Jew lover. I'm not willing to tolerate that and neither are other officers in this camp. But what you don't know is that the commandant, Major Sloan, is himself a Jew and he and Colonel Reichmann are now friends. I heard them talking and laughing. They were telling each other what they did in civilian life, where they lived, how many people were in their families. I almost vomited."

Von Steuffel had cornered Gruber as he sat outside his hut reading.

Major Gruber sighed, "I don't know what you mean you're not going to tolerate it. You have no choice. I told you about the special long-time relationship that the colonel had with the doctor. It doesn't prove he's a Jew lover. It proves that he owed that particular man his life and, as an honorable man, he repaid that debt. I've told you once and I'm not going to tell you again, if you have a bone to pick with Colonel Reichmann, you take it up with him. Don't sneak around his back and whine to me," Gruber said angrily. "As far as a Jew being the commandant of this camp—I don't like that anymore than you do, but I can't do anything about it. I also don't like the desert. I don't like being a prisoner of war and I don't like being away from Germany and my family. I can't do anything about those things either."

"But—" Von Steuffel started, but was immediately interrupted

"Enough," Gruber put up his hand to stop Von Steuffel. "When, and if, we ever get back to Germany, and if we have won the war, and if the National Socialist Party is still in power, you can tell your story about Reichmann to the authorities. Under those circumstances, Reichmann probably will be punished—perhaps even shot—even though he is a German war hero in two separate wars. In the meantime, he, like us, is a prisoner of war. We have no authority to conduct a war tribunal, much less mete out punishment. Now that is the last I want to hear about this."

Von Steuffel walked away without another word with his head down like a whipped dog. Captain Juergen Felsheim—known to be a good loyal officer, but not a fanatical Nazi—was sitting close by.

"I hope we have heard the end of all that," he said to Gruber.

"I hope so, too," said Gruber with a sigh.

"What is your problem, Steuffel?" shouted Lieutenant Kronstadt after Von Steuffel had walked away into a group of officers. "You look like you've lost your last friend."

Kronstadt and three or four other junior German officers were aimlessly kicking a scuffed-up, underinflated ball around in the sand.

Von Steuffel walked over to them. "You should look the same way. Reichmann is not only a Jew lover, but our revered commandant, Major Sloan, is also a Jew. He and Reichmann have become close friends."

The young officers stopped playing, but said nothing. "Well, I suppose our shame is now complete," said Von Steuffel. "We're not only in a camp, but we are the inmates and the Jews are the guards rather than the reverse. We are in exactly the same position as the Jews in our concentration camps."

Several of the others, but not all, nodded in agreement—despite the fact that Von Steuffel's statement was a monumentally gross and vicious overstatement. There was only one Jewish guard, albeit he was the commandant and, more importantly, the Germans were being treated humanely under the provisions of the Geneva Convention—unlike the Jews in the German concentration camps who were not being treated as humans at all.

"What do you intend to do about it?" said Schlechter, one of the other football players.

"What do *I* intend to do about it?" repeated Von Steuffel. "Shouldn't that be 'What should *we* do about it?'"

"All right—what should we do about it?"

"I don't know, but I'll think of something."

"We can, and should, do nothing," said Felsheim. "The

man did what he thought was right for someone who had saved his life. Even if that is wrong—who ordained that we were to be his judge, jury, and executioner? As for thinking, Steuffel, stay away from it. You'll overtax your brain and hurt yourself. Stick to football. That's an area you know something about."

CHAPTER FORTY-THREE

CAPTAIN LASSITER CAME RUNNING into Sloan's office, panting and totally out of breath.

"What is it, Jim?" Sloan said, jumping to his feet.

"It's Reichmann. He's been stabbed. He didn't show up for this morning's roll call and we found him lying on the floor of his hut. He had a knife wound in his back."

"Is he alive?"

"Barely. It must have happened last night. There's blood everywhere."

"Where is he now?"

"I called for an ambulance. He's on his way to the base hospital."

"Corporal Evans," Sloan yelled at the top of his lungs.

Evans was close by and quickly came in.

"Get the Jeep right away. Double time."

Evans brought it around. Sloan pushed Evans aside, jumped into the driver's seat, and tore off toward the hospital.

"Colonel Reichmann, German officer. Is he here yet?" he asked the nurse at the front desk.

"Yes, sir. He's in pre-op. Three doors down on the right," she replied.

Reichmann was lying face down on a gurney. He was not conscious and what could be seen of his face was as white as the sheet that covered him. There were three other men in the room—all on gurneys and all awake. Two were sitting up and the third one was having what appeared to be an injury to his arm looked at by a doctor in a white jacket.

"Doctor, are you responsible for determining the order of treatment for the men here?" Sloan asked.

"I am. Who are you?" asked the doctor.

"I am Major Sloan, commandant of the POW camp—and who are you?"

"I am Captain Reynolds. I am the doctor currently here in triage"

"I am not a doctor, but I understand that triage is a procedure for deciding the order of treatment for wounded personnel based on severity of injury. Am I correct?" asked Sloan.

"You are," responded Reynolds.

"Is this German officer the most seriously injured person you have here in triage?"

"Well, I haven't examined him yet—but, yes, he appears to be."

"Well, then, why isn't he being treated first?"

"Ordinarily we treat our own men first before we treat the enemy."

"You're a doctor, not a combatant. Your duty is to give priority to the most severely wounded—not to determine who is a friend and who is a foe. I have no medical training, but it looks to me that the rest of these men are not in immediate danger, but Colonel Reichmann is. He was stabbed last night and has lost a lot of blood. He should be taken care of at once."

Reynolds walked over to Reichmann, pulled back the sheet, and called for the orderly. "This German is first. Take him to operating room number one and notify Dr. Abbot that this is an immediate emergency." The orderly wheeled the gurney out of pre-op and down the hall.

"And now, Major, I would ask that you leave. Pre-op and triage is for patients and medical personnel only," Reynolds said coldly.

"I'll wait outside. I would appreciate an update on Colonel Reichmann's condition when that is available," Sloan responded just as coldly.

After he left, the young soldier with the arm injury said to Reynolds, "Did you ever hear anything like that before, Doc? A British officer wanting to have a bloody Kraut taken care of before our own boys."

"No, I didn't, but the German is probably not going to recover from his injuries anyway. Now let's take a look at that arm."

Chapter Forty-Four

SLOAN SAT OUT BY the nurses' station most of the morning. There were murmurings among some of the hospital personnel as to why a British officer would be so concerned about the condition of a German prisoner that he would sit around for hours and await word as to his condition. Nobody said anything to him about that, although the desk nurse did offer him a cup of tea around mid morning, which he gratefully accepted.

Around noon, Dr. Abbot came out still wearing his operating room garb.

"Major Sloan?" he asked.

"Yes," said Sloan.

"I am Major Abbot, chief surgeon here. I understand you have been asking about Colonel Reichmann."

"Yes, I have. Will he recover?"

"Well, it's still touch and go. The wound was quite deep. Fortunately, it missed his heart by a very small margin. The real problem is an enormous loss of blood. He must have suffered the stab wound to his back some hours before he arrived here. We have given him several pints of blood and have repaired the damage. Despite his age, he's not a young man, he appears to be very fit, which is in his favor. Only time will tell."

"May I speak to him?" asked Sloan.

"He won't recover consciousness for some time and, when he does, he will be groggy from the anesthesia and quite weak. May I suggest you come back tomorrow?"

"Thank you, Doctor. I appreciate the information." Sloan was grateful that Abbot had not questioned him about his seemingly unusual interest in the German's condition.

He left the hospital and went immediately to the German compound. Captain Lassiter had assembled all of the prisoners in the mess hall and had posted armed guards at strategic locations around the room. The prisoners had been fed and those who needed to visit the lavatory were permitted to do so while accompanied by an armed guard.

"Jim, have you found out anything?" asked Sloan outside the mess hall.

"Nothing, Bernie," Lassiter replied. "I haven't completed questioning them, but I have taken about twenty of them individually into Barracks A. Each of them denies any knowledge of what happened and claim they never heard anything. I'll talk to the rest this afternoon, but I doubt if I'll learn anything."

"Have you talked to Major Gruber?"

"Not yet. I thought you might like to do that."

"Thanks. I think I would like to."

"How's Colonel Reichmann?"

"He had surgery and they won't know anything for a while."

Sloan went back into the mess hall. "Major Gruber, I would like to have a word with you. Please come with me." Gruber followed Sloan into Barracks A.

"What do you know about the attack on Colonel Reichmann?"

"If you are asking me who did it, I can only say that I honestly don't know for sure—but I have my suspicions which I will not share with you. If you are asking me what led up to it, I have a conjecture—but I hasten to say it is only a conjecture," Gruber said in very clear, albeit accented, English.

"Tell me your conjecture."

"I must start back a number of years. Colonel Reichmann and I were young officers during the First World War and have been friends ever since. A Jewish medical officer named Meyer Helstein was in our unit. I know you are aware of Colonel Reichmann's interaction with Dr. Helstein. What you don't know is that in addition to saving Colonel Reichmann's life, he also saved mine. The prisoners in this camp know of those incidents and know that Colonel Reichmann was instrumental in aiding Dr. Helstein and his family to escape into Switzerland. They also know that you and Colonel Reichmann have become quite friendly and that you are a Jew. I won't tell you how the prisoners in this camp came to learn all this information. Just accept the fact that they do know. We are Germans and we are loyal to our Fuehrer and to the Third Reich. I do not disapprove of what the colonel did in saving the Helstein family, but I will not denounce the policies of my government. That may sound like a contradiction, but I will not argue the point with you. There are many officers in this camp who are angered by what the colonel did for the Helsteins and for his apparent friendship with the Jewish commandant of this camp. I believe that the attack on Colonel Reichmann was conducted by one or more prisoners as a result of that anger. I have let it be known that crimes, if they are crimes, committed by Reichmann or any other prisoner before our capture is not a subject for punishment by the prisoners. With that said, I will conduct my own investigation into the attack on Colonel Reichmann, but neither I nor—I believe—any other prisoner here will cooperate with our captors in this matter."

"If Colonel Reichmann is your longtime friend and has been brutally attacked by a coward who stabbed him in the back and maybe has murdered him, why would you not want to see the culprit punished?" asked Sloan.

"I didn't say I didn't want to see the culprit punished. I just said I wouldn't cooperate with the British in identifying and punishing him. Now having told you all that, will you please tell me of the condition of Colonel Reichmann."

CHAPTER FORTY-FIVE

"Could I see the German officer, Colonel Reichmann?" Sloan had returned to the base hospital early the next day.

"I'll page Major Abbott, sir," the desk nurse said.

"Good morning, Major Sloan. I understand you are asking about Colonel Reichmann," said the white-coated Abbott.

"Yes, I am. How is he doing?"

"He survived the operation quite well. The knife penetrated the upper portion of the left lung, but did no other significant damage. It missed his heart by a couple of centimeters. We gave him several pints of blood. The blood loss was very extensive. He's a strong man. Many much younger men would have succumbed, but he has a good chance of making a full recovery. He's not completely out of the woods yet though."

"Thank you, Doctor. May I see him?"

"You may, but first, may I ask you a question?"

"Of course."

"Since you were here yesterday there has been a lot of talk in the hospital about the amount of interest that a British officer showed in the condition of an enemy officer. Would you mind explaining that to me?"

"Certainly. I could say that, as the commandant of the POW camp, all of the prisoners including, but not limited to, Colonel Reichmann are my responsibility and leave it at that. But that would not be the complete answer to your question."

"What then is the complete answer?"

"You're a busy man so I will give you the abbreviated version." Sloan then outlined the saga of Reichmann's rescue of the Helstein family.

"That is truly a fascinating and extraordinary story," said Major Abbott who had been listening intently. "It proves that acts of honor, humanity, courage, and indeed nobility can be found in the most unexpected places and performed by some of the most unlikely people. Thank you for sharing it with me. Although my treatment of patients does not depend on their nobility or lack thereof, the story you have told me can't help but make me look at Colonel Reichmann in a totally different light. Let me show you the way to his room."

"Colonel, you have a visitor. I'll leave you two alone and I will check back with you later," said Abbott as he left the room.

"I understand that you're doing much better," said Sloan.

"Thank you. I feel a little weak, but much better than I felt last night. It is kind of you to come and see me," replied Reichmann in a surprisingly strong voice.

"Of course I was worried about you and I wanted to visit, but I must confess that's not the only reason I'm here. I want the man who did this to you and I want your help in finding him. What can you tell me?"

"Not a lot. I had made my rounds of each of the barracks as I do every evening and had returned to my hut. Whoever attacked me must have been behind the door and struck me as I came in. I fell forward on my face. I never saw him—although I heard his footsteps as he left. I tried to get up, but I lost consciousness and remember nothing until I woke up here after the surgery and a very lovely nurse was leaning over me."

"Was there anyone who might have had a grudge against you or have had any reason why he might want to hurt you? Can you think of anything—anything at all—that may have a bearing on what happened?"

"I can only speculate. There are no secrets in a POW camp. It would not surprise me if my helping the Helsteins was known to my fellow officers. Obviously Major Gruber knew Dr. Helstein and knew that he had saved my life and that the doctor and I were close personal friends. Of course he also saved Gruber's life. Many of the prisoners would not look with favor on my being a friend of a Jew and particularly would be outraged by my helping a Jewish family escape from Germany."

"Do you think Major Gruber could do this?"

Reichmann hesitated and did not answer directly. "Gruber had served with Helstein in the First World War and Helstein had saved his life. Nonetheless, it would be unlikely that Gruber would approve of my helping Helstein to escape. Gruber and I are not close personal friends, but we have served together in two wars and seem to have been able to adjust to the fact that our philosophies differ markedly. I would be surprised if he had done this. He is a stickler for rules."

Sloan was puzzled by Reichmann's circuitous answer, but did not pursue the matter.

"What about other officers in the camp. Would they be constrained by the same rules that apparently govern Major Gruber's concept of what, if any, punishment can be administered in a POW camp?"

"I don't think so. I don't know, but I believe that there are officers in the camp who would have no compunction about stabbing me if they had believed I had helped a Jew escape from Germany."

"Can you list those prisoners who you believe could do this?"

"No. I don't think so."

A female nurse came in. "I am afraid you will have to leave now. Doctor's orders are that the patient can only have visitors for a brief time."

"I'll come back and see you later. See if you can come up with something about who could be responsible."

As he got out of his Jeep, Sergeant Buckley met him. "Colonel Corcoran called. You're to report immediately to General McCaudle."

"Did he say what for?"

"No, but he emphasized *immediately*. Do you want me or Evans to drive you, sir?"

"No, I can manage."

Chapter Forty-Six

"Go right in, Major. The general's waiting for you," said the corporal in McCaudle's outer office.

"Hello, Bernie," said Corcoran. He had arrived some time before and was seated in one of the two chairs in front of the general's desk.

McCaudle angrily interrupted. "Never mind the greetings. I have a complaint about you, Sloan, from one of the doctors at the base hospital. He said you busted into pre-op and ordered him to stop treating a wounded British soldier and instead treat a German prisoner. Who the bloody hell do you think you are busting into the hospital and telling doctors what to do?"

"General, I didn't 'bust in' and I didn't 'order' anyone to do anything. I went to the hospital because I had been informed that a German prisoner, for whom I have responsibility, had been knifed and was in serious condition and had lost a lot of blood. There were four patients in pre-op—three British soldiers and the German. Two of the soldiers were sitting up on gurneys laughing and talking. A doctor was tending to an arm wound on the third British soldier. Meanwhile, nobody was attending to the German. When I asked why the German wasn't receiving attention, the doctor told me that it was their practice to treat British wounded before attending to the enemy. I told the doctor that my understanding was that the most seriously injured were to be treated first—whether they were British or German—and that there was no question but that the British soldiers were in no danger and that the German was going to die if not treated immediately. The doctor turned his attention to the German."

"Why are you so interested in the health of this Kraut?" demanded McCaudle.

"As I said, General, all of the enemy prisoners are my responsibility as commandant of the POW camp. It's not only my duty to make sure they don't escape, it's also my duty under the Geneva Convention to be sure they are fed, housed, and that they receive reasonable medical attention when needed—and nobody needed medical attention more than Colonel Reichmann."

For some reason, Sloan decided he would not share the Helstein story with McCaudle.

"Well, at least your concern for the German proves you're not a Jew. No Jew would care whether a German lived or died. I had wondered whether you were and I'm glad you're not. I don't like having Jews in my command. They're good at some things, like making money, but they're not loyal, they have no courage, and I wouldn't want any fighting alongside me," snorted McCaudle.

Sloan turned bright red, his veins stood out in his neck. He was within an inch of going across the desk and grabbing McCaudle by his flabby neck. Corcoran looked at him and imperceptibly moved his hands in a gesture. as if to say 'calm down. "I am a Jew," said Sloan.

"What with a name like Sloan! I never knew a Jew with

that name. What did you do—change your name so you could pass as an Englishman?"

"I am an Englishman and I would be so if my name were Sloan, Goldstein, Cohen, Corcoran, or even McCaudle. When my father immigrated to England, he started a tailoring business in the East End of London. His shop was small and narrow. He wanted to put his name on the front, but it was too long to fit so he shortened it."

"Well maybe you're different from the rest of them. I suppose some are okay," McCaudle reluctantly conceded.

"General, you can't generalize about people—if you'll forgive the unintentional pun. I have found that people must be judged on their individual merits and demerits—not by their race, religion, etc. For example, it wouldn't be rational to claim that all generals were raving anti-Semites because one general was."

Now it was McCaudle's turn to get red in the face. He leaped to his feet. "You insolent bastard," he yelled. "I'll see you in the stockade for this. Get out of here. You too, Corcoran. I'll talk to you about this later."

When they got outside, Corcoran put his hand on Sloan's shoulder and could feel him trembling. "Don't worry about the miserable, old bastard. He's not going to do anything about it. There's been rumors circulating about his anti-Semitism for some time. He has aspirations. He wants a knighthood and a seat in parliament after the war. A scandal about his bias wouldn't help. He knows I heard it all and I wouldn't be on his side. In any event, he is to be transferred. They're sending him back to England for something. I think to head up a new armored division that's being formed."

"Thanks, Joe. I wanted to punch him in the mouth."

"Let me ask you something personal. Since you arrived

in the Middle East, have you deliberately not said anything about being Jewish?"

"No. Why should I. It's nothing I'm ashamed of. Nobody asked me. When you are discussing the war or what's going on in England with fellow officers, do you say, 'Oh, by the way, I'm a Christian.'?"

"Good point. Just asking."

Sloan paused and said, "No, Joe, you're right. It isn't lost on me that at the supply dump, at my current HQ, in the officer's mess, and the officer's club, I am the only Jewish officer. Perhaps subconsciously I am pleased my name is Sloan rather than Goldberg and maybe I haven't said anything that would reveal my religion because I don't want to be looked on as different or even ostracized by some. But believe me, I am not ashamed of being Jewish and I don't wish I was something else."

Corcoran gripped Sloan's shoulder tightly. "Look, Bernie, I don't care if you're a Jew, a Catholic, or a whirling dervish, I like you. It's early, but I have the key to the officer's club. Come on, I'll buy you a beer."

CHAPTER FORTY-SEVEN

BERNIE SLOAN'S ANGER AT the confrontation with General McCaudle had only slightly cooled down, but what had not cooled down was the intense desert heat. The rifle range was not the most comfortable of places—and it was the last place that Sloan thought he would be on a sweltering afternoon. All soldiers had to qualify with the rifle—regardless of rank and whether or not they were infantry. Sloan had shipped out of England on very short notice and had not satisfied this obligation. A clerk at Eighth Army headquarters had noticed this non-compliance and had brought it to the attention of the officer in charge of these matters. Sloan had put off the inevitable for as long as possible—despite repeated reminders from HQ, but his delay finally brought a pointed and not altogether polite "request" from that senior officer that he qualify as soon as possible.

Along with several cooks, a couple of clerks, and a quartermaster corporal, Sloan found himself looking through the sights of a rifle at a target that seemed miles away. He had emptied two clips without coming remotely close to even the outer ring of the target. The other qualifiers had completed their firing successfully and were getting ready to leave. The range sergeant sighed loudly. He was looking forward to a cold beer or two at the NCO club and, with each errant shot from Sloan, those beers seemed further and further away.

"Major, I'll make a deal with you. Get just one bullet anywhere on the target and I'll qualify you. Just don't tell anyone." He paused for a moment and added, "If you can't do that with the next clip, I may have to have you fix bayonets and charge the target," he said facetiously—at least Sloan thought he was joking.

The third bullet of the next clip struck the target and in fact almost made it into the bull's eye. "Sheer luck," muttered the sergeant under his breath, "but I'll take it. Well done, Major. You qualify. I'll send in the papers."

Sergeant Buckley, anticipating that Major Sloan would be on the range for some time, had settled back for a nap. The metallic rasping of the phone jolted him awake and almost made him fall over backward off his metal chair.

"Sergeant Buckley," he announced.

"Sergeant, this is Dr. Abbot. Is Major Sloan available?"

"I'm afraid not, sir. He's on the rifle range. I'm not sure when he will be back."

"Is his exec around?"

"Yes sir. I'll get him."

Captain Lassiter was in the mess tent and hurried over to the phone.

"Doctor, this is Captain Lassiter. How may I help?"

"We have a critical situation here at the hospital. The German officer, Colonel Reichmann, has taken a bad turn and we are going to have to go in again. He has a rare blood type and we are running dangerously low. Please go to the POW camp and see if anyone there is AB negative and ask if such persons will donate a pint. If not, try the Italians.

The operation will be tricky even with an adequate supply of blood. Without it—" his voice trailed off.

Major Gruber dutifully assembled the German prisoners dutifully asked if there were any of them with AB negative blood. and dutifully asked any man with such a blood type to step forward. Nobody did. Gruber shrugged, dismissed the men, and went back to his quarters.

Lassiter had no better luck at the Italian compound. One officer was AB negative, but he recently had a bout with hepatitis and was told his blood could not be used.

Lassiter ran back to the phone and was in the process of telling Abbot about coming up empty when Sloan walked in. Lassiter asked Abbot to hold and explained the situation to Sloan. Sloan grabbed the phone. "Doctor I'm AB negative. I'll be right over." Without waiting for an answer, he hung up and rushed out the door.

Lassiter yelled after him, "General McCaudle won't like this. He barely accepts that the Geneva Convention requires that we give prisoners medical treatment. He's going to hit the ceiling when he finds that one of his officers has given one of them blood."

"Too bad!" yelled Sloan.

"Your funeral!" shouted Lassiter.

"Either mine or Reichmann's," Sloan yelled back, but he was out of earshot.

Reichmann had several difficult days after the surgery and there was a moment when his survival was in serious doubt, but he rallied—thanks in part to the infusion of Sloan's blood. On the fourth day, Sloan visited. Reichmann was pale and had lost weight.

"I hear I am again in your debt," Reichmann said and held out his hand, which Sloan took.

"I am glad you are recovering so nicely and I am particularly pleased that my blood helped. Of course, you may now develop an overwhelming craving for gefilte fish." It was a corny old punch line that Sloan remembered from a long-forgotten joke told to him when he was a boy. Reichmann smiled, remembering meals that Hanna Helstein had cooked for him years ago.

General McCaudle's reaction was uncharacteristically mild when he heard. He threw his arms in the air and, in a frustrating voice, said to no one in particular, "Lunatic. I should make him wear a uniform with the Star of David on one sleeve and a Swastika on the other." The fact that he was packing for his reassignment in England and that Sloan would now be somebody else's problem probably had something to do with the mildness of his reaction.

LONDON, 1941
PART TWO

Chapter Forty-Eight

"WHAT DO YOU WANT, son?" a heavyset man said to Tom.

The man was standing behind what looked to be a counter in a big room on the second floor of the Scotland Yard building. Tom had left home that morning a little earlier than he usually left for school. His mother liked him to walk with Rebecca, but he made the excuse that he had to finish a paper that he had left in his desk before his first class and had to get there a half hour early. He jumped on a bus, got off at Bethnal Green station and took the Tube to the Embankment. From there, it was a short walk to Scotland Yard. He didn't go in immediately. He walked down the Embankment towards the Inns of Court. There were a lot of people on the sidewalk. Barristers, some with wigs and robes, were on the their way to and from the Inns. He saw workmen with helmets on their way to jobs on damaged buildings and roads. There were office workers headed for the government buildings, men and women—some uniformed and some not—coming and going from Scotland Yard. The river was busy with barges taking their cargoes to and from the wharfs at Wapping, Limehouse, and other places on the south side of the river. For a half hour, Tom walked up and down, summoning his courage and silently rehearsing what he was going to say. Clutched in his hand was Leuzinger's letter. Finally, Tom went into the building after convincing the police officer on duty outside that he had business there.

"Well, what is it?" the heavy set man said impatiently as Tom stood silently. "I haven't got all day."

"I want to see the man in charge," Tom stammered.

"Oh, you want to see the man in charge, do you?" the man said sarcastically. "Did you hear that?" he turned with a smile to his colleagues who were in the room. "He wants to see the man in charge." He turned back to Tom and said, "Look, son, this is a busy place. We have lots of work to do and we don't have any time for silly little boys playing silly little games. Now be off with you."

"Sanders, have you finished the report on the Lawrence matter yet," an older, slim grey-haired man who had been looking at some documents he had pulled out of a filing cabinet said sharply.

"Not yet, sir," replied Tom's initial contact in a more subdued and respectful tone.

"Well, get on with it. I want it first thing tomorrow morning without fail. Do you understand?"

"Yes, sir. I'll get on it right away," and he walked hurriedly toward a small desk in the far corner of the room.

The gray-haired man walked over to Tom. "Now, what's this all about?" he said in a kindly voice.

"Are you the man in charge?" Tom asked.

The man smiled. "Not entirely, but I am Chief Inspector Andrew Dixon."

"Could I speak to you in private?"

"Come into my office."

Dixon took him down a long hall to a large corner office

with windows on two sides. One window overlooked the river. Tom's father told him that men in corner offices were usually important. The room was furnished comfortably, but inexpensively. There was a couch along one wall. A large desk faced the river. There were several chairs and wooden filing cabinets. There were pictures of London on the walls and a dark red carpet on the floor.

Dixon sat down behind his desk and motioned Tom to sit on one of the chairs facing the desk.

"What's your name, lad?"

"Sloan, sir. Tom Sloan."

"Well, Tom, tell me why you wanted to see me."

"I found a German pilot in a bombed-out house. He has broken his leg."

"That's very good, Tom. The more German pilots who are killed or captured the better. They don't have an endless supply of pilots any more than we have. But why do you come to me? We can't pay any reward for information which led to the capture of an enemy flier."

Tom paused, trying to choose his words carefully. "He's not been captured. At least not just yet."

"What. Are you telling me he escaped? Was that before the police arrived or after they grabbed him?"

"The police never came because I never told anybody about him until just now when I told you."

Dixon paused and looked startled. "How long ago did you find him?"

"Quite a while ago. I've lost track. I'm not exactly sure."

"He's been there for what you say is 'quite a while,'" Dixon said in amazement, hardly believing what he was hearing. "Are you sure he's still there?"

"Oh, yes sir. I know he is."

Dixon hit a button on the intercom. A female voice answered, "Yes sir?"

"Betty, bring your pad in and ask Sergeant Graham to come in."

Both arrived within a minute. Chief Inspector Dixon made the introductions. "Tom Sloan, this is Detective Sergeant Ernie Graham, my trusted right-hand, and Mrs. Betty Stoddard, my long-suffering secretary. Tom has started to tell me a remarkable story. Some time ago, he found a German pilot with a broken leg in a bombed-out building. Before telling me about it this morning, he has not told a single person and the pilot is still in the bombed-out building—or at least was as late as last night."

"Blimey," exclaimed Graham. "Now I've heard everything. Son, you are in big, big trouble."

"Now hold on, Graham. I want to hear the whole story," said Dixon.

"But shouldn't we send a car out to pick up the Kraut now before he gets away," said Graham.

"Not just yet. As I said, I want to hear the whole story first before we do anything. Tom, Betty is a very skilled shorthand typist. She is going to take down what you say. I want you to start at the beginning and tell us everything. Don't leave anything out. All right?"

Tom took a deep breath, swallowed a couple of times, looked down at Leuzinger's letter, and began. He took Dixon and Graham through the story starting with finding Leuzinger. Mrs. Stoddard sat with her pad and pencil taking everything down, occasionally asking Tom to repeat something she had not heard correctly. From time to time Dixon, and once in while Graham, would ask a question. How did Leuzinger get enough food (Dixon smiled about the can of beans) where did he wash (in the bathroom wash basin); was he still in his uniform (he was); how did they fix his leg (with the make shift splint); how did Tom get in and out without being seen (he was seen by the ARP Warden once and he used the alley after that). For the most part Dixon allowed Tom to tell the story in his own way, at his own pace, with only the occasional interruption.

He related for them the tales Leuzinger told of his sick wife, his young children, his farm, his hatred for Nazism and his great sympathy for the plight of the Jews in Germany and in occupied Europe. He told of Leuzinger's claimed burning desire to get to Ireland, knowing that he might be interned in that neutral country but that there would be a strong possibility that his wife and children could join him there. He related Leuzinger's story of his long close friendship with the Irish pub owner, Eamon Shaughnessy and his claim that, while Shaughnessy had no sympathy for the Germans, he would and could help Leuzinger get to Ireland. He told of Leuzinger's inability to get in touch with Shaughnessy because he had lost his wallet which contained that contact information.

They had been listening to Tom for the better part of an hour.

"Let's give Betty a rest. We've been going for a while. Tom, would you like a cup of tea?" Asked Dixon.

"Thank you. I would."

Betty always got tea for Dixon, but Graham stopped her.

"You rest, Betty. I'll get it," he said.

Mrs. Stoddard looked at him gratefully. "Thank you, Sergeant. I could use a little time."

Graham's initial anger at Tom had softened somewhat.

As they drank their tea, he said, "So you thought you were helping a decent chap with a sick wife and a family. Did you, Tom?"

"That's what I thought," said Tom.

"And that's why you didn't tell anybody?" asked Dixon.

"That's right," answered Tom.

"So why did you come and tell us now," asked Dixon. "What changed your mind?"

"I was just getting to that when we stopped for tea," said Tom.

"Betty, are you ready? Nice and rested, are you?" asked Dixon.

"I'm ready, Chief," she said with pad in hand and pencil poised.

Tom then told of finding the wallet, giving it to Leuzinger, and Leuzinger explaining how he had encoded Shaughnessy's contact information; how he brought him pen, paper and envelope and then how he took the letter sealed in the envelope home with him with the intent of posting it the next day.

"Did you post the letter?" asked Dixon.

"It rained last night. The envelope got wet and smeared. You could still read it but it was a bit difficult. I wrote a new envelope and opened the smeared one to put the letter in the new one. My mother told me never to read other people's letters which were not addressed to me—but I did read Captain Leuzinger's letter and after reading it I decided I had to come here and show it to you."

"Where is it, Tom?" asked Dixon.

Tom silently handed it to Dixon. He read it slowly and carefully and then, just as silently, handed it to Graham. He also read it slowly and carefully and, as he did, he shook his head back and forth.

"Let Mrs. Stoddard read it, Ernie," said Dixon.

After reading it, her reaction was totally unexpected, at least to Tom. "Oh, Tom. You poor dear boy. You were doing something so kind, so thoughtful, and so dangerous without caring for yourself at all and this monster, this evil man lied to you, deceived you, and betrayed your trust. I'm so sorry." The tears welled up in her eyes. She put her pad and pencil down, came over to Tom, and put her arms around him. The silence in the room was broken only by tough old Detective Sergeant Ernie Graham, a hardened veteran of thirty-two years at Scotland Yard rather loudly blowing his nose.

"Shall I send a car to pick up Leuzinger now, Chief?" asked Graham.

"No. I don't think so," mused Dixon. "We might have bigger fish to fry here. So many of these downed German pilots are avoiding capture and managing to get out of the country and back to their units. This might be a breakthrough. If we can track the people who come to pick him up, we might uncover the whole escape organization. It's worth a try."

He looked long and hard at Tom. "I'm going to ask you to do something, Tom. It could be dangerous and I have no right to ask a young boy like you to do this, but I'm going to anyway. I want you to go on as you have before as though nothing happened. Keep bringing food to the German. Don't let on that you read the letter. Tell him you posted it. Are you up for it?"

"You mean I'm not going to prison? I'm not going to be hung?" said Tom.

Everyone laughed. "No, Tom, you're not going to jail and you're not going to be hung. But you cannot give Leuzinger the slightest hint that you're on to him. Can you do it? Will you do it?"

"Yes, sir."

"You can't breathe a word to anyone about this—not a single word. Promise?"

"I promise."

"I have to talk to your father about this."

"My father is in the army. He is a major in the Middle East. He is the commandant of a German POW camp." Tom said.

"Well, that is ironic. You must be very proud of him. I must talk to your mother. Can she be trusted to keep a secret?"

"She can keep a secret, but why must you talk to her? She will be very angry with me."

"I can't let you do this without her permission. It's too dangerous," he said.

He turned to Graham. "Ernie, we are going to mail this letter. We have to be careful. First the envelope. The escape cell will be suspicious if they notice that the handwriting on the envelope doesn't match the handwriting on the letter. Get in touch with our decoding people. I know they have handwriting experts who can do a good job copying Leuzinger's handwriting. Also, we need to post the letter near the bombed-out house. We don't want to have a postmark on the envelope miles away—and particularly not near Scotland Yard. We will also have to set up surveillance on the house and wait for our friends from the Midlands to come calling. Ernie, I want that letter posted tomorrow so get going on getting the handwriting chap on it. I'll drive Tom home, meet his mother, and set up the surveillance."

As he pulled on his overcoat, Dixon thought, *Sometimes the frequent rain in England is a godsend. Let's hope it is now.*

Chapter Forty-Nine

DIXON AND TOM SAT in the back of the Humber Super Snipe. The driver was introduced to Tom as Detective Fredericks. He was a young sandy-haired man with a ready smile and a strong Scottish brogue. Tom had only been in a private car a few times in his life. His father never had a car even before the war. His Uncle Reuben had an old beat-up Morris and he had been in that, but he had never been in such a slick, shiny vehicle like this one.

Dixon called Detective Sergeant Graham from the car. Tom couldn't believe it. Of course, he had seen it at the cinema, but there he was in a car with the ability to call people. What a day this had been—and it promised to get even more exciting!

"Ernie, I am on my way to the Sloan house. I should be back in a couple of hours. Get the Blue Team together in Conference Room E. Give them a briefing on the Leuzinger matter and keep them there until I arrive," said Dixon on the phone.

The Blue Team was a counterespionage unit at Scotland Yard. One of their projects had been to try to ferret out the Nazi spy ring that had, among other things, been instrumental in spiriting German airmen who had parachuted out of crippled aircraft and had managed to escape capture back to the Fatherland. In addition to other duties, Dixon had overall supervision of the Blue Team.

As they drove toward the flats, Dixon asked Tom, "Does Leuzinger have a weapon?"

Tom thought for a moment. "I don't know. I didn't notice."

"Some German airmen carry a pistol, most frequently in a holster at their waist. You didn't see such a holster did you?"

"No, I didn't, but I really wasn't looking for it. Maybe he took it off to get more comfortable."

"If and when you go back in the room see if you can see it. Don't make it obvious and don't ask him if he has a gun. Okay?"

"Okay."

"When you fixed him up with the splint, was he able to get around?"

"We—I—cleared a path through the rubble so that he could get to the bathroom. It was just a short distance. I only saw him go to the bathroom a couple of times and he hopped on his good leg."

As they approached the area where Tom lived, he gave final directions to the driver. "Fredericks, drive slowly down Fleming Street. Don't stop. I want to look at the apartment building opposite the bombsite. Then turn right at the corner and let us out. We don't want to stir up any unnecessary curiosity by parking this car on Tom's street. Tom and I will walk the rest of the way. You wait for us where you let us off."

Tom knocked on his front door. Immediately, his mother

opened it. "Why are you knocking? Don't you have your key and why aren't you in school?" She then saw Dixon standing a couple of feet behind Tom. She stopped and looked inquiringly at him.

"Mrs. Sloan, I am Chief Inspector Dixon of Scotland Yard," he said pulling out his credentials and showing them to her.

Her eyes got like saucers. "Tom, what have you done?" she gasped. "Have you been arrested?"

"Don't be alarmed, Mrs. Sloan. Tom is not in any trouble, but I do need to talk to you. May I come in?"

Speechlessly, she stood aside and Tom and Dixon went into the flat.

"Is it about my husband? Has something happened to Bernie? Is he all right?"

"It's not about your husband or any of your family. Let me explain what I have come about."

Miriam, Tom, and Chief Inspector Dixon sat down around the small kitchen table.

"Please excuse the mess. I haven't had time to clean up."

The kitchen was as neat as a pin without a single thing out of place. If the world were coming to an end in ten minutes, Miriam would make sure everything was clean and tidy and would apologize for the "mess." It was a standing joke in the Sloan household and Bernie would rib her about it good-naturedly.

"What I am about to tell you is highly confidential. You must promise that you won't tell anybody about it—not even your daughter. Will you promise me that?"

"Yes, yes I promise. Now please tell what this is all about and what it has to do with Tom."

"Some time ago, Tom discovered a wounded German pilot hiding in a bombed-out building on Fleming Street. He has been caring for him, tending to his broken leg, and bringing him food ever since. He told nobody about it until he told me this morning," Dixon started.

Miriam had just begun to put water in the kettle to make some tea. No visitor ever escaped her flat without having the mandatory cup of tea. On hearing what Dixon had just said, she felt faint, put the kettle on the sink, and sat down.

"Tom, how could you do such a thing? Whatever possessed you to help a Nazi?" Miriam was on the verge of hysteria.

"Calm yourself, Mrs. Sloan. As it turns out, Tom may have done a great service for his country."

"I don't understand," said Miriam.

"The German pilot, Captain Leuzinger, is a clever, cunning sort of bloke. He convinced Tom that he is anti-Nazi and that he has great sympathy for the Jews who are being persecuted in Europe. He also convinced Tom that his wife is dying of some disease and that if he doesn't escape, he will never see her alive again. He told Tom that he has an Irish friend living in England who could help him get to Ireland where he might be interned for the duration of the war and, since Ireland is a neutral country, his wife and family could join him there. Yesterday, quite by accident, Tom found out that Leuzinger has been lying to him; that he is a Nazi and a virulent anti-Semite. He has no wife or children and no Irish friend. He had written a letter that he wanted Tom to send to his friend. It got wet in the rain last night. Tom opened the envelope, read the letter, found out the truth, and that it was written to a secret Nazi spy organization in this country. This spy ring we believe has been responsible for sending classified information to Germany and has been aiding German fliers who have bailed out over England to return to Germany. Scotland Yard has been trying, without success, to uncover this ring and capture its members and particularly its masterminds. Tom's contact with this German pilot might provide us with an important breakthrough. We need his help."

Miriam was deeply relieved to find out that Tom was not in trouble and had, in fact, been of substantial help to Scotland Yard.

"Tom will be of whatever help he can. His father is a major with the Eighth Army in the Middle East."

"I am sure you are justifiably proud of your husband and I think you can also be proud of your son. But what we are asking your son to do does have an element of danger," said Dixon.

Miriam stiffened. "What kind of danger?"

"We will mail the letter Leuzinger wrote. We expect, probably in a week or maybe a little short of a week, the spy ring I mentioned will send people to get him. Those people will probably be lower-level members of the ring. We will allow them to pick up Leuzinger and we will then track the vehicle wherever it goes. In that fashion, we may very well find the leaders of the ring."

"How does Tom fit into all of this cloak and dagger stuff?" Miriam said with a puzzled look on her face.

"Tom has been to see Leuzinger virtually every day since he first found the German. If he now stops going, Leuzinger is going to get suspicious. He may conclude that Tom opened his letter and read it. He may also conclude that the authorities now know the whole story and they are doing exactly what we plan to do. That may lead to one or two things. Maybe Leuzinger will try to escape on his own. That will be difficult and he probably won't choose that option. He has a broken leg and he's wearing a German uniform. He has no way to warn the spy ring in advance of their coming so he will warn them when they arrive. That may cause them to leave the house without Leuzinger or, if they take him, they won't lead us to their HQ."

"So you want Tom to continue doing what he has been doing so that Leuzinger won't get suspicious?"

"Exactly," said Dixon. "The danger to Tom is if Leuzinger detects that Tom's attitude has changed or that he is more nervous than before, he may suspect that Tom opened the envelope, read the letter, and informed the authorities. If he comes to that conclusion, I can't predict what he will do. It wouldn't help him to hurt Tom—even if he thinks Tom has turned him in—but I can't guarantee anything. My guess is that he would be livid, but he wouldn't do anything to Tom. It wouldn't help him to escape and he clearly wouldn't be treated as a prisoner of war under the Geneva Convention if he was captured and if he harmed Tom."

It wasn't lost on Miriam that Dixon kept using the term *harmed* rather than the more drastic term: *killed*.

"Mum, I'm not afraid of him. I won't be nervous and I won't let him know I'm on to him. Remember you said I did a good job when I acted in *Hamlet* in the school play."

"This isn't a play and it isn't *Hamlet*. This is real life," said Miriam.

"He used me, Mum. He hates Jews and he used me. You have to let me do it. You just have to," he said pleadingly.

She sat there deep in thought for the longest time while no one said a word. Finally, she spoke, "On one condition," she said shaking her finger at him. "If he even looks hard at you or if he says the slightest thing that might suggest he is worried about something, you turn and run right out of there. You don't wait. You don't stop to think. You just run right out as fast as you can. Do you understand?"

"Yes, Mum."

Chief Inspector Dixon got up, shook Miriam's hand, and thanked her. "You're a brave woman with a brave husband and a brave son and I'm sure your daughter takes after you. With your permission, I will take Tom back to Scotland Yard with me now. There are some things I need to go over with him and I will bring him back later this evening."

After they had gone, Miriam sat quietly, alone with her thoughts. *Have I done the right thing? What if something goes wrong? If only I had talked to Bernie. We're Jews. We're maligned in our own country. We're called names and beaten. We're blamed for all the bad things that happen. Many Jews who can trace their ancestry in England for a number of generations still don't think of themselves as English. Many of them still refer to non-Jews as English to identify them as non-Jews. Many Jews say goodbye to each other with the saying "Next year in the Holy Land"—even though there's no chance of that happening or any real desire that it would. My husband is an officer in the British army putting his life on the line for his country and still we get abused. My son may be putting his young life on the line for his country and we will still be abused.*

She got up, put the kettle on, and thought, *This is my country too—mine and Bernie's and Rebecca's and Tom's. I am English and always will be—no matter what all the bigots and all the anti-Semites in the world say or do. My country needed my husband and he did his duty and now it needs my son. He will do his duty and I am proud and happy with that.*

203

CHAPTER FIFTY

IN ADDITION TO DETECTIVE Sergeant Graham, there were
ten other men in Conference Room E when Dixon and Tom
arrived.

"Have you briefed them, Ernie?"

"I have, sir."

"Good. Now chaps, thanks to Tom Sloan here, we may
have our first big break in the spy ring investigation. So far
it's been one blind alley after another. I have a number of
assignments to hand out. We don't know when they will
come to pick up the German, but my guess is that it will
be somewhere around a week or ten days after we mail
Leuzinger's letter, which we will do tomorrow. Ernie, did
we get a handwriting chap to do the envelope?"

"We did, sir. There's a bloke in the cipher section who's
an expert in it. I gave him the letter and he's working on it
now."

"Very good. We're going to have to move quickly."

Dixon walked to the end of the room pulled open two
side-by-side curtains, revealing a blackboard.

"Tom, come over here please. Take a piece of chalk and
draw what the inside of the house looks like. Don't worry

about doing it to scale or neatness. I want to know where Leuzinger is in the house and what the front and back of the house looks like. Stoneman, take your note pad and copy down what Tom is drawing. You are going to be in charge of surveillance from the front of the house."

Detective Sergeant Roger Stoneman, fiftyish and bald as an egg, was a veteran of many stakeouts and knew the routine by heart. He had been a promising middleweight boxer thirty years earlier, but was now quite a few pounds over his ideal fighting weight. He took pencil and paper and followed what Tom was doing.

"Now, Tom, draw how you got into the house from the front and from the alley and the paths you took from the front and back to reach the room where the German is," said Dixon.

Tom dutifully drew the street, the rubble-strewn route from the front door to the back room, the damaged wall in the alley, and the wire fence with the hole in it between the two houses. Stoneman took it all down.

"Tom, you told us that Leuzinger has a broken leg. Do you think that he could get out of the house by way of the alley?" asked Dixon.

Tom thought for a moment. "It would be very difficult for him. There's a wall he would have to climb over about three or four feet high."

"What about if he had a couple of fellows to help him?"

"That would make it easier," said Tom. "But what good would that do? Once he was in the alley, he would have to go quite a way to the end. There's so much rubbish and debris in the alley that you couldn't get a car or lorry up there."

"That's helpful," said Dixon.

"I looked at the flats on Fleming Street across the street.

The building is six stories with a flat roof and a visible door on the roof. Roger, you, Fullmer, Regis, Smithers, and Platt will maintain surveillance on the Fleming house from the roof of the flats across the street. You will take turns. You will check out home guard uniforms, helmets, binoculars, and walkie-talkies. You are going to be impersonating aircraft spotters. As you know, there are a large number of spotters on roofs and other high places all over the country identifying enemy planes and calling in information. You should have no trouble blending in, but keep out of sight anyway. The last thing we want to do is spook the 'Rescuers.' Having spotters on the roof, even if they are seen by the tenants, won't raise their curiosity. There will be two of you up there at all times."

There was a pause as tea was brought in. No matter how intense and dire the circumstances, it was still unthinkable to get past four o'clock without tea.

"An unmarked van will be parked around the corner with two of you in at all times. It has an AR7 tracker installed. You will check out another one from our supply room. It will be on the roof with the spotters. Given that Leuzinger has a broken leg, they undoubtedly will take him out the front way and not through the alley. As Tom said, an escape route through the alley is very unlikely. To ensure that, I am having barriers erected at either end of the alley with danger signs posted.

"As soon as the rescuers go into the house, one of the spotters will run down the stairs and place an AR7 under the bottom of the back of the rescue vehicle. There's a strong magnet that will hold the AR7 firmly against the metal undercarriage of any vehicle. It will emit a constant series of signals that will be received in the van that will be able to follow without getting too close. Whoever affixes the AR7 will have to do it in a real hurry—down the stairs two at a time and across the street on the dead run. It will take some time for them to help Leuzinger out, but not that much time. If they see you putting something under the car, the jig is up. You need to do it and get back out of sight as fast as can be. Roger, are you up to this? I want you involved, but when it comes to affixing the AR7, let your partner do it."

"Chief, you cut me to the quick. I'm as fast as I ever was," Stoneman said, tongue firmly in cheek.

"That's what I was afraid of," retorted Dixon. There was laughter all around. Dixon was well liked and, more importantly, widely respected.

"Lambert, I want you to get in touch with Chief Constable Simons of the Burton-on-Trent Police Department. He's an old friend of mine. Tell him that you're coming up to do a stakeout on the post office that has the PO box that Leuzinger used. I want a tail put on anyone who opens that box. Take Stern and Frawley with you. Simons will give you some men to help. But don't have them in on the tailing. They are probably good officers, but they aren't skilled in this type of work and one mistake and the jig is up. We will dress up one of our chaps as a postal clerk and keep one eye on the box. I don't want the person who opens the box confronted. When our man sees the box opened, he can give a prearranged signal that won't be detected except by our people. I'm not expecting too much from that surveillance. They are much too clever to just pick up the letter and go back to their hideout with it. We won't have time to use the AR7 plan. Whoever picks up the letter will be in and out before we have time to attach it. He or she probably won't park a car directly outside the post office anyway. Too obvious. Our big hope is Fleming Street. But we must leave no stone unturned."

"Tom, since you started going in to the house, has anybody else been there to your knowledge?" Dixon asked.

Tom was startled. He hadn't mentioned Josh and didn't have any intention to do so now.

"I know boys like to go through bombed-out buildings looking for shrapnel. Incidentally a very bad idea and quite dangerous," said Dixon.

"No, I haven't seen any. There were some the first few days after the bomb fell, but the house has been pretty well picked over now. I don't think anyone else will go in there."

"How is it none of those boys found Leuzinger and you did?"

"The door to the back room where he is was jammed shut. Probably by the bomb. Apparently nobody tried to open it. When I went in by myself, Leuzinger cried out for help. I think he was afraid to do that when he heard a lot of people. But when he heard what must have sounded like one person and his pain had gotten real bad, I think he decided to call out. It was hard, but I finally forced the door open."

"Nonetheless, as a precaution, I think we should put wooden barriers around the front of the three houses with danger signs on them. It won't keep out the rescuers, but it will deter the casual intruder. Those of you to whom I haven't yet given an assignment get the Civil Defense people to do that."

Dixon looked around at his men who were feverishly writing notes about assignments and the like. "Any questions?"

Simpson put his hand up. "Yes," said Dixon.

"Suppose after they pick up Leuzinger, they stop

somewhere and change vehicles. We will have lost the ability to track with the AR7."

"That's simple," said Dixon. "You go up to the new vehicle and ask the driver if he wouldn't mind waiting a minute while you transfer the tracking device. I am sure he will be most cooperative—particularly if you are very polite."

The room burst into laughter and Simpson turned a bright red. Dixon held his hand up and the room went silent.

"I'm not making fun of you. Actually, that is a very good question. Unfortunately, there is no very good answer. They have been highly successful so far and I'm hoping they have become somewhat complacent. I am not assuming that. I always assume that my adversary is at least as smart as I am. That way, if he is, I am not taken by surprise and if he isn't, then that is an unexpected bonus. However, the AR7 is new and the spy ring is probably not anticipating its use. If they do change vehicles, you will know they have stopped. You will have to move in closer to see what is going on and see which vehicle, if any, they have switched into. If they have switched, you will have to follow more closely and risk detection. There is no perfect solution unfortunately. Any other questions?" There were none.

"Fredericks, drive Tom home. Again park around the corner. Don't leave him off on his street." He handed Tom a card. "Here is a number. You can reach me there at any time—day or night. Don't hesitate to call me if anything happens and call me once a day after you have seen Leuzinger—whether anything of note happens or not. Okay, Tom?"

Tom nodded. Dixon added, "This will be something to tell your grandchildren one day. But wait until then before you say anything to anyone."

CHAPTER FIFTY-ONE

"HELLO, TOM. I'VE BEEN waiting anxiously for you."
Leuzinger was sitting up on the couch his broken leg propped
up on a large piece of lumber. "Did you manage to post the
letter to Eamon?"

Tom had been rehearsing in his mind all day how he
would react to Leuzinger. It would be the first time he would
meet the German with the knowledge he had obtained in the
letter. He was not able to concentrate in school. Twice, he
had his knuckles rapped for inattention, once in geography,
usually his favorite class, and once in algebra, not one of his
favorites.

"Yes I did," he answered, hoping his voice didn't sound
as nervous as he felt. "Letters are taking longer than normal.
My mother got a letter from her aunt in Torquay and it took
five days to reach us."

"Well, we will just have to be patient," said Leuzinger,
apparently not detecting any change in Tom's attitude. "By
the way, I heard some noise outside the front of the house,
sounded like men talking and some hammering. Do you
know what it was?"

"Not for certain," answered Tom. "I came in the back

way through the alley. I think it was probably the Civil Defense people putting up barriers outside the three houses warning of danger. The BBC said last night that two boys were seriously hurt by a falling beam in a bombed-out house in Islington. They were looking for shrapnel. The Civil Defense is apparently putting up barriers all over the place to keep boys out."

"It won't stop Eamon getting in, will it?" Leuzinger said anxiously.

"Oh no, they are real low. You can step either over or around. It's just a warning. I'll look down Fleming on my way home, but I'm sure it won't be a problem."

After the first few minutes of nervousness, Tom was starting to relax. He was surprised that, as much as he hated the man in front of him and as much as he knew that man hated him, he was not having any trouble carrying on a normal conversation. He had brought a piece of fish and some boiled carrots from school wrapped up in a couple of pages from his notebook.

"You had better eat the fish soon. My mother says that fish spoils very quickly if it is not kept in a refrigerator."

"I will," Leuzinger smiled, "and thank you for bringing it. I've always liked fish. We have a pond on my farm and it has some trout and carp that we catch."

"I had better run home," said Tom. "My mother will start wondering where I am. I'll come tomorrow. We're having sausages for lunch. I'll bring you one. I think they're mostly sawdust, but they're better than nothing—although not by much."

Leuzinger laughed. "I'm certain they will taste wonderful. Hunger improves the taste of even the foulest food. Not that your sausage will be foul."

Just as Tom was getting ready to leave, Leuzinger shifted his weight and a small pistol fell off the couch. Tom went over and picked it up.

"That is such a little gun. Is it a toy?" asked Tom.

Leuzinger laughed. "No, it's not a toy. Be careful with it Tom. It's loaded."

Tom looked at it more closely, being careful not to touch the trigger. He handed it back after Leuzinger had explained some things about it and where he got it. Tom promised he'd be back the next night and left, very relieved and, in fact proud, that he had been able to act completely normal and not cause Leuzinger to be at all suspicious. It was dark and the alley was empty and quiet. He ran home as fast as he could.

"You know, Mum, if it wasn't for Colonel Reichmann, I wouldn't be involved in any of this." On arriving home, he had found his mother alone. Rebecca was upstairs with her friend doing homework. Miriam was relieved beyond words that Tom's encounter had been essentially uneventful.

"Are you talking about the German colonel your father wrote about? The one who saved that Jewish doctor and his family?"

"Yes," said Tom.

"What on earth has a German POW in the Middle East got to do with your dealings with Captain Leuzinger?"

"Well, before dad met Colonel Reichmann and heard what he had done for that Jewish family, dad hated all Germans and all things German—and I did too."

"And therefore what?" said a puzzled Miriam not knowing where Tom was headed.

"Well, if dad hadn't told us about Reichmann, I would still believe that all Germans, without exception, were evil and I would have turned Leuzinger in to the police the first day I found him. So in a strange way, the fact that dad found a "good" German made me help Leuzinger, who turned out to be a "bad" German.

CHAPTER FIFTY-TWO

THE ARRANGEMENTS AT THE post office in Burton-on-Trent had been carefully and skillfully planned. Because of wartime regulations, the post office was only open from ten to three Monday through Friday and closed Saturday and Sunday. Dixon had arranged to place a detective from the Yard dressed as a postman whose duties caused him to be in the area of the boxes giving him a clear view of anyone who opened the target box. As luck would have it, the postman who regularly filled that position became ill with flu and Dixon was able to replace him with the detective without raising suspicion among the other postal workers.

In the street directly opposite the post office, two other detectives dressed as workers in overalls had placed wooden barriers around an open manhole cover in the center of the street. One of the men was down the hole while the other busied himself around the top of the hole handing tools down, seemingly working on something and talking about the work to the man in the hole. There was a van parked in front of the hole with local county counsel markings on it. The casual passerby would find nothing unusual about the goings on.

If and when anybody opened the target box, the detective inside the post office was to walk outside and light a cigarette as if he was on a break. While the pedestrian traffic into and out of the post office was ordinarily quite sporadic, in order to avoid confusion, that detective was to take the cigarette out of his mouth and hold it in the direction of the person exiting the post office who had opened the box. The officer outside the hole was to shout to his compatriot down the hole that he would go back to the shop and get the larger size pliers that were required. He would then get into the van and follow the person who had opened the box while making sure there was no hint that he was following that person. Since Dixon believed that the tail from the post office was much less likely to bear fruit than the tail from the bombed-out house, the detectives at the post office were strongly ordered not to take any chance of raising suspicion and to err on the side of cutting off the tail.

Days went by and no letters were delivered to the box and nobody opened it. As was customary in long, drawn-out stakeouts, there was an odd mix of boredom and nervousness. Through long hours, all three detectives had to be alert, but as the time passed it became more difficult and required greater effort. Leuzinger's letter was delivered to the post office on the third day of surveillance and immediately placed in the box. Two more days passed.

At ten minutes to three on the third day after the letter had been placed in the box, the inside detective appeared outside the post office and lit a cigarette. He took a puff, removed the cigarette from his mouth, and held it in such a way that it casually pointed to a tall, slim man wearing a green smock frequently worn by grocery clerks and a tweed workingman's cap pulled down so that most of his face was not visible. The detective, Stern, at the top of the hole yelled down to his mate, "I don't have the right pliers. I'll have to go back to the shop. I'll be back in a jiffy." The man in the hole yelled back, "Don't be long—I can't do anything with this pipe without it."

Stern got into the van and turned on the engine. There was a white van with a ladder attached to the top parked about fifty feet down the street and a black car parked about twenty feet in front of it. Stern thought that the man was almost certainly headed for the white van. He planned to wait until the van pulled away from the curb and then would follow from a distance. The man had undoubtedly heard him yell to his mate and would not be surprised to see the county council van behind him.

To Stern's surprise, the man walked right past the white van and stepped off the curb between the van and the black car. Suddenly, the man reappeared from between the two vehicles riding a bicycle. He pedaled rapidly down the street with Stern following. Halfway down the block the bicycle turned right into an alley. As he approached the alley Stern realized that it was too narrow to accommodate the width of his van. He continued down the street to the corner, intending to turn right and right again to pick up the trail of the bicycle. There was a bus stopped in front of him. This was a two-lane street and a taxi and a lorry approaching slowly on the other side prevented him from going around the bus. "Blast," he said as the bus slowly discharged and picked up passengers. By the time he had made the two rights, there was no sign of the bicycle. He drove around for five minutes, but could find no trace of the bicycle or its rider. In fact, the only vehicles he saw during those five minutes were two vans, a horse and cart, and a taxicab. He went and looked for a public phone.

"Not your fault, Stern. Our plan was a good one. If anyone is to blame, it's me," said Dixon. "It should have occurred to me that the messenger might use a bike and find an escape route that a car or van couldn't follow. I don't know whether they were devilishly clever or just lucky."

"Shall the three of us continue the stake out? He, or somebody, will probably come back for other letters later," asked Stern.

"We'll give it a couple more days. We can't keep that barrier in the center of the street much longer. It's bound to raise suspicions sooner or later. These enemy agents are no fools. Also, I imagine that they periodically change post offices and get new post office boxes and safe houses and notify German intelligence of the new locations. But hang on there a bit longer. Oh, and one other thing, get a bike and put it inside the van. If they try the same trick again, follow—but not too closely," said Dixon.

CHAPTER FIFTY-THREE

IT WAS THE EASIEST five quid Bill Craddock had ever made—or ever would make. It had taken five minutes and had worked out exactly as that Irish bloke had told him it would.

Three days earlier, he was in the Crown and Thorn on Radley Road having a beer by himself in the back bar. He had been released from Cromwell prison the Saturday before, having served three months for snatching a woman's purse in Lakeview Park.

He'd have gotten away with it too if he hadn't tripped on a raised paving stone and fallen. A bunch of teenage boys playing football had heard the woman cry out and had jumped on him and held him down until the police came. Bloody paving stone, he could have broken his neck. He ought to sue, he thought. All day he had been out looking for a job. With the war on and all young people in the military, it ought to be easy to get a job. Once they find out he is an ex-con with three prior snatch-and-grab convictions, they lose interest.

"May I sit here?" A heavyset bearded bloke with dark glasses and a full beard had asked him in a pronounced Irish accent. He was a rum-looking cove with his beard and dark glasses, particularly in the dimly lighted bar.

"It's a free country—at least for some people," Craddock said.

"Want another beer?" the man said.

"I've no more money for beer or anything," said Craddock.

"My treat," said the bearded bloke. "I'll get them." He waved to the waitress and two pints quickly appeared.

"How would you like to make five quid for five minutes work?"

"Who do I have to kill?"

The Irishman laughed. "Nothing like that. I'm involved in a real ugly divorce. My wife is out to take me for everything she can. I know she has some bloke following me. A private investigator or something like that. I've had a friend send me some papers to a post office box close by here. They will help me prove she's been carrying on with some geezer over in Thurston Hills. I have a hearing in court next week and those papers will help me a lot. My wife's solicitor has been trying to find me to serve some papers on me. I don't want that to happen before the court hearing. If he can't find me, he can't serve the papers."

"All very interesting, but where do I come in and how do I get the five quid?" said Craddock, looking closely at his now empty glass.

The Irishman signaled to the waitress to bring Craddock another one. "I'll give you the key to the post office box in the post office on Thurston Road. You go over there three days from now at ten minutes to three. No earlier and no later. Pick up any letters in the box. After you have opened the box, you can push the key into one of the envelopes, if there is more than one, by opening it just an inch. Don't open the envelopes further and don't look at the contents. Walk out the front door, turn right, and about fifty yard down the road, there will be an old bicycle against the curb. Ride it as fast as you can in the same direction it is pointed. Halfway down the block, there is a narrow alley on the right. Ride down that alley and, when you get to the end, turn right. As soon as you turn onto the road, there will be a taxi by the curb. Hand the envelopes to the woman driver. Then ride off immediately. You can ride a bike can't you?"

"Of course, I can," snorted Craddock. "How do I get the fiver?"

"I'll give you two quid now and the taxi driver will give you the rest when you give her the envelopes—provided the envelopes have not been opened. It's important that you not be followed. If you think you are, just ride straight past the taxi and keep going. If that happens, we'll pick up the envelopes from you later at your house and give you the three bucks then. If you do it the way I've said, there is little chance that anybody will be able to see you give the envelopes to the taxi driver. Is it a deal?"

"Yes, it's a deal. What do I do with the bike afterward?"

"It's an old piece of rubbish. You can keep it if you want or just leave it somewhere. What is your name and address?"

Craddock gave him the information. "What if I have to reach you?" he said to the Irishman. "What's your name and address?"

The Irishman smiled, "You won't need to reach me. Just do what I say and I'll have the papers and you'll have your fiver."

As he got up to leave, the Irishman fished out two one-pound notes, handed them to Craddock, and, without another word, walked out of the pub.

Chapter Fifty-Four

It was nine o'clock the night after Craddock had delivered the envelope to the taxi driver. Two men were sitting at a table in the kitchen of a farmhouse thirty miles away and deep in the Staffordshire countryside. One man was in his sixties, gray-haired, and balding. The other man was much younger, dark-haired, and bespectacled. A woman, also in her sixties, was washing dinner dishes in the sink. She was stout with gray hair pulled back severely into a bun. She also wore glasses and appeared matronly with very little makeup. The farmhouse sat in twenty-five acres of heavily forested land and was reached off a country road by a long, winding dirt path. The property had been purchased through a straw man several years before the war in anticipation of its possible use as a spy headquarters. To outward appearance, it was owned and occupied by a retired couple and their three sons.

While the retired couple kept much to themselves, they were occasional visitors to the village ten miles away where they patronized the few shops and frequented the lone pub in the area. Sometimes one or more of their sons accompanied them. Locals thought little about them. They were not there often and while they had their beers in the pub and didn't talk much to other patrons, they were not unfriendly. The elderly gentleman had a brogue. His wife sounded more cockney. The sons' accents were more English than Irish, but were difficult to place. The older man was known as George Duggan and the older woman was identified as his wife Irene. The sons were named Henry, Jimmy, and Fred.

It had been raining steadily all day and there was a thick fog that reduced visibility to a few yards. The sound of a car was heard coming down the dirt path leading to the house. The young man reached for a pistol in a drawer in the kitchen table. "Put that away, you fool," hissed the older man. Sheepishly, the younger man complied. The car engine was turned off close to the house and, a few minutes later, the man Craddock had met in the pub in Burton-on-Trent came in, shaking the rain off his hair. He no longer wore the dark glasses or the worker's cap. His beard, which was a clever fake, was gone—as was the padding that had made him appear heavyset. In fact, he bore no resemblance to the man involved in the messy divorce. The change in appearance was startling. The beard had hidden a prominent scar that started just below his left ear and ended at his chin.

"Well, did it go off well?" asked the older man.

"Have you eaten, Heinrich?" asked the woman. "I have some stew left over if you'd like some."

"Not now," said George impatiently. "He can eat later. I want to know what happened and don't call him Heinrich. His name is Henry. Remember that. It's always Henry, never Heinrich."

"But nobody is here but us," she pleaded.

"Don't you understand. I've told you time and again we can never let our guard down. We've got to use the names we have been assigned at all times—not just when we are with outsiders. The slightest slip will betray us. Don't ever forget that. We are only a very short step from the gallows."

"I'm sorry, George. It won't happen again," she said quietly with her head down.

"Well, see that it doesn't," he angrily retorted.

"Go ahead, Henry," he said, turning his attention back to the new arrival.

Henry detailed his meeting with Craddock and the instructions he had given.

"Good," said George. "Fred should be here soon and we'll find out what he's got. In the meantime give him something to eat, Irene."

About a half an hour later another car was heard coming toward the house. This time Jimmy knew better than to reach for his gun. The "female" taxi driver came in—only "she" was no longer wearing a long blonde wig or makeup and his appearance, similar to Henry's, was totally different from what Craddock had seen.

"Everything go smoothly?" asked George.

"Couldn't have been easier," said Fred.

"Do you think there is any possibility that Craddock could identify either one of you?" asked George.

"Not a chance with me," said Fred. "He stopped his bike for a split second to give me the envelope, there was only one, and I gave him the money. He barely looked at me.

"What about you, Henry?" asked George.

"It was dark in the pub. With the cap, the padding, the beard, and the glasses, my own mother wouldn't have recognized me."

Irene smiled as she put some food in front of Fred. As motherly as she appeared, she wasn't the mother of Fred, Henry, or Jimmy.

"We ought to kill Craddock any way just to be sure," said Jimmy.

"Don't be an idiot," snapped George. "We kill Craddock and there will be inquiries and an investigation. There are probably people in the pub that saw Henry talking to Craddock. Right now nobody has or will focus on that, but they might if something happens to Craddock. Where that would lead, nobody can know. I think we are all right the way it is. Let me see the envelope, Fred."

Fred handed it over. "Was it open when you got it from Craddock?" asked George.

"Just a slight slit sufficient for Craddock to be able to slip the key in," answered Fred.

George read Leuzinger's letter and handed it to Fred who then handed it around so that everybody read it.

After everybody had read it, George said, "Very interesting. It doesn't sound like the Jew boy suspected anything. The only fear I would have is if he opened the envelope and read it before it was sent. Fred you took that course in Munich about handwriting. Take a look at the writing on the letter and compare it with the writing on the envelope. Do they appear to be the same?"

Fred looked carefully at the writings. "They look the same. Of course, the boy might have steamed open the envelope and resealed it later. It doesn't look like that was done, but it might have. The boy might have taken the letter to the authorities and they might have steamed it open. I doubt it, but it could have happened."

"Nothing in this business is without some risk, but I think it is most probable that the boy did not open the letter. According to the letter, Leuzinger had told the boy quite specifically what was in the envelope. Obviously, the boy trusted Leuzinger who is clearly a very clever fellow. He wouldn't be curious about the contents because Leuzinger had described them. I'm satisfied the letter was never opened before it was sent. Anyone disagree?" asked George. Nobody did.

George sighed. Communications concerning their clandestine operations were always fraught with danger. While letters unrelated to those operations such as bills for electricity and water routinely came to the house, communications concerning such operations had to be channeled through less dangerous means. Telephone calls from agents or other sources in Ireland or Great Britain were sometimes used, but were disfavored by the High Command as being too easily traced. Radio communications were necessary and employed, but could conceivably be intercepted. Letter communication via Irish and English sources through different boxes at different post offices had recently been implemented by the High Command and had occurred sporadically in the last few months. Such use was signaled in advance by coded radio transmissions.

George did not like this method of communication. Apart from the obvious danger involved, he never knew for certain whether any letters would be in any particular box on any particular visit. Once the coded message came in by radio, the boxes would have to be checked periodically until a further coded radio message temporarily terminated the procedure. That is how it came about that pickups were made over the past several weeks at different locations by unsuspecting "mules"—including Craddock.

CHAPTER FIFTY-FIVE

"JIMMY, YOU GET ON the radio and check Leuzinger's bona fides with Berlin," ordered George.

Jimmy immediately got up from the table and went into a back room. George was obviously not one who brooked delayed responses to his instructions.

George turned back to Fred who was still tackling Irene's stew. "You are quite sure no one followed you after Craddock slipped you the envelope?"

"I'm quite sure. There was no traffic on the street when Craddock gave me the envelope. I watched him continue and turn and I saw no one follow him. I pulled away from the curb, drove around several streets, and kept a look in the rearview mirror. I'm quite sure I wasn't followed."

"What about the taxi?"

"I replaced the license plates with the original ones and returned the taxi to Sid Olson." Sid was a person that Fred had gotten to know. They had many drinks together and had gone to a number of football games. They had become very good friends. Sid was an independent taxi driver, owned his own cab and, innocently, had been very useful to George and his "family." Sid had loaned his cab to Fred on Fred's explanation that his car was in the shop and he needed to run some errands. It was believed by George and Fred that the use of a cab in the Craddock exchange would be less conspicuous and that Craddock would not be able to describe a particular make and model of a private car if he was ever questioned.

"Henry, you went in the post office and also walked by it the day before Craddock picked up the envelope. Did you see anything out of the ordinary?" asked George.

"No. Of course I would have called it all off if I had. No, there was nothing at all strange."

"Good. Well, we will wait for Berlin to tell us about Leuzinger," said George.

"Come to think of it, there was something, but not really out of the ordinary," said Henry.

"What?"

"There were workmen—I think two—working in a sewer or something across from the post office. They had a manhole opened. They were from some county repair something or other. At least that was what I recalled was on their van," said Henry vaguely.

George stiffened. "That could have been a plant. Fred, you're quite sure you didn't see such a van. If it was the police or some other law enforcement agency, they might have followed Craddock with that van."

"You're sounding a bit paranoid. We never pick up letters from the boxes ourselves. We always use some unsuspecting stranger and we never get caught."

George bristled. "Listen, being paranoid is what has— and will—keep us alive. It doesn't sound as though those workers and that van were a plant, but we won't take a chance. We won't use that box again. We'll get a new drop somewhere else and notify Berlin.

A half hour later, Jimmy came back into the kitchen. "Berlin says Leuzinger is legitimate. Everything checks out."

"All right. We'll go get him. It will take two of us. He has a broken leg. He'll need help. We'll use a van with markings that identify it as a water and power vehicle. We'll have suitable overalls. It won't create any suspicion because work crews are frequently at bombsites repairing gas or water leaks. We'll probably have to do it in broad daylight since most repair work is not done at night. Henry, pull out some of those uniforms from the shed. We'll need an extra one for Leuzinger."

"What if someone sees two of us go in and three of us come out?" asked Henry.

"Good question. We'll park the vehicle directly in front of the bombsite. Two of us will help Leuzinger toward the front of the house through what must be a lot of rubble and debris. Then one of us will help him the rest of the way to the van. The other one will go over the wall at the back of the house into the alley and we'll arrange a rendezvous point after we look at the map. That way, if any nosy neighbor is looking, she'll see two people go into the house and two come out."

"What about the fact that two able-bodied men might be seen going in and one will come out limping?"

"Another good question," said George. "Bomb-damaged buildings are notoriously unsafe. It probably won't surprise anybody to see an uninjured man go in and an injured man come out. It might even be helpful. We're going to be coming out very quickly. Probably too quickly to have done any repairs. If an injured man comes out, that might explain the quick exit. We've got to go get medical help and can't finish the job. No more questions? Good. Henry, don't forget a toolbox. We need to look as workmanlike as possible. We'll plan on going down to London the day after tomorrow. Just in case something comes up."

Chapter Fifty-Six

"WHAT THE BLOODY HELL is all the noise about?"

A disheveled man in his pajamas, bathrobe, and slippers had just appeared on the roof of the building across from the bombed-out site. Regis and Platt in their home guard uniforms were on duty. Regis looked at the man and was hard put to keep from laughing. The man's few strands of gray hair were tousled and standing on end. His glasses were perched precariously on the end of his nose and it looked as if, in his rush to register his complaint, he had grabbed his wife's flowered robe, which would have fit the man if he was forty pounds lighter.

"We're enemy plane and fire spotters," explained Regis.

"You sound more like fire dancers," retorted the man.

"Well, it's cold up here and we walk around to keep warm."

"The roof on this building is as thin as parchment. My wife and I can hear every blooming step you take. Sounds like a bunch of elephants in football boots marching up and down. Why on earth are you spotting from this building anyway? It's only six stories high and your view is cut off on two sides by much bigger buildings. We've never had spotters on this roof before and it makes no sense to have them now."

Regis wanted to say, "This is the only building we can see the German when he comes out, you silly bastard—and get the hell out of here back to your nice warm flat while we freeze our arses off." Instead he bit his tongue and said, "We don't make the rules. Our superiors shift the spotters around from time to time to get different views. We'll probably be moving on in a few days."

"That makes no sense at all. Stupid bureaucrats. They have their you-know-whats stuck up their you-know-whats."

"We agree with you," said Platt, "but what can we do. We're just following orders."

"Well, one thing you can do is stop jumping around and disturbing everyone's sleep. What with the bombs keeping us awake half the night and you keeping us awake the other half, we are never going to get any sleep. If it keeps up, I'm going to report this to your superiors. Mark my words," warned the man.

"Yes, sir, we'll try to be quieter," Platt said. He thought, *Go back to your bed and, if you come up here griping one more time, I'll bounce you off the roof if my frostbitten hands will let me get a grip on your fat neck.*

After the man left, Regis said, "We had better stop walking around. I know the chief warned the Home Guard commander in this area what we would be doing, but if that old geezer complains, somebody who doesn't know the plan might tell him there isn't anyone from the guard supposed to be up here. We'd better tell Dixon. I don't know what he will do about it. The fewer outsiders who know about this, the better."

They had already done three shifts on the wall and

nobody had come or gone into the house. They knew Tom had been there, but he went in and out over the back wall.

Tom had called Dixon on the three evenings following his trip to Scotland Yard. In each call, he reported that everything with Leuzinger was the same as before. The calls were quite brief, the report short, and the thanks coming from Dixon were short, but heartfelt. This evening's call was a little longer for two reasons. First, Dixon told him that Leuzinger's letter had been picked up, but the attempt to tail the man who picked it up had failed. He also told him that it was probable that members of the spy ring—some or all of whom might be Irish—would be coming to get Leuzinger shortly, perhaps within the next day or two.

When he had been at Scotland Yard, Dixon had told Tom that some of the German agents in Britain were from the Republic of Ireland. His conversation that night with Dixon reminded Tom of that. Tom had learned in his geography class a couple of years earlier that that Ireland was made up of Northern Ireland, which was part of Great Britain, and the Republic of Ireland, which was not. He had learned how the two parts had at one time not been divided, but were partitioned many years ago because of a number of reasons, including religious differences and animosity toward England by many people who were now citizens of the Republic. What he hadn't learned in his geography class was why certain citizens of the Republic of Ireland were willing to be German agents.

In his report to Dixon that evening, he had asked him why Irish people were willing to be agents of Germany against Britain. Dixon tried to explain, recognizing that Tom was only fourteen years old and, even though he was obviously very advanced for his years, he was still a boy.

"Almost all the citizens of the Republic would never help the Germans. Although their country is neutral, they know how dreadful Nazis are and what terrible things they have done. However, traditionally, many Irish citizens have not liked the English because of the way they feel the English have treated them. Many have actually hated the English. Some—not a lot, but some—have been willing to help the Germans. Not because they agree with what the Germans are doing, but because the Germans are at war with England. Tom, there is an old saying—'the enemy of my enemy is my friend.' Do you understand?"

"I think so."

"Continue to be very careful, Tom. Scotland Yard detectives are on the roof of the flats across from the house twenty-four hours a day. Remember that the men who come to get Leuzinger may arrive when you're there. I hope not. But if they do, just act the way you have been acting. I'm sure they won't hurt you. It would not help their escape if they did."

Just as they were about to hang up, Tom remembered something. "You wanted me to see if he has a gun. He does. I saw it. It's very small. I thought it was just a toy, but he told me some things about it and it was real."

CHAPTER FIFTY-SEVEN

GEORGE DUGGAN SAT BY himself in the kitchen, drinking his third cup of strong coffee. Irene, Jimmy, Henry, and Fred had long since gone to bed. He had agonized over which two to select for the Leuzinger mission. He could go. Pre-war, it might have looked a little strange for a man of his age still actively working in a job requiring strength and physical dexterity. Nowadays, with most of the younger men in the service, it was not unusual to see older men called back to perform work requiring hard labor.

The five of them were an odd group. He was German. His real name was Wolfgang Steiner. He had been a staunch fascist from the early days—even before the formation of the brown shirts. He had served several lengthy prison terms in Germany for fascist activities before the rise of Hitler. In the thirties, he had been sent undercover to England to form a spy cell in anticipation of what turned out to be the Second World War. He had successfully integrated himself into English life. His forged papers were perfect and impenetrable and his English had a touch of the Midlands and no German accent. His "wife," Irene, was actually Heidi Russlander. She was born and raised in Linz, Austria, and had also come to fascism early in life. She had worked for various right-wing extremist organizations well before the Austrian Anschluss. She was actually a distant relative of the Fuhrer and had even been a guest at the Eagle's Nest in Bavaria. She had been sent to England in the thirties to blend in and become part of a spy cell and had acquired a perfectly acceptable English accent. She was ostensibly the wife of George, but that relationship was non-sexual and purely business. She and George were dedicated without reservation to Nazism and the Fuhrer and were both lifelong virulent anti-Semites.

Unlike George and Irene Duggan, Henry (Heinrich von Bernheim) was a blue blood—born to Prussian nobility and brought up in the lap of luxury. He was classically educated, having taken firsts at Oxford in Latin and seventeenth-century English literature. Similar to George and Irene, he was a dedicated Nazi and anti-Semite. He had been recruited into the spy business while still at Oxford. He had returned to Germany after being awarded his degree at Oxford and was spirited back into England with false papers before the start of the war. He brought a variety of talents with him. He was fluent in English, French, German, Spanish, and Italian. He was a master of accents and could easily pass for a cockney, a Scotsman, an Irishman, or any number of European nationalities. He was also a master of disguises, choosing to create his own and those of his compatriots. He was an accomplished actor who had performed lead roles in theater companies at Oxford and in Germany.

Jimmy (Liam Grady) and Fred (Sean O'Flaherty) were citizens of the Republic of Ireland. They had both been born and raised in Dublin and had made their living as construction workers. Their passion, however, was acts of terrorism (or in their view, acts of patriotism) against the British troops (or in their view, illegal occupiers of Northern Ireland). Both had been involved in clandestine operations against the Black and Tan (the British constabulary so named because of the color of their uniforms and characteristic belts). Fred was a well-reasoned, highly intelligent, and thoughtful person—despite his lack of much formal education. Jimmy's talents lay elsewhere. He was by no means as bright as the others were. He was, in fact, a cold-blooded assassin whose skill, and indeed pleasure, was killing the English. Neither Fred nor Jimmy were Nazi's or particularly anti-Semitic. Their value to the German high command was that they were courageous, loyal, and totally anti-English.

George had made up his mind. There was never a question about Irene. She had been helpful in various missions in the past and would be again in the future, but this project required two men. He would not go. He was still strong and plowing through the rubble of the bombed-out building would not prove any obstacle for him. He prided himself on his physical ability and stamina, but this would be a project better handled by younger men. Besides, if the mission failed and the two men were taken, it would be better if it were not him. Not that he was a coward, far from it. But he had more value to the organization than the others did.

The big decision was which of the three younger men to drop. They were all talented and they all brought different strengths to consider. Suddenly, he got up from the table. He would drop Jimmy. It would annoy him, but so be it. Jimmy was the best in the event of a fight. He was an expert with any type of weapon. He was ruthless and would take as many with him before they finished him, but he sometimes let his anger and strong antagonistic feelings govern his common sense. George couldn't allow that. This was not a project that required muscle. It required quick thinking and smart decision-making. Those were not Jimmy's strong suits. No, this was a task for Henry and Fred.

The decision made, George let out a big yawn. He looked at his watch. Somehow or other it had gotten to be three o'clock in the morning. He headed for bed. At his age, he found that three or four hours of sleep was enough. He would keep Jimmy busy by having him communicate with Germany about Leuzinger's evacuation. They had experienced luck with transportation to Ireland and occasionally with pickups by U-boat. Captain Leuzinger would be at the farmhouse soon. George looked forward to meeting him. He was apparently a highly decorated war hero. It would be good to talk with a German officer—even for a short time—who had recently been in the Fatherland. George was asleep almost before his head hit the pillow. That was one of his many talents.

Chapter Fifty-Eight

"Jimmy, I'm going to send Henry and Fred to pick up Leuzinger," George told the assembled group at breakfast the next morning.

Seeing the disappointment on Jimmy's face, he said, "I have an important task for you. I want you to radio our contacts at the German High Command. Tell them we will shortly have a highly decorated German pilot who parachuted into London when his bomber was shot down. Tell them we have already verified that the pilot is Captain Leuzinger and that HQ has confirmed the identity. Finally, tell them that we recommend a U-boat pickup—if that is at all possible—as the safest method but, if we must, we will try the riskier avenue of fake credentials and passage to Ireland by ferry. We will provide them more updated information in a day or two and get coordinates for a U-boat pickup—if that is to be the method."

Turning to Henry and Fred, George said, "Leuzinger has told the boy that the letter was to be sent to his Irish friend, Eamon Shaughnessy. The boy has been told extensive details of that friendship and, if one of you trips up playing Eamon, we could be in trouble and we might then have to dispose of the boy, something I don't want to do."

George anticipated that Henry was about to detail his acting ability and his facility with accents. "I know you could play the part very well, Henry, but you will be under a lot of pressure and you will have a lot of other things to remember. This mission will not be played on the stage at the university. If the boy happens to be present, tell Leuzinger that Eamon dearly wanted to come, but his wife is about to give birth to their first child. She has had a difficult pregnancy and the doctor says both her health and the health of the unborn child are at severe risk. It's possible that Leuzinger will pretend that one of you is Eamon before you are able to say that Eamon couldn't come. If the boy is there, we can't do anything about it. If Leuzinger addresses one of you as Eamon, that will be your cue to be Eamon. If he just says hello without specifically identifying one of you as Eamon, then Henry, you're the actor, you'll have to be Eamon."

"Very well," said Henry. "What about disguises?"

"You'll use the van without any signage. Once you are close to London, find a quiet, secluded spot and put the London County Council Water and Power signage that is in the back of the van on the frames on both sides of the van. You remember that we made those signs and used them when we picked up that pilot—what was his name, Driezen or Friesen?—in London a while back. It would not do to put the signage on now. Driving a London County Council vehicle through Staffordshire would be unusual and suspicious. Don't forget to remove the signage in a quiet spot on your way back. I'll leave it to your expertise, Henry, to create appropriate disguises for you and Fred. Don't overdo it. Water and Power workers don't ordinarily have thick beards and dark glasses. The suitable work clothes are in the shed. Don't forget to bring a set for the pilot. Be sure to take your identification papers and your driver's licenses." George paused and lowered his voice. "And don't forget to carry your cyanide pills. The end result of our work in this country is to kill the English, not kill ourselves. Only use those pills if absolutely necessary. Finally, do not draw attention to yourselves, drive within the speed limit. The headlights are slits as required by blackout regulations so that should cause no problem. Any questions?"

"If the boy is present, wouldn't it be wise to kill him? He might get suspicious," asked Jimmy.

"Absolutely not," said George, visibly irritated. "I have lived in this country a long time and I've learned a lot of things. One is that Jewish parents are cautious about their children's safety. They expect them to grow up to be doctors or moneylenders or something like that. If their child is not where he or she is supposed to be within a set timetable, they will organize a search, call the police, and raise Cain. The last thing we want is a brouhaha and the police searching for the boy. We want to slip away nice and quietly and, with any luck at all, the authorities will never know Leuzinger was ever in that house or that we came and got him. Henry, you and Fred will leave first thing in the morning. Now, let's get the map out, pinpoint exactly where the house is, and calculate the best way to get there."

CHAPTER FIFTY-NINE

SOME TIME INTO THE trip Henry had spelled Fred at the wheel after Fred had driven for the first few hours. They were getting closer to London.

"Keep a look out for a good place to pull off and put on the London County Council signs," he said.

"Wait a while. We're still too far from London. We don't want to do it too soon," answered Fred.

They drove on in silence for the next half hour—both of them chain-smoking cheap cigarettes. "There's a sign for a lane two miles ahead on the left," called out Fred who had been monitoring the road signs. "That's as good as any and we're close enough."

Henry nodded and slowed down so as not to miss the cut off. It was difficult to see. The approach to the cut off was obscured by trees and dense underbrush. He turned in and traveled about a quarter of a mile when he saw a flat, grassy area partly hidden by bushes.

"Perfect. Let's get it done here."

They had inserted one of the signs on the side of the van closest to the road and were about to insert the other which was lying face up on the ground when they heard the sound of a motorcycle approaching from the direction they had come. It pulled up behind the van and a police constable wearing a leather jacket, helmet, and boots got off and came toward them.

"Let me do the talking," hissed Henry. "Good day, constable. Anything wrong?"

"I saw you chaps turn off the motorway and reckoned that maybe you were lost. There's nothing down this lane but two or three small farms. Were you on your way to one of them? You're not having trouble with your van, are you?" he said in a friendly voice. Before Henry had a chance to answer, the constable looked down at the sign on the ground. His voice became a little less cheery.

"What's all this then? Why are you putting those signs on the van and why did you come down this lonely road to do it? Show me the registration for this van and let me see both of your driving licenses."

"Certainly, constable," said Henry as he dug in his wallet. "Fred, get the registration and show the constable your license."

Fred got back in the van and, while pulling out the registration papers from the glove compartment, he reached carefully under the seat and loosened the Luger pistol hidden in a space carved out in the upholstery. He would have no hesitancy in killing the officer. He was no novice. He had killed before—several times—but this would be more than a little dangerous. It would not be long before the constable was missed and there would be police everywhere.

While all this was going on, Henry was thinking as fast as he could. "See, constable, here's the way it is. My mother lives in Burton. She is very ill. Cancer—the doctor only gives her a few weeks. Fred here and me work for the London

County Council. We're repairmen. Mostly investigating and fixing leaks. With all the bombing in London, we have to work long hours with no time off. There's an awful lot of water in bombed buildings."

"Well, I'm sorry about your mother and how hard the two of you have to work. Working double shifts on this bloody motorcycle is not exactly a picnic, I can tell you. What has your mother and your hard work got to do with you being out here changing signs on your van?"

"Our supervisor let me borrow the van to go see my mother, but told me to take the signs off when we left London and put them back on when we came back. He only let us go for a day. We left London last night and will be back tonight. Outside of London, we would be away from our jurisdiction and that's the reason the signs came off and now are going back on. Fred came along to keep me company."

The constable examined the licenses and registration papers slowly. Fred, who was back in the van with his hand, now sweaty, on the Luger, said nothing. "Why didn't you just pull over on the motorway and change the sign there?"

"It just seemed a little safer to do it away from the traffic."

"I never knew that government vehicles could remove and replace their identities with sign changes put in those slots on the sides. I thought the identification was painted directly on the vans. I never saw anything like this," queried the officer.

"I never had either," agreed Henry, "but with the war and everything and so many vehicles being damaged and destroyed by the bombing, the various agencies have to borrow from each other. To avoid confusion, some of the vehicles have this ability to change signs to reflect which agency is operating the vehicle. I think it's only done in London."

"Well, I suppose that makes sense—although I can't say I fully understand it. You had better get going—it's still quite a way to London."

Fred relaxed his grip on the Luger and smiled at the constable as Henry retrieved the licenses and registration, replaced the remaining sign and climbed into the driver's seat. They said their farewells, told him that they wouldn't be coming back to Burton for some time, and the constable roared off back to the motorway.

Fred and Henry didn't speak for a while. Finally, Fred said, "How did you dream up that blarney? I couldn't have come up with that in a month of Sundays. Must be your university education. Do you suppose he bought it entirely?"

"I think so, but if he checks on this nonsense about government agencies switching signs, he's going to find out that it's a lie. We've got to get Leuzinger quickly and we'll have to return to the farm by a different route. We don't want to run into that officer again. I wish we could change vans or at least repaint this one, but we don't have time."

Officer Ferguson returned to police headquarters at the end of his shift. "You know, Sergeant, I ran across a strange thing tonight," he said to his supervisor. "Two fellows on Lomond Lane were putting London County Council signs on a van. Said they worked for the County Council and had permission to use the van to go see his ill mother, but they were not to have the signs on the van while out of London. Sounded like a cock-and-bull story, but I let them go. What do you think we should do? Maybe call somebody at the London County Council. I could do it now if you think I should."

Sergeant Ramsey was tired. He had worked a double shift and had to finish some paperwork before he could go home. He never raised his head from the papers and barely heard what Ferguson had said.

"Maybe they were German spies on their way to London to blow up Buckingham Palace." He laughed out loud at his lame attempt at humor. "Go on home and get some sleep. Remember you're back on duty tomorrow afternoon."

"All right, Sarge. I'm off."

Sergeant Ramsey grunted something without stopping with the never-ending paperwork.

If he doesn't care, I'm sure I don't, Ferguson thought as he climbed back on his motorcycle and headed home.

CHAPTER SIXTY

AS THEY APPROACHED LONDON's East End, Fred was studying the map as Henry was driving. "Left at the next turning then two miles down Hackney Road and then a couple more turns and we're there. I'll tell you when to turn."

Henry followed the directions. After a couple of wrong moves and some swearing by Henry at Fred, they arrived at Fleming Street. Henry parked the van directly in front of the house. They both got out. Fred took the Luger out of its hiding place and placed it in the front pocket of his overalls. He walked to the rear, opened the back door, and took out a rectangular dark brown tool case. Ordinarily it would have contained pliers, bolts, hammers, and a number of other items necessary for repairing leakage. On this occasion, it contained nothing but an extra set of work clothes for Leuzinger. It was half past three in the afternoon. Henry got out of the driver's side and waited for Fred to close the back door of the van.

Outside the flats on the opposite side of the street was a horse and cart with a deliveryman carrying bags of coal into the flats. He was about to lift a large bag off the cart when he looked over in the direction of Fred who was just closing the back of the van after retrieving the toolbox and Henry who was standing next to the driver's side.

"'Hello, mate," he called out in a loud cockney voice. "Got some work to do in that building, do you?"

"Yes," said Henry in a cockney accent that rivaled that of the coal man "We've got to check for water leakage."

"Well, you be very careful, you hear. That place is a deathtrap. I was here yesterday and there was a lot of creaking. You get hit with one of them beams and you won't be fixing no more water leaks."

"We'll be careful. Don't you worry. We've been in a lot of these buildings and we're still here."

The coal man waved, picked up the bag of coal, swung it onto his shoulders, and disappeared into the flats. Fred took a look around. There was no one else on the street. He and Henry walked quickly around the barriers and into the house. They picked their way carefully through the rubble toward the back of the house. As they got to the back room, they heard voices; one was that of an adult—the other the voice of a boy. Fred and Henry froze in their tracks and looked at each other.

Blast, thought Henry. *The young Jew is here.* Before going into the room, Henry said in a loud whisper, loud enough to be heard in the room, but not loud enough to carry much further, "Don't be afraid. Eamon sent us." Later he would wonder why he didn't think of that earlier. Calling out that Eamon sent them before they went into the back room would have precluded all the instructions of George as to what to do if Leuzinger greeted one of them as Eamon before they had a chance to forestall that by saying Eamon couldn't come.

George is supposed to be the leader and the brains of the outfit. Why didn't he think of something this simple instead of going through the rigmarole of what to say if Leuzinger identified Eamon first. Well, thought Henry, *in this business, you can't think of everything, but when your ruddy life may depend on it, you had better try.*

CHAPTER SIXTY-ONE

SMITHERS AND PLATT HAD worked a double shift on the roof of the flats. They had been there since midnight and it was now almost half past three in the afternoon. The two detectives who were supposed to relieve them at nine in the morning had been called off on some other urgent project. They were tired, cold, stiff, hungry, a little wet (it had drizzled for an hour or two in the early hours of the morning), and extremely irritable. They had been warned not to walk around more than was necessary for fear that the old geezer who lived on the top floor would stir up a hornet's nest if they again disturbed his sleep.

Platt wiped his reddened eyes with his handkerchief and resumed peering through binoculars at the face of the bombed-out house. Gazing at the same view for hours on end caused the eyes to play funny tricks. The scarred and broken brick façade seemed to change colors. The shattered remnant of the roof seemed to straighten out and then curve. Platt became fascinated by two birds that had made a nest on the side of the chimney that rested at a crazy angle on what was left of the roof. All morning what must have been the male bird had flown back and forth with pieces of twigs in its beak while the female remained seated—presumably about to produce a family in their new abode. *At least some living creatures were performing something of value,* thought Platt. Periodically, Platt would turn the binoculars up and down the street. People, mostly women, would come and go, usually with shopping bags. Occasionally, a tradesman would deliver something. Once in a while, a van or a car would go up or down the street. None stopped outside the bombed-out house.

A horse and cart delivering coal pulled up outside the flats. Platt, who was about to pass the binoculars to Smithers, watched idly as the coal man got down off the cart, put a feed bag on the face of his horse, and started to get a bag of coal off the cart. Platt yawned and stretched. A van turned onto Fleming and stopped outside the house. Two men got out. One went to the back and opened the door. The other stood by the driver's side. There seemed to be a short conversation between the coal man and the two men from the van. The coal man took a sack and went into the flats. The two men from the van went into the bombed-out house, one carrying a tool case.

"It's them!" Platt said to Smithers. "It's them. Go! Go! Go!" Smithers grabbed the AR7 and ran down the stairs. Platt grabbed the radiophone and plugged in numbers. "Yes," a voice said. "Activate the AR7. They're here." Without waiting for a reply, he disconnected and plugged in another number. It was a direct line to Dixon. "Two men in a brown van just went into the house. License plate CKY 498. It has a sign on the side 'London County Council.' I've notified the trail vehicle and it is activating the AR7. Smithers is placing the other unit under the van now."

"Good work, Harry," Dixon said. "We're on it."

Smithers careened down the stairs two at a time. At the bottom, he bumped Mrs. Lowenstein who was just about to go into her ground floor apartment. She dropped her carrier bag and the sparse results of her long shopping trek spilled out on the floor. Smithers didn't stop, but said "sorry" as he sped outside.

"What do you mean, *sorry*? Look what you've done. Running into an old lady like that and not even stopping to help. Didn't your mother teach you anything?" she yelled at him as she painfully bent over and scooped up her pitifully few items. She looked up in time to see Smithers kneeling down behind the van and reaching far underneath while seemingly attaching something to the bottom of the van. He then got up and ran back inside the flats.

As he ran by her and back up the stairs, she called after him, "What were you doing to that van? That's not your van, is it? I'm going to call the police about this, you rude man."

Smithers stopped halfway up the first flight of steps and turned. "No, it's not my van. I'm with the Home Guard. We're spotting for fires and enemy planes. I saw the randomizer fall of that van and I thought I'd do a good turn and put it back on for them. I was a boy scout you know." He smiled.

"What's a randomizer?" she asked.

He had no idea—he had blurted out the first thing that came to mind.

"It's a newfangled gadget they've just come up with that's supposed to increase petrol mileage."

"I thought I saw you bring that thing down the stairs with you?" she said.

"Oh no. You must be mistaken. I was just holding my coat. That randomizer was lying on the ground just under the van."

"Well, be more careful next time, young man. You can't go around knocking old ladies down."

Without another word she went into her flat, by no means entirely convinced by his explanation.

Chapter Sixty-Two

LEUZINGER REACHED UNDER THE pillow he was sitting on and pulled out the small pistol that Tom had picked up after it fell off the couch.

Leuzinger pointed the derringer at the door and said, "Come in slowly with your hands straight in front of you, palms up and open."

They came in, obeying Leuzinger's instructions. "All right, who are you and where is Eamon?"

"We're good friends of the dear man," said Henry in an Irish accent that no citizen of the old sod would have faulted. "His poor wife is about to deliver his child. She is proper poorly and the doctor says it will be touch and go with both the woman and the child. He sends his undying regrets and hopes you'll forgive him this once, but he had to stay with her."

"And you two?" asked Leuzinger, still pointing the derringer at the newcomers who remained still, arms outstretched and hands open.

"I owe Eamon my life," said Henry. "He came to my rescue in a fierce fight where three thieves would have killed me for my purse if it had not been for Eamon. He asked me to come and help you and I could deny him nothing."

"What about you?" Leuzinger turned to Fred, still holding the derringer.

"I had no money. No job. No place to stay when I came from Ireland. Eamon loaned me money and gave me a room to live in until I got on my feet. He's the finest man I know. I would die for him. There is no one like him." Fred's accent was as convincing as Henry's, which was no great accomplishment since—unlike Henry—he was Irish.

Now satisfied that the charade—performed for Tom's benefit—was successful, Leuzinger put the gun in his pocket and motioned to Henry and Fred to put their hands down.

"Forgive me, gentlemen, for my rudeness, but in my position one can't be too careful. I am indeed eternally grateful to both of you and—with God's help—our mutual friend Eamon and his wife and child will all be well," Leuzinger said. "This young lad is my close friend, Tom Sloan. Without his help, I would now either be dead or in a British POW camp and would never see my dear wife again."

Henry and Fred dutifully shook hands with Tom and smiled broadly at him. "It's a brave lad you are and no mistake," said Henry. "What you have done is indeed noble."

"What's the plan?" asked Leuzinger.

"We have a van outside. The two of us will help you to the door," said Henry "I will go with you to the van. My friend will go out the back way—over the wall into the alley—and we will pick him up in a spot he and I have arranged."

Looking momentarily puzzled, Leuzinger asked, "Won't that waste valuable time? Why don't the three of us go out the front way?"

Fred chimed in, "If someone saw two of us go in, they might find it suspicious if three of us came out."

"Good idea. I hadn't thought about that. What about the fact that two able-bodied men came in and two came out, but one is now limping?"

"Nothing we can do about that. We decided it would be too difficult taking you out the back way. Anyway, it will probably look like one of us got hurt in this dangerous building. I'm sure it happens all the time," said Henry.

Leuzinger turned to Tom and said, "You'd better get going out the back way." He stuck out his hand then pulled it back. "A hand shake is not enough." Clumsily, he got to his feet and gave Tom a big hug, which both of them secretly found infinitely distasteful, but for enormously different reasons. "A simple thank you is totally insufficient, but it's all I have at the moment. I promised you before and I promise you again that we'll see each other again."

Tom thought, *Yes, we would like to see each other again— with you it would be me in a concentration camp and with me it would be you at the end of a hangman's rope.* but instead He said something that he nonetheless meant, "I hope I do see you again. Good-bye."

With that, he went out the back, through the wire fence, and over the wall. He ran as fast as he could down the alley, around the corner, and home where his mother gave him a hug of relief—the second hug he had received within ten minutes, but one that was not distasteful.

CHAPTER SIXTY-THREE

"ARE YOU SURE THAT lad is a Jew?" said Fred. "Sloan is not a Jewish name. I knew several Sloans in Ireland. None of them were Jews."

"He told me he was a Jew," said Leuzinger. "Besides—I can smell them a mile off."

"He didn't even look Jewish and I didn't smell anything," replied Fred.

"Hadn't we better get out of here?" said Leuzinger, now tired of the conversation. "Take my word for it—he's a Jew, all right. Let's get out of here."

Henry went to the front of the house and cautiously peeked outside. There did not appear to be anybody on the street.

He came back hurriedly and said, "Let's get going."

Fred and Henry supported Leuzinger by looping his arms over their shoulders. It was difficult going. Leuzinger had received no medical attention for his broken leg and the homemade splint was only of rudimentary help. He was weakened by his enforced inactivity over a number of days, making it even harder to move him to the front of the house. The obstacles created by fallen beams and other debris didn't make it easier. Finally, they got within a few feet of the front door.

"Okay, Fred, you nip out the back and we'll meet you in five minutes where we arranged," said Henry.

Fred carefully extricated himself from Leuzinger's arm and went toward the back of the house. Without Fred's help, Henry's burden of getting Leuzinger to the van was much more difficult. After a struggle that left both men covered in sweat, they got to the van unseen—or so they thought.

Mrs. Lowenstein had been watching their painful progress to the van. *That poor man*, she thought. *They should never make them go into those dangerous places. He could have been killed. I am going to tell them that a man put something under their van. It might have been a bomb for all I know.*

Henry had helped Leuzinger into the passenger seat and had climbed into the driver's side. He started the engine and pulled away from the curb. Mrs. Lowenstein came running out of the flats shouting, "Stop! Stop! Somebody put something under your van."

Through the rearview mirror, Henry saw an old woman running down the pavement toward the van, waving her arms, and shouting something. She was about thirty yards away.

"What's she saying?" asked Henry.

"I can't make it out," Leuzinger replied as he rolled down the window. "Can you slow down?"

Henry braked, rolled his window down, and put his head out. "What did you say?"

Mrs. Lowenstein didn't hear Henry, but she shouted again much louder, "Somebody put something under your van."

Chapter Sixty-Four

Rose Lowenstein had been a pretty decent runner in her younger days. She had won several medals in school and, after graduation, while running for Burnham Harriers. She was mostly a quarter-miler, but she had come third on two occasions running the 220. She was now seventy-eight and had not run a step in more than fifty years. After only fifteen yards, she was spent. Her legs were like rubber. She was breathing like a freight train and her face had turned scarlet. She stopped cold, feeling as though she was going to faint.

Henry called out again, "Are you calling to us? What did you say?"

Mrs. Lowenstein said nothing. She couldn't. It was all she could do to gasp for breath.

"Let's go," said Leuzinger impatiently. "She probably saw the sign on the van and wanted us to fix her toilet or her washbasin. We can't hang around here."

"You're right," responded Henry. "She certainly could run for an old lady." They both laughed as Henry accelerated and turned the corner.

Mrs. Lowenstein rested for a few minutes and then walked slowly back to her apartment. She got a cold wet towel, put it on her forehead, and sat down on the one comfortable chair in the house.

"Well, it didn't blow up, so it probably was just a randolizer, or whatever that rude man said it was, that fell off," she said out loud. She had seen an American picture at the Odeon several days earlier where some gangsters had attached a bomb to a car's ignition and, when a member of another gang had tried to start the car, it exploded in flames.

The trail van was parked around the corner from Fleming Street. Detective Randolph called the chief. "We've activated the AR7 and it's picking up a signal. The van just passed us and stopped on the corner of Lyman Road and Woodruff. It picked up a man who hopped in the back and took off north on Woodruff."

"Okay, Randolph, keep well back, but get going. The AR7 has a workable range of two and a half miles, so there is no reason to get close. It will also chart what the distance is between the two AR7s. Whatever you do, don't let them see you. If you do come into visual contact, drop back. We have moved out in two cars. We'll stay well behind you, but keep in touch and let us know the direction they're traveling. Oh, and tell Platt to pack up the roof surveillance and drop over and make sure young Sloan got home all right."

"Will do, Chief," replied Randolph.

The procession of motor vehicles continued winding their way through London. Henry was driving the brown van, Randolph and Hennessey were in the trail van, Randolph driving and Hennesey wearing headphones and monitoring the signal from the AR7 and the two Scotland Yard cars each containing four men took up the rear. From front to back, there was a distance of about four miles, with Randolph being about a mile behind the brown van.

It was a long, slow, and tortuous journey to get out of London. Bomb damage and emergency vehicles caused numerous road closures and difficult detours. Fred was continually reviewing the map to navigate for Henry and to suggest roads he might take to avoid some of the trouble.

Finally, after two hours, the caravan got through the worst of the traffic and proceeded north through open country. For a considerable period of time they encountered little traffic and were able to maintain a reasonable speed. Fred cautioned Henry that they were approaching the alternate route that would cause them to avoid the main road. They did not want to run into the same motorcycle officer they had encountered on their way into London again.

"A mile on the right. It's a street call Walham Cross. Take that and we go about four miles on it."

As they approached Walham Cross, they saw flashing red lights at the turn and a police car blocking it. They pulled off the main road and stopped close to the police car.

"Can't we go on Walham Cross?" asked Henry.

"No. There's an unexploded bomb about half a mile toward the Hightree Junction. No one can pass. The bomb squad is working on it," said the officer. "Where are you chaps going?"

"Just north of Burton," replied Henry.

"Why in the world would you want to go down Walham Cross? That will take you miles out of your way. Just continue on the main road north."

"Somebody told us Walham Cross was a shortcut."

"Whoever that somebody is either doesn't know the area or is pulling your leg."

"Thank you. Officer,""

Henry pulled back onto the main road.

"What do we do now? We don't want to meet up with that motorcycle officer who saw us changing the signs again. We got away with that last time. I don't want to chance our luck a second time," said Fred

"We have no choice. There is no detour other than going back about twenty miles and picking up the east coast route. That will take hours. We'll just have to chance it. That blighter can't be on duty twenty-four hours a day and in the same location," replied Henry.

About fifteen minutes later, they hit a deep pothole. The van swerved, jumped in the air, and came down with a bang. A hubcap went clattering across the roadway. Leuzinger hit his broken leg against the dashboard and cried out in pain. Fred was bounced around in the back of the van and jammed his hand on the bare metal side. Henry momentarily lost control, but quickly straightened out the van and resumed speed and direction.

"Sorry. I didn't see that pothole. It gets dark early these days and bloody slits for lights make it almost impossible to see the road. Are you all right, Captain?"

"Yes, I'm all right. I took a bang on my leg, but it's starting to feel better. What about you, Fred?"

"I'm fine," said Fred. "For a moment, I was careening around like a snooker ball."

Distracted by the inability to take the Walham Cross route and by the slamming into the pothole, neither Fred nor Henry remembered to pull over and remove the London County Council signs from the sides of the van.

Chapter Sixty-Five

"They've stopped," Hennessey yelled.

Dixon cried, "Everybody stop *now*! Pull over to the side of the road. Randolph, how far are you behind the van?"

Hennessey looked at the AR7 screen and said, "A little over a mile."

"Chief, we're a little over a mile behind," said Randolph.

Dixon turned to Detective Stephens in the back of the car. "You know this road. What's up ahead where they could have stopped? Is there a petrol station or a café or something?"

"Chief, there's nothing for miles. Not a house—not even a turn off. It's nothing but forest," replied Stephens.

"Are you quite sure?" asked Dixon.

"I know this road like the back of my hand. My parents live about twenty miles further on. There's nothing until you get to Ladbourne Corner, which is about fifteen miles from where we are and about ten miles from where the van stopped," answered Stephens.

"Maybe they are just changing drivers. We'll wait."

Ten minutes went by. "Anything happening, Randolph?" asked Dixon.

"Nothing. They haven't moved an inch."

"It can't be a change of drivers or a lavatory break. It wouldn't take that much time. They are too smart to have run out of petrol. Maybe they got a flat tire," speculated Dixon. "We'll give it another five minutes."

Another five minutes passed and the AR7 measured no movement. "They could have changed all four tires, changed drivers, and had lavatory breaks by now. Randolph, move up. If you see the stopped van, go on by and keep going."

Randolph pulled away from the side of the road. After a mile he suddenly swerved to avoid a big pothole in the middle of his lane. An object on the side of the road caught his eye. He stopped got out and ran over to look at it. He ran back to the van with the object in his hands and called Dixon.

"Chief, bad news," he shouted excitedly.

"What is it? Out with it, man," shouted Dixon.

"It's the AR7. I just found it by the side of the road. They either detected it and removed it or it fell off. Their van is gone. It's nowhere in sight."

CHAPTER SIXTY-SIX

"RANDOLPH, YOU GO AFTER them. They probably have twenty miles or more on you by now, so you'll have to pour it on. We'll assume for the moment that it fell off, although I don't know how. Try to avoid detection if you can. If you catch sight of them, don't lose them," Dixon ordered.

"In this rain with the reduced visibility and the slit lights, it will take quite a while to catch up with them—if we ever do—but we'll do our best. Incidentally, we just avoided a large pothole right where we found the AR7, so be careful," Randolph said.

"Don't worry about us—just get going."

The two Scotland Yard cars reached the pothole and Dixon told the driver to pull over. The area was heavily wooded as it had been for a number of miles. The rain was coming down even more heavily. There was no moon and it was extremely dark. There were huge rain puddles along the side of the road. The pothole was deep. There were skid marks in front of it and shreds of what looked like pieces of rubber caught on its edges.

"Looks like at least one vehicle has hit this hole pretty hard. Probably caused by the heavy rain seeping below the roadway and undercutting the covering," Dixon said. A metallic object on the side of the road caught his eye. Surely, Randolph hadn't left the AR7 there. He walked over. It wasn't the AR7. It was a shiny hubcap. It probably hadn't been there long. It looked too big to have come from a passenger car.

He went back to his car and called Randolph. "Listen, Randolph. I'm convinced they did not find the AR7. I am almost certain they hit that pothole—and hit it very hard. It would take a pretty good knock to dislodge the AR7, but I think that's what happened. I found a hubcap that probably got knocked off at the same time. I'm sure they don't know we're onto them. At least that's what I'm guessing. If you manage to catch up with them, try to avoid them seeing you if you possibly can. It's rotten luck, but we'll have to handle it the best we can. We'll be following you. Keep in touch."

Dixon was torn. He could call ahead to local police departments, give them a description of the vehicle, and give them a chance to tail it. If they were discovered, they could go ahead and apprehend the occupants of the van. The probability was that Randolph and Hennessey would not catch up with the van and there would be no arrests at all. The van occupants were clever and experienced. Local police would do their best, but surely they would be detected. That avenue almost certainly would not lead to the apprehension of the ringleader or leaders. Dixon sighed. He would gamble. He would not involve the local police. He would hope against hope that Randolph and Hennessey would pick up the trail. If they didn't, they would lose the German pilot and two lower-level spies. If they did, the prize might be the top Nazi agent in Britain. If he succeeded, he would be the toast of Scotland Yard. If he didn't, he would merely be toast.

Chapter Sixty-Seven

Constable Ted Ferguson was not a happy man. It was a cold rainy night and he had been at home enjoying a roaring fire, a pint of Guinness stout, and the newspaper when the phone rang. His wife answered and he heard her say, "All right. I'll tell him."

It was the desk sergeant. "Joe Collins has come down with the flu and you have to take his shift. You have to be at the station in half an hour. Oh, and by the way, the sergeant wanted you to know he's sorry."

"Sorry is he! He's not as sorry as I am. Why couldn't he pick on someone else? Collins always seems to come down with something on nights like this."

That's how it came about that Ferguson was in a police car at the Ladbourne Corner intersection with his lights turned off. At least he was in a car and not on the motorcycle. He would stay at this corner for fifteen minutes at a time looking for speeders and drunks. He would then patrol for a while before coming back to Ladbourne Corner. There was very little traffic and nothing to relieve the boredom.

He was idly watching the occasional lorry or car go by. With the heavy rain, no one was driving very fast and no one appeared to be drunk. Suddenly something stirred him out of his boredom. The brown van with the sign 'London County Council' on the side went by heading north. *Here, here, here—what's all this then? This is the same van and probably the same two blokes who I talked to earlier today on their way to London. I thought there was something wrong with their story and now I know there is.* For a moment, he thought of putting on his red lights and pulling them over, but something told him not to. He decided to follow the van at a discrete distance and call in to Sergeant Ramsey.

"Sarge, you remember I told you about with those two blokes putting London County Council signs on a van and telling me they had been visiting the mother of one of them who was very ill?"

"Yes. So what?" said a disinterested Sergeant Ramsey.

"That same van with the same signs just passed Ladbourne Corner going north—this morning, they were going south. I'm following them, trying not to be seen."

"That's more than a little odd," said a suddenly more interested Ramsey. "Keep following them. I'll call the London County Council and see if they know anything about one of their vans being up here twice in one day. I'll call you as soon as I can."

Ten minutes later Ferguson's radiophone rang. "London County Council said that van is not one of theirs. They put me straight through to Scotland Yard and to a detective sergeant whose name was Chesney or Chesley, something like that. He gave me the radiophone number of a Chief Inspector Dixon who knows something about the people in that van. You are to call him right away."

Dixon picked up the radiophone as it buzzed. "Yes, this is Chief Inspector Dixon. Who is this?"

Ferguson related his two encounters with the brown van.

"Good work, Ferguson," said Dixon. "Do you have the van in sight right now?"

"Yes, I do, but it is difficult to see very far with the rain and no moon."

"Keep after him, but try not to get too close. I don't want to raise suspicions. Keep this frequency open and call me with any developments. How far past Ladbourne Corner are you?"

"About four miles. I'll call you back soon."

Dixon called Randolph and relayed the development to him. "This may not work. Ferguson sounds like a bright lad, but I doubt that he has much experience with this sort of thing. You keep moving along and I'll get back in touch with you."

CHAPTER SIXTY-EIGHT

LEUZINGER SHIFTED UNCOMFORTABLY AND let out a slight groan. "You all right, Captain?" Henry said with concern in his voice.

"I've stiffened up a bit and I have a dull ache in my leg."

"We should have brought some pain medicine. I quite forgot. I'm sorry."

"I'll be all right. Do we have much farther to go?"

"Probably less than an hour. It would have been quicker, but this rain has slowed us down. We're not too far from Grigsby. Once we're past that small town, we make a series of turns down secondary roads and country lanes. This area is honeycombed with them. You must be looking forward to a hot bath and a comfortable bed after your long stay in that house."

"Thank you. Don't think I am unappreciative. On the contrary, I am forever in your debt. But I would be looking forward with more pleasurable anticipation if the hot bath and comfortable bed were in the Fatherland."

"I understand perfectly," said Henry. "Rest assured that plans are being formulated to get you to Germany as soon as possible. We have had great success in the past in getting pilots back to Germany and we are confident we can do the same for you."

Leuzinger smiled weakly, rested his head on the seat back, and closed his eyes.

Ferguson had checked in with Dixon a couple of times and had reported that he still had the van in sight—although the rain had increased in intensity and visibility was limited. He also told Dixon that the van was a few miles from the small farming town of Grigsby.

"Chief, do you think there is much chance for Randolph and Hennessey to get within visual distance of the van in the next seven or eight miles?" asked Stephens.

"I really don't think there is any chance. What's so important about seven or eight miles?"

"I estimate that Grigsby is about that far away from where the van probably is now. I could be wrong, but that's my best estimate."

"Why is Grigsby significant?"

"Just beyond Grigsby there are a large number of secondary roads and country lanes. Down those roads and lanes there are numerous additional offshoots. I assume that the van is going to branch off on one of those roads or lanes shortly after it passes Grigsby. If it does that and nobody follows it, they'll be impossible to find. The land is dotted with small farms and tiny villages. Some of the roads and lanes lead somewhere and some lead nowhere. It's an incredible maze. As a matter of fact, some of the locals call the area 'the Maze.'"

"Surely, with time and patience and enough men and cars, we could cover the whole area?" asked Dixon knowing in his heart that the answer would not be favorable.

"It would even take an army several months. I'm afraid if they get off this road unseen, we're finished."

Detective Dan Anderson was driving Dixon's vehicle. He had only been with the Yard for three years and was much younger than any of the others were. During the trip, he had said virtually nothing. When Stephens had finished his pessimistic appraisal, Anderson laughed.

"You have a very peculiar sense of humor, Anderson," Dixon said angrily. "I fail to see anything the least bit funny in what Bert has just told us. Perhaps you will let the rest of us in on the joke."

"Forgive me, Chief. I am not laughing because I see anything funny. I am laughing at the irony of the situation."

"Explain yourself," said Dixon, clearly not satisfied with Anderson's answer.

"We have ten Scotland Yard detectives in pursuit of this van. We have the might and the capabilities of the Yard behind us. We have used the most intricate and modern tracking devices. We have used the services of the Yard's best handwriting expert. We have had surveillance performed by the most experienced experts available and we have the Yard's top anti-espionage person leading the chase. With all that, our only chance of finding the spy HQ and the Nazi's top agent in Britain is in the hands of a village policeman who undoubtedly has no technological expertise, no surveillance experience, and no investigatory background. We are in the hands of a policeman whose days are spent catching speeders and drunks."

Dixon said nothing for a long time and then smiled wryly.

"Good analysis, Anderson. The only thing one can rely upon is that there is always the unexpected. There's hope for you yet."

CHAPTER SIXTY-NINE

"I DON'T KNOW FOR sure, but someone may be following us." Fred had been looking out of the back window of the van. Henry had taken a right turn on to a secondary road about two and a half miles past Grigsby. He had then passed three or four country lanes and made a right turn.

"Watch him carefully. I'm going to slow down. See if he does too."

Henry slowed from fifty miles an hour to about thirty and went another mile. "What's he doing?" Henry yelled turning his head toward Fred.

"I can't tell yet. It's so misty that I can barely make him out. He's just a blur back there. Wait a sec. It looks like he's slowing too," said Fred.

"Okay, now I'm going to speed up. Give it about twenty seconds and tell me what he does."

The radiophone beeped and Dixon picked it up. "He slowed for a while and now he's picked up speed again. I slowed when he did, but I haven't picked up speed again. What should I do?" said Ferguson.

"Keep going slowly and turn off as soon as you can. Don't continue to follow them. They're either onto you or they are at least suspicious. Tell me where they are and which way they are heading."

"They turned left off the main road two and a half miles past Grigsby on a secondary road called Gemstone Lane. They went three miles down Gemstone and turned right on Farm Lane and they had gone four miles on Farm when I let them go."

"Where are you now?"

"I pulled off Farm onto a one-lane dirt road called Lime Passage and I stopped about a quarter of a mile up Lime."

"What's your first name?"

"Edward—Ted—but everyone calls me Ace. Don't ask why. It's not because I'm a crack pilot."

"Ace, you stay exactly where you are. We'll catch up with you. I want you to help us figure out where they might have gone."

"I pulled over on the right side. There's a little clearing here. It won't be easy to find them. There are several options off Farm Lane."

Dixon notified the other car and Randolph's tail vehicle what had happened and arranged that they would all meet Ferguson on Lime Passage.

Ferguson was awestruck by the company of a chief inspector and nine other Scotland Yard detectives. After Dixon had introduced everybody, Ferguson said, "I'm very sorry, sir. I probably shouldn't have gotten as close to them as I did, but I was afraid I would lose them and I don't have any experience in this tracking business."

"You've got nothing to apologize for, Ace. You're a godsend. If it hadn't been for you we would have no idea where they've gone. You've given us a chance to find them, which we never would have had without you," reassured Dixon.

Ferguson beamed. "Thank you, sir. We do have one edge. Although there are a lot of forks off Farm Lane further on than I went, there is no way out the other end. A few of the turns have some additional forks, but all of the forks and sub-forks end up being cul-de-sacs. If anyone wants to get out of there and head north, south, east, or west, they have to go back to the road you just came from."

"That is a break," said Dixon. "Do you have any way of knowing how many houses or farms are in the area?"

"It would be the wildest of guesses, but probably near a hundred. They are pretty well spread out—mostly on ten or more acres. There's a good deal of vegetables grown down here, some sheep and pigs, some retired people. There's a couple of lakes. There some good trout fishing."

"Our people saw two chaps coming out of the building. We think one of them is a German pilot and the other one is a member of a Nazi spy ring who no doubt lives around here. He has probably been in deep cover here for years and got himself established in the area. He may be known to some of the local people. How would we go about finding people to who might know the man?"

"There's a little village down Farm Lane another few miles. It's the only one for miles around. There's a small grocery shop, a feed and grain store, a chap who's a barber and a lady's hairdresser, a small post office, and a pub. Not much else. The fellow that owns the pub has been there for years, name's Jack. I used to come down here and fish Blair Lake, but I haven't been down here for some time. He knows most everyone in the area. He'd be the one who might be able to identify the man."

"Here's what I think we should do. We'll give Ace the description we got from our surveillance team and let him go to the pub to ask Jack if he can identify him. Just one man known to Jack is less likely to stir up much curiosity. We ought to get you in some other clothes. Going in wearing police uniform is not the best way."

"I've got some clothes in the back of the car," said Ace. "I'll change into them."

"See if you can do it confidentially and make sure that Jack keeps the inquiry to himself. The man we want identified is tall—maybe six foot one or two, thin—maybe twelve stone—with light blond hair. He's probably in his early thirties. Most important, he has a very noticeable scar. It starts right below his left ear, goes down the side of his face, and ends just short of his chin."

"You can count on me, sir. This is real police work. Not like what I usually do," said Ferguson eagerly.

"We'll just wait here. You take whatever time you need."

CHAPTER SEVENTY

"Hello, Jack. How are you, you old buzzard?" said Ferguson as he walked into the small pub. There was a bar, three tables, and three booths. The owner was rinsing some glasses behind the bar. Two elderly men sat at the bar wearing overalls and drinking beer. One table was occupied by a man and woman, but there was no one else. A large fire added to the cozy atmosphere.

"Ace! Ace Ferguson, where the bloody hell 'ave you bin. Got too snobbish to come see yer old mates have yer," the rotund, rosy-cheeked bald owner yelled cheerfully.

"I've been busy arresting rascally old pub owners who've been watering beer," responded Ace laughing.

"Come and have a beer. On the house. I owe you one. How's the old lady?" said Jack, pulling the Guinness stout handle and filling a pint mug.

"She's well. You remembered my favorite beer," said Ace.

"As I remember, you lapped up anything what was free," chortled Jack.

The banter continued for a while until Jack said, "What

brings you out this way? Bit off your beat ain't it? And the trout ain't in season yet."

"Could I have a word with you Jack—in private?" Ace said seriously.

"Certainly. Come over to that far booth. Nobody will disturb us there. Rainy night like this, there's not many customers."

"What's it all about then?" said Jack after they got settled in the booth.

"I'm looking for someone. A tall fellow, maybe six one or two, around twelve stone, fair-haired. Do you know any one fitting that description?"

"There's a lot of blokes around here who could fit that description. Is that all you have?"

"I forgot one thing. He has a scar. Goes from his left ear to his chin."

"Sounds like Henry Duggan. Can I ask my missus?"

"Certainly."

"Mary," he shouted. "Get out here a minute."

"What you want, Jack," she yelled back. "I'm just listening to the news."

"You remember Ace Ferguson, don't you?"

"Certainly I do. What do you think, I'm senile or something?" she playfully scolded. "How are you Ace and how's your better half? I ain't seen Daisy for ages. Why don't you bring her around more often?"

"Will you stop your nattering and sit down. Ace is looking for a bloke—tall, thin, fair-haired, with a scar down the left side of his face. Does that remind you of anyone?"

"Of course it does, you silly old fool. You had to drag me in here to ask that question. It's Henry Duggan. That's who that is. How is it you didn't know that, Jack?"

"I thought it was, but I wasn't sure."

"Where does he live?" asked Ace.

"What do you want to know for?" asked Mary.

"It's just routine police business. Nothing serious. But please don't tell anyone I was asking. All right."

"My lips are sealed," said Jack.

"So are mine," said Mary.

"He lives not too far from Blair Lake," said Jack. "You know where that is, Ace. You've fished there enough. You go down Farm Lane about two miles from here. Turn on Jasper. You can only go one way. Then about one mile down there till you come to Redgrove. Turn right and Duggan's place is about a half mile down on the right. There's a dirt road off to the right. You go up that road about half mile and his house is there. He lives there on and off with his mum and dad and his brothers, Fred and Jimmy. Quiet family. Keep a lot to themselves. They come in here once in a while for a beer."

"How do you know where they live?"

"When Roy Browning goes on holiday, I deliver the post. Pick up a little extra money, you know."

Ferguson finished his beer, again swore Jack and Mary to secrecy, promised that he and Daisy would visit soon, and returned to where the Scotland Yard detectives were waiting.

CHAPTER SEVENTY-ONE

"WELL DONE, ACE! YOU'VE done a smashing job! You ought to get a medal. I can't promise that. I can't even promise any recognition at all given that we are dealing with something here that is top secret. Maybe after the war," exclaimed Dixon.

All ten Scotland Yard detectives were gathered on Lime Passage having listened to Ferguson report his discussion with the pub owner and his wife. Ferguson had not only picked up the tail on the van when Randolph had lost it, he had discovered the identity of one of the spies and the exact location of the ring's HQ.

"I don't want any recognition. It's enough that I'm involved in something of great importance. See, I was too young for the First World War and I'm exempt from call-up now because of my police job. I did try to volunteer, but they wouldn't take me."

"We'll take it from here, Ace. We must let you get back to your duties. I don't want to incur the anger of your police department for depriving them of one of their officers. We have to reluctantly let you go with our undying thanks."

Although it was getting dark, the disappointment in

Ferguson's face was clear to all. "My shift is almost over and I don't have to be back on duty until the day after tomorrow. I had called in before I turned off the main road. My sergeant knows what I am doing so he's not going to expect me back today or tomorrow. I really want to stay involved in this. It means a lot to me. I know I'm just a country policeman, but I can help."

"You're a top police officer in my book, Ace, and I'd love to have you involved. But this is different from anything you have been involved in. It will be very dangerous. Some of us, including you, could be killed. These people are not speeders or drunks. They're trained assassins. If they are captured, they will almost certainly be hanged. They have nothing to lose and I'm sure they will not allow themselves to be taken alive if they can help it. We're trained for this. You're not. We can't afford any slip-ups. It's just that simple."

"You wouldn't be here if it wasn't for me. You said that yourself. You would never have found them if it wasn't for me. You know that. Given all that, surely I've earned the right to be in on it. I won't slip up. I promise."

Dixon paused for a long time and looked searchingly at Ferguson.

"Obviously it's your call, Chief," said Simpson, "but if you want my advice, and you probably don't, I'd let him stick around. It's not like he's a bus driver or an accountant. He's a trained police officer even though he hasn't been involved in this type of thing. There's ten of us here and several of us, although trained in counterespionage, have never had firsthand experience in anything quite like this."

Dixon looked at Simpson, "You're right." Simpson smiled. "I probably don't want your advice." The smile vanished. "But you do have a point. I hope I don't have cause to regret it, but you can come along, Ace—on one condition. You do exactly and precisely what I say—nothing more. Is that understood?"

"Yes, sir," Ferguson said excitedly. "I promise you won't regret it."

"The most important thing we can accomplish is to get into the house quickly and with the utmost surprise in order to get documents and equipment intact before they have an opportunity to destroy anything. I'd like to take them alive, but knocking over their operation, killing their top man—if we can't capture him—and the recovery of documents and equipment are paramount. If they discover us, they will try to kill us to avoid capture. If they can't do that, they will try to destroy everything—probably including themselves. It won't be easy. They have been in deep cover for many years and have established themselves in the community and you might think that has caused them to become complacent. Maybe it has, but I don't think so. I always assume that my adversaries are at least as smart as I am. That way if it turns out that they are, I'm not taken by surprise and if they are not, then that is an added unexpected bonus. They haven't survived this long by being careless and we'd do well to assume they won't be careless tonight. Now let's go over how we are going to do this and your assignments."

"Anderson, you're the youngest and fittest. You get the most important assignment. We'll drive our vehicles up Jasper and stop about a quarter of a mile past Redgrove. We'll park along the side of the road. That way if anyone is driving to Duggan's place, they will have to come up Jasper and turn on Redgrove without seeing us further up Jasper. Anderson, you will walk to the Duggan place and, very, very carefully, scope out the best way to approach the house and maximize our chances of surprising them. Don't approach the house too closely. I understand from Ace that the site is heavily wooded. Stay behind trees and shrubbery. I doubt that they have any type of alarm system that will pick up movement. This area probably has a lot of wild animals—deer and the like. Isn't that right, Ace?"

"Yes, sir. The woods around here have a lot of deer, badgers, squirrels, and a lot of other animals. If they had an alarm that went off every time there was movement outside their house, it would be going off all the time. There are also people that would come to their house who are not part of their ring. The postman, some tradesmen, the coal man, and others," said Ferguson.

"Okay. Now, Anderson, empty your wallet of everything except your driver's license and your money. If they get you, I don't want them to tie you to Scotland Yard. Tell them you were trying to find the home of a friend and you got lost and want to use a telephone. You had never been up this way before. Scribble a name, "Joe Russell' on a piece of paper and a telephone number and put that in your wallet. They probably won't believe you, so your best chance is not to get caught in the first place."

"I'll try to remember that," Anderson said wryly. "May I take a weapon?"

"Afraid not," replied Dixon. "If they capture you, your only chance to have them let you go is to make them believe your story of being lost. If you convince them—and they will be very suspicious—they might let you go because they would just as soon not have law enforcement agencies investigating a missing person in their area. But if they find a gun on you, there would be absolutely no chance of you getting away. The rest of us will wait here and we'll defer further planning until Anderson gets back with an explanation of the layout. Off you go, Dan—and good luck, lad."

CHAPTER SEVENTY-TWO

DAN ANDERSON HAD NEVER felt more alone in his young life than he did walking up a dark, damp Redgrove Lane. The roadway was pitted with holes and covered in many places with mud that had run off from the banks of the adjoining properties. He moved slowly and carefully. A sprained ankle or a broken leg would certainly not help the cause.

He had done very well in his university studies. His parents had expected him to opt for the law or a career in banking. His father was a prominent company director and would have had little trouble, with his connections, in establishing his son in a promising position in the city. It therefore came as a surprise and somewhat of a disappointment that Dan had chosen a career with Scotland Yard. Dan had joined Scotland Yard before the war with no intention of avoiding military service. Like Ace Ferguson, he had tried to enlist, but like Ace he was rejected because of the need for his services in law enforcement.

He passed several properties. The houses were set back a long way and were not visible from the road. No lights from the houses could be seen through the dense forestation. The only indication that there were people living off this lane was the presence of some dirt paths leading from the lane and signs containing the names of the occupants. Because he had no flashlight and there were no streetlights, he had to get within a few inches of the signs to make out the names. The paths were set far apart, indicating that the individual properties were very large and there must have been considerable distance between the houses. The fourth path he came to had, similar to the other houses he had passed, a post with a small square piece of metal attached to the top. This piece of metal contained the name of the occupants, as the others had—only this one, unlike the others, had the name "Duggan."

The hair stood up on the back of his head and he felt a tingling down his spine. He told himself that it was not fear, but excited anticipation. Unlike most of the others, his field experience was relatively minor. After training, he spent a little more than a year in a desk job at the Yard. He then had a series of tasks that mostly involved interviewing potential witnesses and getting written statements. It had only been fairly recently that he had been assigned to counterespionage, but as yet his involvement with that unit had been relatively excitement free.

At one time there had been a gate blocking the entry to the Duggan property. It had apparently fallen into disuse and hung on one hinge. Anderson easily got past the gate onto the property. As if on cue, the rain, which had been little more than a drizzle, suddenly began to come down heavily. He did not go down the path, but decided to go into the dense forest to the left of the path. Making his way in the darkness through thick wet underbrush while stepping into puddles of mud and water and skirting numerous trees dropping large drops of moisture on him, he made progress very slowly and, occasionally, noisily. He tried his hardest to make as little noise as possible, but the going was difficult. It wasn't long before he was soaked to the skin with mud all over his shoes and trousers. The rain was a mixed blessing. On one hand, he was soaked and miserable. He had not come dressed for this type of weather. On the other hand, the rain created its own noise, which he hoped would muffle the noise of his unavoidably clumsy progress.

He halted, frozen in his tracks. The dense forestation and thick underbrush stopped suddenly and Anderson found himself about thirty yards from the house, but still behind the last of the trees. The house was a large sprawling one-story building. The trees and underbrush had been cut back uniformly to create a clear area of about thirty yards on the front and both sides of the house. Anderson could not see from where he was whether that same pattern extended to the back. What halted him in his tracks was not the sight of the house, the clearing around it, or the abruptness with which it appeared. It was the fact that the van they had been chasing for hours was sitting in the clearing just fifteen yards from where Anderson stood. Even that was not the most arresting sight. A man was standing beside the van. If Anderson had taken a few more steps, he could have touched him. The man had been removing some things from the sides of the van. He stood up, turned in Anderson's direction, and looked directly toward him. The man then turned toward the house and shouted "Henry, get out here. Do you hear me, Henry? I need you right now."

Anderson's legs turned to rubber. He had heard of such things, but this was his first encounter with it. He wanted to turn and run, but he couldn't move. Even if he could move, he had no weapon and the occupants of the house would gun him down anyway. When he was three years old, he remembered believing that he could hide from his older brother by holding a dinner plate in front of his face. If he couldn't see his brother and he kept perfectly still, then his brother couldn't see him. His brother, who was several years older and a good sport, would go along and pretend that he did not know where Danny was. "Danny, where are you? Mum, Dad, have you seen Danny? I can't find him anywhere." His parents thought it was adorable. Years later, they would relate the story, sometimes in front of his friends, to his chagrin. He felt as if he was again trying to hide behind a dinner plate. The only thing between him, the Nazi agents, and almost certain death was a thin tree that only partially hid him. He kept perfectly still.

Chapter Seventy-Three

Henry came running out of the house with a pistol in his hand.

"What is it Fred? What did you hear?"

"I didn't hear or see anything. Put the gun away. I've got these blasted signs stuck. You have to help me get them unstuck so I can pull them out."

"That's what all the shouting was about? These bloody signs. I thought you were being attacked. You'd better calm down."

"I'm calmed down. I just don't see why I'm the one that has to do all the dirty work here."

"Come on. Let's get the signs put away. It's wet out here. Whatever you do, don't tell the old man we forgot to take the signs off until we got here."

After ten minutes of tugging and pulling, Fred and Henry got the signs off of the van and into a small shed to the right of the house. They shook the rain off and started to go back in the house when a woman's voice rang out. "Both of you take your shoes off. Don't be tracking mud in here. I just cleaned the carpet."

The ten minutes seemed more like ten hours and Anderson

was sure he had aged ten years. After a few more minutes he moved up behind the van, shielded from view from the house so that he could get a better look. The curtains were open and he could see into what looked to be the main living room. This far from London and deep in the country, the blackout was not observed as strictly. There was a table quite close to the window. Two men were sitting on opposite sides. The one facing the window appeared to be the German pilot. The man that the pub owner and his wife identified as Henry Duggan was the chap who had come out of the house to help the first man with the signs. The man with his back to the window seemed to be heavy. His hair was gray—or what there was of it. They each had a tall glass in front of them with what looked like beer. In the background, a woman who appeared to be in her late fifties or early sixties was sitting in an armchair reading a book. Her gray hair was pulled back tightly and she wore horn-rimmed glasses. The two younger men were not in view. There was a roaring fire in the fireplace on the left side of the room. The entire scene was one of domestic tranquility. A doting father and mother with their sons, enjoying a comfortable family evening in the English countryside beside a warm fire on a cold, rainy night. If one wandered on this cozy scene, one would never guess that this was the hub of a Nazi spy ring whose members were instantly capable of cold-blooded assassination.

Anderson concluded that it might be difficult to get into the house—or perhaps even close to it—without being detected. He inched his way around to the back to see if the access would be any easier. The trees and underbrush were perhaps ten yards closer to the house than they had been in the front and sides. The entry to the house was through a front door that seemed to open directly into the main room. There was also a back door—more or less centered and there were several windows at the back of the house. The lights were on behind just one, which was about seven or eight yards from the back door. There were shutters that were not completely open on the inside of that window. Anderson could not see in the window from the edge of the underbrush. He took a deep breath and tiptoed up to the side of the house. He sidled past the darkened windows at the back and stopped right before the lighted window.

He got down low and looked between two slats of the shutter. There was barely an inch and a half opening. The room was quite small and, unlike the main area, was sparsely furnished. Against the far wall was a table. A man sat at the table with his back to the window. His body obscured what—if anything—was on the table. He was wearing headphones. In all likelihood, Anderson thought, the man was connected to a sending and receiving radio. Two steel filing cabinets stood against the wall by another table containing several black binders.

Anderson felt his leg cramping and shifted. He must have caught a twig with his foot and it cracked loudly. The man at the desk whipped off his headphones, turned toward the window, and yelled out, "What's that?" Anderson moved back along the wall away from the lighted window. He heard the shutters being raised and the window opening. A head came out and looked around. Another voice said, "It was probably a rabbit or a squirrel. Close the window. It's cold." The window closed and the shutter was pulled back down. Anderson had not seen the man at the radio before. He was not one of the two men who had removed the signs from the van. There were at least five men and one woman in the house. There might be more, but that was all he had seen.

He had seen enough and didn't want to press his luck any more than he already had. He carefully picked his way back toward Redgrove Lane. On his way he stepped into a big hole that was completely hidden from view. For a terrified moment he thought he was stuck, but with considerable effort, he was able to pull himself out on his hands and knees. He was now covered in mud from head to toe. Ten minutes later he saw the Scotland Yard vehicles and Ace Ferguson's police car. He had never seen a more beautiful sight.

"That was quick," said Dixon. "Did you get anything of value?"

"You might think it was quick, but it was actually a lifetime. There's five men that I saw. One was Henry Duggan, the man identified by the pub owner. One I think was the German pilot. There were two or three other young men that we haven't seen before. There was an older man. I could only see his back, but he had gray hair. There was also an older woman. There may have been others, but that's all I saw. I can draw a map of the layout and where the radio and files are. One of the men was on the radio. We had better act fast. I'd guess they're going to move the pilot very soon."

Dixon smiled, "There's no hurry, Dan."

"What do you mean there's no hurry?" Anderson blurted out, forgetting in the excitement that he was being very brash with a man who was light years ahead of him in the Yard hierarchy. "If we don't get a move on, that pilot is going to escape."

"That's exactly what we want to have happen. We want the pilot to escape."

THE NORTH AFRICAN DESERT, 1941
PART THREE

CHAPTER SEVENTY-FOUR

"IT'S CAPTAIN LASSITER ON the phone. He sounds excited. He says it's urgent," Sergeant Buckley called from his desk.

"All right, Sergeant. I'll take it," Sloan said, picking up the phone. "What is it, Jim?"

"This is bad, Bernie. Real bad. On routine rounds this morning, we found a dead German officer in the latrine. He's been hanged."

"Who is he?"

"It's a Lieutenant named Von Steuffel, Heinrich Von Steuffel."

"I'm on my way. I'll meet you there in five minutes."

The latrine was empty except for Captain Lassiter and two military police NCOs—Sergeant Stafford and Lance Corporal Kendrick. The body was still hanging from the rafters. It appeared that bed sheets had been ripped up to use as makeshift rope.

"Who discovered the body?"

"We did, sir," said Stafford. "Me and Kendrick. We were making rounds at seven and found him. I had Kendrick support the body while I immediately checked for a pulse.

There was none. I thought we should not cut him down until you and Captain Lassiter had seen him."

"Anybody send for a medical officer?"

"I did. He should be here any minute," said Lassiter.

At that moment, an officer wearing a white jacket and a stethoscope around his neck came in. "I'm Captain Askew, Eighth Army Medical Officer."

Askew gave a cursory examination of the body. "Any reason why he hasn't been cut down?"

"We wanted to let you see the body the way we found it in case there was anything you can tell from that position," said Lassiter.

"Not a bad idea, but I don't think there is anything I can determine from the present position. Please cut him down."

Lassiter said to Stafford, "Get some more of your men and examine every bed in the compound. See if any bed is missing a sheet or has one that has a strip torn out."

On his knees, Askew studied the body from all angles. Finally, he got to his feet and looked at his watch. "From the stage of rigor mortis and discoloration of the extremities, I'd say he's been dead for approximately eight to ten hours. It's now 8:30. He was probably killed somewhere after nine and before eleven last night. That's fairly rough. There's a good-sized hematoma at the base of his skull. It looks like he took a pretty good whack on the back of his head with some form of blunt instrument—the butt of a pistol, a metal bar, or a lump of wood. It would have stunned him. Maybe knocked him unconscious for a short time, but it wouldn't have killed him. Obviously he died from asphyxiation as a result of the hanging."

"Would there have been blood on the instrument that struck him?" asked Sloan.

"Probably not. There is blood that oozed from the wound, but the weapon was in contact with the head for a split second and almost certainly had been withdrawn by the time the bleeding started—although the bleeding started very quickly after the blow."

"Could it have been suicide?" asked Sloan.

"You're probably asking the wrong man. I'm no forensic scientist. But with that reservation, I would say it's unlikely given the whack on the head."

Lassiter looked around. There was a small wooden box against the wall about six or seven feet from where Von Steuffel's body had been found. He took a rough measurement of the piece of sheet still attached to Von Steuffel's neck and the piece still hanging from the iron bar. He estimated Von Steuffel's height and the dimension of the box.

"He could have stood on that box, tied the sheet to the bar, and kicked the box out from under him," said Lassiter.

"It would have taken a ferocious kick. He wouldn't have needed to use that much force to get it out from under him," said Askew.

"Von Steuffel was a professional football player in Germany. I vaguely remember him. He was known for his powerful shot. I'll bet he could have kicked that box a lot farther," said Lassiter.

"We're guessing," said Sloan. "Jim, you had better notify the Army Intelligence chaps. They're the ones that must investigate this. In the meantime, quarantine this latrine. Nobody comes in or out. I don't want anything disturbed until the investigators have finished their work. Doctor, will you take care of what has to be done with the body?"

Lassiter left to call Army Intelligence. Askew said he would arrange to have the body picked up. There would have to be an autopsy, although the cause of death was obvious. Stafford reported back that all the beds had their requisite number of sheets. None had tears and that the one used in the hanging must have come from the storage cabinet. Stafford was ordered to post guards around the latrine. Prisoners who needed to use the latrine would be escorted to the one in the Italian compound.

Sloan met Gruber in Barracks A, which had been emptied of occupants.

"Major Gruber, I want you to tell me all you know about the death of Lieutenant Von Steuffel. Please understand that I am not conducting the formal investigation. That will be conducted by British Intelligence, but as commandant of this camp, I am required to delve into this."

"Major Sloan, I don't want to sound arrogant or uncooperative, but I must explain something. First, I don't want you to assume that I know anything about this unfortunate event. But I will say that you can send in British Intelligence, Scotland Yard, the French *Surete*, the American FBI, and any other investigative body you choose. They could spend years investigating and you will still never learn how or why this happened."

"I don't know why you would ever think that I believe you to be arrogant or uncooperative," Sloan said sarcastically.

Gruber ignored the studied sarcasm. "Understand that I'm not saying for one moment that this is what happened. But let's assume, just for the sake of argument, that Lieutenant Von Steuffel was the one who stabbed Colonel Reichmann and later, in a fit of remorse, decided to commit suicide. Why don't you just leave it at that?"

"You and I both know that he didn't commit suicide. He's been struck on the back of the head and he couldn't possibly have kicked a heavy box halfway across the room. If he stabbed Reichmann, it was no accident and why would he feel sorry he did it—sorry enough to kill himself. Your supposed hypothesis makes no sense at all."

"Suit yourself, Major. He was playing a ferocious game of football yesterday and could have accidentally been hit in the head. He was a professional football player before the war. He was a center forward with a powerful shot. He could have kicked that box a lot further than six or seven feet. I'm no psychiatrist, but I think it's a known fact that people perform acts that, on reflection, they later regret. I'm sure that, under some circumstances, that regret may cause enormous emotional difficulties—particularly in a case of attempted murder."

"I'm not buying any of that. If he had any regret, it was probably because his attempt wasn't successful. In any event I'll leave it up to British Intelligence. I'm sure they won't need the help of Scotland Yard, the FBI, or the French *Surete* to discover what really happened and who was responsible."

Sloan started to leave when Gruber called him back. "One piece of advice just between us. Don't send Colonel Reichmann back here after he recovers. There are still many officers in this camp who do not like what the colonel did for those Jews. I'm not saying they would do him any harm, but we know somebody did and I certainly couldn't vouch for his safety if he came back. Hansi and I go back a very long way. We fought side-by-side in two wars and have been close friends throughout. I wouldn't want anything to happen to him."

CHAPTER SEVENTY-FIVE

"HOW ARE YOU FEELING, Colonel?" Sloan had stopped by the hospital to see Reichmann who was up and walking around.

"I am feeling very well. I think I am ready to go back to the camp."

"I am sorry to have to tell you this, but there has been a very serious incident at the camp. Lieutenant Von Steuffel has been hanged."

Reichmann sat down suddenly and covered his eyes. "That's terrible. Have you any idea who could have done it?"

"We are making inquiries, but Major Gruber, who is temporarily the senior German officer, thinks we will never find out. He's worried about you coming back to the camp. He fears that there may be others in the camp who might want to hurt you. As a longtime friend of yours, he wishes that you would be transferred to another camp where the prisoners would not know about your rescue of the Helsteins."

"So that's what Gruber told you, did he?" Reichmann said with a curious smile that Sloan had not seen before. "I have no fear of going back to the camp and I'm ready to do so as soon as possible. I do thank you for your concern, but please don't worry about me."

"Is there something about your relationship with Major Gruber that you are not telling me? He says that you and he are very close friends. Is that not true?"

Reichmann again smiled strangely. "I would rather not comment. Let's just say that we have known each other for a long time and we have become used to each other."

On the way back to his office, Sloan stopped by to see Corcoran and told him about the killing at the camp.

"There is something quite peculiar about the relationship between Gruber and Reichmann. Gruber claims they are close friends. Reichmann squirms around when asked if that is true and never concedes anything other than they have known each other for a long time and have become used to each other. Whatever that means. Joe, I wish there was some way to place Reichmann, somewhere he wouldn't be in danger. Transferring him to another POW camp may not be adequate. There are no secrets in POW camps, so I have been told. Even if we move him, there is no guarantee that word of the Helstein episode won't leak out."

"Let me send a letter to my father. He might have some ideas and you know he has a lot of connections."

Chapter Seventy-Six

DRIVING BACK TO HIS office from a meeting near the docks, Sir Rupert Corcoran decided, on a whim, that he would stop by and see the Helsteins. His route to his office took him very close to their street in any event.

Dr. Helstein opened the door and broke into a broad smile when he saw who it was.

"Sir Rupert, how marvelous it is to see you again. Please come in." The doctor had read a story in the paper which included references to Sir Rupert's charitable work and had told his wife that the proper method of address was "Sir Rupert" and not "Mr. Corcoran."

"It's very rude of me to show up unannounced like this, but I was in the area."

"Not at all. Not at all. You're always most welcome. Hanna, look who has come to see us."

Hanna Helstein came running from the kitchen, wiping her hands on her apron. "I'm so very glad you stopped in. Please sit down. I have the kettle on for tea and I made some wonderful little tarts. They're from an old family recipe."

"Please no. I don't want to eat up your rations."

"A little tart is nothing. Besides, at our age, we don't eat as much as we used to."

Sir Rupert ended up eating two tarts and drinking three large cups of sweet, strong tea. The tea was good and the tarts were delicious.

"Mrs. Helstein, I just don't know how you do it. That was wonderful. It's the best thing I've eaten in years."

Mrs. Helstein beamed. "I'm so pleased you like it. You must come more often. Even with rationing, I'll cook you a dinner you won't believe."

They all laughed.

"What of Hansi?" said the doctor. "Have you heard anything more about him?"

"Yes. There was a little something. Nothing to worry about. He's going to be just fine. One of the other prisoners stabbed him. It wasn't serious. It was in the dark and no one saw who it was. He's healing nicely and is back on his feet."

Sir Rupert wisely decided he would not trouble them further by telling them that Reichmann's aid to the Helsteins probably motivated the attack.

The concern showed on both of their faces. "Who would do such a terrible thing? I hope they catch the man," said Hanna.

"In the meantime, the second most senior officer in the camp—a longtime friend of the colonel's—has suggested that the colonel should be moved to a different camp for his safety."

"What a nice friend to have," said the doctor. "What is this friend's name? I knew most of the officers who were in the same unit with Hansi during the First World War. I was in that unit myself."

"I remember you telling me that the last time I was here. The friend's name is Gruber, Major Gruber."

Dr. Helstein's face, which had been pleasant and smiling, suddenly darkened and the smile evaporated. "You're talking about Karl Gruber who was in the old Thirty-Second Regiment in the First World War, aren't you?"

"I don't know what outfit he was in, but my son tells me his name is Karl Gruber and he served with Hansi in World War I and now in World War II. Is there something wrong?"

Corcoran knew that Dr. Helstein had treated Gruber, as well as Reichmann, for injuries during the first war. To tell him that would mean that the relationship was discussed in the camp. Corcoran didn't want Helstein to put two and two together and conclude that the stabbing might have been as a result of Reichmann's aid to him and his family.

"Gruber's no friend of Hansi's. He hates Hansi. He always has."

Sir Rupert was stunned. To this point, it had been his understanding that Reichmann and Gruber not only had served together in two world wars but were also close friends.

"Why?"

"Hansi is a brilliant man. He was always highly regarded as a soldier and a leader of men. He was awarded the Iron Cross First Class for heroism. Gruber was always jealous of him. There's no comparison between the two. Gruber is very deceptive—but not very smart—and has no leadership ability. Hansi came into the army after Gruber, but was promoted before him. Gruber was always making up lies to hurt Hansi's progress but, in truth, they hurt Gruber and not Hansi. If Hansi had not been captured, he would have ended up being a general—maybe even a field marshal. How Gruber got to be a major is beyond me. They must have been very short of officers."

"This is very interesting. Did you know Gruber very well?"

"Oh yes. I operated on him. I probably saved his life. He is a rabid anti-Semite. He took a bullet in his chest. If I didn't get the bullet out and cauterize the wound, he would have bled to death before they could have gotten him to a field hospital. He kept screaming, "I don't want this Yid touching me. Get me a real doctor." I told him that there was no other doctor for miles around and, if he didn't let me treat him, he would certainly die. He finally passed out and I did what I had to do. When he recovered and came back to the unit, he not only didn't thank me, but he swore at me."

"Don't misunderstand me. I'm not doubting the accuracy of what you just said, but are you sure you're not exaggerating just a little because you don't like him? My son has not indicated that he has any inkling of what you have just told me."

"Oh, I don't like him all right, but I'm not exaggerating. If anything I'm downplaying it. I could tell you a lot more about Karl Gruber. Gruber would do almost anything to get ahead of Hansi. There's no way that could happen fairly. But if Gruber could do something unfairly to get an advantage, believe me, he would do it. Now you say he is the acting senior German officer. It's not a leadership position in the field, but it is a leadership role. No doubt he would like to make it more permanent and getting Hansi transferred or worse would do that."

"Even if Hansi was transferred, there is always a possibility that another officer senior to Gruber would be captured and imprisoned in that POW camp and Gruber wouldn't be the leader anymore."

"I wouldn't think that too many colonels are captured and, in any event, Gruber would have gotten rid of what he sees as his nemesis and would have had his moment of what, in his mind, he would think of as glory."

"The information I am getting from my son makes Gruber seem like a fair-minded man. Not as selfless as Hansi, but no anti-Semitic beast."

"As I said before, Karl Gruber is not very smart, but he's also not stupid. He is devious and he can put on an act if he thinks it will help him."

"If all this is true, why didn't Hansi tell the British military about it when they talked to him after the stabbing?"

"You'd have to know Hansi. He has the deepest level of honor and loyalty of anybody you will ever meet. Sometimes it seems a little misguided. It would be totally out of character for him to have revealed what he knows about Gruber."

As Sir Rupert drove away after thanking the Helsteins for their kind hospitality, he wondered what his son and the other British officers would think—and, more importantly, do—when they got this surprising information.

CHAPTER SEVENTY-SEVEN

"COLONEL REICHMANN, WE NEED to discuss a couple of matters with you."

Joe Corcoran and Bernie Sloan had come to see Reichmann at the hospital. His convalescence was almost complete and he would be well enough to return to the POW camp in a few days.

"It's nice to see both of you. Please sit down if you can find chairs. Now what is it that you wish to discuss?"

Corcoran closed the door to the corridor. "Bernie tells me you were in the cavalry for a short time at the start of World War I. Is that correct?"

"Yes, that is true. Unfortunately, my stay in the cavalry was all too brief. I love horses and my great passion when I was younger was riding. However, I was quickly transferred to an infantry unit and stayed there for the rest of the war. The cavalry, as I knew it, is now no more. Now they call tanks and half-tracks cavalry. Hardly the same thing."

"My father and grandfather would agree with you," said Corcoran. "My grandfather was a cavalry officer with Kitchener in the Sudan and my father was with the horse-drawn artillery in the First World War. My father has a big estate in England. He has retained his love of horses and has a number of them on his place. As I think you know, my father is quite prominent and has a lot of connections. He has been discussing your situation with our War Office and he has prevailed on a high ranking official there to place you in his care and custody. With your agreement, you will be transported to his place and stay there for the remainder of the war. Your duties will be limited to taking care of the horses and riding them to your heart's content. You will have the run of the place. There will be no guards, no barbed wire, and no other prisoners. It is a very unusual and unique opportunity. It may not be a position commensurate with your stature, but it will keep you comfortable and, most importantly, safe from any attack on you by any fanatic in a POW camp who has issues with your aid to the Helsteins. What do you think of that?"

"I am indeed overwhelmed. Your kindness and concern for my wellbeing are truly breathtaking."

"There is only one condition which the War Office insists upon and I think and hope it is one you will find acceptable. You must promise not to try to escape. It is of course understandable that the War Office is not willing to place an important senior German officer in a situation where escape would be easy without such a commitment and without certain assurances and observations Major Sloan and I have given about you. Apart from anything else, they would have a hard time explaining why they allowed a high-ranking and important officer such an easy opportunity for escape. They are going out on a very long limb and are only willing to do so based on the highly unusual circumstances we have told them about."

"Please don't misunderstand me. I am most grateful to

both of you and to your father, Colonel Corcoran, but I could not sign such an agreement."

"It will not be necessary for you to sign anything. Your verbal promise is quite adequate. We recognize you as a man of honor who would not violate such a promise whether or not it was in writing."

"Forgive me. I am not making myself understood. My inadequate command of the English language has perhaps let me down. There are many things happening in my country at the present time with which I am in strong disagreement. However, I am a loyal German officer. What I did for the Helsteins was not, in my view, an act of disloyalty to Germany. Possibly I am wrong about that. So be it. As you know, it is the duty of every captured soldier to attempt to escape. It makes no difference if that soldier is English, French, German, or some other nationality. I cannot—and will not—abandon that duty and I cannot—and will not—agree not to attempt to escape if I get a chance."

"Is that your final decision? Would you like to think about it? It's not necessary to make up your mind today. We can certainly wait a day or two."

"That is kind of you. Of both of you. But, I can assure you my decision would not change no matter how long I had to think about it. Please thank your father for me. Perhaps one day after the war, I might have the opportunity to visit his estate and see his horses."

"Very well. That is your decision to make, but whether or not you go back to the POW camp you came from or go to another one is my decision to make," said Corcoran. "I have decided that if you reject our offer to let you go to my father's estate, I will transfer you to another camp. Von Steuffel might have been the only danger to you, but I am not willing to take that chance—even if you are. I will also ensure that no one from this camp ends up in your new one."

"That's not necessary. I am quite willing to go back to the present camp and I am sure nothing will happen."

"My decision is not open to further argument and so the discussion of that issue is closed. I want to discuss a different matter. The attack on you is still under investigation and has been expanded to include the death of Lieutenant Von Steuffel. We believe both incidents are connected. We have learned that Major Karl Gruber bears a longstanding animosity toward you. We are told that it stems from jealousy as a result of your success in the military and his more mediocre record. We are looking into whether the attack on you and the death of Von Steuffel are related in some way to Major Gruber. I do not want to tell you where we got our information, but I assure you it is reliable."

"You don't have to tell me. Your father got it from Meyer Helstein. Meyer is the finest man I have ever known and he was treated shamefully by Gruber. Meyer saved Gruber's life and Gruber repaid him with cruel and awful insults. Meyer is an honest man and he would not consciously exaggerate, but subconsciously Gruber's attacks on him must have influenced him. I know it has influenced the enormity of my loathing of Gruber. Gruber is an avid anti-Semite and I am quite sure the aid I gave to the Helsteins disgusts him. Nonetheless, I can't believe he would try to kill me. In addition, why would he kill Von Steuffel who is at least as big an anti-Semite as he is?"

"I don't have any answers at the moment, but I assure you we will get to the bottom of this. In the meantime, I will arrange your transfer. It may be that we won't see you again, so we will say good-bye and wish you well."

They shook hands warmly and the two English officers departed.

LONDON, 1941
PART THREE

CHAPTER SEVENTY-EIGHT

"CHIEF, I DON'T THINK I understood you," queried Anderson. "How can we want the pilot to escape? We've staked him out for days. We've got ten Scotland Yard agents involved in pursuing him. We've chased him for miles and almost lost him. I almost got killed being sure he was in that house. If I don't die of pneumonia, I'll be very lucky and now we're going to let him go. What is he—a British agent and not a German pilot?"

"He's not a British agent. He's a German pilot. While you were gone, we were in touch with the Yard. They have heard from Whitehall. The British High Command and the War Office are very excited about our discovery of the spy nest. They want to capture or kill all the Nazi agents, but they want to get their hands on the German radio and whatever files there are in that house. They feel there is a chance that we can break their code or at least discover the identity of other Nazi agents in Britain. They don't care about one rotten German pilot. If we prevent his escape and German intelligence doesn't hear from the spy ring, the Germans will know—or at least suspect—that we've found their HQ. They will immediately change their codes and warn their other agents. Even if we capture their radio and files intact, we may not be able to break their code quickly enough to continue communication uninterrupted. If that happens, we will be too late. But it's worth gambling one German pilot for the chance of a bonanza."

Anderson looked down at his feet. "Sorry, Chief. I was so focused on the pilot that I didn't see the bigger picture."

"Don't feel bad, Anderson. To some extent, neither did I. I was thinking that we could probably successfully use the element of surprise to kill or capture everyone in the house and get the radio and files. I knew that the quicker we could get someone working on decoding the material in the house, the better it would be. Quite frankly, I hadn't concentrated on the time we would buy in deciphering the stuff by letting the pilot go. It was elementary and it should have occurred to me, but it didn't."

Anderson felt better and his facial expression reflected it. "What's the plan?"

"Two of the Yard's crack decoders are flying up here with all of their equipment. They should be landing at the Sidley RAF base thirty miles from here in the next hour. Logistically, we are in a bit of mess. We can't attack until after the pilot is out of there and the enemy agents who take him wherever he is going are back in the house. We don't know when that will be. We can take turns sleeping in the back of the van and in the cars. I have sent Ace to get some food and drink for all of us. We will just have to wait here. That brings me back to you, Dan. I hate to ask you to do this, but I'm going to anyway. I want you to go back to the house and replace the AR7 under the back of the van. We checked it out while you were gone and it is still operational despite being jarred off by that bump. Randolph will tail the van.

It will let us know when it leaves, where it goes, and—most importantly—when it comes back. We don't want to pounce until all the birds are back in the nest. It may also help us in the future if we discover where the pickup point in this case is. Did you see any other vehicles while you were snooping around?"

"No. There was no garage on the property. There was a shed, but it was far too small to accommodate even a small car. I went all the way around the house. I am sure there were no other vehicles of any sort besides the van."

"Good. I wouldn't want to be waiting for the van to leave with the pilot and find out they must have used a different vehicle. Off you go then, Dan. I don't have to tell you to be very careful."

Anderson's second trip to the Duggan estate was completely uneventful, unlike the first. The old bloke and the pilot were still at the table and the older woman was still reading. There was no sign of the three other young men. Anderson planted the AR7 securely under the rear of the van without incident. The rain had tapered off and he stepped in no holes on the way in or the way out.

Twenty minutes after Anderson got back to the Yard vehicles the two cryptographers arrived. After introductions, Dixon instructed Anderson to get some sleep. He needed no second invitation. He was totally exhausted, despite his youth and remarkable physical fitness. Slogging through the damp and resistant underbrush on the two trips had taken their toll, but the primary enervating factors were fear and excitement. Anderson knew from his sports career that adrenaline builds up before a game but that, after the game, when the adrenaline rush stops, fatigue sets in. This was the same feeling. The back of the van was not exactly the Savoy.

There was a blanket and a couple of pillows. Simpson was already asleep on one side of the van. Anderson removed his outer layer of clothes and, while still damp, fell fast asleep.

CHAPTER SEVENTY-NINE

OFFICER FERGUSON RETURNED WITH the food and drink. Considering he had no ration books with him, he had done well. There were some tinned sardines, two loaves of bread, cheese, tomatoes, ten packages of crisps, and a box of biscuits. He also brought several bottles of orangeade.

"Well done, Ace," said Dixon appreciatively. "A feast fit for a king—or at least a tired old detective. You haven't met our decoders. They just arrived. Joe Mason, Ron Tyler, I'd like you to meet Ace Ferguson, a local policeman who saved our bacon on this venture."

There were handshakes all around.

"Joe and Ron were about to explain to us what they hope to accomplish if we can get the material from the Duggan house. Go ahead, chaps."

Joe, the older of the two decoders, looked a bit embarrassed. "We really can't discuss it in front of Officer Ferguson. He doesn't have the required top-secret clearance and this is very hush-hush stuff."

"You don't have to worry about Ace. He's become one of us. We wouldn't be where we are without him," said Dixon.

"It's really no reflection on Mr. Ferguson and certainly there's no offense intended. I'm sure he understands and I know we are all immensely grateful for his help, but orders are orders."

Dixon turned to Ferguson. "I'm sorry, Ace, but would you mind sitting in one of the cars for a while. This won't take long. Why don't you have a bite to eat while you're waiting?"

Ferguson left and Mason started to explain. "I don't want to get too technical."

"Please don't. Some of these younger men may be more advanced, but my technical knowledge is limited to starting a car and filling a fountain pen with ink," replied Dixon.

"Well, we are quite far along in deciphering the German method of encoding and cryptography. The Germans are very clever and extremely careful, but they are not as adept at creativity. They tend to be more predictable and have a more definable pattern of changing codes than we do. That is an enormous exaggeration, I'm afraid. I don't want to give the impression that uncovering their code is as simple as solving the *Sunday Express* crossword puzzle. It is far more complex than that. What we need, and what we haven't had, is access to a fully operational German transmitter. Again, without getting too technical, our ability to test such a machine would be a big breakthrough."

"Our man was not able to see the transmitter and we don't know for certain that there *was* a transmitter. However, he did see a man sitting at a desk wearing headphones. His body obscured any view of what was attached to the headphones."

"What he saw was probably connected to a radio transmitter. I understand there may also be files. Our experience would indicate that they would be less useful than the radio itself, but we won't know until we see them."

Dixon turned to one of his men. "Stephens wake up Anderson and ask him to come here. I want to debrief him on the house and the best way to get to that radio, if that's what it is."

A disheveled and sleepy-eyed Anderson quickly appeared.

"Sorry to wake you so soon, lad, but we need some information from you."

At Dixon's request, Anderson took a piece of paper and drew a map of the approach to, and the surroundings of the house. He also drew, among other things, the location of the back room where he had seen the man with the headphones.

"The obvious access is through the back door, but that is probably not the best idea," said Dixon. "It is some distance from the radio room and we can't tell exactly how quickly we can get through that door and into the room. We probably should go through the window. It would be ideal if we could time it when there is no one in the back room. Having a simultaneous distraction at the front of the house is a double-edged sword. On the one hand, it might draw everyone away from the back. On the other hand, they may immediately see it as a diversion and several of them might head for the radio room. To get through the window, we will have to smash not only the window, but also the shutters that Dan told us are on the inside of the window. We don't know how firmly attached they are or how much difficulty we will have smashing through them. I want to think more about it. We have time. We will wait for the German van to leave and return before we make a move. In the meantime, I can't offer you decoders much in the way of creature comforts. Please wait in your vehicle. I want to discuss strategy with my people. Officer Ferguson was kind enough to fetch us some food. Please take some."

"That's kind of you chief inspector, but we had something to eat before we left London," said Tyler.

After they left, Dixon sat in one of the cars by himself for a long time. *This is not going to be easy,* he thought.

An hour later his thoughts were interrupted by Stephens rapping on the window. Dixon rolled the window down.

"What is it?"

"The German van is moving."

CHAPTER EIGHTY

RANDOLPH HAD TAKEN ROY Thompson with him to track the van. Thompson would drive while Randolph watched the instruments and kept in radio contact with Dixon. Thompson was a six-year veteran of the Yard. He had earlier received well-deserved plaudits for his involvement in tracking down and arresting the infamous "Debonair Bandit." The Debonair Bandit was so named because of his expensive, high-style clothing, his elegant manners, and the variety of colorful masks he wore. He had a six-year run of bank robberies before Thompson had finally captured him in, of all places, the Old Vic Theatre, where the bandit, whose real name was Lionel Bronson, was enjoying a performance of King Lear accompanied by two beautiful young ladies. Thompson had recently been transferred to the counterespionage unit and had been working with Dixon for six months.

"They're heading northeast, probably going to bypass Nottingham, although I can't be sure," reported Randolph.

Dixon was looking at a map as he talked with Randolph. "My guess is they are heading for the North Sea Coast, probably north of Skegness, but it's too early to tell. Keep after them, but not too close," ordered Dixon. He called the rest of the group together and told them to get as much rest as they could. As soon as Randolph reported that the van was on its way back from wherever it had gone, he would call them back together and give them their assignments for the raid on the Duggan house.

Randolph reported in sometime later that the German van had indeed bypassed Nottingham. It had stopped in that vicinity. Dixon speculated that perhaps they had dropped off the pilot, but he quickly discounted that possibility when the van started again about ten minutes later and proceeded in the same general northeast direction. Dixon assumed the stop was for petrol. Randolph had stopped at about the same time and for the same purpose. The route of the van was not consistent with them heading for any good-sized town and it was becoming more apparent that the ultimate destination was a more-or-less deserted area along the North Sea coast.

It had been a long time since Dixon had gotten any sleep and he was beginning to feel it. *This is a young man's game,* he thought, *but even a young man needs sleep once in a while.* He pushed the car seat back as far as it would go, closed his eyes, and dozed off.

The beep of the radiophone woke him abruptly. He sat up straight with a groan. His right leg was numb and his back was aching. He looked at his watch. He must have been asleep for over two hours.

"They've stopped again," said Randolph.

"Where are they?" replied Dixon.

"They are pretty close to where you predicted they would be. They're north of Skegness and south of Grimsby—closer to Skegness. We're about two miles behind them and we've stopped, too. They must be at the coast or very close to it."

"Find a place to pull off the road. After they drop off

Leuzinger they'll almost certainly come back the same way and I don't want them to see you. Let me know the moment they start moving."

An hour went by and then two and the van had still not moved.

"Any chance the AR7 is not working or they've found it?" asked Dixon.

"It's possible, but not likely," said Randolph. "I pulled our van out of sight, but I can see the road from where I am and they haven't come back this way. I don't think there is any other way out of where they are and, even if there was another way, why would they take it?"

Another half an hour later Randolph reported, "They're moving again. We're behind some bushes thirty yards off the road. I'll see them when they go by, but they won't see us."

"Stay on the radio and let me know when you see the van."

Ten minutes later, Randolph called in, "There they go. They're heading back the way they came. They've dropped off Leuzinger. My guess is that a dinghy from a U-boat picked him up. This is a very desolate area of coast and there's not much around here."

"I think you're probably right. Give them a big lead before you start after them. It'll take them about three or four hours before they get here. We'll wait until it gets dark again and then we'll move in on them.

Chapter Eighty-One

Seven Scotland Yard detectives, two cryptographers, and a village police officer were gathered in a circle around Chief Inspector Dixon.

"There are thirteen of us in total. Probably the most important of us are our worthy cryptographers, Mason and Tyler. When we start the raid, the two of you will remain here. We'll bring you in after we subdue the occupants and secure the premises. I'd never hear the end of it from the decoding section at the Yard if I got any of their precious chaps hurt."

Everybody laughed, including Mason and Tyler, although their laughter was more of the relieved variety.

"Anderson will lead us in. He's now made two trips and knows the way. He has promised me that he has sufficiently explored the mud holes and will be sure to have us all avoid them this time."

Everyone laughed again. Over the course of many dangerous missions both before and during the war, Dixon had developed the ability to ease tension with teasing lighthearted banter while not deviating from outlining for his men the nature of the mission and the assignments. It was a great talent and was one of the factors that had made him tremendously effective and had caused his men to be fiercely loyal to him.

"Ernie," Dixon said, turning to Detective Sergeant Ernie Graham, "you will be in charge of the front of the house. Hennessey, Stephens, and Kravitz will be with you. I will lead the group at the back of the house. Anderson, Strawbridge, and Simpson will come with me. I'll brief Randolph and Thompson when they get back from tracking the van. Randolph will take up position in the underbrush on one side of the house and Thompson on the other side. Ernie, you keep your men back in the trees until you hear us break into the back room. We will try to make our move into that room when there is nobody in there. Maybe we will get lucky when we first move in. Otherwise, we will wait a short while. We can't wait long and, if we have to, we will crash into the room with it occupied. As soon as you hear us smashing the windows and shutters, move into the front. I will distribute handguns to all of you. It would be a bonus if we can take any of them alive, but don't count on it. They know that if they are taken alive, they will almost certainly be hanged as spies. They will not allow that to happen if they can possibly avoid it. If they can't kill us and if they can't escape, they will take lethal pills. All their agents are provided with them. Do not hesitate to kill them if you must. Believe me, they won't hesitate to kill you. Any questions?"

There was only one.

"What about me?" asked Ace. "You haven't given me an assignment."

In fact, Dixon had completely overlooked Ferguson in the development of his strategy, but he thought fast.

"I have a most important assignment for you, Ace. I want

323

you to stay in the bushes by the gate on Redgrove Lane. You will be our rear guard."

Ferguson was nobody's fool and he knew he was not really to be an integral part of the operation. Nonetheless, he was a good officer and wasn't going to pout about it.

"Do I get a weapon? I've been checked out on handguns, rifles, and shotguns. I've never actually used one in police work, but I scored very well with a handgun on the police range."

"Of course you will be armed and we are counting on you to watch our backs. Now all of you get your weapons and check out that they are loaded. Take several additional clips with you. Put on the black jerseys and blacken your faces and hands. You'll find everything you need in the boot of the first car. There are two very sharp axes in the boot of the second car. Strawbridge, you take one. You will be responsible for smashing through the window and shutters in the back room. Stephens, you take the other for use on the front of the house. Neither of you are to use the axes until I give the word in the back and Graham gives the word in the front. Simpson, you and I will flank Strawbridge when he bashes in the window. Don't let anyone destroy anything. Kill them if you have to. Ernie, make sure nobody gets out of that front room. From the moment we start walking up Redgrove Lane until the attack starts, there will be absolute silence—no talking. Walk carefully and watch where you're going. As Dan has explained to me, the route we take will put us in the front of the house first. Ernie, you and your group will be immediately behind Dan and you will deploy your men when we get there. When Dan was there, the van was parked close to the main room. When the van returns, it will probably be parked in generally the same area. If so, you might use the van as cover."

"Right, Chief," said Graham who, along with the rest of them, had been listening intently to Dixon's instructions.

"After Dan has led Ernie's group to the front of the house, Dan will wait for the rest of us and we will proceed to the rear. All of you will get to your positions, staying as long as possible in the trees and undergrowth. After you have checked your weapons you can relax. The German van won't be back for some time."

CHAPTER EIGHTY-TWO

THREE HOURS LATER RANDOLPH and Thompson returned. They reported an uneventful trip tracking the vehicle to the Duggan property.

"We'll wait until it gets dark and then give them another two hours to allow them time to have something to eat and hopefully go to bed. It is quite possible that there will be no lights on. Dan, without lights, will you be able to determine which one the radio room is?"

"That will be no problem," said Anderson. "I could find it with my eyes closed."

"I'm sure you could, but let's have you keep your eyes open this time. I will have a flashlight with me as will Sergeant Graham. We won't use them until needed."

For the next hours, the eleven men who would participate in the raid busied themselves with donning dark jerseys, blackening their faces and hands, checking and re-checking their weapons, and engaging in quiet occasional chitchat. They then rested. Although most of them had previously been in dangerous situations, this was different—potentially more dangerous than anything they had done before and probably far more important. The two cryptographers stayed out of the way for the most part. Dixon had told them that, as soon as the house was secured, he would send somebody back for them and they were to get to the house in one big hurry.

The hours finally passed. Never had time passed so slowly. "Let's go," hissed Dixon and the eleven men moved quickly until they got to Redgrove Lane. Once they turned onto Redgrove, their pace slowed and became more cautious. The night was very overcast. Neither the moon nor stars could be seen. That, coupled with the dark clothing and blackened faces, made an orderly movement difficult. On one occasion Stephens got too close to Hennessey and tripped on the back of Hennessey's shoe, causing it to come off. Instinctively Hennessey let out a loud curse. "Quiet," growled Detective Sergeant Graham.

They moved into the Duggan property and inched their way toward the house, staying off the driveway and remaining deeply in the surrounding forest. Once in a while someone would step on a twig. The crack was not loud, but to the raiders it sounded like thunder. They got to the clearing in front of the house. The van was parked almost exactly where Anderson had seen it on his two prior visits. Detective Sergeant Ernie Graham silently signaled his team to take up positions along the side of the van, screening them from the house. There were no lights visible from the house. Anderson signaled the other team to follow him through the underbrush to the back of the house. There were no lights visible there either. Dixon beckoned to Anderson and both of them approached the window of the room that contained the radio and other materials. To their surprise, the shutters had been folded back against the inside wall. There was nobody in the room and the radio was now clearly visible. Dixon again beckoned to Anderson and the two of them retreated into the wooded area.

Dixon motioned to his team to retreat farther back into the woods. When he calculated they were well out of earshot, he whispered to them that the shutters would not be a problem and they would be able to smash through the window and get into the room quickly. The noise would undoubtedly awaken the occupants and bring them running into the room. He told them that as soon as the window was smashed, he would turn on his flashlight and Anderson, who was the youngest and most athletic, would enter the room and position himself beside the door so that he could intercept anyone coming in. Simpson was to follow and take up a position on the other side of the door. They would try to disarm and immobilize anyone that entered the room. Strawbridge and Dixon would stay outside the window and would fire on any entrant who avoided the attempts to capture them alive.

Dixon whispered, "Remember, it would be a bonus if we could capture one or more of them alive, but it is not top priority. This is a highly dangerous operation at best and I don't intend to take any chances that we don't have to. We will err on the side of killing them if there is the slightest chance that we can't control them. Let's go."

What happened next would be etched in the minds of those who took part for the rest of their lives. Years later, Anderson would tell people that it was like an out-of-body experience. Although the whole episode took less than a minute, everything seemed to move in slow motion.

He seemed to float into the room the moment the axe splintered the window and its wooden frame into a hundred pieces. Dixon switched on his flashlight and, simultaneously, the lights in the room were snapped on. Jimmy, the radio operator, was first into the room, screaming at the top of his lungs. Anderson came out from behind the door and swung the butt of his pistol at his head. Jimmy moved sidewise at the last moment and the pistol struck him a glancing blow. He fell, momentarily stunned. Fred ran in firing his pistol. Simpson swung at him and missed. A bullet struck Strawbridge and he went over backward. Dixon fired point blank at Fred and killed him instantly. Jimmy, still lying on the floor, fired wildly and the bullet struck the wall. Simpson fired two shots; the first hit Jimmy in the shoulder and the second in the back of the head. The back door opened and Henry ran out. Dixon turned and emptied his clip. Henry staggered, reeled away from the door, and fell forward onto his face.

At the moment that the axe crashed through the back room window, Graham signaled his men to open fire. A barrage of shots was directed into the front room, which remained dark. Thompson and Randolph opened up from opposite sides of the house into darkened rooms without seeing any specific target. Heavy fire was being returned from the front room. Graham motioned Hennessey and Kravitz to move laterally and to approach the house at an angle. They reached the wall at the front of the house and fired at close range into the room.

Ferguson, from his post at the gate on Redgrove Lane, heard the gunfire. It sounded like a whole battalion was involved. *Maybe there are a lot more people in that house than anybody believed. I'd better help,* he thought. With his pistol in hand, he raced straight down the driveway until he was in sight of the house. The gunfire was less now. He stopped abruptly. A surprised look came on his face and a small hole suddenly appeared in the center of his forehead. He went down on one knee and slowly keeled over. The man known affectionately as Ace who was not one—the village police officer, the man who had picked up the chase when advanced technology failed, the man principally responsible for finding the German spy ring—was dead.

CHAPTER EIGHTY-THREE

"CEASE FIRE," SHOUTED DIXON. Graham also yelled for his team to stop. There was sudden silence. Dixon ran over to Strawbridge who was awkwardly getting to his feet.

"Where are you hit?"

"It's just my shoulder. It's nothing. I'm all right."

"Hang on. We'll get you help soon."

"Don't worry about me," protested Strawbridge "Do what you have to do in the house."

"Anderson, run back to the cars and get the decoding chaps over here quick. Tell them we've captured everything intact."

"I'm on my way," said Anderson as he came back out of the rear window and broke into a run.

"Simpson, what about the two down in the room?" asked Dixon.

Simpson leaned over and felt for a pulse in the necks of the two fallen men. "They're both dead."

"Stay there in case anyone else is alive in the house and tries to destroy the radio."

Dixon walked over to the man he had shot exiting the back door. He could see three bullet wounds; one had torn a hole in his throat, the second had entered in the center of his chest, and the third lower down in the abdomen. Probably any one of the wounds would have been fatal.

"Johnny, he called out to Strawbridge, "think you're okay to watch the back door from where you are?"

"Piece of cake," said Strawbridge.

"Good lad."

Dixon came around to the front. "Ernie, keep two men on each side of the house. Leave the rest of your team out front and let's you and me go in and see what else we can find."

Graham shot out the lock on the front door and he and Dixon carefully entered the house with guns drawn. The gray-haired man lay face up on the floor of the main room, his eyes wide open. A woman of approximately middle age sat slumped in an armchair beside the fireplace. Dixon knelt beside the man. There was no sign of physical injury, but he was dead. Graham pushed the woman's head back. She was dead, but also had no sign of physical injury. There was a strong smell of almonds around both bodies.

"Cyanide," said Dixon. "All German agents are issued cyanide pills. Let's look in the other rooms. I think we've seen all of them, but let's be sure."

A hallway to the right of the main room led toward the back of the house and to the other rooms. Everything in the kitchen was neat and tidy. Shiny copper pans hung on hooks. In an alcove, a table was set for breakfast. There was not a dirty plate or a dishcloth out of place. There were four other rooms and two bathrooms. The first three rooms contained beds, wardrobes, and chairs. The beds were made with military precision. Although Dixon had waited a couple of hours in the hope that everyone in the house would have gone to bed, obviously nobody had. Clothes were hung in the wardrobes in neat rows arranged by color. The bathrooms sparkled, towels were folded, and bathrobes hung on hooks.

"Apart from being a master spy, Mrs. Duggan—or whatever her name was—certainly was a bloody good housekeeper," observed Graham. "I wonder what she was going to fix for breakfast."

They opened the door to the last room and got the shock of their lives. There, sitting on the bed with his hands up, in full Luftwaffe uniform, was a very-much-alive Hauptman Heinrich Leuzinger.

Chapter Eighty-Four

"ERNIE, LEAVE FOUR MEN outside covering all sides of the house. Bring everyone else in."

"Right, Chief," responded Graham as he hurried out.

Dixon kept his pistol pointed at Leuzinger. "Now, Captain, why didn't the U-boat pick you up last night?"

"My name is Heinrich Leuzinger. My rank is Hauptman and my serial number is 184396."

"When and where are they going to make another attempt to get you?"

"My name is Heinrich Leuzinger, Hauptman, 184396."

"Why didn't they pick you up last night?"

"My name is Heinrich—"

Dixon angrily interrupted. "I know your name. I didn't like it when I first heard it and I don't like it now. Don't tell me what it is again. Do you understand?"

"I understand perfectly, but my name, rank, and serial number is all you are going to get from me."

"We'll see about that."

Graham came in. "You had better come out here, Chief."

"What is it?"

"You need to come in the other room."

"Stay here, Ernie. I'll send Simpson in to help."

When Dixon came into the main room, all his men were present except the four guarding the exterior of the house and Graham.

"Gentlemen, the German pilot is not on any U-boat. He is here in one of the bedrooms." The assembled detectives looked at each other in amazement and a buzz of conversation started among them.

"Quiet down," shouted Dixon. "Mason, you and Tyler better get to the radio in the back room. Simpson, go help Graham guard the pilot. Kravitz, gather up the German weapons and put them on this table. There should be two in the back room—one outside the back door next to the German I shot and the weapons that the two older people had in this room. Now what is it that Ernie wanted me to come out and hear?"

"It's Ace, Chief," said Anderson.

"What about Ace?"

"He's dead."

"He's what? Are you sure?"

For the first time since the operation started, Dixon was momentarily unable to cope with what he had been told. He walked to the window, stood there for a moment staring out at the woods without saying a word, but quickly pulled himself together.

"How did it happen? He was all the way out to the road. There was nothing going on out there."

"He wasn't out by the gate. I found him much closer to the house. He must have decided to help and took a bullet in the head. He must have died instantly."

Dixon was a hardened, crusty veteran of the dangers of

law enforcement. He had lost men before, but it had never affected him the way the news of Ace Ferguson's death was affecting him. He turned away to brush tears from his eyes with the back of his hand.

"Why didn't he listen to me? I told him to stay out by the gate."

"Don't blame yourself, Chief," said Simpson. "We all heard you tell him what to do. He just wanted to be part of the action."

"It was just damn bad luck. If that bullet had struck him anywhere else, it almost certainly wouldn't have killed him," said Anderson.

"How can you say that?" said Dixon, looking at the weapons Kravitz had piled on the table. "They are all large-bore handguns. They would have blown a large hole wherever they hit a man. Look at Strawbridge's shoulder."

"Ace wasn't killed by any of those guns," said Anderson, gesturing at the pile on the table. "The hole in his forehead is small and was caused by a small-caliber bullet."

"I want that weapon," said Dixon. "Make a thorough search of the house and find it. A couple of you bring Ace's body and put it on one of the beds. Randolph, I want you to take Strawbridge to the RAF station. Bring up one of the cars. They have medical facilities there. As soon as we are through here I'll get in touch with the Yard to make arrangements about Ferguson."

Ten minutes later, the team reassembled. They had not found the small-bore weapon. "All of you go outside. Search in the proximity of the house. I want that gun," demanded Dixon.

Twenty minutes later, Kravitz came running in,

triumphantly brandishing a small pistol above his head. "I found it, Chief." he said handing it to Dixon.

Dixon looked it over very carefully. The chamber could hold two bullets. It was not loaded, but appeared to have been fired—how recently was hard to tell. Somebody had carefully scratched the letters "R.W." on the butt. There was no other identification.

"It's an old derringer. Where did you find it?"

"It was in some tall grass right before the underbrush took over. Looks to me like someone might have thrown it there. Maybe from one of the bedrooms. That's just a guess."

"You might just be right."

Dixon took the now-empty derringer into the bedroom. Leuzinger was still sitting on the bed. Graham and Simpson were standing in front of him with their guns pointed at him.

"This is your gun, isn't it, Captain?" Dixon said as he handed it to Leuzinger.

"No, it's not," Leuzinger responded quickly. "I never saw it before. See there," he said pointing, "Somebody has scratched their initials on the butt. They're not my initials."

"You killed a non-combatant. You'll hang for that," said Dixon.

"You can't scare me," said Leuzinger. "That's not my gun. I didn't fire it and you can't prove differently."

"You'd better tell me when and where that U-boat is coming to pick you up or you will hang."

"My name is Heinrich Leuzinger. My rank is—"

Dixon stalked out of the room and Graham followed.

"Can he be executed if we can prove he killed Ferguson?"

"I don't know. I think so, but I'm not sure. I'll bet Leuzinger doesn't know either."

"Why did he come back here? Why didn't the U-boat pick him up? Do you think it is still planning to come and get him?"

"Those are three excellent questions," said Dixon, "and I don't know the answer to any of them. I am just going on the assumption that some unexpected problem prevented the U-boat from coming this time, but it still plans to come and get him. If that assumption is right, we need to find out when and where."

"How can we prove it's his gun?" asked Graham.

"I don't know that either. We could have the crime lab check for fingerprints but we are running out of time."

They sat at the table for some time caught up in their own thoughts.

Suddenly, Dixon slapped himself on the forehead. "That's it—Tom Sloan."

"What about Tom Sloan?"

"When we first met Tom, I asked him if Leuzinger had a gun. He said he didn't know. In a later visit, Tom saw that the German had a small gun."

"Ernie, call the Yard. Have them pick up Tom Sloan and fly him up here right away. I am betting he can identify that gun."

"But it's two o'clock in the morning."

"Make the call now."

CHAPTER EIGHTY-FIVE

"WHO'S THERE?" SAID A female voice through the door.

"It's Inspector Micelli from Scotland Yard, Mrs. Sloan."

It had been a quiet night in London as it had for a week. German bombers were concentrating their raids on the shipyards in Tyneside and the industrial cities in the north. Micelli had to bang on the door for five minutes before waking the occupants.

"It's three o'clock in the morning," protested Miriam.

"I know and I'm extremely sorry, but it's important that I talk to you and Tom right away."

She opened the door simultaneously with Mrs. Goldstein opening her door across the corridor, dressed in a shabby old dressing gown with her hair in curlers. "What on earth is going on and what's all the banging about? We finally get a little relief from the bombing and we still can't get any sleep," groused Mrs. Goldstein.

"Go back to bed, Mrs. Goldstein. I'm sorry you were disturbed," said Mrs. Sloan. "Come in, Inspector. What's this all about?"

Mrs. Goldstein muttered something uncomplimentary under her breath and retreated back into her flat.

Tom joined his mother and Inspector Micelli in the tiny kitchen. Characteristically, Rebecca had not awakened.

"Is there something wrong?" Miriam asked anxiously.

"No, nothing is wrong. Quite the contrary. We have captured the German pilot. For reasons, which I can't divulge at the moment, we need Tom to come with us to the house in the Midlands where we are holding the German. We would like to take him with us now—with your permission of course."

"Is there any danger? You know Tom was in great danger in helping Scotland Yard track this man down. I don't want him to be in danger again."

"I can assure you, Mrs. Sloan, that he will be in no danger whatsoever."

"What about his school? By the time you drive him up there and back, he's going to miss a lot of school."

"We're going to fly him up there this morning and we'll have him back by tonight."

Tom's eyes opened wide. "We're going to fly. Gosh. Mum, you have to let me go."

Micelli smiled. "Have you ever flown before, Tom?"

"Golly no. I've only even been in a car a few times."

"All right, Tom. Go and get dressed—and be sure to put on warm clothes," said Miriam.

"May I make you a cup of tea for you while you wait, Inspector?"

"That's very kind of you, Mrs. Sloan, but no, thank you. We have to get going as quickly as possible."

"Hurry up, Tom," shouted Miriam.

Five minutes later, they were on their way to Croydon where a plane was waiting to take Tom and Micelli to the Midlands.

The flight took a little less than two hours. As a special treat, the pilot let Tom sit in the cockpit for a while. The sun was just coming up when they landed at the RAF base. Randolph, who had delivered the injured Strawbridge to the infirmary on the base, was waiting for them with a car. It was seven o'clock in the morning when they got to the Duggan house. Tom was very nervous at the thought of seeing Leuzinger in the hands of Scotland Yard. At that point, he did not know whether Leuzinger was aware that he had turned him in.

CHAPTER EIGHTY-SIX

DIXON LOOKED AT HIS watch and mused about the tasks ahead. *Tom Sloan should be here in within the hour. It's too early to call Sir Giles Willoughby at the Yard. He wouldn't get in for another couple of hours. I'll see how the decoding chaps are doing.*

He went to the back room. Mason was reading documents in the binders while Tyler seemed to be performing some kind of examination of the radio.

"Well, any headway?"

"Good news and bad news, Chief," replied Tyler.

"What's the good news?"

"The radio and the materials are intact. The German agents obviously did not have the opportunity to sabotage anything. Given enough time, we will have a working knowledge of the German communication system with their agents in this country."

"Good. What's the bad news?"

"It will take time. There's a lot of tedious trial and error tests we must perform."

"How much time?"

"Hard to say. We'll work very long hours, but it's going

to take three or four days. Here's what we see as the problem. For some reason, the U-boat didn't pick up the pilot last night. We don't know why. I doubt very much that the pilot knows why either. It could have been as simple as an engineering malfunction—or perhaps it was weather or maybe they were spooked by some Allied naval activity. It could have been any of a number of things. We don't know for sure, but we think it's likely that they will quickly make another attempt to get him out of England and probably by U-boat—although that's by no means certain. We think it will be within the next twenty-four hours—although we don't know that either. They won't pick the same spot again, but they will want to do it soon. Those arrangements have probably already been made and, though it's unlikely that the pilot knows why he wasn't picked up last night, it is likely he knows, that if another attempt is to be made, when and where it will occur."

"Assuming we find out where and when they are planning a second attempt—a very difficult assumption to make—how does that help us with the time problem in deciphering the German code?" asked Dixon.

"The Germans keep their radio communications to a minimum. It's always on an important time-sensitive basis. Our understanding, which is admittedly sketchy, is that typically there may not be contact for days—sometimes even weeks. If Leuzinger just doesn't show up for the prearranged second attempt, the Germans will naturally be very concerned and suspicious and will definitely initiate a call to this radio. If they don't get an appropriately coded answer, they will know this nest has been compromised."

"What's your solution—assuming there is one?"

"It's a long shot. If we can discover the rendezvous and

the pickup time, maybe we can have the navy intercept the sub and either drive it off or destroy it."

"How does that buy us any time?"

"It may not. If Leuzinger doesn't show up, the Germans will know there is something wrong. If the sub gets intercepted or sunk, the Germans may conclude that it was coincidence and plain bad luck that the sub ran into Allied vessels. They know that the coast is heavily patrolled and they also know that there is danger in rescuing downed fliers or picking up agents in this fashion. Bottom line—Leuzinger doesn't show up and the sub is not intercepted—100 percent of our decoding will be too late and ineffective. If the sub is intercepted, driven off, or sunk when Leuzinger was to show up, they may not believe this nest has been compromised and may not immediately initiate a call to this radio. It's a long shot, but it's the only shot we have."

"Of course that long shot—slim as it may be—depends entirely on getting the information from Leuzinger—a very doubtful proposition."

"That's all we have, I'm afraid," said Mason.

Graham opened the door. "There's a car coming up the driveway. It's probably Randolph, Tom Sloan, and whoever picked up the boy in London. I've got our people with their weapons at the ready in case it's some more of Leuzinger's friends."

Graham and Dixon went to the front door. The car door opened and out jumped Tom Sloan.

"It's good to see you, Tom," said Dixon shaking him by the hand. "Sorry we had to get you up so early this morning. How did you enjoy the plane ride?"

"It was terrific, sir. I've never been in a plane before. You could see all the way to the sea. Wait till I tell the boys at school. Will they be jealous."

"I'm afraid you can't tell the boys at school. You know that we are on very hush-hush police business. Just like the whole thing with the bombed-out building, you have to promise me you won't tell anyone."

Tom was crestfallen. He was looking forward to bragging to his friends about the flight. "I promise," he said.

"Good lad," said Dixon. "Come in the house with me. I want to show you something."

He took Tom into the main room, picked up the derringer from the table, and handed it to Tom. "Have you ever seen that before?"

"Yes. It's Captain Leuzinger's," Tom quickly responded after looking at the butt of the gun.

"Are you sure, Tom?"

"I'm absolutely positive."

"This is very important. How can you be so sure?"

"Remember when you first asked me if I had seen a gun with Captain Leuzinger at the bombed house and I told you no. Remember that a few days later the captain had moved on the couch and the gun fell on the floor. Well, he showed me the gun. He said he had it a long time and pointed out the initials 'R. W.' scratched on the butt."

"The Captain's name is Heinrich Leuzinger. His initial are 'H. L.'—not 'R.W.'—if it's his gun, why would he carve somebody else's initials on it?"

"That's easy. He told me that the gun belonged to his uncle who was a pilot in the First World War and flew with the Red Baron. His uncle's name was Rolf Werner. I remember it very clearly because when he told me his uncle's name he pronounced it 'Verner.' I asked him why his uncle carved "R. W." when his last name started with a 'V.' Captain Leuzinger explained that his uncle's name did start with a 'W,' but Germans pronounced a 'W' as 'V.' That's why I remember it so clearly."

Stephens and Thompson were in the bedroom guarding Leuzinger with the door closed. Mason and Tyler were in the back room attempting to decipher the German code. Strawbridge was in the infirmary at the RAF base. All the rest were in the room listening to Dixon's conversation with Tom.

"That does it. Leuzinger killed Ace," said Simpson.

"Seems conclusive to me," agreed Graham.

"If this was a usual murder case, you'd get a conviction every time with Tom's testimony and the characteristic smell of gunpowder on his hand " said Randolph.

"I found the derringer on the verge of the underbrush in line with the room where we found Leuzinger. He could have taken a couple of shots with it and, when he heard us entering the house, he could have thrown it out of the window," said Kravitz.

"Sounds to me like you have all convicted him," said Dixon with a wry expression. "Now if I can convince Leuzinger that we've got him, maybe we can get something out of him."

He turned to Tom. "You must be hungry." Without waiting for an answer, he said to no one in particular, "I think we have some food left over from last night. One of you take Tom out to the car and get him something to eat. I want to talk to the superintendent before we confront Leuzinger."

Sir Giles Willoughby was the superintendent at the Yard and the top man. He was born with the proverbial silver spoon in his mouth and came from one of the oldest and most respected families in England. He was Eton and Oxford educated and lived in a five-hundred-year-old restored castle on two hundred acres in a prime area of Buckinghamshire. He was haughty and aloof and could be curt and sarcastic with subordinates. He did not suffer fools easily. He was a perfect example of a real blue blood. He belonged to all the right clubs and was on the A-list for invitations to parties hosted by the so-called elite of the country. For all that, he was a skilled and highly respected policeman. He had distinguished himself in the First World War and had been awarded a DSC for bravery. His knighthood was earned.

Dixon got Willoughby on the radiophone and explained the whole story ending with the capture of Leuzinger and the German radio and binders.

"Good show, Dixon. Jolly good show. We'll make a detective out of yet."

Willoughby's weak attempts at humor were usually at the expense of someone and this was no exception. "Did any of your men get hurt?"

"We lost one man. Ace Ferguson was shot in the head and killed."

Dixon could hear Willoughby thumbing through some papers.

"Ferguson, Ferguson—I don't see the name of Ferguson as one of our men."

"I'll explain that later, if I may. Strawbridge also took one in the shoulder, but it isn't serious. Here's what I want to do. We know Leuzinger killed Ferguson. We can prove it primarily through the boy, Tom Sloan, who I told you about. I think that the shooting of a non-military person by an escaped combatant is a hanging offense, but I don't know for sure. I want to convince Leuzinger that he will likely hang for the killing, but that if he tells us when and where the U-boat will pick him up, we won't hang him. If we find out, we can have our navy intercept and sink the U-boat or drive it off before its rendezvous. That may buy us some time, which we won't have if the U-boat is there and Leuzinger doesn't show up."

Dixon explained Mason's theory at some length and said "If the U-boat is sunk or driven away, a story can be planted in the papers and on the BBC that the naval vessels were in the vicinity quite by accident and it was just good fortune that the U-boat was found. Maybe the Germans will buy it and will lie low for a while and won't contact the radio for a few days. By that time, our boys may have broken the code. It's a long shot, but better than nothing."

"Not much better," grumped Willoughby. "I'll get on to the War Office and see what they say."

"Tell them it's urgent. We need clearance right away. One last thing. Very important. Ask him if I can promise him that he won't be hanged if he gives us the information we want."

"I will. I will." Willoughby was not pleased at being told what to do.

Twenty minutes later, Willoughby called back. "The War Office approves. Go for it." Dixon knew that, with Willoughby's connections, he would be able to slice through government red tape very quickly.

"The navy has to be careful. It mustn't look like they have been lying in wait. If the Germans get word that it's an ambush, we're out of luck," cautioned Dixon.

"They know that, Dixon. It's really not necessary for you continually to say the obvious," Willoughby said testily.

"We're out of luck, as you say, if you can't get the bloody German to give you the when and where."

"Yes, sir. That fact has been obvious to me for some time now," said Dixon, gently pushing in the needle. Dixon was a legend at the Yard and he was the one man at the Yard who had absolutely no fear of Willoughby—or anybody else for that matter.

"Can I tell him he won't be hanged if he gives us the information?" asked Dixon.

"Yes, you may—although there is a great deal of doubt as to whether they would hang him anyway. Keep me advised."

Tom Sloan and Detective Thompson walked in to the room shortly thereafter.

"Did you get something to eat?"

"Yes, sir. It was really good."

"Good. Are you ready to go in and see Captain Leuzinger?"

"I am."

"I'll go in first and talk to him for a few minutes. You wait here in the main room and I'll call you."

CHAPTER EIGHTY-SEVEN

"CAPTAIN LEUZINGER, I BELIEVE this is your gun and it is the gun that killed a non-combatant—a local village policeman. That, Captain, is a hanging offense," Dixon said to the German.

"That's not my gun and you can't prove it is. Show it to me again."

Dixon handed it to him. "See, I already told you once. It has the initials 'R. W.' and my initials are 'H.L.'—you had better come up with something better than that," Leuzinger said with a smirk.

"Oh, I have something much better than that," Dixon retorted. "Tom, will you come in here please."

Tom Sloan walked in. Stephens, who had been guarding Leuzinger, moved to one side so that Tom could get closer.

Leuzinger frowned and then smiled. "Tom, what a surprise to see you again and what a pleasure. What on earth are you doing here?"

Tom didn't answer, but Dixon did. "Tom is going to prove that this gun is yours and some of my men are going to prove that you used the gun to kill the policeman."

Leuzinger paled, but did not abandon his cocky bravado.

"I repeat it's not my gun and neither Tom nor anyone else can prove otherwise. Besides, Tom is my friend. He helped me and he knows that I am a good person who hates this war and would not have shot the gentleman. He's not going to help you hang me."

Dixon paused. It was what was known as a dramatic pause. It lasted almost a minute, but seemed longer. During that time, Dixon stared directly at Leuzinger. Nobody moved or made any noise. Finally, in a very quiet monotone, Dixon said, "Tom read your letter."

His bravado quickly evaporating, Leuzinger made a last effort. "What letter?"

"Don't be so dense, Captain. You know the one about your mythical friend Eamon Shaughnessy and your nonexistent wife who was supposedly dying of some mysterious illness."

Leuzinger's face contorted in anger and, despite his leg, he came off the bed and lunged at Tom. Stephens moved quickly and threw him back on the bed.

"You dirty little Jew bastard. Don't you worry, we're coming and you and all the Jewish vermin in this country will end up in concentration camps. You sneaky little rat—you opened my letter. I'll get you. You wait."

Leuzinger was totally out of control. His face was bright red. The veins in his neck looked like rope. As he spoke, saliva spewed from his mouth. Dixon was as angry as any of his men had ever seen him. He took a menacing step toward Leuzinger and would have struck him, but for Ernie Graham stepping between them and gently pulling him away.

"All right now, you listen to me. First, if it wasn't for the English weather, you would probably never have been caught," said Dixon.

Leuzinger's anger still showed, but it was now mixed with puzzlement.

"You see, Tom never intended to open your letter. On his way home, he got caught in the rain and the envelope got wet. It smeared the address and Tom decided, to be sure it got to your 'friend,' that he would take the letter out and put it in a new envelope and copy the address. When he took it out, the letter fell open and he saw reference to your filthy anti-Semitism. When he saw that, your days were numbered. You look a little faint—would you like some water?"

Dixon gestured to Thompson who went to the kitchen, came back, and handed the glass to Leuzinger who, still defiant, threw it on the floor.

Dixon ignored it and went on. "Now for the proof that it is your gun. Tom is prepared to testify that you showed him that very gun; that you told him the initials R. W. are those of your uncle Rolf Werner; that you told him that Ws in German are pronounced as Vs and that your uncle Rolf gave you that gun. Is that right, Tom?"

Tom nodded affirmatively.

"So much for proving that it's your gun. Oh, and by the way, Captain, in this country—unlike yours—the word of a Jew is as good as the word of anyone else. Now to the proof that you used that gun to kill a civilian. That proof comes in several parts. First, it was your gun. Who else would use it? Second, despite your protests that you never fired a gun in this house, several of my men are prepared to testify that they smelled evidence on you that you had recently fired a weapon. Third, my men collected all the weapons used by your comrades—all of whom are dead and had their weapons close to their bodies. None of them had a derringer. Fourth, Detective Kravitz found your gun thrown out of this window and close to the underbrush. Finally, Constable Ferguson was killed by a small-bore weapon. Yours is the only weapon here that fits that description. That's it. The prosecution rests. In this country we don't like Nazis killing our civilians while trying to save their own murderous necks. Oh, you'll hang all right." Dixon walked out followed by the other detectives—except the two who were on guard.

"We'll let him stew for a half hour and then we'll give him the cooperation option."

CHAPTER EIGHTY-EIGHT

"BRING LEUZINGER INTO THE main room," Dixon told Stephens.

Stephens brought Leuzinger out of the bedroom and plopped him down in a chair opposite Dixon. All the fight was gone out of him and he looked hopelessly defeated.

"I want to discuss a proposition with you," Dixon said.

They were seated at the large table where Anderson had first seen him with the older German agent. The rest of the team sat around the table or stood in various places in the room. Tom was seated in the armchair next to the fire where Anderson had seen the older woman reading.

"If you tell us exactly when and where the U-boat will make its second attempt to pick you up, we will send you to a POW camp and you won't be hung. There are several additional conditions, however. First, I want your answer in the next half hour. If you reject the proposal or you don't give me your answer within the half hour, it will not be repeated. You only have the one chance to accept and I emphasize we won't repeat the offer. Second, if you agree and the U-boat does not appear when and where you tell us, we will consider that the same as if you had rejected the offer. So, in summary, if you reject the offer or you don't respond in thirty minutes or if you accept the offer and the U-boat does not appear when and where you told us, you will be hung. Are you clear on the proposal and do you have any questions?"

Leuzinger looked around the room and drummed his fingers on the table. He was no longer defiant and his bravado had completely left him.

"I am a German officer and it was and is my duty to try to escape and that's all I was trying to do. I demand that I be treated under the Geneva Convention as a prisoner of war."

"You don't have the right to be treated as a POW or to have the protection of the Geneva Convention if you kill nonmilitary personnel. Any other questions?"

"Even if I have the information and I give it to you, I have no ability to guarantee that the U-boat will show up. You already know that it was supposed to pick me up last night and, for whatever reason, it didn't arrive."

"I thought I made it clear that you will be executed if you give us information and the U-boat doesn't appear. We will assume you gave us false information. That may sound harsh to you, but those are the terms and they are absolutely non-negotiable. Any more questions?"

Leuzinger shook his head. "Take him back in the bedroom."

After Leuzinger had returned to the bedroom, Anderson asked what everybody thought the chances were that Leuzinger would crack.

Graham said, "I think he would have agreed if he thought he could get away with giving us incorrect information. Now that you've made it clear that it has to be provably legitimate, I don't know."

Thompson said, "He may think you're bluffing about

hanging him, but it's a big chance for him to take. Of course, he has to realize that if he gives the proper time and place, it is quite possible that a German sub will be sunk and most—if not all—of the more than fifty sailors will die. I don't think he would allow that to happen in return for his life."

Randolph said, "I'm betting that he won't agree. He apparently has been decorated—presumably for bravery—and he's a fanatical Nazi. He's a rotten swine, but I don't think he's a coward."

"You might be right, Randolph," said Graham, "but I found it a little odd that he raised the issue of his inability to ensure the arrival of the U-boat. If he wasn't thinking of accepting, why raise that issue?"

"That's easy. You said he would give us false information if he could get away with it. He was probably thinking he could have it both ways—give us false information and not be executed. He's now found out that is not an option," responded Randolph.

Dixon looked at his watch. "We could sit here and speculate for the rest of the day, but we won't have to. We'll know in precisely twenty-two minutes."

CHAPTER EIGHTY-NINE

AFTER FIFTEEN MINUTES, THOMPSON came out of the bedroom. "He's ready to talk."

"Bring him out here."

"He wants to talk to you alone."

Dixon went into the bedroom. Leuzinger was sitting on the bed and looked as if there were tears in his eyes. *The master race,* thought Dixon. *He looks like the master disgrace.*

"What is it going to be—yes or no?"

"I want to talk about it."

"There's nothing more to talk about. You give us the information we want or you don't—it's just that simple."

"What if I give you the information and your navy sees the submarine, but it gets away?"

"If they see the sub and it gets away, you're off the hook. If they don't see the sub, you're dead."

"What if your navy sees the sub, but says it didn't."

"Our naval personnel don't lie. If they see it, they'll say so. If they don't, they'll say so."

"Do you solemnly promise that if they see the sub, I will not be executed?"

"I do." *This is beginning to sound like a wedding ceremony,* Dixon thought.

"Will you put it in writing?"

"No. An Englishman's word is his bond."

Leuzinger paused, his face taut and pale. "All right, I'll tell you."

Leuzinger appeared to Dixon as though he had aged ten years in the last two hours. *Strange,* thought Dixon, *he looks smaller than he was when I first saw him. Panic will do that to a man.*

"The sub is to pick me up tomorrow night twenty-five miles north of Skegness. There is a deep-water cove. I think they call it Rogues Cove or Bogues Cove. I don't remember which. I wasn't in contact with Germany. I don't know the code. There was a fellow here named Jimmy who was in charge of that. He told all of us about the location when we got back last night."

"When is the pickup?"

"Tomorrow night between eleven and midnight. There is no moon. A dinghy will come in to pick me up on the shore. I'm to be standing by myself, in uniform, on the beach in the middle of the cove."

"What's the signal?"

"The U-boat will flash three times. I'm to flash twice."

Dixon opened the door. "Thompson, come in here and watch him."

He hurried to the car and entered a coded number. A woman's voice answered, "Sir Giles Willoughby's office."

"Put him on," he said more brusquely than usual.

"He's in a meeting and can't be disturbed," the voice said more icily than had been the initial greeting.

"Well, disturb him," he growled. "Tell him it's Dixon and I have to talk to him right now."

"Oh, Chief Inspector, I didn't know it was you." The sweeter tone suddenly returned. "He told me to interrupt him if you called. Wait just a minute."

Almost immediately, Willoughby came on the phone. "What have you got, Dixon?"

"The pickup is tomorrow night between eleven and midnight in a place called Rogues Cove or Bogues Cove, he didn't know which, although I think it is probably Rogue. It's twenty-five miles north of Skegness. Somebody can look on a map. It's a deep-water cove apparently. They will expect Leuzinger to be standing on the beach in the middle of the cove between those two times. The sub will flash three times. Leuzinger is to respond by flashing twice. We must have a man of Leuzinger's height wearing a Luftwaffe uniform standing there. He is about six foot one or two tall and maybe thirteen stone. I know we talked about it, but it is essential for us to have any chance at all to crack the German code that the German's don't suspect that the attack on the sub was a planned ambush."

"Got it. I'll put the War Office on it right away." For once, Sir Giles had no peevish criticism of Dixon telling him what to do.

CHAPTER NINETY

ABLE SEAMAN ALFRED "ALFIE" Roberts, wearing the uniform of a German Luftwaffe pilot, stood shivering in the middle of Rogues Cove holding a flashlight that was turned off. It was half past eleven and he had been there in the cold, drizzling rain for an hour. Three of his mates, armed with rifles, were hidden behind rocks on the beach. Alfie was thinking what a strange day this had turned out to be. If anybody had told him when he got out of his bunk that morning that later that night he would be standing on the beach dressed as a German pilot, he would have thought they were barmy. His destroyer, *The Braxton*, was in port for routine maintenance. Chief Petty Officer Lambert had told him and his gunnery crew that they would be cleaning the ship's six-inch guns and they had better put their backs into it or he would put his boot into their backs.

Halfway through the morning, a formation was called. Three blokes in civvies that he had never seen before went up and down the line of sailors, looking them over. They pulled five sailors out of line, including Alfie. They gave those five another once over; had a whispered conversation, and then beckoned Alfie to follow them. In the captain's cabin they told him of the plans to attack a sub that was coming to pick up a German pilot and that someone impersonating that pilot would have to be seen by the sub standing on the beach. They had decided that Alfie fit the description best. The three civilians, who did not identify themselves, told Alfie that it was a matter of national security and that he was not to say a word to anyone about it. The ship's captain, who was present, told him sternly that if he did tell anyone, he would be court-martialed. One of the three civilians told him that if anyone asked what it was all about, he was to tell them they needed someone for a police lineup. Later, they picked him up on the dock in a van and drove to Rogues Cove. On the way he put on the German uniform.

The destroyers *HMS Lysander* and *Cranbrook* lay three miles apart on either side of the cove. Two torpedo boats were deployed on either side of the destroyers. The engines on all four vessels were stopped and no lights showed. The crews were instructed that absolute silence was to be maintained. Gun crews on all vessels were in place with the guns loaded. Torpedoes were loaded on the torpedo boats and their operators in place. Sonar operators on the two destroyers listened for any sound and watched their screens. Officers on both ships looked over the operators' shoulders.

Suddenly and simultaneously both operators called out, "Contact approaching from west-northwest. Distance 2000 yards and closing." Commander Stratton on *The Lysander* commanding the small flotilla ordered, "Wait for it." His radio operator tapped out the message. The sonar operators called out 1,500 yards, then 1,200 yards, then 1,000 yards. A few minutes later the lookout on one of the torpedo boats called out, "Periscope off port bow," and then "Submarine breaking surface," and gave the coordinates.

Night glasses on all the vessels were now focused on the U-boat. It came to a stop, surfaced, and the hatch on the conning tower opened. The number 137 was clearly visible on its side. It flashed a light three times. On the beach, a nervous Alfie, his fingers numb with cold, fumbled with his flashlight. Finally he was able to flash twice. Two men were seen to launch a dinghy from the sub and row toward the beach. Stratton shouted, "Start engines." Simultaneously, all four vessels, lights now shining, converged on the U-boat. "Fire at will," ordered Stratton. Messages were relayed to all vessels. Guns on the destroyers were maneuvered into position. Gunnery officers shouted, "Shoot!" and the guns roared again and again. The torpedo boats swung into firing position and, on order, let loose with their deadly ordnance. On board the U-137, Captain Jurgen Steiner yelled, "Dive! Dive," but it was too late. A shell smashed into the conning tower. Another hit the bow. A torpedo caught the doomed sub amidships. It was all over within minutes. A series of explosions racked the sub. Fire broke out. It rolled over on its side and went down rapidly. Nobody got out.

CHAPTER NINETY-ONE

THE DINGHY WAS ABOUT two hundred yards from the U-boat when the attack started. Lieutenant Dieter Mannheim looked back in horror. "My God," he gasped.

"What shall we do?" cried petty officer Kurtz

"Stop rowing." The U-boat was on fire and the sound of explosions was earsplitting. It was clear that the sub could not survive.

"Let's wait a minute and see if anyone gets out." They sat in the dinghy and watched as the sub went down. They waited another five minutes. Nobody surfaced.

"Nobody got out but us. They're all dead. Row for the shore. If we get to land, maybe we can get away. I don't know, but one thing's certain. We can't row back to Germany."

On the beach, Alfie Roberts watched the attack in amazement. It was like the fireworks display they used to have at the Blackpool Pier before the war. He could see the submarine as it burned. It was a sight he wouldn't soon forget. He wasn't sure what he was supposed to do now. The civilian blokes had told him where to stand and when and how many times he was to flash his flashlight. He knew that was supposed to lead up to an attack on the sub and it had.

What they hadn't told him was what, if anything, he was supposed to do after the attack. *I suppose they don't really care what happens to me after the attack,* he thought.

"Hey, Bert," he yelled at one of his mates who was still behind the rocks. "What the bloody 'ell are we supposed to do now?"

"I dunno," replied Bert. "Nobody told me."

"Me neither," said Alfie.

"'alf a mo," said one of the other sailors "There's a dinghy coming. See it? Straight ahead. About a hundred yards out."

"Get back here, Alfie," said Bert. It's probably survivors off the sub or the blokes what were supposed to pick up the Kraut. Duck down behind these rocks."

The four of them watched as the dinghy approached. There were only two men in it. It beached almost directly in front of them.

"Let's take them," whispered Bert. The two men had gotten out of the dinghy and were wading ashore.

Bert stood straight up and leveled his rifle at the Germans. "All right, you two. Put your hands up—and no monkey business." The other three British sailors also stood up and three rifles pointed to the Germans. Kurtz, who could speak no English, pulled a pistol from his waist. Three rifles fired at him and he fell dead. Lieutenant Mannheim raised his hands.

The four Englishmen walked toward Mannheim. Alfie called out in his North Country accent, "Keep your hands up and walk toward us slowly. Try anything funny and your dead."

Mannheim was stunned. *Who is this fellow wearing a German Luftwaffe officer's uniform,* he thought.

"You're not a German officer. You're not Captain Leuzinger, are you?"

The four Englishmen laughed. "You're bloody right. I'm not Captain Whatshisname. And who are you?" said Alfie.

"I am Lieutenant Dieter Mannheim. Serial number 347623."

Just then, Dixon, Graham, and Kravitz came down to the beach.

"Well done, men," said Dixon. "Take this officer up on the bluffs. There are military policemen there who will take him from you. Your chief petty officer is up there, too, with a vehicle to take you back to your ship."

CHAPTER NINETY-TWO

"THIS IS THE BBC and this is the six o'clock news. Stuart Hibbert bringing it to you. German bombers were out in force last night hitting targets in London and the Southern Counties after a seven-day respite. Anti-aircraft fire brought down three of the bombers. This morning, a large number of Messerschmitt fighters were engaged by squadrons of Spitfires and Hurricanes. Eleven of the German planes were shot down and several others severely damaged. Four of our planes were lost. The pilots of two of them have been saved."

"A German U-boat was discovered by a flotilla of British warships on routine maneuvers close to shore on the North Sea Coast. It was on the surface with its engines stopped. The submarine was sunk by cannon fire and torpedoes. No German submarine has ever been spotted that close to the English coast, particularly with its engines stopped. The War Office has stated that it has no explanation for the submarine's presence."

"In other news—" Dixon turned the radio off.

The early edition of the *Evening Standard* quoted Commander Stratton of *HMS Lysander* as saying that coming upon a German submarine that close to the coast, with its engines stopped and on the surface, was a complete surprise and that he had never seen or heard of such an occurrence before.

Both the news broadcast and the newspaper article occurred the day following the U-boat sinking. Dixon went to the back room of the house. Mason and Tyler were still working on decoding tasks.

"Possibly we bought some time, but I'm not sure whether we have and, if we have, how much" Dixon told them about the news stories. "How are you coming?"

"We're making headway, but it's more difficult than we thought. Unfortunately, the Germans are not quite as predictable as we thought."

"Do your best. That's all we can expect."

Dixon closed the door, went into the main room, sat down, and wearily ran his hands through his hair. Micelli had left with Tom Sloan to fly back to London. The bodies of the German agents had been removed. They would be buried secretly in a remote location. Stephens had driven down to the RAF infirmary to pick up Strawbridge. Doctors at the infirmary had told Dixon that Strawbridge was well enough to travel and Stephens would drive him to his home where he would convalesce and be treated by his own doctor.

Simpson, Randolph, and Hennessey had left with Leuzinger before the sinking of the U-boat and with strict instructions not to tell Leuzinger any news—when and if it broke—about the attack on the submarine. Leuzinger was to be detained temporarily in a holding cell at the Yard, pending his transfer to a POW camp. Dixon told his men to make sure that neither they nor anyone else talked to Leuzinger about the sub. Dixon wanted to be the one to discuss the matter with the German pilot. He was disgusted by the German both because of his vicious anti-Semitism and because of his astonishing and totally unexpected display of cowardice. He had convinced himself that, as the senior man, it was his duty to inform Leuzinger of the sinking of the sub and that—as a result—the British would not hang him. Secretly, he knew that he was motivated, at least in part, by his hatred for the man and his willingness to let him suffer for a while longer.

Other than Graham and Kravitz—who had accompanied him to pick the Leuzinger impersonator and had been on the bluffs above the beach during the attack on the sub—all the rest of his men had left.

He had one more sad duty to perform. Ace Ferguson's body had been taken to funeral directors in his hometown. Before that, he had called Ace's chief of police and told him what had happened. The chief, who explained that he had known and worked with Ace for many years, said that it would be best if he broke the news of Ace's death to his wife. Dixon decided he would drive down to the Ferguson home on his way back to London with Graham and Kravitz to offer his condolences to Ace's widow. He said good-bye to Mason and Tyler and instructed them to notify him of any developments, then he, Graham and Kravitz left.

So as not to overwhelm Mrs. Ferguson with a number of strangers, he left the other two in the car and knocked on the door. A fiftyish man answered the door. "Would it be possible for me to talk with Mrs. Ferguson for a few minutes?" he asked.

"Does she know you?"

"No, she doesn't," Dixon responded.

"I am her brother and she just lost her husband. She is really in no condition to see strangers."

"I am Chief Inspector Dixon of Scotland Yard. I was with Ace shortly before he died and I can tell her things that might be of some comfort to her."

"Come in," he said, opening the door wider and standing aside.

There were eight or nine people in the small drawing room. Mrs. Ferguson's brother said, "Daisy, this is Chief Inspector Dixon of Scotland Yard who was with Ace right before he died."

A tall, thin, handsome woman in her late forties or early fifties with dark circles under her eyes got up off a chair and came toward him.

"Mrs. Ferguson, I am sorry, deeply sorry for your loss. Unfortunately, I did not know your husband for very long. That was my loss. But I knew him long enough to know that he was a fine, courageous human being. I am not now at liberty to tell you the details of what was going on at the time of his death. At some time in the future, I hope I will be able to. I can tell you this. He died in the service of his country and his actions may well prove to be of immeasurable assistance to our war effort. I wish I could tell you more and I know this is not a great deal of comfort, but I hope it is some."

Tears welled up in her eyes. "Thank you for coming and for saying what you have just said. It is indeed a comfort and I am deeply grateful. Won't you please stay for a while?"

"I wish I could, Mrs. Ferguson, but I am afraid I must get back to London." In a gesture that surprised him, he gave her a quick peck on the cheek. "God bless you," he whispered and walked out. He got in the front passenger seat and said to Kravitz, "Let's go."

CHAPTER NINETY-THREE

KRAVITZ AND GRAHAM WERE not sorry that Dixon had asked them to wait in the car while he went in to pay his respects. These matters were always difficult and there was no easy way to handle them. Dixon got back in the car after ten minutes.

"How did it go, Chief?" asked Graham.

"How do you think it went?" snapped Dixon. Graham was not offended. He and Dixon went back many years and had worked together on so many occasions that it was hard to count. They were good friends and were so close that they almost always knew what the other was thinking.

"It wasn't your fault, Chief. You told him to stay out at the gate and he just didn't do it. You couldn't have done anything else."

Dixon's tone softened. "Thanks Ernie. I didn't mean to bark at you. I'm just having a hard time with it right now."

Very little else was said on the long drive back to London. They stopped once for petrol and went into the little café adjoining the station. They had not eaten since the prior evening and were ravenous. The pickings in the café were sparse. They had sausage rolls and a couple of cups of tea.

Graham drove the rest of the way while Dixon and Kravitz dozed off and on. It was almost midnight when they got to Dixon's house. His wife, Edith, didn't know if he was coming home that night. She never did, but she had waited up for him as she always did.

"Come to bed, dear," she said. "You look so tired." They had been married for more than thirty years and she knew not to ask him anything about his work.

"I will in a few minutes. I think I will just sit here for a little while and have a quick drink."

"You just relax. I'll fix it for you." She knew his preference was a shot of Johnny Walker Black Label and a splash of soda with no ice.

He sipped on it and said, "You go to bed, dear. I'll be up in a little while." She gave him a kiss on the cheek and left. He sat in his favorite armchair in front of the fire, which had long since gone out. He was physically and emotionally drained. He had known Ace Ferguson for such a short time and yet his death was like a great weight on him. Good old Ernie always knew exactly what to say, but this time it was not much help. *I should have sent Ace home the moment he came back with the information from the innkeeper. I know it would have upset him, but I should have done it.* He saw the surprise on Ernie's face when he told everyone to keep the sinking of the U-boat from Leuzinger. Ernie knew that instruction had nothing at all to do with proper police work. It was an act of vindictiveness. He wanted Leuzinger to suffer. It was not right. He knew that. What's more, Ernie and probably all the rest of them knew that. In all his years with the Yard, he had never before let his feelings control his judgment. Strangely enough, he was not sorry.

He finished his drink. He thought momentarily about

having another, but dismissed the idea. He went up to bed, being careful not to wake Edith. He usually fell asleep the moment his head touched the pillow. Not this night. He spent hours with his eyes wide open. The faces of Ace, Daisy, Tom Sloan, and Ernie Graham passed before him—as did the dead faces of the German agents. Finally, at close to three o'clock, he fell asleep.

He was usually in his office by eight, but this morning he was late. He had overslept and Edith had not wakened him. He pretended to castigate her for letting him sleep past his normal time, but both of them knew he didn't mean it. She even gave him a soft-boiled egg for breakfast. He hadn't seen a real egg in months and he refused to eat the powdered variety. He said powdered eggs tasted liked paint scrapings.

"Where an earth did you get it?" he exclaimed.

"Len, the grocer has been promising me a couple of real eggs for the longest time and yesterday he finally came up with two of them. I'll give you the other one for breakfast tomorrow."

"You'll do no such thing. You'll have it yourself."

"We'll see," she smiled.

As soon as he got to the Yard he went to see Sir Giles. There were several other men in Willoughby's office when he opened the door. "I'll come back later," said Dixon.

"No. Come on in now. You know all these chaps," Sir Giles said, rather abruptly ushering them out.

"Come sit down and tell me all about it." Dixon recounted the whole episode starting with the stake out at the bombed out house and ending with the sinking of the U-Boat. Sir Giles was familiar with most of the story, but had not had it related to him in an uninterrupted chronological fashion.

"Jolly good work. How about the decoding? Are they coming along?"

"Mason and Tyler were hard at it when I left. It's proving to be more difficult than they had anticipated. I'll get an update later this morning. In the meantime, I have Leuzinger in a holding cell here. I'm going to tell him that the U-boat was sunk and we won't hang him. I'll have him transferred to a POW camp right away."

"That hanging bit was a bit of a stretch—if you'll pardon the pun. We almost certainly wouldn't have hung him even if there was no U-boat," said Willoughby.

"You and I knew that, but he didn't."

"That's what I like about you, Dixon. You're as sly as a fox and just as devious."

"I'm not sure whether that's a compliment or not, sir."

"It's as close to a compliment as I've ever given. Your method was certainly close to the line, if not across it, but it worked. Off you go then."

Dixon picked up Ernie Graham and they went down into the basement where the few holding cells were located. A uniformed officer opened the cell and they found Leuzinger sitting on the narrow cot. The cell was tiny—eight feet by six feet and the cot was the only thing in it. Leuzinger looked a lot better than the last time Dixon had seen him. He had taken a shower and shaved. His hair was neatly combed. His broken leg had been placed in a cast and he had been provided with a pair of proper crutches in place of the makeshift ones that Tom had put together.

He looked up anxiously as Dixon and Graham came in. Dixon said immediately, "The U-boat showed up."

The relief on Leuzinger's face was palpable. "Thank you," he said. "Am I to be sent to a POW camp?"

"Aren't you the least bit interested in what happened to the U-boat that came to rescue you?" Dixon said scornfully.

"Of course, I am. I'm hoping you're going to tell me that it got away."

"That's a forlorn hope. The U-boat was sunk. Two men got out. They were the two who were rowing to shore to pick you up. One was shot. The other was captured."

Dixon looked long and hard at Leuzinger. "Do you understand what I'm telling you? I don't know what the complement of a U-boat is—fifty or sixty men, maybe more. They came here to save you—and all but one of them died. The British sunk the sub and their guns and torpedoes ultimately caused their deaths, but you and I both know who was primarily responsible, don't we?"

Leuzinger looked down at the ground, but didn't say a word. Dixon had prevented Leuzinger from getting information about the sinking to prolong his pain. For a moment, he thought he would tell Leuzinger that he probably wouldn't have been hung even if he hadn't told about the U-boat, but for some reason decided not to. He did, however, get in one last shot.

"Please understand that the sinking of the U-boat doesn't mean you won't be killed."

"What do you mean? You promised me if I gave you the information and the sub showed up, I would not be hung. You promised. You can't go back on that now."

"I promised that *we* wouldn't execute you. We will live up to that promise. I didn't promise you that your own comrades wouldn't do so if they found out what you had done."

"Who would tell them?"

"I don't know. Probably no one. But I'm told that there are very few secrets in a POW camp. If I were you, I'd watch out. Good-bye, Captain Leuzinger, and thank you for your very valuable information. I'm quite sure we won't see each other again."

LONDON AND NORTH AFRICA, 1941
HONOR AND DISHONOR

CHAPTER NINETY-FOUR

THE POW CAMP IN Victoria Park, which ironically was only a half a mile from the Sloan's flat, was vastly different from the one in the desert. Victoria Park had green grass, flowers, and trees—and no sand dunes. The climate was cool with frequent rain rather than oppressively hot and dry. There were similarities. There were barracks, latrines, and mess halls. There were the omnipresent barbed-wire fences and machine gun towers at each side with guards around the perimeters. Similar to the desert camp, Victoria Park was limited to officers and there was a senior German officer named Major Ernst Feldheim. His reign as SGO ended, however, upon the arrival of a colonel. Feldheim, a short, bald, overweight, red-faced man was only too pleased to relinquish the position. In civilian life, he had been an accountant in Leipzig. In the army he was in the financial corps responsible for army payroll and payment for provisions. His duty post at the beginning of the war was well behind the lines. One day, in an uncharacteristic display of bravado and without authority, he traveled to the front on a supply lorry to, in his words, "see what it was like." He quickly found out. The vehicle he was riding in came under fire and the occupants evacuated it and were promptly captured.

"Colonel, I am occupying the hut reserved for the SGO, but I can get my things out this afternoon."

"There's absolutely no hurry, Major. I can move in tomorrow or the next day. In the meantime, I can bunk in one of the barracks."

That's very thoughtful of you, sir, but I don't have much stuff and it will be no trouble for me to be out of there in a couple of hours. To be honest, I'm glad you're here. Command is not what I'm trained for. Columns of figures are more what I'm used to."

"And I'm sure you're very good at it," said the colonel with a smile.

"There are several new men who came in this morning. It's customary for the SGO to meet with new men and let them know what's expected of them. May I leave that up to you?"

"Of course, Major. Would you be good enough to tell them I'll meet with them first thing in the morning after breakfast?"

There were four officers lined up outside the SGO's hut after breakfast the next morning—three were Wermacht, one was Luftwaffe. The new SGO came out of his hut and the four men came to attention and saluted.

"At ease, gentlemen. Please tell me your names."

"Captain Rudolf Bergen."

"Lieutenant Franz Gleber."

"Lieutenant Fritz Joenblach."

"Captain Heinrich Leuzinger."

"I am Colonel Hans Dieter Reichmann and I am a new man here myself. I just arrived yesterday as I think all of you did. I need to learn the ropes myself. I'm sure I will be getting a visit from the camp commandant so I'll keep this short. I'd like to welcome you here, but I think that's hardly the right thing when you're entering captivity." Reichmann looked around to be sure that no enemy guards were present. "One of the things I will be looking into is the question of escape. I'm sure there is an escape committee and I'll be talking with them. I'll get back with you soon. Dismissed."

The four men saluted and moved away. "Oh, Leuzinger, just a minute."

Leuzinger froze and turned to face Reichmann. "I just noticed you looked a bit pale and shaky. Are you feeling all right? I am sure I can get you medical attention."

"Thank you, sir. I am all right. I think I have a bit of a cold."

"I assume you were recently shot down."

"Yes, sir. I was hiding out in a bombed-out building for a while. It was very damp. I probably caught something."

"They found you in that building, I suppose."

"Yes. I'm afraid so."

"All right. Let me know if you need any medical attention."

"I will. Thank you, sir."

Two days later, one other captured officer was brought in. He was a naval officer.

Reichmann interviewed him in his hut. "I'm new here myself. Only been here a couple of days, but I don't think there are many naval personnel here. In fact you may be the only one. What is your name?"

"Lieutenant Dieter Mannheim, sir."

"I'm Colonel Reichmann. How did you get here?"

"My submarine was on a mission to pick up a downed

pilot. We had done this a couple of times before without incident. This time was different. We were ambushed."

"Tell me about it."

"I don't know much about the build up, but there's an organization, or was, in England that helps get pilots who were shot down out of the country. Sometimes submarines pick them up. Sometimes they try to get them out in different ways. This time the pilot was to stand in the middle of a cove on the English North Sea Coast. We give him a signal. If he returns it correctly we use powerful night glasses to see if a pilot in uniform is standing where he's supposed to be. He was. I was detailed to pick him up along with a petty officer. We launched a dinghy and started to row away from the boat. We'd gone maybe 50 yards when all hell broke out. Gun fire and torpedoes hit the sub and in minutes she rolled over and sunk. No one got out. We continued to the shore. Three British sailors or marines, I'm not sure what they were, jumped out and pointed rifles at us. My petty officer pulled his pistol. They shot him dead. There was nothing I could do, so I put my hands up. Three civilians came down from the bluffs. Now here's the curious part. The fellow in the German pilot's uniform started talking to the others about what was to be done next. He wasn't German. He was English. He certainly wasn't the Captain Leuzinger I was supposed to pick up. It was a set up. We were set up."

"Wait a moment. What did you say his name was? The fellow you were supposed to pick up."

"Leuzinger—Captain Leuzinger."

"First name Heinrich?"

"I think so. Yes, Heinrich. That's it. Captain Heinrich Leuzinger."

"Well, I've got a surprise for you. He's here. He came in a couple of days ago."

"Colonel, there was one other thing. Probably most important. When I was taken to the top of the bluffs, two soldiers—I think they were military policemen—grabbed my arms and marched me across a street where there were several vehicles. You couldn't see them from the sea or from the beach. As we were nearing the first car, I saw a man sitting in the driver's seat. He was talking on some kind of radiophone. I heard him say, "Leuzinger was slot on, or spock on. I couldn't quite make it out."

"Could it have been 'spot on'?"

"That's it, 'spot on.' That's what he said 'spot on.' What does it mean? My English is not so good."

"It's an English expression. It means accurate or correct. Something like that. 'Leuzinger was accurate.'"

Mannheim exploded, "The bastard sold us out. He told them when and where we were coming. I'll kill him! The miserable traitor. Sixty-five men—all dead because of him. We have to kill him. Let me do it, Colonel. I want him to die nice and slow."

CHAPTER NINETY-FIVE

CORCORAN AND SLOAN WERE meeting with two Army intelligence officers to get an update on the investigation into the stabbing of Colonel Reichmann and the death of Lieutenant Von Steuffel.

"We've had a substantial breakthrough," said Major Drummond. "Von Steuffel was very well liked by many of the other German officers. He was a professional footballer before the war. He was very good. I remember him. He was a center forward and scored a lot of goals. Very powerful right foot. He even played several times for the German national team. Scored the winning goal against a very good Hungarian side."

Colonel Corcoran looked at Drummond and smiled. Drummond's face reddened. "Sorry for the digression. I am a great fan. Season ticket holder at Arsenal. Anyway, he was almost idolized by a lot of the other prisoners. He wasn't the smartest officer in the German army. No education. Probably only got a commission because of his footballing fame. On the other hand, Major Gruber is not well liked. He is a bit of a martinet, always pulling rank on more junior officers. He couldn't wait to assume the mantle of the senior German officer—calling formations and reprimanding the others for whatever little transgression he thought he saw. Ordinarily, discipline is pretty lax in a POW camp. Perhaps not to the same extent as you've seen in the Italian compound. Anyway, he was not too well liked before he became temporary SGO and his popularity has not improved since."

Captain Jurgenson took up the story. "The officer in the next bunk to Von Steuffel, name of Wolf, told us that Von Steuffel bragged to him that Gruber had promised him a medal and a promotion if he killed Reichmann; that Gruber had said that Reichmann was a Jew lover and that killing the traitor would make Von Steuffel a hero in the Fatherland. Wolf didn't take him seriously. Von Steuffel was known to tell some wild stories and was a bit of a prankster. After Reichmann was stabbed, Wolf said that Von Steuffel had given him a nod and said with a smile, 'Can you guess who did it?' He then looked around and pointed to his own chest. It was well known that Von Steuffel was a virulent anti-Semite. That fact would not have adversely affected his popularity in the camp nor would Gruber's similar anti-Semitism have increased the dislike felt for him."

Major Drummond then came to the most significant evidence. "On the night Von Steuffel died, Lieutenant Schoenfels went to the latrine shortly before lights out. All prisoners have to be in their barracks by lights out although there is no roll call at that point. The next roll call is at formation at seven. Guards come around and secure the barracks at lights out. When Schoenfels went into the latrine, he saw Gruber and Von Steuffel arguing. He heard Gruber shout at Von Steuffel, "You clumsy fool. You made a mess of it and now you won't keep quiet." They both then saw Schoenfels and stopped talking. Schoenfels completed his toilet and left. Gruber and Von Steuffel were still there. Von Steuffel was not seen alive again."

Sloan said, "Sounds like there is very compelling case against Gruber. What is the next step?"

"We'll report the results of our investigation to Eighth Army command. There almost certainly will be a military tribunal. I have been informed of the information that Sir Rupert Corcoran obtained from Dr. Meyer Helstein. That establishes a motive. Coupled with the testimony of Schoenfels, Wolf, and others, I think there is a strong case against Major Gruber and our investigation is not completed. Colonel Reichmann has been transferred to a POW camp in London. If necessary, we can bring him here. Alternatively, we can get a written sworn statement from him. I think the tribunal would admit it under the circumstances. We're sure there will be further evidence. Gruber had motive and opportunity and those are the two key factors in a criminal prosecution.

Chapter Ninety-Six

Colonel Reichmann called Lieutenant Mannheim into his quarters. He knew he was going to have a very hard time convincing his fellow POWs to agree to his plan as to what should be done about Leuzinger. He also knew that without Mannheim's support, obtaining that agreement would be virtually impossible.

"Lieutenant Mannheim, I want you to promise me something. I'm not going to ask you to keep this matter to yourself. I couldn't—and I wouldn't, even if I could. I am going to ask you to hold off doing anything until I have spoken to all the men. I'm going to assemble them in the mess hall and I am going to tell them the whole story. I want you next to me so that the story comes out right. I'll then make a suggestion as to what we should do. I am going to ask you to support what I tell them. While that's going on, I'm going to put Leuzinger in here by himself. Will you listen carefully to what I tell the men and not make up your mind about it until I finish? Will you do that?" asked Reichmann.

"I'll wait to hear what you have to stay, sir. Beyond that I can't commit."

"Good man."

First thing after lunch Reichmann sought out Leuzinger. "Please come with to my hut." After they arrived, Reichmann said, "This morning, a naval officer off the U-137 arrived at the camp. He was the only survivor of the sinking of that boat by the British. He knows you told the British the time and place where the sub was to pick you up."

Leuzinger looked as if he was going to faint. He sat down heavily in the only chair in the room. "I did no such thing," he protested.

"It's no good, Leuzinger. He saw the Englishman dressed up to look like you. He heard another Englishman say that your information turned out to be accurate. I'm going to try to keep the men from tearing you apart. Quite honestly, you deserve it. I might even like to help them. The reason that I want to stop it is to prevent them from being executed by the British for murder—not to save you. Do you understand?"

Leuzinger nodded mutely. His face was the picture of abject despair.

"Now you stay here and don't move until I tell you."

Sitting in the SGO quarters, Leuzinger's misery was complete. He had been undone by a combination of a young Jewish boy, the rainy London weather, and the sole survivor of a U-boat.

The mess hall was packed to the rafters. Even men on sick call showed up. They all knew that there was something in the wind, but only two of them knew what it was. The air of expectancy could be cut with a knife.

Reichmann cleared his throat and began, "Gentlemen, I have something very serious and even more terrible to tell you. I want you to listen quietly to what I have to say and I want no disturbance whatsoever. Is that completely understood? All right. The officer standing next to me is Lieutenant Dieter Mannheim. He is the sole survivor of the U-137 that was sunk a few days ago. The story I am going to tell you is more completely understood by Lieutenant Mannheim because he was there and I wasn't. If I state the facts incorrectly I have asked him to so state.

"The U-137 was detailed with the responsibility of attempting to rescue a German pilot whose plane was shot down while on a bombing raid over London. That pilot was captured by the British before he could be rescued. For reasons that we don't yet know, the pilot revealed to his captors the time and place that the U-boat would attempt the rescue. The U-boat was attacked by a number of British warships and sunk with all hands except two men—Lieutenant Mannheim and an enlisted man who was killed by British troops on the beach. The only reason that Lieutenant Mannheim survived is because he was in a dinghy proceeding to shore to pick up the pilot when the U-boat was attacked."

There was an immediate hubbub in the hall.

Reichmann cleared his throat, held up his hands for silence, and paused for a few seconds. He continued, "Two days ago, that pilot was brought to this camp."

The place exploded in noise. The meeting was momentarily out of control. Shouts erupted all over the room.

"Where is the bastard?"

"Bring him in."

"String him up."

"Kill him."

"Gentlemen, gentlemen, you promised silence. I need you to cooperate."

An infantry captain, missing his right arm, couldn't contain himself. "The man's a filthy cowardly swine. He deserves to die. We should kill him now." There was a loud chorus of approval accompanied by a rhythmic pounding on the mess hall tables.

Reichmann held up both hands for silence. After some time the noise died down.

"Captain, you and the rest of you are partially right and partially wrong. He is a filthy cowardly swine and he does deserve to die, but I want to convince you that we should not kill him."

A chorus of boos and hisses broke out. Again, Reichmann held up his hands for silence. This time, it took longer before the noise died down. No one in the audience liked what they were hearing.

"I have two reasons why we should not kill this man and the reasons are related. First, we do not have the legal authority to convene a court-martial—much less kill the man without a court-martial. Second, if one or more of you do kill him, I can assure you the British will hunt you down and, when they find out who did it—and they almost certainly will—they will execute you. This man is not worth any of you dying in order to get him. I want to see all of you return to your homes, hopefully sooner rather than later."

"What if we all kill him? They can't execute us all," came a cry from the back of the room.

"Don't rely on that. You're German officers. You are the cream of the crop. Don't debase yourselves by setting on this man like a pack of dogs."

The one-armed officer cried out, "What do you suggest, Colonel? We treat him like one of us. We eat with him. We talk with him. We play football with him. We share our cigarettes with him. We go on as though nothing has happened. You can't ask us to do that. I for one won't."

Shouts of agreement thundered out from all parts of the room.

"I'm not asking you to do that," Reichmann responded, raising his voice and again holding up his arms for silence. "I, for one, won't talk to him. I won't eat with him. I'll arrange where he sleeps so he won't be near any of you. I'll turn my back on him when he comes near me. In short, I won't have a single thing to do with him. When we get back to Germany, I will ensure that he stands trial for his treason. In many ways, what I am suggesting is greater punishment than death. You may not think so now. But after a few months of total ostracism and total contempt, he may wish we had killed him."

Reichmann turned to Mannheim. "Here is the man who lost the most. The men who died on that U-boat were his shipmates and his friends. He had been through a lot with them and now they are all dead. Lieutenant Mannheim, despite your great loss and your feelings of rage, I ask you to agree with what I have suggested. Your agreement is most important."

Mannheim didn't answer for a long time. Finally, he said, "I'd rather see him spread out on an anthill covered in honey."

The murmurings started again. This time it was Mannheim who held up his hands for silence. "But, Colonel, you're a lot older and wiser than I and if you think this is what we should do, I'll go along. I think you should tell the men what name this mangy dog goes by."

"His name is Leuzinger—Captain Heinrich Leuzinger"

CHAPTER NINETY-SEVEN

"MAJOR GRUBER, I AM informed that you have repeatedly rejected the assistance of military counsel in this proceeding. Is that true?"

Gruber, standing stiffly at attention, answered, "That is true." The military tribunal formed to hear the trial of Major Karl Gruber for the murder of Lieutenant Von Steuffel was convened in a converted mess hall at Eighth Army Headquarters. Tables and chairs had been moved to the back of the room. A makeshift judge's bench had been created by placing a long rectangular plank across three empty ammunition boxes and covering it with a large cloth. Counsel tables were placed strategically in front of the bench. A chair with a small, attached platform was to be used for the witnesses. The platform could be used for documents and water. Another chair and a small table were reserved for the court reporter. There were two rows of chairs behind the counsel benches. They were for prospective witnesses and a limited number of spectators. Two armed military policemen stood directly behind Gruber. Two more guarded the entrance to the mess hall. Sergeant William Schultz, a certified German-English interpreter sat next to the reporter.

Colonel Kurt Buchner was the chief judge. The other two judges on either side of Buchner were Major Derek Lowell and Major Reginald Fitzhugh. Both of Colonel Buchner's parents were born in Germany. Colonel Buchner had been born in England, as had his younger sister. Both of his older brothers had been born in Germany, although they had gone to live in England at an early age. The prosecutor was Captain Sturtevant—a King's Counsel and a very prominent barrister in London in civilian life.

"Major Gruber, I strongly urge you to reconsider your decision. You are on trial for your life. Captain Ross is a very experienced and extremely capable trial counsel. In civilian life he is a barrister in England and renowned as a first-rate defense lawyer. He is here in court and is prepared to represent you. I am perfectly willing to put this matter over for a week to allow Captain Ross to confer with you and prepare your defense."

"I refuse. I am prepared to proceed now and I insist on representing myself," said Gruber.

"Very well. That is your prerogative, but I must tell you that it is a most foolish and potentially disastrous decision," said Buchner. "If you change your mind at any time during the trial, let me know. I will have Captain Ross next to you and—even though you don't want him to represent you—he will be instantly available to give you advice during the trial or, if you change your mind, to take over your defense."

"I don't want him or his advice," said Gruber loudly and defiantly.

"Nonetheless he will sit next to you. In light of what you

have just said, he will not offer you any advice unless you ask for it."

"I said I don't want him and I won't listen to anything he says."

"I've decided he will sit there whether you like it or not. That is my decision and I will not listen to any more about it."

The opening statements were made. Captain Sturtevant made a well-organized and persuasive presentation. It included a fulsome description of Gruber's involvement in the plot against Colonel Reichmann, the killing of Lieutenant Von Steuffel, Gruber's hatred and envy of Colonel Reichmann, and Gruber's anti-Semitism. Gruber's attitude had changed dramatically from being calm and reasonable when he was interviewed earlier by Sloan to being angry, emotional, and out of control.

In his opening statement, Gruber ranted for fifteen minutes about the trial being a Jewish plot and barely addressed the issue of his guilt or innocence. He did, however, raise one cogent issue. After the revelation to the prisoners that Colonel Reichmann had aided the escape of the Helstein family, Gruber had ordered that Reichmann was to be shown respect and not to be harmed. Sturtevant had blunted that defense by urging that Gruber's speeches to his fellow prisoners in support of Reichmann were nothing more than attempts to deflect any suspicion from him. At the end of his statement, Buchner again raised the need for Gruber to be professionally represented. Gruber again refused.

Sturtevant then put on the prosecution's case. It methodically demonstrated the almost-certainty that Gruber had killed Von Steuffel. Lieutenant Wolf testified that Von Steuffel had essentially admitted that he had stabbed

Reichmann and that Gruber had put him up to it. Sturtevant had found two other German officers who had heard essentially the same thing. Lieutenant Schoenfels recounted the argument he had overheard in the latrine between Gruber and Von Steuffel the night that Von Steuffel was killed. The German witnesses testified through the interpreter. Some of them were quite competent in English. However, Colonel Buchner insisted on the use of the interpreter. He pointed out that many people were comfortable in casual conversations speaking in a language that was not their native tongue. Where the actual words used could be crucial such as in a trial, speaking in their native tongue would be more likely to ensure accuracy. Captain Askew, the medical officer who certified to the cause of death of Von Steuffel, testified to the cause of the contusion on the back of the dead man's head and the way in which a single individual could have accomplished the hanging of an unconscious victim.

Gruber did manage to establish in his inexpert cross-examination of Schoenfels and other witnesses that after Reichmann's aid to the Helstein family had become known to the prisoners, he had insisted that Reichmann be treated with all military courtesy and respect and that the prisoners had no legal authority to punish Reichmann.

Gruber's efforts were ineffective. Sturtevant persuasively developed evidence that Gruber knew that several prisoners were not staunch Nazis and that his speeches ordering that Reichmann not be punished in any way were hypocritical and mainly directed at the non-Nazis. Gruber was in fact trying to create evidence that he hoped would insulate him from suspicion after Von Steuffel had killed Reichmann. He had overlooked three things. First, that Von Steuffel would fail in his attempt to kill Reichmann and would only wound him. Second, that Von Steuffel would openly brag about having attacked Reichmann and implicate Gruber, and third, that his berating of Von Steuffel in the latrine for that bragging would be overheard.

Captain Lassiter and the MP staff at the camp testified that, while they did not conduct a formal roster check that night, they were able to say that when the men fell out for roll call on the morning after Von Steuffel's death, all of the occupants of their individual barracks—with the exception of Von Steuffel—exited their respective barracks.

Lassiter also testified that all the barracks were locked at lights out and shutters on all the windows were secured. Searchlights played on the barracks all night. Guards on the towers confirmed that no prisoner came out of the barracks that night. Significantly, the only prisoner who was not locked in was the senior German officer. He had his own separate quarters. After Colonel Reichmann was hospitalized, Gruber—as the ranking German—lost no time in moving into the SGO's hut. In the trial's only light moment, Captain Lassiter explained to the court why there was no lock on the SGO's quarters. It seems that the officer who preceded Colonel Reichmann was quite old and, similar to many older men, had the necessity of visiting the latrine several times during the night. At first, the solution was to provide the elderly officer with a pail to use inside his quarters. He complained vociferously about the indignity. The then-commandant relented and took the lock off the SGO's hut. The commandant reasoned that it was virtually impossible for any prisoner to get through the barbed-wire fences and evade the searchlights and guards. Even if that was accomplished, the enemy lines were many miles distant through desert. Nobody had ever escaped. The lock was never replaced. On the night of Von Steuffel's death, Gruber was the only prisoner who could come and go to and from his quarters after lights out.

Gruber's cross-examinations were erratic, rambling, and of no help to him. They were mostly diatribes and not questions. He yelled at witnesses that they hated him and that they were lying or that they were not loyal Germans. He screamed at Lieutenant Wolf, "It's true, isn't it, that your grandmother was a Jew." Captain Ross reached over, touched Gruber on the arm, and tried to whisper something, but Gruber brushed his arm away. Captain Sturtevant objected on numerous grounds. Colonel Buchner, leaning over backward, given that Gruber was on trial for his life and didn't know what he was doing, allowed the witness to answer while urging Gruber to try to ask pertinent questions and to listen to Captain Ross. Lieutenant Wolf reacted to the accusation that his grandmother was a Jew as if he had been accused of murdering babies—and the answer did not find favor with the tribunal.

Sturtevant submitted a written statement signed under oath by Colonel Reichmann. It attested to the fact that he could not identify his attacker and it related his long time relationship with Gruber. The interviewer had attempted to get Reichmann to attest to Gruber's anti-Semitism and to his longstanding jealousy of Reichmann. Characteristically, Reichmann declined.

The last witness was a surprise. It was Dr. Meyer Helstein. As Colonel Buchner was attempting to administer the oath to Helstein, Gruber exploded. "You're not going to let this filthy Jew testify against me. In Germany, no Jew would be allowed to testify against an Aryan, particularly a German officer. You, as a German, should know that."

Finally, Buchner had had enough and he too exploded. "This is not Germany; it's not a German court and I'm not a German. I'm a British officer. Dr. Helstein is going to testify and you're going to be quiet."

As Helstein took the stand, Gruber stood up and turned his back on Helstein. Buchner said, "Major Gruber, you turn around and sit down. If you don't do so, I will have the guards handcuff you to your seat." Gruber sat down. Dr. Helstein testified to his experiences with both Gruber and Reichmann, his medical treatment of both officers, Gruber's anti-Semitism (which, given Gruber's performance during trial, was now superfluous and unnecessary), Gruber's jealousy of Reichmann, and his efforts to damage Reichmann's career. At the conclusion of the direct examination of Dr. Helstein, Colonel Buchner asked Gruber if he had any questions of the doctor. Gruber said, "I don't want to have anything to do with him."

Buchner icily responded, "I'll take that as a no."

Sturtevant rested and Buchner asked Gruber if he wanted to put on any witnesses. Ross asked the court for a moment and leaned over to try to say something to Gruber. Gruber shifted his chair to separate himself further from Ross. Ross looked at Buchner and shrugged. Buchner gave Ross a look of resignation.

"I don't need any witnesses," said Gruber.

Buchner responded, "I'll put the trial over until tomorrow if you want to think about that and I'll have any witness within easy distance of this court brought in if you ask me to do that."

"I need no witnesses. Let's get on with it," said Gruber.

"Very well. The parties may now make their closing arguments."

Sturtevant was methodical and skillful—as he had been throughout the trial. He pointed out all of the testimony that established Gruber's motive to instigate the attack on Reichmann and the killing of Von Steuffel to silence him. He went through the testimony that placed Gruber at the scene of the killing and the fact that he alone had ready access to and from the latrine after lockdown.

In his argument, Gruber emphasized his one good point. He had established his instructions to the prisoner that they were to show Reichmann military courtesy and not attempt to punish him because he helped Jews.

In his rebuttal, Sturtevant urged that such a speech to the camp by Gruber was a charade and was intended to deflect suspicion from him after Reichmann was attacked. While making the speech, Gruber knew that he was going to solicit the attack on Reichmann and that when Von Steuffel had started to brag about being the perpetrator and involving Gruber, he cold-bloodedly killed Von Steuffel to silence him.

After recessing overnight to consider their verdict, the tribunal reconvened the following morning and Colonel Buchner announced the decision of the court.

"Major Karl Gruber, the tribunal, having considered all the evidence introduced in this trial and having listened to the arguments of both sides, unanimously finds you guilty of the murder of Lieutenant Von Steuffel. The sentence of this tribunal is that you will be put to death by a firing squad at a place and time to be set. May God have mercy on your soul."

CHAPTER NINETY-EIGHT

THE POW CAMP IN Victoria Park had been without disturbance of any kind in the two weeks following Reichmann's revelation to the prisoners of Leuzinger's treachery. He was surprised. Leuzinger had not been killed or injured. Indeed, no one had as much as touched him. Reichmann was honest enough with himself to know that it was more Mannheim's doing than his own. Mannheim had lost his ship and all his shipmates as a result of Leuzinger's treachery. Nonetheless, he had been willing to accept Reichmann's counsel and had supported his plea that Leuzinger not be touched. It was hard for Mannheim—very hard, harder in fact than Reichmann knew at the time of the meeting in the mess hall. Reichmann knew, of course, that it was Mannheim's shipmates who were killed. It was not difficult for him to imagine that many of the men on the U-137 were not only his shipmates, but also his friends. What he had not known was that one of those who died on the U-137 was the first officer, Gerhardt Mannheim, Dieter's older brother. Gerhardt was not only Dieter's older brother—he was also his best friend. When Reichmann found this out, he marveled at the young man's ability to set aside the enormity of the loss of his brother and his old shipmates to help protect his new comrades—his fellow prisoners. He had quickly accepted Reichmann's concern that the killing of Leuzinger could only lead inevitably to further killings and that the British would leave no stone unturned to find those who had killed Leuzinger. It wasn't worth it.

Months went by. The ostracism, which had started as complete, remained that way. No POW ever spoke to Leuzinger. At meals, no one would sit with him. If he attempted to sit down at a table that was only partially occupied, the men at that table would stop talking and silently move to another table. If he came near any of them on the yard, they would move away without a word. They had moved the beds closer together in Barracks B where Leuzinger was housed in order to separate themselves as far as possible from him. Once, during a pickup game, the football rolled toward Leuzinger who picked it up and threw it to one of the players. No one would ever touch that ball again. A British guard ultimately kicked it into a corner of the compound that was seldom used. Reichmann prevailed on the guard to give the prisoners another ball.

On a couple of occasions, Leuzinger tried to talk to one or more of the men. He wanted to explain what had happened. He wanted to tell them why he had no choice, but to do what he had done. Nobody listened. Nobody said a word. Anybody within earshot walked away. Leuzinger tried to talk to Reichmann about it. All Reichmann would say was that he could do nothing about it and he too walked away.

The situation was generally understood by the British guards. They knew that somehow Leuzinger had betrayed Mannheim's ship, which as a result was lost with all hands— save Mannheim. They didn't know why Leuzinger had done this or the circumstances surrounding it. They did not know of the German spy ring or the involvement of Scotland Yard, they only knew that, for some reason, Leuzinger was a traitor. Leuzinger had asked several of the British guards that he had come in contact with if they could see about his being transferred to another camp. Nothing ever came off it. On several occasions, Sergeant of the Guard Des Connors had broached the subject with the camp commandant, Major John Wright.

"Major, do you think we should do anything? Leuzinger looks terrible. He's lost so much weight that he looks like a scarecrow. He tells me he's been coughing up blood, but the M.O. found nothing wrong with him. The other prisoners, as you know, won't have anything to do with him."

"I can't justify moving him," said Wright. "Where would I send him? Any place I did, the prisoners would be bound to find out. I'm astonished that no one in the camp has killed him. I can't punish them because they won't talk to him. Would you if you were one of them?"

"I suppose not," said Connors.

"At least they're not hurting him here. If I send him some other place, the prisoners might not be so disciplined. Look at it this way, Des. If somebody in your unit betrayed the unit to the Germans and, as a result, everybody in the unit died, how would you feel? What would you do?"

Leuzinger remained where he was. Nobody killed him. Nobody struck him. The treatment he received remained the same. He was completely and absolutely isolated. He could have been alone on a desert island thousands of miles from civilization rather than in close proximity to hundreds of his countrymen and he wouldn't have been a more solitary figure.

Three months later, two events occurred and ironically on precisely the same day.

In the desert, Major Karl Gruber's appeals had run out and his execution was scheduled. With his hands bound behind him, he was tied to a post driven deeply into the sandy soil. He refused a blindfold. The officer in charge asked Gruber if he wanted to make any last statement. He declined. As the officer ordered the firing squad to aim, Gruber shouted "Heil Hitler" and a volley of bullets tore into his chest.

Thousands of miles away, a totally defeated and emaciated Leuzinger, physically ill and mentally shattered who had sacrificed an entire German U-Boat and virtually it's entire crew to save his own neck, put that same neck in a noose made from a bed sheet, threw the other end over a beam in the deserted latrine, tied it off, kicked out the box he was standing on, and died.

Epilogue

The Germans changed the code before they could be deciphered. The Scotland Yard strategy was, nonetheless, a significant success—albeit a partial one—and the raid on the Duggan house a major victory. An important spy ring that had operated in England for years was destroyed and a U-boat sunk.

When Hans Dieter Reichmann was repatriated to Germany shortly after the end of the war, he got a mixed reception. The story of the Helstein family had preceded him. There were the pro-Nazis who resented what they saw as pure treason. They were however equaled or outnumbered by those who were relieved that the war was over and were guilt ridden by the horrors perpetrated by the Third Reich. As time went by, the legions of pro-Nazis dwindled and the voice of a younger generation became predominant. A broken and defeated country had very few heroes emerging from the war. Hans Dieter Reichmann was one of those few. His stature continued to grow and he was in fact widely lionized. A groundswell developed strongly favoring him to be the new German chancellor. He declined, preferring to retire to the peace and quiet of a farm in rural Prussia.

A young state of Israel named Reichmann as one of the "Righteous" and invited him to come to their country for a ceremony of gratitude and to have a tree planted in his honor. He accepted and traveled to Israel with his wife and children. They flew to London from Frankfurt and from there to Tel Aviv accompanied, at Reichmann's request, by former Brigadier General Joe Corcoran, former Lieutenant Colonel Bernie Sloan and by Dr. Meyer Helstein and his family. On the way home, as promised, the Reichmanns spent a long weekend at the estate of Sir Rupert Corcoran where he and his sons rode horses.

The Helsteins elected to stay in England and not return to their native Germany. The friendship of Meyer Helstein and Hans Dieter Reichmann never faded. They visited each other frequently and their visits often included Miriam and Bernie Sloan.

In 1950, Rebecca Sloan married out of the faith. Had she been old enough to have wed before the start of the Second World War, her father would have disowned her and forbidden his wife and Tom to attend the ceremony. Instead, her father hosted a large-scale party and was honored to give away the bride. The ceremony was conducted by both a Rabbi and a Church of England minister. The cake was selected by both Miriam and Bernie Sloan with the approval of the bridal couple. In place of the traditional figures of a bride and groom, the cake was topped with a Star of David and a crucifix. Among the many guests were Joe Corcoran, his family and his father and mother, Hans Dieter Reichmann and his wife, and Dr. Meyer Helstein and his wife.

In 1953, young Dr. Tom Sloan, interning at St. Luke's Hospital, was paged. He was told that a Mr. Dixon was on the phone. "Who is Mr. Dixon?" he asked the telephone operator.

"I don't know," she said. "He sounds like an old geezer."

Tom got on the phone. "Yes, Mr. Dixon. What can I do for you?"

"You probably remember me better as Chief Inspector Dixon."

"Chief Inspector, forgive me. I will never forget you until my dying day. How are you?"

"For an old man, I'm not too bad, Tom. I'm retired chief inspector these days. I hope I didn't catch you at a bad time, but I had something I wanted to tell you."

"For you, Chief Inspector, there never could be a bad time. What is your news?"

"The Duggan house raid; what led up to it and what followed, including the destruction of the spy cell and the sinking of the U-137 came off the Secrets List. The Queen's Honor's List just came out and Ace Ferguson is posthumously to get the highest civilian medal for bravery for the effort he put in on the raid. You know we would have failed miserably if it wasn't for him. His wife will receive the award from the queen at Buckingham Palace on June 3. I thought you would like to come. All the Scotland Yard detectives who were in on the raid will be there. The Queen has made an exception to the number of people who can attend. Oh, and I am to be knighted. I am sure it must be a mistake, but I'll take it anyway."

"I'd be delighted and I know your knighthood was more than well earned. My heartiest congratulations. The award to Ace Ferguson is just so wonderful. I'm overwhelmed."

"By the way, I almost forgot—you had better plan to bring your entire family," Dixon said stifling a laugh.

Tom was puzzled. "I know my father and mother would love to see the inside of Buckingham Palace, but I thought the number of friends of the honorees was limited."

"Didn't I tell you, Tom," Dixon said with a chuckle "You're to get an MBE."

"I'm to get *what!*" cried Tom.

"Let me read you the citation: 'In the early years of the war, Thomas Sloan, then fourteen years of age, established a relationship with a downed German pilot and aided Scotland Yard through such relationship in discovering and destroying a major Nazi spy ring in Britain and in being of invaluable assistance in helping the Royal Navy in locating and sinking a German U-boat. Dr. Sloan's actions demonstrated the most extraordinary courage in the face of extreme danger and were of invaluable help to the British war effort. Her Majesty is pleased, on behalf of a deeply grateful nation, to make this award to Dr. Thomas Sloan and to make him an honored Member of the British Empire.'"

The tears streamed down Tom's face at the magnitude of what he had just heard. The chief inspector could not see the tears, but knew they must have come. "You deserve it, Tom. Without you, we would not have had a chance. I'm looking forward to seeing you at the palace."

And so it came to pass that, on a warm, sunny June afternoon, the entire Scotland Yard party that raided the Duggan house—and the Dixon, Ferguson, and Sloan families—stood proudly in the spacious garden of Buckingham Palace, watching the honors being presented to Mrs. Ferguson, Sir Andrew Dixon, and Tom Sloan. They then all talked to the Queen and sipped tea with members of the royal family.

On that same day at the Globe & Crown pub in Sheffield, Alfie Roberts was being treated to free beer as he regaled his audience with the story of how on one night during the war, he was transformed from a Royal Navy seaman to a German pilot. Those who had heard the story many times before, which was most of them, listened good-naturedly.

A year later, Tom was married to a young American who he had met in medical school. Again, the invitation list was long. This time a seriously ill Hans Dieter Reichmann was not able to make the trip. The cake was again the centerpiece. The top was, as in the case of Rebecca's wedding, different. This time it had three small flags. They were the British Union Jack, the American Stars and Stripes and the pre-Third Reich Imperial flag of Germany.

One of the guests, Phil Shapiro, a long time friend of Bernie Sloan nervously approached Sloan.

"Bernie there is something I have to ask you that has puzzled me and a lot of your guests. I hope you won't be offended."

"Go ahead Phil. What is it?"

"We know that the flags on the wedding cake of Great Britain and the United States are to honor the countries of birth of Tom and his bride. But why the German flag?"

Sloan didn't answer immediately, looked thoughtfully for a few seconds at the three small flags, then said quietly, "I found out a lot of things during the war that I never understood before. One of the most important lessons I learned is that honor knows no borders."